# HER STORY

K. S. MOORE

For Nancy—
Many blessings!
K.S. Moore

HEARTSHINE
PUBLISHING

HER STORY BY K.S. MOORE

Published by Heartshine Publishing

ISBN: 979-8-9875800-5-9



Cover and Interior design by Kathryn Moore, kathrynsuemoore.com

For more information on this book and the author visit: KathrynSueMoore.com



Brought to you by the creative team at Heartshine Publishing LLC.

Library of Congress Cataloging-in-Publication Data Moore, K. S.

Her Story/K. S. Moore 1st ed.

Printed in the United States of America

*For my father. I miss your unfailing encouragement and steadfast belief in me, more than words can express.*

# MIRACLES

**June 2014**

Tomorrow will alter the trajectory of our lives. I feel it, like I feel the storm coming.

"Think she'll stay this time?" Aiden's face shines innocent and optimistic. I flip on his Sheriff Woody night-light and tuck him into bed. He scoots to make room so I can sit.

"God willing," is all I can say. He always asks tough questions, ones I can't answer.

His brows scrunch together. "When does what we want get to matter?"

"We did our best this week, Buckaroo. That's all a person can do." I know he's in sore need of reassurance, but all I have is a hug.

"Don't worry, Dad. Love never forgets." He smiles that crooked grin of his, but doubt shadows his eyes.

His compassion is beyond his years, and I feel like a horrible father for the loss he's endured. We're both afraid to voice the other possibility, but it hangs in the silence between us like the worst possible verdict.

I hear a light knock and the screen door squeaks open.

Aiden perks up. "Going for a ride tonight?"

The question hits me like a splash in the face. He knows about my late-night rides. "Yep, but Avery's here in case you wake up." I won't be gone long. My niece has school tomorrow.

He smirks as if to say, aw, Dad. "I'm too big for a babysitter. I'm almost double digits now. 'Sides, Uncle Isaac and Aunt Bella are just a holler away."

"I know, but it makes me feel better." I ruffle his hair. For the first time, I glimpse the young man he'll become, and I'm blindsided by another wave of guilt. Am I condemning him to the same life of loneliness and despair by wanting him to love this ranch as much as I do?

Uncertain who will be more disappointed tomorrow, him or me, if Samantha leaves again, I ease the door closed, and greet the sitter.

I take a moment to sit and ask her about prom, her boyfriend, and college applications. Most nights, Aiden and I dine with my brother and his family in the big house, so we talk often, and like everyone on the ranch, I'm sure she knows about Samantha's return six days ago and wonders how things have gone this week. But she doesn't ask. She may think it would hurt me to talk about it, and knowing myself as I do, I suspect she's right.

When I stand to leave, she squeezes my hand and smiles, and I wonder what this means.

I slip into my Carhartt, don my Stetson, and ease open the screen door.

"Mac," Avery says.

I glance back and her hands are pressed together as if in prayer.

"Thank you," I say with a catch in my throat, and I slip out the front.

My boots kick up a cloud of dust as I cross the gravel drive. It's been so dry lately I could start a fire with the spark in my eye.

Lights are on in the big house. Isaac and Bella are still up. I consider talking to my brother and his wife about Samantha's manuscript, but it's too late for that.

In the barn, I pass the four-wheelers and snow machines, and Buck, my chestnut quarter horse, nickers and turns my way. He knows where we're heading and stomps with anticipation. I think he loves these late-night rides as much as I do.

Beneath a dark Colorado sky, I head off across the meadow, my way softly lit by a half-moon, hanging like a busted lantern above the eastern horizon. I lean forward in the saddle to pat Buck's neck, a small comfort to my anxious heart. We enter the pitch-black woods and he snorts. I can't see squat but it doesn't matter. It's a trail as familiar as the way to the barn. I nudge the horse forward.

Of all the evenings I've made this ride, this time feels different, hopeful somehow. Will it happen tonight? It's the possibility that keeps me going.

My life has not been the joy-filled wonder I imagined it would be. I have the ranch, brothers and cousins, in-laws, nieces, and nephews, but they're no substitute for the love of a wife and full-time family of my own. I have a scant two months more with Aiden before he returns to his mother in Houston, but I've learned over the years, to focus on making the most of our time together, instead of dwelling on his departure at summer's end. The other nine months of the year, I work from dawn to dusk to avoid my empty cabin and the solitude that has been thirty-seven years in the making. I once read that a person can get used to anything, if given enough time. I must be an exception.

The trail winds up and up, and minutes later we reach the top of the ridge. I dismount, wrap the reins around a branch, and look over the valley spread before me. Slivers of light outline the windows of the small cabin below, and my pulse quickens as hope floods in. She's reading the story she wrote, the story I have read a hundred times. Will she remember? Or will she read about her heroine's lover and fall all over again? If only I could will it so.

My father used to tell me a happy man is one who perseveres.

He's not smarter, more gifted, or any luckier. The man simply tries harder, doesn't give up. He knows where his happiness lies and does whatever it takes to wrangle it.

My happiness lies in that old hunting cabin, right down there. She's everything I ever wanted. Nothing makes sense without her, like waking up in the dark. And I've waited three and a half years for her to return to my mountain.

It was divine providence that she wrote a story that summer—our story, her parting gift to me. And aside from that one afternoon beneath the cottonwood, she'd captured the essence and entirety of the man I am with her delicate prose.

Sometimes there's a whole lot of truth in fiction.

While I'm confident the path I've chosen to follow has always been the right one, I know I'm nothing special. But I have loved a woman – two women, actually – with all of my heart, and regardless of how tomorrow goes, it will have to be enough. I won't put Aiden through this again. I won't put myself through this again.

I lie on the ground, relax against the log stretched sideways to the ridge, like we did four summers ago. Has it really been that long? I close my eyes and feel her warmth beside me, hear her gentle laughter. The way her eyes lit up when I shared the constellation story squeezes my heart. She didn't say so, but I'm fairly certain that was the night she fell in love with me.

She's forgotten everything about that summer, but it doesn't matter, so long as she remembers the way I made her feel. At day's end, that's all that counts. That quiet ease that turns a friend into a lover.

I gaze at the stars, one of the few constants in my life—the vast sky, as desolate as my emptiness. The moon understands, hanging in the dark, yearning for its other half, that missing slice of light to complete the circle of its waning life.

A gentle breeze whispers through the woods, setting the pungent scents of aspen and pine swirling in the dry mountain air. It's cool and eerily quiet. Even the cicadas sound muted tonight, conserving their energy for another hot day tomorrow.

Like the wildlife, silent in the darkness, I rest against the log as my mind churns with tomorrow's possibilities, and I try to convince myself I haven't lost her yet. There's still hope.

The way she kissed me earlier this evening lingers on my lips like the start of an all-night-long, slow kiss. I am no longer a stranger to her, yet I ache for so much more: to hold her, to have her, in my life, my heart, my soul. The love we shared consumes me, shrouding me in a gut-wrenching fear that I'll never feel that way again.

Hot tears sting my eyes as I rise to my knees, and I can barely make out the cabin below. I bow my head and pray for the strength I know I will need and the hope that has come to dominate my life —that she'll remember what we'd found that summer and we will never part again. My voice catches on the ragged edges of my heart, and I suck in a breath as deep as the valley below.

A stick cracks in the woods, and I spring to my feet. In an instant, I'm at Buck's side, drawing my rifle silently from its scabbard. The horse snorts and stomps. Each second ticks away a heartbeat. Silence stretches out, filling the space between us, the whole mountaintop. I smooth Buck's neck for reassurance—his and mine. Probably a mule deer. No rain for weeks, the mountain's as dry as a tinderbox. I don't linger to find out. I mount and turn toward the ridge for one last look at the cabin below, the thin strips of light outlining the windows. My heart lifts. She's still reading.

Maybe, just maybe, she'll remember how she once loved me.

# PART I

## BROKEN FENCES

June 2010
(4 years earlier)

*"The farther one gets into the wilderness,*
*the greater is the attraction of its lonely freedom."*

– Theodore Roosevelt

# 1

# MICAH

**June 2010**

A hush fell over the packed courtroom as the judge took the bench. "Will the defendant please rise?"

Micah Daniels glanced at the clock on the wall, leaned back in his chair, and folded his hands in his lap.

Doc Grady, a rotund little man with kind eyes and hair more salt than pepper, stood on unsteady legs at the far counsel table and buttoned his suit jacket. With a steely resolve, he lifted his gaze to the judge.

"Doctor Robert B. Grady, the jury has found you guilty as charged of thirteen felony counts of shooting livestock of another. Counselor Daniels, on behalf of The Homestead Ranch, has requested leniency despite the significant loss of property and expense of these proceedings. Do you have anything to add before this court proceeds with sentencing?"

Doc Grady shot Micah a nod of gratitude. "No, your honor."

"Very well." The judge perused the papers before him. "This court hereby sentences you to time served, twenty-five hundred dollars restitution and two thousand dollars fine per animal, and five hundred hours of community service."

Doc Grady exhaled and turned to his attorney, hand extended, while Micah breathed his own sigh of relief. As bad as it was, it could've been much worse. Besides the restitution, each charge carried up to two years in prison. Micah shook the district attorney's hand, and then turned to the rail where his Uncle Will stood beside Katrina Sloan, the sharp young associate assigned to the case by the Colorado Ranchers Association. He shook his uncle's hand, then Ms. Sloan's. "Thank you for your help."

The judge's pronouncement, "Court adjourned," faded into the sudden melee of the crowded courtroom.

While his uncle glad-handed everyone within reach, Ms. Sloan leaned into Micah with a fresh scent of berries and citrus. "I know a quiet little table for two down the street where we can celebrate," she said, a suggestion of something more in her wide doe eyes.

They were eyes a man could drown in, cool, dark, stunning. In her slim tan suit and crisp white blouse, her long black hair pulled back into a sleek ponytail, Katrina Sloan exuded polish. And she was an excellent litigator. Serious and intensely persuasive, her round feminine tones had held the rapt attention of the whole courtroom as she'd argued on behalf of the Colorado Rancher's Association.

Micah pulled back, his gaze darting everywhere except at the lovely young attorney in front of him. "My uncle and I'll be heading home tonight." He tipped his hat. "Another time, perhaps."

She tilted her head, captured his gaze, and grinned. "I'll take you up on that, Counselor."

Micah turned back to the table and packed up his briefcase. Sometimes he longed to be the kind of man who'd enjoy a one-nighter with a beautiful woman. She could've been a lot of fun.

"You did a fine job in there today," his Uncle Will said, slipping into the cab of the truck. "Your daddy'd be proud."

Micah glanced over at his uncle in the passenger seat of his late father's old Ram pickup. With his thin white hair and deeply etched face, he looked all of his seventy-some years. "Thanks, Uncle Will. I was glad to have your help." From the courthouse parking lot, he turned toward the highway leading home.

"You're ready to take over, you know."

Micah cringed. His uncle was referring to more than their legal battles. He meant everything: the ranch, the family, the whole kit and caboodle.

Squaring his shoulders, Micah felt the full weight of the responsibilities being placed upon them. "Think so?" he asked with a nervous chuckle.

"This fight, the ranch, they need the strength of youth, Micah. You and Cody, maybe even Nick, should take on the next case."

"Nick?" Micah shot his uncle a side-eye.

His cousin, yeah. Responsible and conscientious, Cody cared about the ranch with the heartfelt sense of family and heritage passed down religiously from generations past. But Nick? Nick was as irresponsible and uninvolved in the family business as if he'd been born a flatlander. Truth be told, Micah's little brother would be a prodigal son if only they had the cash to turn him loose.

What Micah wouldn't give to be that unencumbered.

"Aw, come on now." Uncle Will let go a hearty chuckle. "The boy just needs a sense of purpose. Give him a chance. He'll come into his own. Every man marches to his own beat. Some just take longer to join the band."

Micah disagreed, but out of respect for his uncle, didn't argue. Eager to change the subject, he returned to the trial, a huge win for them personally and for all western ranchers. "How much longer you figure we have until they outnumber us and we lose this fight?" By *they*, he was referring to the national group of near-manic environmentalists who believed Colorado's open range laws to be absurd in the context of modern culture and took every opportunity to stir up public opinion against them. During the trial, they'd gathered on the courthouse steps with their signs and bullhorns, and each day their numbers seemed to have grown.

Uncle Will took so much time to answer, Micah wondered if he'd fallen asleep. He glanced his uncle's way as he merged onto the interstate.

"The open range land definition's been around a mighty long time," his uncle said. "It isn't likely to change anytime soon. Lawmakers can't mandate fencing 'cause the federal government can't afford it. But they won't give up the income from our leases either. And we sure can't look to Brazil or the Asians to grow our beef like they manufacture our hard goods, so they can't risk putting us out of business either. Hell, what will people eat when we're no longer around?"

Micah nodded, not entirely reassured by his uncle's reasoning.

"We're sure going to miss having Doc Grady in town. He was a fine doctor, despite getting a mite hot-headed about the animals from time to time," Uncle Will said. "I think his sentence was fair enough, though, don't you?"

"Yeah, but it should've never come to this." Micah hadn't even gotten a chance to diffuse the situation before it had escalated. As a family-run business, they strived to be good neighbors and conscientious ranchers, diligent about keeping the fences in good repair, even the ones constructed by others. But all it took was one weak section, one strong storm, or one determined animal to break through.

"We had a rock-solid case," Uncle Will added.

Micah nodded. "Yep. The law's on our side, for now, anyway. But it won't be long before this kind of publicity turns folks against us."

"Well, as long as the CRA keeps hiring talent like Ms. Sloan, I'd say we got nothing to worry about."

Micah gazed ahead to the mountains in the distance, awash in so many myriad shades of blue, it was hard to tell where the far-flung peaks ended and the sky began. He thought about Ms. Sloan's untoward excitement over the outcome. For her, it was one more shining victory added to her already stellar career scorecard, but for the Daniels family, ranching was a way of life, and the trial was yet another attack on their livelihood.

They'd been raising cattle in these hills and valleys for six generations—since the end of the Civil War—and for them, these cases were an all-to-frequent threat to their heritage and everything they held dear. It was only a matter of time before they lost one, and it was Micah's responsibility now to ensure the ranch survived it.

"Where are you, Micah?"

Micah shifted to face the woman on the couch beside him. He'd grown accustomed to the sadness that shadowed her eyes, but it riled him all the same. On the television, credits were rolling, and he couldn't remember the movie they'd been watching.

"I'm right here, Janie." He forced a smile and squeezed her hand, but his gaze returned to the glow of the moonlight spilling through the front window, luminescent white against the black night sky. Beckoning.

His neck bristled beneath her unrelenting stare and he struggled for the words to ease her troubled heart. She was beautiful and loved him deeply, but for reasons he couldn't fathom, he didn't feel the same, and questioned if he ever would.

She was young, only twenty-two, when she'd lost her husband, a smoke jumper, in a relentless wildfire. Micah was there for her after the accident, a friend and a shoulder to cry on. For reasons he never questioned, he continued to check on her and fix things around the house.

In his mid-thirties, Micah was older, but despite their age difference, it had seemed perfectly natural when, after almost a year, it had grown into something more—a romantic relationship, at least from her side of the couch.

But like she often reminded him, it wasn't enough. Micah's

indifference left a *gaping hole, an emptiness that yearned to be filled*, her words.

"You're not here, Micah." Her voice broke under what that truth meant to her.

He took a deep breath, reining in his patience as he looked into her bottle green eyes, and despite her best efforts, the tears pooling there. It was a conversation he'd long ago grown weary of, and he found it near impossible to mask his frustration. For reasons he didn't understand, he simply couldn't give her what she needed from him.

"It's been a long day." He stood, stretching his long frame, and turned to offer a hand up. As he kissed her forehead, a single tear escaped down her cheek. He winced and brushed it away. "I'm sorry, darlin'." It wasn't even close to what she needed to hear, but it was the best he could offer.

MICAH MADE his way up the dark, narrow trail, his shoulders heavy with guilt. He should have stayed over. Janie was about to invite him. Again. Why couldn't he bring himself to sleep with her? She was a pretty little thing, all feminine curves and honey-sweet goodness.

He hadn't been with a woman since ... Elizabeth.

His breath caught when he emerged into the clearing at the top of the ridge, and all thoughts of Janie—and Elizabeth—evaporated like drips from a coffee pot onto a bare, hot plate.

The expanse of lonely meadow shimmered in a multi-hued palette of pale luminescent gold beneath the light of the full moon. It brought a warm comfort to his heart, as it always did whenever he gazed over Moonglow Meadow on a night like this.

He was thankful he hadn't missed it. Spread out before him, the land was stunning in its vast emptiness, several miles long and half a mile wide, isolated between gently rolling hills and dense tree-lined ridges that rose to great solitary peaks in the distance: Mount

Agner, a stark barren rock face to the east, and Sleeping Giant, a massive lone figure of solid granite lying prone to the west.

A broad shallow stream, briefly transformed to a raging river by the springtime melt, meandered through its center, glistening in the moonlight like a thin silver streak painted by an artist's unsteady hand onto the smooth wheat-gold canvas of the vacant valley floor.

This was where he belonged.

His breath came in huge, desperate gulps, his lungs starved for the clear mountain air that he'd missed the past few days while in Denver for the trial. The heady aroma of pine, aspen, and fir, mixed with the pungent smell of molding leaves long buried by winter snows and now exposed to the warm spring air, filled his nostrils with the welcome scents of home.

Dismounting, he patted the neck of his horse, Buck, looked down the valley, and offered up a silent prayer of thanks for the amazing gift spread before him.

Would there ever be another soul with whom he could share this simple beauty? His heart longed to experience the wonder of it with someone special, to savor its glory and splendor with someone who could appreciate it as fully as he did.

He'd never thought to invite Janie to join him. She didn't understand the way he felt about the land, and besides, she'd be too frightened to ride through the densely wooded Colorado Rockies on a moonlit night.

*Janie.* He lifted his Stetson to rake a hand through his hair. She deserved so much more than he could give her. He wanted to love her; he'd tried to convince himself he might in time, but why hadn't it happened?

Sweet and kind, and a mountain girl, born and bred, she'd hinted at her desire to live on a ranch someday. Why wasn't all of that enough?

He squeezed his eyes shut against the decision he was now forced to make. Deep down, he knew he needed to let her go. She deserved to be loved. Didn't everyone?

She was still young; it wasn't too late for her to find someone.

She'd be heartbroken, but once she thought it through, she'd agree it was for the best. He hated himself for the way he'd left her, the pain he'd seen in her eyes, the tears that were solely his doing. They were always his doing.

He'd miss her something awful. He had no one else.

*The hardest thing is usually the right thing*, his daddy always said.

# 2

# ARRIVALS

On her knees in the back of her SUV, struggling to offload a fifty-gallon water tank, Samantha Jamison barely glimpsed the vehicle that roared by, kicking up a massive white cloud of dust in its wake. She covered her face with her sleeve and turned away, but it did little good. She'd forgotten how dry it could get in the mountains.

Fifty yards past, the pickup skidded to a stop, then backed up, churning up another maelstrom on the gravel road. The driver, sporting aviator sunglasses and a well-worn Stetson, lowered his window, rested an arm on the edge, and leaned out. "Howdy. Need a hand with that?"

"Hi." She waved away the cloud of dust as the man and his beat-up white truck slowly emerged from the fog. "I think I can manage, but thank you."

She turned back to her task, tipped the large cylinder on its edge and inched it toward the rear of the SUV. When she paused to wipe the sweat from her brow, the cowboy was still there, watching. She jumped down and eyed the water tank, then the ground, knowing full well she lacked the strength for the task at hand. She hadn't expected it to be so heavy.

The man stepped from his truck, slammed the door, leaned against it, and crossed his ankles and arms. He wore a smug smile, as though fully entertained.

She detested that look, the same one her husband used whenever she felt reduced to ask for his help with something manly. She studied the tank and considered her options.

Resigning herself to the inevitable, she swallowed her pride, brushed a wisp of hair from her face, and turned to the cowboy. "On second thought, I could use your help."

"Sure thing." He swaggered across the road to join her. He moved like the wind, graceful and silent, effortless. At least four or five inches over six feet, lean and muscular, he wore blue jeans, cowboy boots, and a Carhartt jacket. He tipped his hat as he approached and a bright white smile lit up his sun-bronzed face. He may have been close to her age, or ten years younger, impossible to gauge in a man who made his living outdoors.

"Micah Daniels," he said, shaking her hand. "My ranch is up the road a piece." He had a seductive voice, deep and masculine, the kind she could imagine whispering in the dark.

"Samantha Jamison." She leaned against her SUV, exhausted. "Nice of you to stop."

"Wouldn't be much of a gentleman if I didn't, now would I?" The smugness was gone, and he seemed genuinely pleased to offer his help. "Where are you going with that?" He nodded to the water tank. Beneath the Carhartt, he wore a red plaid flannel, a small V-shape of a white undershirt barely visible above the top button.

"Anywhere on the ground. It doesn't matter where it lands, as long as it's upright and won't roll away."

He studied the faint two-track that wound through dense aspens and pines to land at the small cabin a hundred yards down the mountainside. Sam followed his gaze, trying to envision her new home through a stranger's eyes. It was barely more than a shack, a small rectangle of rough sawn pine sporting a green metal roof. If not for its straight lines, it might have disappeared into the surrounding woods. Exactly what she'd hoped to do. She wondered if he realized this barrel of water was the only plumbing her little hovel could lay claim to.

He flashed her that gleaming smile again, removed his jacket, tucked his sunglasses into the breast pocket, and hung it on a nearby branch. His eyes were cloaked beneath thick, dark lashes. They were distinct eyes, the kind she'd remember, with an upper eyelid that angled down ever so slightly at the outer edge, puppy-like. He handed her his hat, turned to the water tank, and set to the task before him. He had no trouble easing it to the ground, and within minutes, he'd secured it against a nearby tree, the spigot within easy reach.

"How's that?" A comma of wavy brown hair fell over his forehead and he raked it back.

"Perfect. Thank you so much, Mr. Daniels." She extended his hat, and he settled it back in place.

"My pleasure, but please, call me Micah." His warm brown eyes sparkled like a whiskey and coke.

"Thank you, Micah."

He retrieved his jacket and scrutinized the trail down to her cabin. "Just moving in?"

She nodded. "Got in this morning."

"If you need anything from town, I'm headed that way."

"That's nice of you, but I just came from town myself." She hitched a thumb toward the bags of groceries in the back of her SUV. "I think I'm all set for now. But thanks."

"All right then, if you're sure you've got everything. Nice to meet you."

"Same here."

He walked the short distance to his truck, slipped behind the wheel, and settled his sunglasses back in place. When he caught her stare, he grinned and touched his hat. Unfazed, she waved back and continued to watch as the white pickup disappeared down the dusty road.

She collapsed onto the tailgate and glanced down at his boot prints in the dirt, dancing with her own.

Her inner smile disappeared, replaced by a sorrow so deep it stung her eyes. She couldn't remember the last time she'd danced.

Near panic circling his heart, Micah searched the arrivals board at the Elk County airport, found his son's flight, and stepped back as relief washed over him. The plane was on time and so was he. Normally, Micah would fly or drive to Houston to fetch his little boy, but this year, Aiden somehow persuaded his mother he was big enough to travel alone, and she convinced Micah their five-year-old son would be fine for the short, direct flight.

Despite the airline's policy of assigning a designated flight attendant to young passengers, Micah bristled as he paced the length of the terminal, waiting for the plane's arrival.

The airport, so small you could almost spit from one end to the other, included two concourses, four gates each, and served as a major hub for the Steamboat Springs Ski area. Typically packed in the winter months, now in early June, it was near empty. When Micah stopped pacing long enough to catch his reflection in the glass wall, he recalled a frigid October night when he had stood in that very spot and waved goodbye to Aiden's mother, not realizing it would be Elizabeth's last time in Providence.

His breath caught, the lake of regret so huge, he felt like he was drowning. Sometimes, in the lonely fall and winter months, Micah suffered nightmares where all he could see was water and sky and he didn't know how much longer he could swim.

A female voice broke his reverie to announce his son's flight, and beyond the glass wall, a small regional jet taxied to a stop. The steps lowered, and within minutes, a steady stream of passengers disembarked then dwindled, no Aiden. His insides tight as a knot, Micah whirled to scan the people now filling the terminal. Had he missed seeing his son descend the steps? He raced to the open door at the front of the concourse. Only when he saw Aiden, walking down the steps, accompanied by one of the cabin crew, a young man with bright eyes, caramel skin, and a friendly smile, did Micah realize he'd been holding his breath.

He couldn't believe how much the boy had changed since Christmas. His jaw seemed more defined, his cheeks less chubby, and he had to have grown six inches. Was he still only five years old?

Micah's gaze followed Aiden across the tarmac and into the building. When Aiden caught sight of his father, he pulled free of the crewmember's hand and ran forward. "Daddy!"

On a knee, Micah caught his child in his outstretched arms, and held on tight as he relished the warmth against his heart. After a moment, he released Aiden, ruffled his hair, and gazed into his own warm brown eyes. "Golly, I've missed you, little bear."

"Me too, Daddy." Aiden's face beamed with pure joy.

Micah stood and took the boy's travel bag from the young man, showed him his ID, tipped his hat, and thanked him for tending to his son. He gripped Aiden's small hand and received another sunbeam smile. Then, with a renewed lightness in his well-worn boots, he led the way through the airport to his truck, determined to make it a summer to remember.

# 3

# YEARNINGS

Sam spent the entire day making the cabin livable. First, she hooked up the propane tanks for the refrigerator and stove, then trekked back up the hill on foot to uncoil the mound of hose she'd dropped off earlier and connected it to the cistern in the loft to provide water to the sinks and toilet—simple gravity-fed plumbing, but better than nothing.

After that, she mounted the solar panel on the roof to power the one and only electrical outlet, checked the fridge temp—cool enough—and stowed her groceries. She moved the grill and deck chairs outdoors, removed the furniture covers, dusted, then swept up the zillions of flies and other dead insects that had found their way inside. As the sun dipped low over the mountains to the west, she cleaned the windows to a sparkling shine.

Physically exhausted, her little dog asleep inside, and a glass of red wine on the small table beside her, Sam collapsed into a lawn chair on the back deck to catch the sunset. She stretched her neck one way, then the other, and rolled her shoulders. The ache felt good, real, productive.

On past visits, her husband Brent, always did the heavy lifting. This time, she'd done it all on her own. Well, almost all, she thought with a smile, remembering the friendly cowboy who'd offloaded the water tank.

As she looked across the valley spread before her, the wide stream that cut through it, and the great peaks beyond, a feeling of contentment settled over her. She loved this place, the way the air smelled: thin, crisp, and cool. And the barely there sounds: leaves whispering in the breeze, hummingbirds zipping everywhere. With a deep breath, she took in the unspoiled beauty, as the sun set leisurely behind the distant mountains. She reached for the glass of wine, then remembered the importance of drinking plenty of water to help her body adjust to the change in elevation. She'd made that mistake before—the intense headaches and nausea of altitude sickness were unforgettable.

After trudging inside for a water bottle, she stopped on her way back to grab the rifle she'd propped in the corner of the living room. Outside on the deck, she leaned it against the cabin beside the door, within easy reach.

Apprehensive about staying in the cabin alone, she'd brought along a handgun and a rifle, even though she dreaded having to use one. It wasn't the two-leggeds that worried her, it was the four-leggeds: bears and mountain lions. Things she didn't worry about back home.

She glanced at the time on her phone. If she were back in Michigan, she'd be driving home from the office about now, unless she was working a writer's conference somewhere. As an acquisitions editor for a Grand Rapids-based publishing company, she attended a few conferences a year, and when she wasn't traveling, she logged fifty to sixty-hour work weeks.

It wasn't a great job—the pay was mediocre at best—but it came with decent benefits, and it was a steady income to offset the ebb and flow of her husband's real estate business. That financial security had come at a price though—one she no longer wished to pay. But too late for that now.

Tears welled in her eyes and she blinked them away, and brought up a photo of her family, a Christmas card worthy selfie she had taken the morning she and Brent had dropped the kids off at the Young Life camp in Southern Indiana where they'd signed on to be youth counselors.

Finished with their freshman year in college, her twins had put forth a conjoined effort to convince them it was a worthwhile way to spend their summer, each speaking in partial sentences that the other finished, as they so often did. It was like listening to a well-orchestrated debate delivered in a canon—one song, two voices.

"We won't make very much money," her daughter said.

"But we'll be leading other young kids to Christ," her son finished.

"Which is more important?" they'd chimed in unison, like the cherry on top of their well constructed sundae-sweet argument.

The young adults they were becoming filled her with an indescribable pride, the long-sought epiphany every parent yearned for, the reassurance she'd done something right. They were the sunshine that brightened her darkest days. And God knows she'd had plenty of those lately.

The photo showed the four of them, ridiculously happy, looking straight at the camera, Brent's smile that could fix anything. Only not this time. Oh, God, his smile. It was her favorite thing about him, but now it made her heart hurt. Now, the idea of using the image for their Christmas card this year seemed ludicrous.

Was that only two weeks ago? She ached for the early years of her marriage, before work, kids, and sports schedules ruled, before life's busyness squelched the joy right out of it. She missed the comfort of her husband's smile, her children's hugs and carefree giggles, but they would never again be the family they once were.

EARLY ONE MORNING, Micah stopped at the North Ridge to gaze across the valley below, as he often did. He shifted in the saddle and stared at the panorama of green and gold grasslands undulating in the breeze and the glimmer of the wide stream rambling through it.

He leaned forward to pat his horse. "Now would you look at that, Buck? How could we ever survive anyplace else?" This was what he lived for, the raw beauty of the Colorado Rockies. What a blessing. But like every blessing, it came mixed.

Most days, Micah thought little about the time he spent riding fences. He'd willingly owned the responsibility of checking and maintaining their miles and miles of fence line because, unlike his brothers and cousins—and most of their hired hands—Micah enjoyed the solitude. But he'd been alone for too long. He'd mastered the art of keeping people out. Of the ranch and his life.

Buck whinnied beneath the blazing afternoon sun, and Micah had a notion to head down for a drink. He nudged the animal's sides but pulled up when someone approached the creek's edge.

Mesmerized, he sat motionless as the woman shed her top, then her boots and jeans, and ease into the water in her bra and panties. Or was it a bathing suit? Hard telling from so far away.

She pulled her hair free of its ponytail, and the sensuous effect of that simple act sent a mass of long shimmering blonde hair cascading over her shoulders, catching the sun in a golden flash and setting every nerve in Micah's body to tingling.

Samantha Jamison, the woman he'd met on his way into town the other day. While she washed her hair and bathed, Micah wondered how she was getting on in the old Baker cabin, and if she was married. He hadn't thought to check for a ring.

He considered riding down anyway, but didn't want to intrude on her bath. Still, she was awfully pretty, and he'd love to see her lithe body up close, feel the softness of her skin, the gentle curve of her hips, the silkiness of her freshly washed hair as it dried in the sun.

His body caught in the throes of responding to his wonderings, Micah cleared his throat and pushed his hat up on his head as he struggled to break free.

He knew he should turn around, go another way, get back to mending fences, but he couldn't pull himself away.

When she stepped from the stream, dried off, and glanced around, his heart nearly stopped. He reined his horse backward, sinking further into the tree line. He felt certain she couldn't see him clear up on the ridge, but he sure didn't want to get caught.

Wrapped in her towel, she spread a blanket in the sun, then stretched out on it, arms wishboned beneath her head.

Micah stilled and remained silent, barely breathing, until sometime later—it could've been five minutes or twenty-five, he had no idea—after she'd dressed, rolled up the blanket, and hiked back up to her cabin.

When she disappeared from sight, Micah let out the breath trapped in his chest and slapped his hat on his thigh. "Whoa."

# 4

# BEAR

"Bear, sit," Sam instructed her dog as she pointed a finger to the floor. Bear sat, and she clipped on his leash.

"Good boy!" She patted his head. With his leash in one hand, she checked her sidearm with the other.

Sam often took the rifle when she left the cabin, but looking forward to a long walk with Bear in the meadow, she thought the sidearm would be easier to carry. The leather holster belted around her waist felt comfortable, the handgun much lighter than the heavy rifle, but every bit as powerful in case she happened upon a bear, a real one.

People often laughed when they heard her dog's name because he was anything but what the name inferred. Her Yorkie was a tiny thing, six pounds with a mass of soft amber brown and black Ewok-looking hair, but as a puppy, he'd looked like a wild bear cub. When the kids had suggested the name Bear, it stuck. No further discussion needed.

He was Sam's dog now that the twins had gone to college, and she hadn't thought twice about bringing him with her to the cabin. Brent had warned her of the dangers, but she'd insisted, and her husband, not thrilled about the added responsibility of caring for the dog, had easily given in.

From the back deck, Sam scrutinized the meadow and the sky for predators, and with Bear trotting ahead of her, headed down the path toward the stream. Bear loved walks and practically bounced along, jumping more than running as he traipsed along the trail. So cute, Sam laughed out loud.

As the trail opened onto the meadow, a shadow fell across Sam's shoulder and she turned as an enormous bird swooped past and silently snatched up her little dog. Bear yipped.

Startled, Sam held tight to the leash and yanked as hard as she could, gasping as both animals tumbled to the ground ahead of her. The bird thrashed wildly in the tall grass, then stilled. Bear let out a pitiful whine. Sam rushed forward and picked up her dog.

Cradled in her arms, Bear went crazy, barking and growling and trying to free himself, but she held tight and whispered, "No bark." The dog settled. She pulled her revolver, eased the hammer back, and leveled the gun as she eased forward to inspect the bird—a golden eagle she could see now. The eagle fluttered slightly, trying to right itself, but its wing lay at an awkward angle.

When the bird stilled, Sam holstered her gun and eased forward for a better look.

Lying on its side, it stared back at her with its one beady black eye.

She covered her mouth with her free hand, but a small "Oh!" escaped.

Bear whimpered, and she looked down at her puppy, limp in her arm while a growing red splotch soaked her white T-shirt. The eagle's talons had cut into his flesh, laying open wide gashes on his shoulders.

Panicked, Sam raced to the cabin and wrapped Bear in a towel. Then, grabbing her keys and purse, she laid him on the passenger seat of her SUV. As she swung the door closed, she remembered the bird.

Since she was taking Bear into town to find a vet anyway, she might as well try. She dashed back into the cabin and scrambled up into the loft for a piece of burlap she'd seen earlier. Returning to where the eagle lay motionless, she threw the fabric over it. It didn't so much as flutter, so she cautiously bundled it up, and using a ponytail holder from her wrist, secured it. She carried it to the SUV, surprised it weighed little more than her pup, and eased it into Bear's dog cage in the back.

Terrified, she sped down the dirt roads and found the veterinary clinic on the main street in the small town of Providence. While a prayer circled in her heart for the vet to be in, she burst through the door with Bear in her arms.

A woman with a mass of wavy auburn curls and plump pink cheeks skirted the counter to lead them into an examination room. A Wyatt Erp-looking gentleman joined them within minutes and introduced himself as Doctor Daniels. "So this is Bear," he said with a chuckle.

Ignoring his laugh, Sam described in a rush what had happened while the doctor examined her dog, lying limp and silent on the table in the center of the small room. "Please, please," she murmured to Bear as she stroked a paw.

"He'll be fine," the vet said, his voice soft with kindness.

Sam sighed with relief.

"But he needs stitches, so I'll have to put him under."

"Okay," she said, nodding.

Sam waited anxiously at Bear's side while the vet administered the anesthetic. As the long needle emptied into her little dog, she glanced at the doctor, his face tender and compassionate, focused on his work.

When he finished with the shot, he gently patted Bear, then turned to dispose of the syringe in a bin on the counter. "So, what kind of bird was it?"

"An eagle, a golden eagle, I think. I have it in my SUV." Sam rested a comforting hand on Bear.

"You what?" He turned to her with an incredulous glare. "You brought in the bird?"

Sam wondered what she'd done wrong. "What? I should've left him there to die?"

"You know eagles are protected, right? You can't just go out and kill one." His obnoxious tone inferred she knew no such thing.

Her jaw tensed and her eyes narrowed. "I know that, and it's not dead. At least it wasn't when I put it in my vehicle. Also, I didn't go out intending to hurt it. It attacked my dog."

"Still, you could get in trouble for injuring an eagle. I'll have to report it to the DOW."

"The DOW?"

"Division of Wildlife."

"Oh, that's great. Do what you need to do, Doc." Didn't he realize she was only trying to help the poor bird?

She crouched to murmur to Bear, nearly asleep on the table. With his head in her palm, she stroked him and whispered, "Good dog," until his trusting eyes closed.

"I'm sorry," the doctor said. "I know you thought you were doing the right thing, but you should've left the bird, as cruel as that sounds."

Stunned by his advice, she shook her head. "I couldn't."

He shot her a sympathetic smile, and she could've sworn she'd seen the warmth of those brown eyes before. Doctor Daniels—right. Probably related to the friendly cowboy she'd met. She wondered if it was a curse or a blessing, those dark good looks the Daniels men seemed to share. "Me neither," he admitted. "Let's see what kind of damage you did to that fella, shall we? Can I go get it?"

Sam handed over her keys. "Black Escalade. It's in the back."

Over the course of the next several hours, Doctor Daniels stitched up Bear's cuts, then operated on the bird's wing.

When the DOW agent showed up, he took Sam's statement and informed her that since she'd acted in self-defense, he wouldn't file formal charges. "But I wouldn't walk your little dog in open meadows anymore if I were you, not up there in the mountains, anyway."

"Right. I'll be more careful about that," she said. "Will the bird be all right?"

"When Doc's done fixin' her up, I'll take her with me. She'll be well taken care of while she recovers, and as long as she can fly again, she'll be returned to the wild."

Sam smiled, relieved they'd been able to save it.

Settled in her SUV, she glanced over at her little dog asleep on the passenger seat, a clean white bandage wrapped around his torso. Thank God he was still there to keep her company.

She couldn't endure losing one more thing she loved.

"I've got a good one for you today," Cody said as they crossed the drive from Micah's cabin to the barn.

"You don't say." Micah chuckled. Leave it to his cousin with his flair for embellishment to turn a simple vet visit into a funny story.

"This pretty blonde walks in with a little Yorkie wrapped in a towel," Cody began. "Turns out a golden eagle swooped him; its talons really did a number on him. But get this, that flatlander yanked the eagle right out of the air along with her dog." He laughed and looked across to Micah, who shook his head. "Snapped its wing right in two. And then, get this, she bagged the bird and brought it in too."

"She brought the bird in?" Micah couldn't believe someone would try to capture a golden eagle, or any eagle for that matter, let alone an injured one. She must have a heart for wounded creatures.

"Yeah. And I think the bird's gonna make it. I repaired the damage—spent over two hours in surgery—and it should heal just fine."

They entered the barn, redolent with the familiar scents of pine, hay, and horse manure, and it took a minute for Micah's eyes to adjust to the sudden dimness. "You're keeping an eagle at your office?" Buck whinnied from his stall while dust motes danced in the filtering light from the open doors at both ends. Micah stopped before Buck's stall, grabbed the bridle from the hook, and opened the stall door. He slipped the tack over the horse's head and led him out.

"No, the DOW took it," Cody said, fetching his horse from the opposite side of the barn.

"You called the DOW on her? That was harsh." They led the horses through the long row of near empty stalls to the tack room.

"Had to. I could lose my license for failing to report something like that. But, hey, it's fine. It was self-defense, so they're not pressing charges."

"Well, that's good at least" Micah placed a pad then a saddle on Buck, flipped up the stirrup, and reached beneath for the cinch. "How's the dog?"

"A few stitches is all." Cody swung a saddle onto his horse and eyed Micah over the top of it. "You should meet this woman. She was something: pure Colorado heart, Vegas legs, California smile. And she ain't afraid of much, that's for sure," he finished with a chuckle.

Micah shot his cousin a side eye as he tightened the cinch. Keeping Aiden occupied was trouble enough, he didn't need a woman complicating things. A sudden image of Samantha Jamison stepping from the stream flitted through his mind. "She was a blonde, you said?"

"Yep, and pretty, too. A real Sunshine Barbie."

Micah laughed. Cody put a unique sparkle on everything. "What was her name?"

"Samantha ..." Cody drew it out, as if trying to remember a last name.

"Jamison?"

"Yeah, that's it. You know her?"

Micah smiled. Yep, she was a beautiful woman. No argument there. "We've met." He stepped into the stirrup and slid up into the saddle.

"Shoulda figured," Cody said with a shake of his head.

For the next several weeks, as Micah headed out each morning to ride fences, he set off toward the North Ridge and the old Baker place. Often, he found Samantha dressed in tight black pants and a tank top doing stretches on her back deck, and he'd stop to watch as she held odd positions for long moments at a time. He enjoyed her graceful movements, like a ballet in slow motion, and he caught himself thinking about her long after he'd moved on, wondering how long she planned to stay, how she was getting along, if her little dog was okay. And if she was married.

He considered being neighborly and dropping by to check on her, but quickly decided against it. The last thing he needed was to get tangled up with a flatlander who'd leave in a month or two, even if she was the most enticing woman he'd met in ages.

Then again, her leaving might be a good thing. He could tangle himself to his heart's content, with no concern for commitment. Yeah, having her around might be nice. Keep him warm at night for the next few months.

He shook his head and pushed the thought away. He could never be that kind of man.

## 5

# STORMS

As the summer days ticked by like a beloved grandfather clock and Bear's injuries healed, Sam found an odd sense of peace in spending so much time alone. She had an odd feeling of being watched, which felt more comforting than eerie, as if someone or something was looking out for her.

Since the eagle incident, every time she coaxed her little dog to go outside, he did his business quickly and wanted back inside the cabin. So, she spent long hours outside alone, doing her Pilates on the back deck, bathing in the ice-cold stream in the heat of the day, and taking long walks in the woods surrounding the cabin.

She enjoyed her solitude. Raised on a farm with five older brothers who to this day, despite her protests, still called her Samantha Jane, there was always someone looking after her. And in college, she'd had roommates, sorority sisters, and then Brent, whom she met her sophomore year of college.

Tall and broad-shouldered, with an organic charisma that made others alight with happiness in his presence, he was the most effervescent person she'd ever met. And he was funny too. She'd fallen for him the first time he looked at her, with his blond hair tumbling down over his forehead and his clear blue eyes that saw through her, around her, inside of her. How magical her life would be if she lived in that circle of light, she had thought. But it wasn't the life she imagined.

Somehow, she felt less alone here, in this tiny little cabin in the wilds of northwestern Colorado, where days went by without a single vehicle passing by on the road above, than she had the last few years of her marriage. She had her little dog, the birds—mostly hummingbirds, eagles and owls—the sky and the clouds, the endless meadow grasses and aspens. The scents of her new home filled her every breath, and it was life-saving, exactly what she'd needed.

Sam passed the first few weeks by doing a deep clean on the cabin. She'd emptied every kitchen cabinet and drawer and washed every glass, dish, utensil, even the canned goods left from prior visits, before returning them to their places. She moved furniture, dusted, swept, and cleaned every nook, cranny, cupboard, and window. Anything to keep busy, to prevent her from dwelling on how bleak, how depleted, her life had become. Exhausted at the end of each day, she'd gaze from the loft at the area below with a sense of pride, then fall into a deep, restful sleep, too tired to wallow in her newfound isolation.

In mid-June, having run out of things to make the cabin more livable, she sat on the deck as a summer storm rolled in over the mountains. Far off, dense purple and black thunderheads hovered and swirled in great masses high above the peaks, rain clearly discernible in the dark blue striations beneath them. It always amazed her how fast the weather could change in the mountains.

The afternoon had been gorgeous, clear and hot, but now, as the clouds rolled in, the temperature dropped twenty degrees, and the wind picked up, bringing with it the line of threatening skies.

It reminded her of a family vacation she and Brent and the twins had taken to the Grand Tetons when they'd gotten caught in a storm while kayaking the Snake River. She'd never been so terrified in her life.

They'd started out on a hot sunny day, and with no sign of bad weather moving in, they'd dressed in swimsuits and brought only life jackets, a few bottles of water and deli sandwiches.

The park ranger who'd helped them decide where to kayak had insisted they scout the pullout, called Dead Man's Bend, before they set out, but for reasons she couldn't recall, they didn't do it. They'd left having no idea what the spot looked like and only a vague sense of how far downstream it was. And if they missed it, the next section was rated expert, highly technical, which meant lots of trees and debris to maneuver around.

For the twins, then fifteen, it was their first time kayaking without a guide. Three hours into the six-hour trip, the storm had moved in, and with it, the temperature dropped to near fifty degrees with a steady driving rain that chilled them to the bone. Accompanied by a wind so strong it almost drove them back upriver, they were all nearly hypothermic by the time they'd gotten to the pullout. And if not for a mother and young son sitting beneath a pine on the bank, waiting for the rest of their family, they may have missed the pullout entirely. Sam shivered just thinking about it.

She missed those fun family vacations, not that one—part of it was a nightmare—but they'd enjoyed many grand adventures through the years.

What she missed most, though, was simply having her children around. Not ready for them to go off to college, she'd been totally unprepared for the heart wrenching goodbyes, the unsettling quiet of their huge lake house. She couldn't even walk past their empty bedrooms without a sharp pain twisting her insides. She'd tried to tell herself it was time, the natural progression of being a parent—the letting go—and while her mind readily agreed, her heart balked at the painful logic.

Coming home to the empty house was miserable, and since Brent worked so many evenings, she found herself staying at the office later and later.

Even before the kids went off to college, she'd been working long hours, often staying well past six o'clock, sometimes seven, and when she'd gotten the promotion to Senior Acquisitions Editor, she'd started traveling more.

That was when she and her husband began to drift apart. Brent was always either working around the house, building something at the barn or maintaining one of their other properties. Even when she was home, she felt invisible.

How did she not see it coming?

Her head fell into her hands as her thoughts drifted back to that stormy night when she'd awakened to a rolling thunder. A flash of lightning illuminated the empty bed beside her and she bolted upright, then searched the house for Brent as an unthinkable dread took root.

While prayers circled in her heart, she paced the foyer in her faded night shirt, and when he finally pulled into the garage, she rushed out to meet him, thankful he was alive. But even in the musty garage, she smelled a strange new scent on him, and when the lightning flashed, she saw betrayal in his eyes.

Weeks later, when the anguish and fury had dulled to a raw ache, she blamed herself. She'd given everything she had to her job, with little left over for him.

When she'd gotten pregnant her sophomore year, she'd had to put college on hold. While the twins were young, she'd taken a few courses, then finished up full-time once they started school. Fast-tracking from there, she felt driven to catch up, make her husband proud, prove to the world she could do it all—be a great mother *and* enjoy a successful career.

Now she felt those days like something sharp in her chest. She swiped at a tear that escaped down her cheek as the first raindrop fell.

What drove her to work so hard? Was it the enormous responsibility that was thrust upon her as the only female in line to make director at her male-dominated company?

Sam felt proud of her accomplishments, but the price she'd had to pay to earn her advancements had been too high. And in the end, it wasn't worth it.

As she stared at the mountains, the tears flowed as steady and unfettered as the cool mountain rain. She tipped her face to meet the sky, welcoming the downpour, letting it cleanse her spirit, wash away the anger and bitterness, the soul-crushing heartbreak of her troubled marriage and life-sucking job.

If only she were young again. If she could start over, she'd do it differently. She wouldn't work so hard. She'd put her family first, always. Instead of a house on the lake, they'd live in a simpler, much smaller home, perhaps on a pond with acreage. She'd have a good job, but she wouldn't be so determined to climb the corporate ladder. She'd gotten close enough to the top to see that what she'd hoped to find wasn't there.

No, if given a second chance, she'd find contentment in a nine-to-five job that would allow her to be home in the evening to make a nice dinner for her family. That nightly meal was important; she knew that now.

"Oh, please God," she begged, the rain coming now in blinding sheets. She raised her palms to the rain, to the heavens. "I need another chance. I'll do it right this time, I promise."

## 6

# SHELTER

"Whoa." Micah reined in his horse downhill from Samantha's cabin. Through the downpour, he could make out her silhouette sitting in a chair on the deck, dark against the dim light of the cabin behind her. Something about the way her shoulders shook as she lifted her face to the rain, cut him deep, and even though he couldn't hear anything over the wind and rain, he felt a sudden urge to race forward, jump from his horse, and wrap her in his arms.

Never had he seen a woman cry so hard, as if her whole heart were splayed wide open. He had stopped, hoping to take shelter, but coming upon her like this gave him pause. Did he dare intrude at such a vulnerable moment? Maybe he ought to ride it out, head on home in the rain. When she stood and disappeared inside, he shook his hat and wiped the rain from his face, his conscience still warring with propriety. And he'd broken himself once chasing a flatlander.

He gave her a few minutes to collect herself, then urged his mount across the meadow and up to the back of her cabin. After tying his horse to the railing on the lee side to give the animal shelter, he skirted around to the front and knocked lightly on the door. A dog barked incessantly from within.

When Sam peered through the window, he waved, hoping she'd recognize him and not shoot him on sight. She dabbed at her face with a towel and opened the door.

"Howdy," he said, touching the brim of his hat. "Micah," he reminded her.

"Right. Hi." She looked sideways, then behind him, while the little dog in her arms continued to bark. "What are you doing here?" she asked, then to the dog, "Bear! No bark." The dog quieted instantly but continued to eye him as warily as its owner.

Micah chuckled and shuffled his feet, immediately feeling the familiar awkwardness he always felt around attractive women. "I was out riding fences and got caught in this storm that moved in sorta quick-like, and well, I was hoping you might take pity on a rain-drenched cowboy and offer me shelter 'til it passes."

A hint of amusement softened her features as he stood there, rain dripping steadily from the brim of his Stetson. "Of course," she said, backing up. "Come on in."

He took off his hat, shook the water from it, and stepped inside.

Closing the door behind him, she again told the dog, "No bark," as she set it down. While the dog gave Micah a thorough sniff, Samantha took his hat and hung it on a hook behind the door. She'd already changed into dry clothes—a dark blue sweatshirt and faded jeans—but her feet were still bare.

Micah bent to let the dog smell his hand, then patted his head. The angry scars along his torso were still visible through the tufts of fur beginning to grow back. "Cute dog."

"Thanks." She eyed it, as though unwilling to meet Micah's gaze. "Please, take off your wet things. I'll get you a towel."

While she disappeared into a small room walled off at the corner, he stripped off his rain slicker and flannel and hung them carefully on the empty hooks beside the door.

She reappeared a few seconds later, handing him a towel as he pulled off his second boot.

"Thank you." He dried his face and hair and draped the towel around his neck, then looked around, amazed at how warm and cozy the little place was.

Except for the tiny room in the corner, it was all one open space, with walls of natural rough-hewn pine softly lit by tapers flickering in brass candle sconces. A few base cabinets and small appliances snuggled together to the right of the front door, providing all the amenities of a full kitchen. While the front half of the room nestled beneath a loft, the other end was open to the timbered ceiling and walled with glass, definitely built with a thought to the view.

There was nothing even remotely fancy about the cabin, but it looked comfortable, clean, and tidy. The scent of the candles, the crackle of the roaring fire, and the soft pelting of rain on the metal roof added to the overall effect, which felt relaxed, warm, and inviting.

"Nice fire you got going there." He nodded toward the massive fieldstone fireplace that dominated one side of the open space.

"Make yourself at home. You must be freezing," she said.

He walked to the fire and rubbed his hands together near the flames. Turned sideways to him, she dried her hair, squeezing the long, wet strands through the towel, and he imagined the cool softness of it threading through his fingertips.

Mesmerized by her natural beauty, he floundered for words and settled for the obvious, "Looks like you got caught in it, too."

"Yeah." She hung her wet towel on a hook near the door and sat on a chair at the small kitchen table to pull on a pair of thick gray socks. When she finished, she glanced up and asked, "Would you like something to drink? Red wine, whiskey, water?"

Without a hint of makeup, her barely sun-kissed skin glowed in the candlelight, and her eyes—the bluest eyes he'd ever seen—sparkled beneath dark wet lashes. She had an earthy grace, much like the land he loved, pure and wild. His breath caught in this throat.

He realized he'd been staring and rubbed the back of his neck. "A whiskey would be great. Thank you."

"I only have water to mix it with," she said, pulling out a bottle from one of the lower cabinets.

"Straight up's just fine."

She pulled two short glasses from a small shelf beyond the sink, poured a couple of inches into each one, and rejoined him at the fire. With an easy smile, she handed him a glass and set the bottle aside, then sat cross-legged on the braided rug, her back to the couch.

He settled beside her and clinked his glass to hers. "To the rain—wait, to rain on a roof." He toasted the ceiling before tossing back the contents.

Sam's eyes grew wide. She took a small sip and grimaced.

Micah rubbed his chin, hiding his grin. She obviously wasn't a whiskey drinker. He pictured her as more of a red wine connoisseur, but maybe, given her emotional state earlier, she wanted something stronger.

She refilled his glass, smiling uneasily.

He eyed the ring on her left hand as she poured, and while a part of him was more than a little disappointed, another part sighed with relief to know she was off limits. He'd never mess with another man's wife. So that was that.

He set his drink aside and relaxed back against the couch, absorbing the heat of the fire as the whiskey warmed him from the inside. "So, tell me Samantha, what's a beautiful woman like you doing here in this little hunting cabin in the middle of nowhere? Are you hiding or searching?"

His compliment drew a small smile, but she looked away as if reluctant to answer. She took another sip, cringing again as she forced it down. "Hiding or searching? Do you really talk like that?"

A soft chuckle escaped him. Definitely hiding. "Apparently, I do."

"I came here to get away and ... to write." She said it like it was the first time she had voiced it to anyone.

The light of the fire danced on her skin, making it glow with a soft radiance, while her bright eyes gazed back at him, drawing him in. He cleared his throat. "Oh, you're a writer?"

"Not exactly. I'm an editor. But I've always wanted to write, change the world with my words."

Micah nodded again. "Are you getting away from something specific or just looking for quiet to get the writing juices flowing?"

"I have a job, but," she took a deep breath and stared into the fire for several heartbeats, "it's not the job I dreamed of. In fact, it pretty much saps the life out of me. I needed a break."

"To write."

"Yes, to write."

He thought she might expound, but she didn't. "How long are you staying?" The cabin was bare bones, and he wondered how long she'd last without running water and electricity.

"I've got the entire summer." She smiled as Bear made himself comfortable in Micah's lap. "He likes you."

"Yeah, dogs always like me. I don't know why. They must know a good guy when they smell him." He shot her a half smile.

Her response was almost a laugh, but it didn't last near long enough.

"Don't you miss the comforts of home?"

Her eyes panned the room. "There's really only one thing I miss."

"What's that?"

"Music," she said. "My solar panel barely produces enough electricity for my laptop, and since I need it to write, no music."

"Really? Music? That's all you miss?"

"Well, okay, I miss bubble baths too," she admitted. "A little."

Micah chuckled. "That's more like it."

Side by side on the worn rug while the fire danced, they drank and continued to dry out as the storm raged and the wind howled outside the cozy little cabin. He asked about her novel then about the incident with the eagle and her dog and told her how he admired her for having the gumption to bag the eagle. When he shared some of Cody's other funny or absurd animal stories, they laughed together.

He couldn't help but stare when she glanced his way. Her eyes were bright and captivating, and several times there was an awkward silence as she stared back at him. They kept the conversation light, but plenty went unsaid.

She refilled his glass again, and when she handed it to him, their fingers touched. Her skin was soft and warm. "Tell me about Mr. Jamison," he said, eyeing her wedding ring.

"Yeah, well." She stared at the ring with a wry smile. "Mr. Jamison decided he wanted a new and improved, and much younger Mrs. Jamison, so—" she let out a weak laugh, "he stayed in Michigan."

There was something about the broken smile and the way she looked away that betrayed her pain, and while his heart went out to her, a small part of him felt relieved she wasn't happily married after all.

"Samantha, I'm sorry." He set his glass on the floor, turned to face her, and took both of her hands in his. "I'm so sorry."

The tears were suddenly there again, pooling in her eyes, as she struggled to hold them at bay.

"Don't feel sorry for me." She sniffled. "I'll be fine."

She certainly didn't seem fine, but he admired her bravado.

"And please call me Sam. All my friends call me Sam."

Micah grinned at that. "Sam, I like that. It sounds much stronger than Samantha."

She pulled her hands away to wipe a tear, then chuckled softly. "Yeah, that's me—strong."

He could tell she wasn't feeling strong. In fact, he felt certain if she were alone, she'd break down again right then and there.

Instead, she forced a smile and finished her whiskey with a cringe and a shake of her head. "Is there a Mrs. Daniels?"

He stared into the flames and relaxed against the couch again. "There was once. She decided she didn't want to be Mrs. Daniels anymore, so she returned to Houston before our son was born. She was young when we married, too young to know what she wanted."

They'd both been incredibly naïve. Terrified at the prospect of having a baby at their remote mountain home, Elizabeth had insisted on going to stay with her parents in Houston, and Micah had no choice but to agree.

Even before then, he knew she wasn't happy at the ranch. A city girl, raised on tennis courts and country clubs, she was a twenty-year-old debutante on vacation with her family when they'd met in Steamboat Springs where he was riding rodeo to help pay for law school.

She had loved The Homestead during their summer visits, but living with the isolation year-round after he passed the bar was a different story. Spending all day alone while Micah tended to business left her lonely and needing something more. He'd hoped a baby would fill what was missing, but when she left, he knew she wouldn't return.

His wife fell in love with Micah Daniels, the rodeo star. Micah Daniels, the rancher-attorney, wasn't enough. Six years later, the memory still brought an ache to his chest.

When Micah glanced at Sam, he was stunned by the compassion in her gaze. Somehow, she had captured a small intimate part of him, a piece he rarely let others see, let alone take hold of.

"You have a son?"

He cleared his throat and pushed Elizabeth to the deep of his heart, where he still held onto her. "Aiden. He's five. Comes to stay with me every summer."

"Five!" Her voice and eyebrows rose simultaneously as if she thought he was too old to have a five-year-old.

Shoot, thirty-eight wasn't too old. Was it?

"You must really miss him the other nine months of the year," she said.

He nodded. "You have no idea."

"Oh, I think I do. My twins went away to college last fall. It's amazing how you spend your whole life building a foundation for them, setting their feet on the right path, and you're so proud of them when the moment comes, it doesn't seem possible to be simultaneously excited about their future and sad to let them go, to embark upon it without you."

Tears hung on her lower lids, and he squeezed her hand in reassurance.

"No matter how much you prepare for it, when it actually happens, it leaves a gaping kid-sized hole in your life." She blinked several times. "I miss them so much. I can only imagine how hard it would be to leave a five-year-old."

He had a sudden urge to hold her, encourage her to let go, yet he sensed she didn't want to cry anymore. He admired her determination, so he waited while she collected herself.

"Do you have other family?" he asked. She seemed so alone, as though she'd lost her last remaining human connection.

"My parents are gone. My dad left when I was sixteen, and my mom passed away a few years ago. I have four older brothers." She eyed his hand, still holding hers. "A fifth one died at eighteen."

"Car accident?"

"Suicide. I was fifteen."

"That must have been tough."

She nodded and her eyes went far away. "We were close."

He searched for words to comfort her, but some pain ran too deep. "Twins, that must've kept you busy."

"And then some. I was looking forward to having them home for the summer too, but they jumped at a chance to be counselors at a Bible camp. What parent says no to that? So, here I am, with three months to myself."

"Well, their loss is our gain."

"Ours?"

"Aiden's and mine, my son. You'll have to meet him."

"I'd like that. Five is a fun age; they still want to play with you."

"Yeah, well, unfortunately, the ranch keeps me pretty busy, and I don't have a lot of time for him. In fact, he's with my brothers and cousins tonight, more than likely playing poker."

"Oh, Micah. Make time for him. Life is short, and childhood is even shorter. Savor every minute because there's nothing more precious or fleeting—" she covered her mouth, as if she'd said too much, "than the love of a child."

Had she sensed his anxiety over his son?

"Trust me on that. The last thing you want is to regret that you didn't ..." She turned away, and he suspected she spoke from experience.

"Honestly, I don't know what to do with him. He wants to follow me everywhere, do everything I do, and it's plain dangerous."

"I'm sure he only wants to know you, to spend time with you."

Micah sighed beneath the weight of his failings with his son. Should he tell her the real reason for the distance between him and Aiden?

Yeah, he thought she'd understand.

"You should have seen him when I picked him up at the airport a few days ago. It was like I was a stranger to him, but he hugged me anyway, seriously hugged me, you know? Like he knows how much I love him. I'm sure he barely remembers me from one visit to the next, yet every time it's the same huge bear hug. I don't know where it comes from, and I'm not sure I deserve it."

"You deserve it, Micah. You're his father, and of course, he knows you love him."

"As hard as it is for me to tell him goodbye at the end of a summer, it's got to be much harder on him. He tries not to, but he always cries. I hate putting him through that every year. I wonder if it would be better—"

"Don't even think it. He needs you, Micah, even if you're only able to give him a summer."

"But my heart breaks every time, and it's ..." He refilled his glass and took a long sip before he continued. "It's like a favorite book with a torn cover. There's no fixing it, and it's only a matter of time before it falls apart. You want to stop reading it, put it on a shelf to keep it whole. When he leaves every summer, it tears a little more."

"You can't put your son on a shelf."

"I know, but you don't understand how hard it is, how it rips me apart to say goodbye every year. The whole summer long, I'm thinking about it, knowing it's coming, dreading it."

"So you don't get too close because that'll only make it harder?"

He nodded, pleased that she seemed to understand. Sam stared into the fire, and he followed her gaze. She looked sad, thoughtful, disappointed even.

When she glanced back his way, he could almost see her mind working. "What are winters like on the ranch?"

He cocked his head, wondering where her thoughts were leading. "They're busy too. We typically overwinter quite a few head of cattle, and even though we move them to lower pastures, they still need a lot of daily care, feeding, water."

"Do you vacation, like around Christmastime?"

"I get to see Aiden every other holiday. For Christmas I stay in a hotel and ingratiate myself with my ex-wife's family for the day. Why?"

"Have you ever considered taking him somewhere, like starting a new father-son tradition?"

"He'll be starting school in the fall."

"I don't know about schools in Houston, but in Michigan, kids get at least a two-week break around Christmas, then another whole week in spring."

Micah smiled as he considered it, then chuckled at the encouragement in Sam's face. "Now that might be a fine idea. He's old enough to travel now. I like that. We could go somewhere fun, do something together, the two of us."

"And it would give you both something to look forward to when you part ways in the fall."

"That it would. Thank you."

She picked at a thread on the hem of her jeans. "I didn't do anything."

Their eyes locked, and Micah had a sudden urge to lean over and kiss her, but his gaze fell to the ring on her finger and the thought vanished.

Sam must have sensed his longing, because she stood and walked to the sliding glass door to peer at the rain. "Seems to be letting up."

He took in the length of her standing there with her back to him, her curves silhouetted against the darkness beyond the glass, then wrenched his gaze away, rubbed his jaw, and set his whisky aside.

"Does the stream down there have a name? It's not on my map."

"Homestead Creek."

"Named for the old homestead?" She turned to face him.

He nodded. "My family's first home when they settled here. Not much left of it anymore. Our ranch is called The Homestead." He stood and set his empty glass on the hearth. "Where's your map?" He glanced around the small room.

Sam walked to the foot of the ladder and faced the wall. "Here."

Over her shoulder, Micah studied the wall map in the dim light of the corner. The faint scent of herbs in her damp hair teased his nostrils, and he leaned closer.

"This section here," he began, using his index finger to draw a large circle on the map, "roughly a hundred and twenty thousand acres, used to belong to my great-great-uncle, my great-grandpa's brother. He had three sons, but they all died. His two daughters didn't want to stay here, so he sold the land to have something to leave them when he passed. My great grandpa bought as much as he could, but unfortunately, Moonglow Meadow wasn't part of it." The familiar regret settled over him for not finding the money when the Bakers put it up for sale.

Sam looked sideways at him. "Moonglow Meadow?"

"Yeah, if you've ever seen it beneath the light of a full moon, you'd appreciate the name." Images of his beloved valley shimmered in his mind.

Sam glanced toward the far end of the room. "I can only imagine how beautiful it is," she said, her voice barely a whisper.

"I could show it to you sometime," he said. "The view from the North Ridge is the best."

"I'd like that."

His heart did an odd little stutter as he imagined the two of them, alone, on the ridge.

Micah peered out the sliding glass door, where scattered rays of pale moonlight filtered across the valley floor. "I think the worst of it's over. I'd best get on home. Aiden and the others are likely wondering where I am." He returned to the front door and pulled on his boots and jacket, then faced her, hat in hand. "Thank you for everything, Sam. I had the best time tonight."

"Me too," she said, with a cute tilt of her head and a light in her eyes.

Funny, he thought, how reaching out to her had eased his own pain, a pain he only now realized he still held onto.

Sam locked the doors, brushed her teeth, and with Bear in her arms, scurried up the ladder to the loft. At the railing, she gazed out the massive windows overlooking the meadow, now softly swathed in moonlight as the shadow of a lone rider crossed the creek and headed up the opposite side of the valley.

"Good night, Micah," she whispered into the darkness.

Her belly fluttered as she recalled the tall rancher stepping into her cabin, how he carried with him the raw scent of the earth, how she'd tried to avoid watching him as he'd stripped off his wet things. How his jeans, soaked through, clung to his thighs, showing every hardened muscle. How his white undershirt fit snug across his broad shoulders, chest, and around his biceps. With a body that worked for a living, not softened by age or lack of use, he possessed a pure male strength she found intensely unsettling.

He was extraordinary, physically, socially, intellectually. By any standards, he was a real catch. Why hasn't he remarried? *Doesn't matter. None of it matters.*

Haunted by his deep voice and sweet easy words, she laid her head on the pillow, determined to push the gentle cowboy from her thoughts, but when his whiskey-brown eyes danced before her, she was struck with a sudden inspiration for a story.

Throwing off the covers, she jumped from bed to retrieve her laptop, and started on her novel. When the first pink blush of dawn peeked over the mountains, she had a rough outline, the first ten chapters, and a hopeful heart.

# 7

# WHITE HORSE

"Hey, buckaroo, give me a hug," Micah called to Aiden.

Aiden hesitated as his cousins continued out the back door toward the sound of yipping puppies. With a huff, he dashed back to his father and threw his arms around his neck.

Micah bent to hug his son for an all-too-brief moment. "You be good for your Aunt Anna and Uncle Cody."

"Always," Aiden said with a grin.

Micah ruffled his hair. "Love you, buddy."

"Love you too, Daddy," Aiden called over his shoulder as he ran out the door, letting it slam shut behind him.

"He'll be fine, don't worry," Cody said. "I'll bring him up tomorrow after supper."

As his son disappeared down the back steps, Micah grinned, pleased that Aiden felt comfortable enough with his cousins to want to have a sleepover.

On his way home, Micah stopped off at the Conoco for gas. As he stood next to his truck while the tank filled, the mail carrier, a stocky bull of a man with a balding pate and unkempt beard, ambled out from the station carrying a cup of coffee. "Hey, Clyde." Micah raised a hand in greeting. "How's it going?"

"Can't complain," Clyde said, heading for his vehicle. He turned back to Micah. "Hey, you go by the old Baker place, don't you?"

"You know I do," Micah said with a chuckle. Clyde had delivered the mail around Providence for as long as Micah could remember. "Got something you need dropped off?"

"If you don't mind," Clyde said.

"Not at all." It wasn't regulation, but it wasn't unusual either for Clyde to take a shortcut now and then, especially on a delivery to a remote address, and Micah didn't blame him one whit.

Clyde ducked into his vehicle and emerged with a large envelope, then waddled over to hand it to Micah.

Micah replaced the gas nozzle, took the envelope, and glanced at the name, Samantha Jamison.

"Really appreciate it," Clyde said.

"Hold up, Clyde. This is certified mail. Don't you—"

"You're a servant of the court, for crying out loud, Micah. I got no problem with you dropping off that return receipt next time you're in town." Clyde headed for his car before Micah could object further.

Despite a niggling unease in his gut, Micah considered the upside as he tossed the envelope onto his passenger seat: It would give him a reason to visit Sam again.

When he slid into his truck, he picked up the envelope, his eyes landing on the return address: Morris, Siegel and Graham, P.C., a law firm.

"Shoot!" He slammed the steering wheel. Micah recognized that type of envelope, and from the information Sam had shared the other night, he had a fair idea what it contained. He leaned his head back on the seat and closed his eyes, wishing he hadn't agreed to deliver it.

Even if she was expecting it, she was bound to be devastated. The image of her on her deck last night, crying in the rain, made him cringe. He knew firsthand, no matter how prepared you thought you were, when the envelope arrives, it still brings you to your knees.

Parked beside her black Escalade, he turned off the engine and retrieved the envelope, stared at it for several moments, imagining the worst and dreading the task before him.

When he knocked on her door, Bear's bark was the only answer. Apparently, Sam was out. Not quite feeling relieved yet, he circled the cabin and gazed across the valley.

She was nowhere in sight.

He returned to the front and considered his options. He ought to have her sign for it, and if he was any kind of friend, he'd try again later to hand deliver it. But would she welcome a spectator for the crash and burn of her marriage, a witness to the humiliation of being cast aside? Compassion overruled his better judgement, and he leaned the piece of mail against the cabin door, a heaviness settling in the pit of his stomach.

Micah sat in a rocker on his deck after dinner, gazed across the broad expanse of valley stretched out before him in the fading light of day, and wondered how Sam was doing. The day he'd received his envelope—he pushed the thought away, refusing to relive the heartbreak.

He let his head fall back against the rocking chair, closed his eyes, and pictured Sam, all alone in that rustic hunting cabin, her only companion, that cute little dog she adored. He considered being neighborly and riding over to check on her and collect that return receipt. Would she want to see him, though? Would she want to see anyone? She could probably use a friend about now.

He knew what she was going through, or thought he did, though his wife hadn't cheated on him. Elizabeth had loved him; he'd always felt certain of that. She just wasn't happy on the ranch and he couldn't live anyplace else.

As he rocked, he tried to imagine how Sam might feel. Likely it bore a semblance to his own misery so long ago. Maybe worse.

He should go see her.

Yeah, he could be the friend she needs.

Minutes later, when he pulled his white pickup to a stop in front of her cabin, the envelope was no longer where he'd left it.

"HEY, MICAH," she said as she opened the door. With her little dog cradled in her arms, she looked as wary as a cornered bronc.

"Howdy." He could tell she'd been crying. The slight redness made the blue of her eyes shine even brighter. "I was just, well, passing by. Thought I'd make sure you were okay."

"I'm fine," she said with a look of confusion, as if wondering why he felt the need to check on her. "Want to come in?" She opened the door wider and stepped back to allow him entry.

He walked in and shuffled his hat in his hands as he glanced around the dimly lit room. A pile of papers covered the table, a glass of wine set off to one side. She pushed past Micah, set Bear on the floor, and collected the papers into a pile, placing them face down on top of the envelope they'd come in.

In jeans and an oversized pale blue sweater, the sleeves stretching to her fingertips, she looked casual and much too pretty for a woman wearing no makeup. She'd pulled her hair to the side, and it hung in a long braid in front of one shoulder, stray wisps curling along her cheek.

When she glanced his way, he gave her a wry smile. "I stopped by earlier and delivered that," he said, nodding to the papers she'd stacked.

"Oh, well, thank you," she said, rolling her eyes. "I guess."

"Divorce papers?" No use pretending he didn't know.

She nodded with a slight cringe and looked away.

He stepped further into the room. "You sure you're okay?"

She took a deep breath, as if collecting the courage to talk about it. "Not really," she admitted. "I mean, I knew it was a possibility. But I don't think I was ready for it."

He remembered the feeling, the shock, the emptiness, the sense of abandonment, wondering what he might've done different. It would stay with him for a lifetime. At a loss for what to say next, an awkward silence settled between them. Then an idea came to him. "Want to get drunk again?"

She smiled and twisted her braid. "No, that'll only make me cry. But I'd be happy to get you a drink."

"If you've got any left." He grinned and returned to the door to hang his hat.

"You're in luck," she said, pulling a bottle from a kitchen cabinet. She poured a glass, handed it to him, then lit the candle sconces around the room.

The cabin came alive with the flickering candlelight, drawing him in to its warmth. "Do you have questions about ... anything?" He eyed the large envelope, the document beneath it. "I can help you decipher the legal jargon, if you'd like."

"Oh, would that be Counselor Daniels?" she asked, stowing the lighter.

He chuckled. "Yes, actually."

Sam stared at the stack on the table and sighed. "Okay. Yeah, I'd appreciate that."

Micah sat, turned over the stack, and glanced up as she eased into the chair across from him. He gave her an encouraging smile and slid her wine glass to her. Then he turned his attention to the pages before him.

Micah leafed through it all, studied the more verbose pages—probably the ones Sam had gotten stuck on—and the detailed accounting of assets and their proposed dispensation.

When Micah looked up, Sam was staring at him. Their eyes locked, and he reminded himself she was still technically married, not a beautiful woman looking for all the world like she wanted him. Or was he imagining that? He cleared his throat.

"It's a settlement agreement for an uncontested divorce,

meaning he hopes to come to terms with you regarding the divorce and avoid a costly court battle. He's giving you the house free and clear." He glanced at the page that began their list of assets, his eyes honing in on the astounding one-point-four million dollar value of that particular asset. Apparently, she enjoyed a much higher standard of living, and he marveled she seemed so at home in the sparse little cabin.

"And the ski boat and jet ski. In exchange, he'll take the vacant land in Collin Township, the cottage on Torch Lake, and the five rental properties. The Colorado properties, since they're held in a real estate investment trust, have to be divided equally between the two of you. He'll take the one with the hunting cabin and pay the difference in market value as a cash deposit into your half of the trust, a sum of thirty-five thousand dollars." When he looked up, her eyes were solemn and vacant, her mind elsewhere.

"Then there's a page of household contents with check boxes for you to indicate which ones you want, and he's checked a few that he wants," he looked back at the list on the page, "the Noritake china, the two ATVs, the contents of the workshop, his office, and the gun room. His grandmother's Americana Fostoria crystal he's noted to go to your daughter. He wants to split the contents of the wine cellar and the Christmas ornaments, furniture and other things stored in the barn." He flipped to the last page. "No spousal support, he'll pay the filing fee, and he's put an expiration date on the offer, if you can call it that, a date of July twenty-fifth."

Sam nodded absently. "Of course, he's a realtor and purchase agreements have expiration dates. But do divorce settlements? Is that normal?"

Micah thought for a minute. "Not that I've seen. But family law isn't my specialty."

Sam stared, stoic and silent, at the pages in front of him. Was she thinking—as he had—about the document's finality and all that it so unemotionally detailed, the fruits of their life together itemized on paper to be parceled out between them?

She blinked several times and turned away to exhale a shaky breath.

He gave her hand a reassuring squeeze and when she looked at him, tears had pooled on her lower lids.

She forced a smile. "Thank you, Micah," she said, standing. "It was nice of you to come by to check on me."

There was a brokenness in the way she spoke, the way her gaze flickered away, the way her whole body seemed to deflate, curling in on itself.

"I thought you could use a friend about now." He stood and skirted the table, not wanting to leave her like this. "I've got a strong shoulder."

She gazed at him, as though considering, and placed a hand on his arm. "You're a kind soul."

He felt the warmth of her touch beneath his shirt, and shame washed over him because he wanted her to cry, so he could hold her, feel her whole soft, warm body against his chest while he soothed her with gentle words.

"You're a strong woman, Sam, whether or not you believe it. You'll get through this." He gave her an encouraging smile. "Every storm runs out of rain. Remember the other night when I stopped by?" He gave her a moment to fetch the memory. "Even the blackest night holds a bright new day."

She studied his face, as if searching to find truth in his words, then her gaze fell away and with a heavy sigh, she picked up her empty wine glass, walked to the kitchen, and stood at the counter, her back to him.

"I thought if I left for a while, he'd realize how much he missed me and ... I guess I still hoped ..." Her voice broke, the rest of her thoughts unspoken.

Micah understood all too well how it felt to lose that last vestige of hope, falling like a spider from its last silken thread, with nothing left to grasp onto.

"So much guilt, regret," she said, as though drowning in it all. Turning to face him, she leaned against the counter and took several deep breaths, as if steeling herself to face the hard reality of her failed marriage.

"I did this. It's my fault," she mumbled almost to herself. "I chose the wrong path long ago. I was so focused on my career I let my husband slip away, and you know what the funny part is? It's not funny at all, actually. It's absurdly pitiful. My company didn't even feel the need to give me a proper title. Not that I've ever cared about titles, but everyone else in senior leadership is a president, VP, or director. I report directly to the CEO, and you know what my role is called? Senior Acquisitions Editor. I worked so hard and for what?" Tears came to her eyes, and she turned away and swiped at her cheeks.

"It wasn't worth it." She leaned on the counter in front of her. "All I ever wanted was to make him proud of me. He was always so encouraging, wanting me to succeed, convincing me I deserved those promotions." She laughed, a sad, bitter sound. "Sometimes you work so hard to achieve that special something you think holds your happiness, and when you get there, it doesn't. And then what?"

Micah's heart went out to her as she fell apart in front of him, and a deep-seated anger grew in him for the husband who had led her to that path, encouraged her upon it, even as it pulled her from him. What an idiot the man must be. Didn't he realize what he was throwing away? She obviously still loved him.

He pulled a handkerchief from his back pocket and stepped forward to offer it. "You can cry if you want to. It's okay."

Sam eyed the red bandana, took it and sniffed into it, then giggled as she peered up at him. "You carry a handkerchief? Few men these days carry a handkerchief."

Micah winked, encouraged by her laughter and totally drawn in by the woman gazing back at him, her eyes glistening with tears. "Yeah, well, cowboys do, real ones anyway. You never know when you'll be pushing a herd across dry dirt, and you don't want to be without one then."

"Right," she said. "Thank you."

Micah tried to imagine Sam's inner struggle but couldn't fathom the depth of her pain. It had to be much harder than what he'd gone through. Her husband had cast her aside for someone younger. How does a woman—anyone—accept being replaced?

Sam dabbed at the corners of her eyes. "What's next for me? Do I sign the papers, just like that, end my marriage? Or do I try to forgive him, move past it? I don't know if I can. I have to return to work but—oh, God, I hate that job!"

Micah felt helpless. He yearned to comfort her but didn't have the answers she needed.

"I want my family back. I can't just give up. How do I stop hoping, believing, praying for everything I've always dreamed my life would be?" She slumped against the counter as tears ran like silent raindrops down her cheeks.

"Come here," Micah said, pulling her into his arms. She collapsed against his chest and wept like a lost child. After several minutes, he led her to the couch and sat beside her.

When she looked at him, her eyes held an unexpected tenderness, as though she'd suddenly realized how hearing these things might bring back the pain of his own failed marriage.

"Oh, Micah." She swiped at her eyes, blinked back her tears, and found a smile. "This is way more than you bargained for. I-I'm so sorry. If you need to go--"

"Shh, it's okay." He eased her head back to his shoulder. If only he had the power to erase her pain. "Sam," he said, his voice so soft it sounded foreign to his own ears, "I'm not going anywhere."

The candles flickered in the wall sconces and Bear jumped down from the end of the couch to curl into his bed beneath the coffee table. "H-how did you get through it?"

Micah breathed deeply, steeling himself to return to his own soul-crushing loss, as he looked beyond her into the dark night and remembered what had gotten him through. He hadn't been able to hear anything in the storm swirling around him as his marriage ended. It was in the hush that followed, when he'd fallen to his knees, that he'd felt God's calming presence.

Micah's voice sounded strong, resolute, as he found his words. "When you can't stand the pain any longer, you kneel." She gazed at him and nodded, so he took her hand, and together they knelt, elbows on the couch.

He prayed for her, for her marriage, for her comfort and patience, for guidance in her life as she braved a new path.

When he paused, Sam took over. "Thank you, God, for my new friend, for his strength, faith, and goodness. Amen."

"Amen," Micah echoed.

They returned to the couch and while Sam rested her head against his shoulder, Micah basked in an inexplicable peace that settled between them. And when the sun rose the next morning, Micah woke to find himself stretched out, Sam spooned in his arms and her little dog snuggled in front of her. She fit so perfectly against him, he hoped she wouldn't wake up, that he could savor her warmth for a few more minutes. It had been so long since he'd enjoyed the quiet contentment of holding someone he cared about and it was a feeling, he discovered, he'd missed. Lulled in intimate languor, his eyes closed, and all the world felt right.

He woke again a short time later when she stirred beside him. "You awake?" he whispered. He bent to rest his chin on top of her head as he reveled in the subtle scent of her hair, like aspen and sunshine.

"Mm-hmm." She nestled deeper into his embrace, and he thought his heart might burst.

"It's a new day," he said cheerfully.

"Yes, it is," she said, and when he rose on an elbow to gaze at her, the pain in her eyes had vanished, replaced by a firm resolve and what looked like a glimmer of hope.

She deserved a happy ending and happy endings always begin with hope.

So why did he feel this ache of foreboding where his heart should be?

# 8

# HOMESTEAD RANCH

Sam's SUV skidded to a stop at the entrance to the Homestead Ranch. A broad timber archway stood sentry over its narrow gravel drive, emerging from the cloud of dust kicked up by her SUV like a harbinger of something important. She pushed the feeling aside and proceeded across the cattle guard.

The winding gravel two-track spilled into a large circle at the center of which sprouted a stand of aspen, an ancient hand pump, and a wooden water trough. A massive two-story stone and cedar house dominated on the left and beyond it stretched a long, low building she assumed was a bunkhouse. Straight ahead, a giant rough-hewn barn stood wide open, beckoning, while paddocks of split rail fencing crisscrossed the meadows beyond like a flurry of tic-tac-toe games.

Micah's truck was parked in front of a small log home, across the drive from the big house, so she pulled in beside it. Why would a born rancher pursue law school? Did he have dreams of leaving the ranch, of someday reclaiming his young wife, the mother of his son?

Micah strolled from the barn as she stepped from her vehicle. "Hey, Sam! What a nice surprise."

He approached with the confident swagger of a man comfortable in his own boots, and her heart skittered. Like the ranch, striking in its orderliness and humility, Micah cut an impressive figure, tall and lean and incredibly sexy in a rugged, masculine way, with a bright white smile that wrinkled at the corners of his eyes. She couldn't remember a man ever looking at her that way, so intensely it made her breath hitch.

She cleared her throat and remembered why she'd come. "I made you a pie." She held out the plate, willing her hands to still. "To thank you for being such a good friend last night. You went way beyond neighborly concern and I really appreciate it."

He gave her a crooked grin, took the pie, and lifted a corner of the napkin to peek beneath. "Looks fantastic!"

"It's a Saskatoon berry pie, and I have to admit I've never made a pie crust from scratch, so," she winced, "please be kind."

He laughed out loud, instantly putting her at ease. "I'm sure it's delicious. Come in, have a piece with me."

He nodded toward the log home and took her hand—he was always touching her—and they stepped up onto the wide wraparound porch. Tucked amidst a stand of towering pines, the cabin looked like it could've sprouted right from the soil, along with the trees, like a Thomas Kincaid painting, picture-perfect in its use of light, asymmetry, and nature-inspired simplicity.

While Micah cut the pie and poured them each a glass of iced tea, she looked around. Like her cabin, only much larger, the main living area was one open space with the kitchen on one side and a seating area on the other. A pedestal table sat in between.

Seated at the table, he took a hesitant bite. "Mmm, delicious."

"Thank you." She glanced out the sliding glass door that led to a back deck. Like the wide plank flooring that ran throughout, the furnishings were all scaled like the man who lived there, large and sturdy.

He paused with a second bite in mid-air, tilted his head, and eyed it. "Where'd you get the berries?"

"In the woods."

"Round here?" He cocked an eyebrow.

"Don't worry. They're safe." She took another bite, but he shot her a side-eye and lowered his fork. Apparently, he needed a bit more convincing. She was an outsider, but she had done her research. He wasn't the only one uneasy about eating wild berries.

"They're Saskatoon berries, and they grow on a bush called serviceberry or western juneberry." She found the picture she'd taken on her phone and showed it to him. "They're like blueberries, only yellow, and they're touted as Canada's newest vogue superfruit."

"Is that so?" He eyed the image looking like he wanted to laugh.

She nodded and shoved another bite into her mouth to show him how confident she was.

"Never heard of them, but, okay." Apparently satisfied, he raised the bite to his mouth. "You know who else likes wild berries?"

"Bears, I know, and I'm careful. I make plenty of noise when I walk through the woods, and I always carry a gun." She'd hate to hurt another animal but would if she had to.

He smiled and nodded, clearly impressed, like he might appreciate a woman comfortable around guns. "This is delicious."

"Thanks." She bit her lip, having second thoughts about sharing something else with him, but plunged ahead anyway. "I wrote you a poem."

"A poem?"

"It's nothing special. Just a thank you. For last night." From the pocket of her jeans, she pulled out a small, folded piece of paper and handed it to him.

He glanced from her outstretched hand to her eyes. "Read it to me."

When she shook her head no, he took it from her, unfolded it, and read aloud.

*I needed a friend*
*You lent a hand*
*And quietly asked me why I came*

*We laughed and we cried*
*Over how we'd tried*
*As we became fast friends that stormy night*

*A pure, caring heart*
*A beautiful start*
*As we shared our broken reveries*

*One really bad day*
*You returned my way*
*Knowing I would need a friend again*

*You tried a warm smile*
*Let me cry for a while*
*And gently wiped my tears away*

*A big strong man*
*Gentle soul, good friend*
*Caring cowboy, willing shoulder*

*You said you would stay*
*Held my hand, we prayed*
*For God's grace, mercy, healing and guidance*

*So safe and so warm*
*I slept in your arms*
*Awoke with a hope of a brand new day*

*And oh, how I prayed for a brand new day*

When he finished, he looked up and their eyes lingered. "This is beautiful, Sam."

He seemed honestly touched by her heartfelt sentiments and gratitude. Her cheeks grew warm, no doubt turning red. She'd shared so much of herself with him the past few days.

He leaned forward. "You know, Sam, this is a really good time to take a hard look at your life, and if you decide it isn't all you hoped for, it's time to stop, turn around, choose another path, one that leads to what's most important in life—the people you love." He placed a hand over hers. "It's never too late to choose a different path."

She glanced at his hand, warm and strong and tender, like the man. Raising her gaze, she could only nod as she stared into the puppy-like eyes of the burly cowboy speaking words of encouragement, and for a minute, she almost believed it could be that simple. But she still loved her husband despite his affair with someone younger. It all just made her feel old and tired—so very tired—and ... unwanted. Yes, that was it—unwanted.

*Choose another path. It's never too late*. She'd needed to hear those words, and she clung to them with newfound hope. "Thank you."

He patted her hand and shot her a reassuring smile. "Can you stay for dinner? I was about to rustle something up."

She chuckled. "We just finished dessert."

"Dessert then dinner. My son and I do it all the time." He must have sensed the *no* coming because he quickly added, "Come on. Please stay."

"Okay," she said, "I'd love to. Thank you."

While he pulled things from the fridge, she scanned the rest of the room. Action figures and toy cars littered the cow-skin rug that anchored the well-worn leather furniture in the sitting area. The fieldstone fireplace took up most of the front wall, and bookshelves full to overflowing with books and toys alike occupied the back wall. Beyond the fireplace, a wooden rocking horse stood next to the stairs. A family, albeit a small one, lived here.

An antique hallstand nestled in a small alcove at the far end of the space, small jackets and hats hung on one side, larger ones on the other. She smiled at the contrast of little-man big-man gear, then turned back to Micah, surprised to find him watching her. "Your cabin is beautiful," she said. The masculine dark tones of the room offset the sunny vistas that shined through every window and door, adding light to the rather austere furnishings, but it had obviously been a while since the place had been privy to a woman's touch.

He tilted his head, glanced around the room, then narrowed his eyes, as though he didn't believe her. "It's home."

She stood and stepped forward. "What can I do to help?"

He handed her a knife, two large potatoes, and an onion.

She cut the vegetables while he lit the grill, prepped two steaks, and refilled their iced teas. Scooping the veggies onto a sheet of foil, he drizzled them with olive oil, generously sprinkled them with the same seasoning he'd used on the steaks, then wrapped it all up.

He picked up his iced tea and nodded toward the deck. "Come on out."

She followed him outside and settled into one of the rockers while he placed the veggie packet on the grill. Returning to sit beside her, they chatted easily about the ranch, the weather, and the amazing view of his own valley. It was all very innocent, but an undercurrent of apprehension made it impossible for Sam to relax.

As though sensing her unease, he patted her knee, then disappeared into the house and returned with a pair of tongs and a guitar. He set the tongs on the platter with the steaks. "You said one of the things you miss most is music, right?" He repositioned his rocking chair to face her and flashed a white-toothed smile.

Sam laughed, suddenly anxious and excited all at once. "Yes," she said, awed that he remembered her telling him that.

"Okay," he took a deep breath and licked his lips, "this is my first time singing this song so," his gaze wandered, as though searching for a memory, "please be kind." He grinned and arched a brow at her.

She laughed again, a nervous flutter in her belly as she anticipated his song.

His music spilled forth, and she quickly recognized it as her poem, except he'd switched out a few of the words to turn it around to be about her goodness and grace and how she was there for him. When he finished, she fell speechless, touched by the timbre of his soft, deep voice and the emotion he'd instilled into her words. He couldn't possibly have needed her as much as she'd needed him. Could he? "That was beautiful."

He stared at her for several moments, seeming to gauge the effect of his music, and his eyes brightened as his grin widened. "My pleasure." He gently squeezed her hand before setting the guitar aside to check on the grill.

With his back to her, he rotated the veggie packet and put the steaks on. They were small movements, but they rippled through his shoulders, his muscles flexing gently beneath his dark green T-shirt, the sleeves taut around his biceps. He wore it untucked, and in his faded blue jeans and boots, he looked relaxed, the raw strength of him cleverly disguised beneath the softness of his clothes, his voice, and the sandy brown hair that fell in gentle waves to his sun-bronzed neck. His jeans were faded in places determined by the work he did, and he didn't carry a wallet in his back pocket like most men.

She wondered how it would feel to run her hands down his muscular back, through his mane of wavy hair, how he'd feel on top of her, stomach to stomach, skin to skin, her legs wrapped around him.

She felt a stab of guilt for thinking of him that way, but she'd done nothing wrong. And yet, it was a guilt born of distant possibilities, and she wondered how the evening would end, if maybe she'd gotten in over her head in coming here.

He seemed like a nice enough man, quiet, even a little bashful at times, not the type to have expectations, especially of a married woman. But oh, the power in that long, lean body of his. As he closed the lid, she reached for her tea, her hands a little faster than her eyes, and the glass tumbled to the deck. "I'm so sorry!" She bent to pick it up, relieved it didn't break.

"No worries. I'll get you a refill." He took it from her with a knowing smile and disappeared back inside.

Thankful for the brief respite, she closed her eyes and took a calming breath, steeling herself for his return. What was wrong with her? She was acting like a starstruck schoolgirl. He was a friend, a neighbor, nothing more.

She shouldn't have come. Too antsy to sit, she stood at the railing, finding an inner calm in the quiet serenity of the grassy meadow rolling lazily away in the afternoon haze.

Quicker than she'd expected, he was back. "Here you go." He handed her the glass and leaned back against the railing to face her, crossing his boots at the ankle, a typical stance for him, she realized. So cowboy.

"Thank you," she said. "So, tell me, who lives in all the other buildings here?"

"Well, across the way, in the main house, are my brother Isaac, his wife Isabelle, and her teenage daughter, Avery. Our little brother, Nick, still has a room there, but more often than not, when he's around, that is, he bunks with the hands in the bunkhouse. That's the long building set back between the house and barn. And then the barn is, well, that's where the horses and any sick animals live." He gave her a teasing smile.

"Looks like you've been here a while."

"Since the end of the Civil War. My great, great grandpa homesteaded on a thousand acres in that place you saw near the bottom of Moonglow Meadow. Over the years, the ranch grew as the family bought more land. Then it got split between sons who moved around a bit, and now, five generations later, pretty near half the county is owned and ranched by the Daniels family."

"You and your brothers?"

"Cousins too. You met Cody. He's the vet. He's got two brothers, Rory and Jonathan. Rory has a degree in animal husbandry and handles the breeding and most of the buying and selling of livestock, and Jonathan's the farmer. He makes sure we have plenty of hay and feed for the animals we over-winter each year."

"Still a family operation, after all this time?"

"You bet."

"What do you and your brothers do?"

"I handle the contracts and accounting, legal issues and property rights, mostly the business end of things. And I ride fences."

"Ride fences?"

"Ride around, make sure there aren't any breaks in the fences, and when there are, I fix them. Keeps the cattle where they're supposed to be and, more importantly, out of where they're not supposed to be. That's what I was doing the night I got stuck in the rain and came by your place."

"Right."

The spark in his whiskey brown eyes made her wonder where his thoughts had gone. Maybe he, too, had found an inexplicable comfort in their newfound friendship that night.

He cleared his throat and glanced away before continuing. "Isaac's the foreman. He runs the daily operations of the ranch, hiring and firing hands, moving the herd, keeping them watered and fed. And Nick, well, he's the family's late arrival, you might say. Ten years younger than Isaac, who's three years younger than me, Nick hasn't quite settled into his own yet. He joined the Marines after high school, served in the Middle East, but since he got back two years ago, he's been a restless soul. I think the death of our father hit him especially hard. He was just beginning to find his place here when Dad died of a heart attack. Since Nick was so much younger, our father had never really had to rely on him. None of us did. Dad had me and Isaac, and I guess he didn't have the patience for another untrained hand."

He paused as a sadness seemed to settle over him. "So, Nick's been living it up on the rodeo circuit—mostly riding broncs and roping. He seems to have a way with horses and does some training too. He shows up here from time to time when he runs out of money or needs a few steady meals."

"And your mother?"

"She died three months after my dad."

"Oh, I'm so sorry."

"Thank you. Yeah, we started losing her when she lost him." His eyes went far away. "You would've loved them. My father taught us to shoot straight, wrangle an errant cow, and how to measure a man by his words and actions, not by what he did for a living or how much money he had. He taught us all the things he thought a man should know, the things his daddy had taught him, the things my mom said made us into good men." He glanced sideways at her and his cheeks flushed.

"And Mom had her own life lessons to share: giving others what they need, respecting folks' point of views, even when they differed from your own, but standing up for what's right in the eyes of the Lord. Things like honor and grace and the importance of family."

"They sound like amazing parents."

"They were. And quite a pair, those two. Met on the playground when he was six. She was five. To hear Grandpa tell it, she was sitting on a swing, her hair all tied in ribbons, and she said, 'I'll let you push me if you want to.' He was smitten ever since. She let him do lots of things for her over the years. It was just her way. She let him carry her books, buy her a soda at the five-and-dime, walk her home. When he went away to war, she let him write to her.

"After he passed, she'd get out those letters and his box of medals and sit for hours, black and white photos of days gone by scattered all around her. She couldn't remember our names by then, but she could tell the story behind every one of those old photographs. I think she missed him and plain willed her body to let go. They loved each other that much. I always thought I'd find a love like that."

All of a sudden, he wasn't the strong burly rancher she'd thought was so infallible. He was simply a man with an emptiness in him that made him real and vulnerable. Her heart ached for his loneliness. "You may still, someday."

He breathed in, long and slow, and then shook his head. "I don't know. In case you haven't noticed, the pickings are fairly slim up here. How many women can bear this much isolation?"

He looked at her like he expected an answer to what she'd assumed was a rhetorical question. "Isabelle must like it here."

He perked up and his easy smile settled back in place. "Yeah. Isaac got himself quite a catch with that one. Spirit of a wildcat, heart of a saint, and a mind to be reckoned with. And she's a fine cook, too. Stole her from The Ore House over in Steamboat Springs, one of the finest and oldest eating establishments in the county. Speaking of food, I expect those steaks are nearly done."

He turned his attention to the grill as he continued to talk. "Most days, Aiden and I eat over there too. But tonight, I'm happy to have your company."

"Where is Aiden?"

"Cody's. He had a sleepover with his cousins last night. Cody'll bring him up after supper." He glanced her way. "How do you like your steak?"

"Mmm." She hesitated, realizing she'd totally missed her opportunity to let him know she was pretty much a vegetarian. It wasn't that she didn't like meat; she was just so picky about meat it was more trouble than it was worth. But his steaks had looked amazing, smelled even better, and she suspected they'd be fresh and lean, likely from his own stock. "Well done, please."

He cringed. "If you insist." He took one of the steaks off and set it atop of the veggie packet, then butterflied the other one and closed the grill. "Two more minutes."

"Want me to make a salad or anything?"

He chuckled. "A salad? No, but thanks. You won't find any lettuce here."

"You don't eat salad?"

"I don't eat anything green."

Sam face-palmed. "Nothing? Seriously? Peas, green beans, broccoli?"

"Oh, darlin'. Don't even get me started on broccoli." He laughed.

"I'll eat corn from time to time. But I don't have any so, it's steak and potatoes tonight."

Minutes later, they were seated at his table, steaming plates before them. He placed a hand on hers, sending a warm current straight through her gut, like fresh warm honey on a hot summer day, coating her insides with a golden glow.

He said a blessing she didn't hear, her thoughts a million miles from God and grace, and when he said amen, she echoed it with a voice exhumed from the jumble of emotions playing tug of war between her heart and her head.

No, she definitely should not have come.

Turning to the meal before her, she got him talking about the ranch again. Better to stay on safe ground. He described the work that went into ranching: calving then branding in the spring, herding the cattle to better pastures or new water sources throughout the hot, dry summer months, the cattle drive in the fall as they sold off part of the herd each year, and building and mending fences year-round.

He spoke of the ever present dangers of drought and wildfires. Droughts were inevitable in the mountains, with mild winters resulting in reduced runoff, streams drying up by midsummer. And if rainfall was lacking too, it all combined to turn the whole landscape into a veritable tinderbox. A wildfire could whip up out of nowhere and totally wipe out thousands of acres, including any livestock in its path.

"We're fortunate to have Homestead Creek running through a large portion of the ranch," he said. "Aside from the parcel that your cabin now occupies, we own most of it. Water rights, typically the number one issue contested in courtrooms across the state, have caused more disputes among neighbors than I like to count. When it comes to water rights, friend or foe, everyone becomes downright un-neighborly."

He described a recent lawsuit they'd been involved in with the town's doctor and then, as though reconsidering mid-story, he ended it abruptly, leaving her to wonder if it was about more than losing a dozen head of cattle, if it was about something much bigger.

"Hey, how about joining me and Aiden at the Fourth of July picnic in town next weekend?" he asked, turning the conversation to a lighter tone. "It's a lot of fun, a huge get-together—we roast a side of beef and a pig or a mutton, sometimes all three. There'll be a carnival and fireworks."

She looked away, searching for the words to reset boundaries, her own most of all. "Micah, you've been a great friend, and I can't begin to tell you how much I appreciate all you've done for me already. But I'm married. And I know things don't look good now, but I haven't totally given up on my marriage."

Micah rubbed his chin as though considering. "It doesn't have to be a date."

"It would be, though." *Wouldn't it?* And how nice that sounded. He'd pick her up, kiss her good night at the end of it, and wrap her in those big strong arms of his again. She thrust the longings back down where they belonged.

He leaned back in his chair. "I understand."

An awkward silence settled between them. "I should be going," Sam said, pushing back from the table.

The sound of tires on gravel drew them both to their feet. Through the front window, an old red pickup eased around the drive and stopped in front of the cabin. A little boy hopped from the passenger side like a raindrop on a griddle, bounded up the porch steps, and dashed into the house, the screen door slamming shut behind him.

Micah bent to greet his son with a hug and turned to introduce him.

"Well, hello, Aiden. It's a pleasure to meet you." Sam knelt in front of him. "My good friends call me Sam," she said in a soft tone. "You can call me Sam, okay?" He looked like a replica of Micah, only smaller, younger, and much less serious.

Aiden grinned and shook her hand with a firm grip and two energetic pumps. "Howdy, Sam."

A pretty young woman with cinnamon hair and green eyes followed him in. She wore a frilly, tiny-flowered sundress and her boots stopped in their tracks when she noticed Sam.

Micah introduced her as Janie, and Sam greeted her politely, but after a somewhat awkward silence, she sensed the younger woman's discomfort, and headed for the door. "Thanks again, Micah, for dinner and your help the other night."

At the door, Aiden tugged at Sam's arm and she knelt again. He leaned in, cupped her ear, and whispered, "Can you keep a secret?" He eased back and eyed her.

Sam considered his serious little face, so much like his father's, and smiled, captivated. "I sure can."

He gave her an excited smile, took her hand in his small one, and with a backward glance at Micah, Sam followed his little guy outside.

## 9

# SECRETS

Through the front window, Micah watched Aiden with Sam, amazed by how quickly and effortlessly she had captured his son's heart. Janie cleared her throat, and he turned back to her. "Thank you for fetching Aiden for me."

"My pleasure. I was heading up here, anyway." Her eyes combed the room, landing on the table: two plates, two glasses, two of everything.

"You were?" Micah pushed in the chairs and stacked the dishes, stabbed by an instant pang of guilt. He should've broken things off with her by now, but he hadn't figured out a way to let her down easy.

"Dropped off a few quilts for Isabelle. Golly, he's grown." She nodded toward the porch. "Still pretty quiet though. Haven't seen you in town in a while," she said, following him to the kitchen. "I've missed you."

With a mustering of resolve, he set the dishes in the sink and faced her. He needed to stop her before she went any further. "Janie—"

Her eyes widened with a flash of fear, and she rushed on. "I was hoping we could go to the town picnic together next weekend."

~

WITH A FURTIVE GLANCE back at the house, Aiden scrambled up into the bed of Janie's truck and handed down a large cardboard box. Whatever was inside scratched across the bottom and Sam could've sworn she heard a faint whine come from within. Aiden's secret was alive.

He jumped down, took the box from her, and hurried onto the porch to set it down, taking great care to do so gently. Then, after a quick peek through the kitchen window, he eased open the top of the box to reveal its contents. Sam peered over his shoulder. Crouched in a corner was a black and white puppy staring up at them.

Aiden looked up at Sam with a smile a country mile wide.

"Oh, Aiden, he's beautiful!" Sam reached in to stroke its soft fur. "Is it a boy or a girl?"

Aiden's face wrinkled in thoughtful consideration and he shrugged. "Border collie."

"Does he have a name?"

"Not yet." Aiden patted the puppy's head.

"I have a dog," Sam said. "His name is Bear, and I bet your puppy and Bear would be good friends."

"Caleb says most dogs don't like other dogs," he said with youthful wisdom.

"Dogs can be very territorial, which means they protect what belongs to them, but your puppy isn't old enough to have learned that yet, and Bear is as soft and sweet as a marshmallow."

Aiden grinned, revealing a missing bottom tooth. "I love marshmallows."

"Me too. Do you know how to take care of a new puppy?" she asked.

A line of worry wrinkled his brow. "You won't tell, will you?"

~

A FRESH WAVE of guilt washed over Micah at the irony of having just invited Sam to the Fourth of July picnic. And despite Sam's refusal, he couldn't go with Janie either. With a heavy breath, he leaned back against the kitchen counter. "You're a beautiful and desirable woman, Janie." He couldn't keep doing this with her. It wasn't fair; she deserved better. But he knew he was going to hurt her.

"But ..." Janie prompted. She moved to stand in front of him, placed her hands on his chest, and caught his gaze, searching for something in his eyes he knew she'd never find. "I'm not the one, am I?"

He looked away, relieved to hear her say what had gone unsaid for far too long. "I'm sorry, Janie."

She squared her shoulders and stepped back, the despair in her eyes deep and dark. Then she moved toward the front window to where Sam knelt before Aiden, their heads bent together. "Is she the one?"

~

"YOUR FATHER DOESN'T KNOW about the puppy?"

Head down, Aiden shuffled his feet.

"Does your uncle know you have the puppy?" Sam asked, concerned he may have taken the dog without telling anyone.

Aiden shook his head, the worried brow returning.

She asked him if anyone knew: his aunt, cousins, Janie? He shook his head no to all of them.

"Oh, Aiden, don't you think your uncle Cody and his family will be worried when they discover a puppy missing? They might be out there looking for him right now, afraid that a coyote or something got him."

Aiden's face was a mask of worry and frustration as he shrugged his narrow shoulders.

~

MICAH FOLLOWED JANIE'S GAZE. "She's just a friend, a neighbor who needed a hand."

A wry smile curved Janie's mouth. "Like you were there for me when Adam died?"

She sounded angry. He hadn't expected anger.

Micah stood motionless as he stared at her profile, the unmistakably sad tilt of her head as she watched Aiden with Sam, and he thought back to when Janie's husband had died. She'd needed someone, and he was glad to have been there for her, but dang-it-all, he wasn't in love with her, and she deserved that. She deserved to be with someone who loved her. He'd been selfish and cruel to keep her hanging on. He knew she loved him, and this was breaking her heart, but it was better this way. Wasn't it?

She turned to catch him staring at her. "She seems really great," she said with a forced brightness she couldn't possibly feel.

"She's married," he said, hoping to dispel the notion she was being replaced. Sam was not the reason for ending things with Janie.

SAM'S THOUGHTS churned as she considered their predicament. "You have to at least tell your father, Aiden, so he can—"

"No! I can't tell Daddy!" He flapped his hands against his jeans.

"Why not?"

"H-He'll ..."

Sam tipped her head, waiting.

"Send me away."

"Away?"

Aiden nodded, and Sam thought he might cry.

"Away where?"

"My uncle's. Or back to Houston." It came out sounding like Hoo-ston and Sam suppressed a smile.

"Oh, Aiden. I don't think—"

"You don't know him, Sam. He'll be mad as a tied bull. He already don't want me around."

"It may seem that way, but he's just busy running the ranch. Your father loves you very much."

Aiden's chin fell to his chest, a dark curl, slipping over his brow.

"Come on. I'll go with you." She held out a hand.

He looked up, his soft brown eyes trusting and hopeful. Then he closed the box and took her hand.

"MARRIED?" Janie's gaze shot to the front porch, then back to Micah. "Where's her husband?"

Micah sighed. "It's a long story. They're going through a rough patch."

She smiled at him thoughtfully. "You should ride a white horse, Micah."

He chuckled, but it held no humor. "It's not like that."

"Isn't it?" When he didn't deny it, she closed the distance between them and tiptoed to kiss him on the cheek. "I'll be seeing you."

"Take care, Janie."

On the porch, she called a cheerful goodbye to Aiden and Sam. At the sound of her pickup starting up and the crunch of tires on gravel fading away down the drive, Micah turned to the dishes searching for a sense of relief but finding only shame and guilt.

Seconds later, Aiden walked in with Sam in tow. "Daddy, don't be mad but ..."

Micah narrowed his eyes at his son while Sam placed an encouraging hand on Aiden's shoulder.

"I got one of Caleb's pups." His eyes darted to the porch. "Can I keep him, please, please, pleeeeze?" He hopped up and down like a sparrow.

Micah resisted his gut reaction to refuse outright, his anger withering at the hope and excitement in Aiden's face and the memory of Sam's words about *fleeting childhood.* "Go empty the dishwasher while I call your uncle," Micah said.

After a brief discussion with Cody, Micah ended the call and turned to Aiden. "You can keep the dog for the summer, so long as you promise to take good care of him." He'd been thinking of adding more chores to Aiden's plate anyway and taking care of an animal was a great way to learn about responsibility and caring for others.

"Promise!" Aiden squealed with delight, hugged his father and then Sam, and dashed outside to fetch his new puppy.

"I'd best be going now too," Sam said as the screen door slammed behind Aiden.

"Thank you for another wonderful evening, Sam."

Sam laughed. "Another? Last night was wonderful for you?"

She had a great laugh, not loud or giggly, but free and easy, like their conversations. "It was, honestly." His eyes captured her gaze and held it.

Her mouth curved upward ever so slightly, her eyes betraying a much different story than her earlier one about not giving up on her marriage. She shook her head as though recapturing her resolve. "Good night, Micah, and thanks again."

LATER, as Micah tucked his son into bed, Aiden asked about Sam, specifically when they would see her again. "I like her, Daddy. She's really nice. And she likes dogs. And marshmallows too."

Micah's heart melted like warm wax as he gazed into the eyes of his child. "I like her too," he admitted.

"She even smells nice. Hey," Aiden bolted upright, "can she come to the picnic with us?"

"I already asked, and she turned me down."

Aiden frowned and plopped back onto his pillow, then his face lit up again. "What if I ask?" he suggested with a gap-toothed grin. "She won't say no if I ask."

Micah laughed. His little guy sure wasn't lacking for confidence—a benefit of being an only child, he supposed. "We'll have to see about that."

Micah kissed Aiden good night, lingering as he always did to enjoy the baby-softness of his cheek and to breathe in the warm, freshly bathed scent of the no-tears shampoo his mother always sent. Now, what excuse could he come up with to stop by Sam's place again so Aiden could ask?

Lying awake in his own bed, Micah's thoughts drifted to Sam—her smile, her laughter, her poem and soft blue eyes. He pictured her stepping from the stream as he'd watched from the ridge, her long slim body dripping wet, the sun reflecting off her skin, shimmering with every movement.

*She's married*, a small voice reminded him. *But she's getting a divorce*. Micah groaned as his heart and conscience wrestled it out.

The bottom line? She was plain amazing, and he wanted her. But she still had a husband and that was reason enough to settle for mere friendship. When her marriage ended—which seemed inevitable—she would need time to get over it, and while the wounds of her loss healed, he'd be there for her, as a friend, nothing more.

The image of her stepping from the stream refused to be subdued. He rolled over and placed a pillow over his head as he fought to push her from his thoughts.

An hour later he threw off the covers, got out of bed, and peeked in on Aiden who was fast asleep, his puppy slumbering beside him in the box on the floor.

In the kitchen, he poured himself a splash of whiskey, stood at the kitchen sink, and tossed it back. He considered having another one, several more if that's what it took, but quickly decided against it. He'd tried once before to drink a woman out of his head, and it hadn't worked. In fact, that whiskey lullaby had almost cost him a brother.

He returned the bottle to the cupboard and climbed back into bed, and when images of Sam flitted through his thoughts, he let them, smiling happily as she filled his heart and mind with remnant memories.

THREE DAYS LATER, on the back deck of her cabin, Sam sat typing away on her laptop, when she heard pounding hoofs racing across the valley. She glanced up as two riders, Micah and Aiden, splashed through the stream and headed up the trail toward her. The sight of horses galloping in the wide-open stirred her heart with yearning for the freedom they embodied. *I've got to capture that in my story.* She breathed deeply; the scene quieting her aching soul.

"Hi, Sam!" Aiden called, waving excitedly as they neared.

Bear barked and ran to the edge of the deck but Sam quickly silenced him. "Stay. No bark." Bear obeyed and stood waving his stubby tail anxiously as the riders approached.

Sam saved her work and set the computer aside as father and son reined in at the front of the deck. "Hey, guys."

Micah had a physique that was tailor made to sit a horse: tall, broad shouldered, slender waist, all anchored in well-worn leather boots. Aiden wore a hat identical to his father's and a grin almost as wide. "My, aren't you two a pair of handsome cowboys!"

"We're going for a swim in the creek and wondered if you'd like to join us," Micah said.

Sam bit her lip as she looked from one to the other of them. "A swim? Sure. Why not?"

"Can I meet your dog?" Aiden hopped off his pony.

"Of course." Sam stood beside Bear as Aiden climbed the few steps. He bent to let the dog sniff his hand before reaching out to pet him.

"You're right, he is like a marshmallow." Aiden rubbed the dog's ears.

"I think he likes you," Sam said.

"He knows a good guy when he smells one," Aiden replied, shooting her a smile.

Sam laughed aloud; he sounded so much like his father. "How's your puppy doing?"

"Good," he answered, totally engaged with Bear.

"Does he have a name yet?"

"Sam," he answered, sheepishly glancing up at her.

Sam glanced at Micah who rolled his eyes. "You named your dog Sam?" she asked, a giggle escaping.

"We still need to talk about that, buckaroo," Micah interjected.

"Are you off-ended?" Aiden asked, obviously trying the word out for the first time.

"Offended?" She shook her head. "No, absolutely not! I'm flattered."

Aiden shot her a huge smile and looked up at his father with a satisfied grin that said, *See, I told you so.* Clearly, they'd discussed it, and Sam wanted to laugh again as she stood there looking from father to son, the full size to the miniature.

"Hey," she said to Aiden, "if you'll keep an eye on Bear, I'll go put my swimsuit on, okay?"

"You bet," Aiden said.

She disappeared inside and returned a few minutes later carrying a beach towel and wearing her suit beneath a pair of jean cut-offs and a white cotton top.

"Bear, come," she called from inside the door.

"Can't he come with us?" Aiden asked as Bear obediently hopped inside.

"Good boy." She patted Bear on the head, removed his lead, and turned to Aiden. "He had a run-in with an eagle the other day and has stitches that need to stay dry. It's better if he stays inside."

Aiden gave a wave. "Bye, Bear."

She slid the door shut, and Aiden mounted his pony.

"Here, climb up behind me." Micah removed his foot from the stirrup and held a hand out to her. "Put your boot here." She did as he instructed, took his hand, and he pulled her right up into the saddle behind him as easily as he'd placed his hat back on his head earlier.

Wrapped around Micah, her inner thighs warmed against his legs, her arms around his waist, Sam breathed in the pure male scent of him—a potent cocktail of earth, sky, horses, and leather. Her insides did a pirouette.

Aiden led the way down the path she and Bear had cut with their earlier walks, a narrow strip of gently trampled meadow grass, a couple hundred yards to where it opened up beneath a large cottonwood. The tree stood on a point bar where the stream arched out in a long lazy bend. While tall reeds, grasses, sagebrush, and boulders bordered most of the water's edge, at this spot the bank was open and afforded a gentle slope into the water.

Unlike the wide, shallow, and rocky spot upstream where Micah and Aiden had crossed, boisterous as it tumbled down the valley, here the water ran smooth, silent, and deep—perfect for swimming.

They splashed around in the cold mountain water, and Sam showed Aiden the breaststroke. He caught on quickly and challenged his father to a race.

Micah let his son win while Sam cheered them on. They were so much fun to watch, Sam lost herself in their merriment until unexpected memories of the all-too-fleeting youth of her own children invaded, and she had to look away.

She ducked beneath the surface, using the water as she came up to make her hair flow back and out of her way. Opening her eyes, she caught Micah's stare, and sent a huge splash into his face, causing his son to giggle with delight.

When they'd worn themselves out, they dried off and lay on their towels beside the stream to warm in the sun. No matter how hot the day or how late in the summer, Colorado mountain streams were always icy cold, the water originating from snow or ice somewhere higher up, days or sometimes mere hours before.

Aiden crossed his arms beneath his head as he gazed up at the crystal-clear blue sky. "Sam," he started pensively, "if I ask you something, promise to say yes?"

Sam turned on her side to study the little boy lying between her and Micah, so relaxed and secure in his surroundings. “No,” she said, playing with him. “I never answer a question I’ve not heard. Would you?”

“S'pose not,” he said, apparently unfazed. He continued to focus on the cloudless sky. A few moments passed, and he flopped onto his side to face her. “So, here’s the question, and I hope you’ll say yes because, well, because I really want you to.” He sounded much more mature than his five years. “Will you go to the Fourth of July picnic with us?”

Sam smiled at the beautiful child staring back at her with hopeful eyes and then glanced beyond him to where his father lay on his back, arms behind his head, eyes closed to the sky, a knowing grin curving his lips. She returned her gaze to the boy. “Aiden—”

“Pleeeeze!”

“You’re a remarkable little man, you know that?” She laughed and pushed him onto his back.

He regained his position up on an elbow. “So, yes?”

How could she say no to that sweet face? And darn-it-all, his father knew she wouldn’t. And honestly, she wanted to go. “Tell you what, I’ll meet you there, okay?”

Aiden cranked his head around to look at his father who gave his son an almost imperceptible nod as his lips curved into an even bigger grin. When Aiden turned back to Sam, a huge smile lit up his face. “Okay!”

She relaxed onto her back. *What am I getting myself into with these two?*

# 10

# FIREWORKS

The entire drive from the ranch to town, Micah wrestled with the idea of Janie and Sam in the same place again. Avoiding Janie altogether was not an option; she always coordinated the church's bake sale, one of the highlights of Providence's holiday picnic.

When he and Aiden arrived at Centennial Park, the whole-town affair was well under way. From across the street, chimes and bells, the screech of metal, and screams of children drifted on the wind from the carnival. Smoke from the roasting side of beef swirled skyward and filled the air with a hunger-inducing aroma. While Aiden ran off to play with his cousins, Micah greeted his family and friends beneath the main pavilion. With Cody's help, he hefted a large cooler filled with soft drinks—his contribution to the potluck—from his truck bed onto the ground at the end of one of the serving tables.

Across a wide expanse of lawn, he spied Janie beneath the church tent, so he made his way over to say hello, hoping to get it over with before Sam arrived. Long tables laden with baked goods awaited while townsfolk came and went, dropping off donations, several lingering to chat with her. Micah felt in the way which was a good excuse not to overstay, so after a quick hello, he said, "Looks like your busy, so I'll leave you to it."

"Yeah, sorry." Janie made room on the nearest table for a plate of caramel drizzled brownies. "Tell Aiden hey for me."

"Sure thing." Micah turned away and spotted Sam walking into the park, looking lost and carrying what appeared to be another pie.

"You invited *her*?" Janie said, her voice half accusation, half disbelief as she stood beside Micah while Sam approached.

"Aiden did." His insides cringed at having to lie. He'd invited her first. He glanced sideways at Janie, but she'd already turned away, moving toward a woman carrying a cake box.

Pushing aside the all-too-familiar Janie-induced regret, Micah waved to get Sam's attention and headed toward her. She perked up when she saw him and when they met in the middle, her eyes sparkled as she took in all the goings-on.

Wearing a flowered skirt, red top, white jean jacket, and cowboy boots, she looked as though she'd lived in the mountains all her life. Her legs were long and lean beneath the frilly skirt and her hair fell in loose curls across one shoulder. He'd never seen her with her hair down before. She usually wore it in a ponytail or braid. It was so lovely he wanted to run his fingers through it, to feel if it was as soft as it looked.

"Hey, Micah," she said, re-anchoring him to reality.

"Howdy, Sam. Here," he took the pie from her, "let's set this on the dessert table." He nodded toward the pavilion where his family bustled about, spreading tablecloths and laying out dishes.

Before setting it on the table, he peeked beneath the napkin cover, pleased to see it was another Saskatoon berry pie. When he turned back to her, a sudden flutter in his gut overshadowed any remnant guilt. "You look—"

"Sam!" Aiden called, bounding up the sidewalk.

She knelt to give him a hug, and he practically bowled her over as he hugged her back. "Hey, little man!"

"You came!"

"I told you I would, didn't I?"

"Yeah, but, oh, I'm happy you came!" he said, barely containing his excitement.

"Nice tattoo," she said, touching the small flag pasted onto his cheek.

"Want one? They're over there." He flung an arm to point off in the distance. "Come on." Without waiting for an answer, he took her hand and pulled her away.

She looked over her shoulder at Micah, who shrugged with a knowing grin and followed. She chose a red, white, and blue shooting stars tattoo, smaller than the flag Aiden had, and she put it in the same spot as Aiden's, high on the cheekbone.

Positioning her face beside Aiden's, she asked Micah, "How do we look?"

"Very patriotic!" he answered with a chuckle. No wonder his son adored her. She was fun.

"Here, take a picture of us." She handed Micah her phone.

Micah snapped the picture, then looked at it. They looked so happy, he couldn't tell whose grin was bigger. Probably his own. He rubbed his jaw. "Send that to me?"

"Of course."

They returned to the pavilion where Micah introduced her to his family—his Uncle Will, two brothers, Isaac and Nick, his three cousins and their wives and children, including Cody, whom she'd already met. He was sure she had to be overwhelmed by the sheer size of his extended family, but she didn't let on. She talked and laughed so easily among them as they ate, Micah couldn't believe she wasn't Providence-born-and-bred.

After dinner, they headed to the carnival, where Aiden led them through the noisy aisles of arcade games, past the tattooed hawkers touting their games of skill and chance, until he stopped before the Cork Gun Shoot.

"Caleb and me been practicing," he said, looking up at his father.

"Caleb and I *have* been," Micah corrected as he laid down the money and Aiden selected a gun. "Chances are, that shooter isn't as sighted in as the one you've been using, so take a single shot, see where it goes, and adjust from there if needed."

After only a few rounds, Aiden's shots hit their mark. When he won enough to earn a small prize, he cast Micah and Sam a proud grin, picked out a small stuffed horse, and handed the rifle to his father.

"Really?" Micah eyed the prizes hanging behind the counter—not much worth laying down more money for.

"Afraid I outshoot ya?" Aiden goaded.

Sam giggled behind them.

Micah waved Aiden aside, pulled out another bill, and sighted down the barrel of the little gun. Every shot hit the mark, and he soon earned enough to win one of the larger prizes. Handing over the rifle, he told Aiden to pick one. His son could've traded up his stuffed horse for one of the biggest prizes, but when he whispered into Micah's ear and pointed to the item he wanted pulled down, Micah's heart warmed with pride.

Aiden took the white cowboy hat from the carnie and, with a toothy grin, offered it to Sam.

"For me?" Her eyes twinkled with delight as she settled it on her head. "Thank you, Aiden." She bent to kiss him on the cheek.

Micah didn't think it was possible, but Aiden's smile grew even bigger.

"Hey, he won it for you," Aiden said, laughing and jerking a thumb toward his father.

Sam straightened, hesitated for a heartbeat, then stood on tiptoe to kiss Micah on the cheek. "Thank you."

An evening full of possibilities, Micah thought as his smile widened, too.

"Can we ride the Ferris wheel next, Daddy? Can we, huh?" Aiden asked, already tugging at his sleeve.

Micah's brows shot up as he turned to Sam.

"Oh, no, not me, thanks. You two go ahead. I'll watch."

"Aw, come on, Sam. It's fun! Look how high it goes! You can see forever!" Aiden reached for her hand, but she pulled away.

She half-laughed, but her eyes went wide, glued to the Ferris wheel. Her mouth fell open, and she took a step back, shaking her head as she withdrew further.

"What? Don't tell me you're afraid of a little Ferris wheel!" Micah teased.

"Little?" Her voice quivered as her gaze traveled warily from the base of the ride skyward.

"Come on, Sam, please, please, please?" Aiden took her hand and tugged.

Micah waited, wondering if she'd be able to say no to his son this time.

Sam knelt in front of Aiden and looked him straight in the eye, her expression serious. After a long pause, as the two stared at one another, she bit her lip, scowled, then forced a nervous smile. "I'm afraid of heights, Aiden." The words tumbled out in one quick breath, and Micah almost laughed out loud.

When Sam glared at him over Aiden's head, he quickly suppressed his grin, replacing it with a look of compassion. How could someone so strong and independent be afraid of a carnival ride? It didn't even go very high, a hundred feet max.

"I would prefer to watch you and your father ride. Okay?" She stood and gave Aiden's shoulder a squeeze.

Aiden gazed back at her and smiled encouragingly. "You won't have to be afraid if you're with me," he said. "Pleeeeze, Sam?"

Sam's expression softened instantly at Aiden's quiet reassurance. She looked at Micah, her eyes silently pleading for rescue, but he could only grin and shrug his shoulders.

Reluctantly, she gave in, and Aiden led the way to the ride, skipping with excitement. But as they waited in line, she grew increasingly tense, tapping her feet, breathing in short quick gasps, and Micah wondered if she'd actually go through with it.

When Micah shot her a reassuring smile, she looked away.

At the front of the line, she hesitated, and Aiden took her hand again. "It's all right, Sam. Come on. You can sit in the middle." He stepped forward to climb on first.

Sam followed him onto the ride, and Micah settled himself on her other side. She stared straight ahead, eyes wide, while her chest rose and fell with her rapid breathing. She blinked, then jumped with a startled gasp when the attendant slammed the safety bar closed in front of them.

Aiden squeezed her hand. "It's all right, Sam, really. It's fun. You'll see."

She let out another nervous half-laugh. "I can't believe I'm doing this."

Micah stretched his arm out behind her as she took off her hat. "Here, let me hold on to that."

"Oh, yes, please." As she held it out to him, their chair lurched forward and up and she grabbed the bar so quickly, Micah had to reach to catch the tumbling hat.

They stopped a few feet off the ground, rocking back and forth, as the seat behind them emptied and more riders got on.

"You okay?" Micah asked.

Sam took a deep breath. She looked like she wanted to scream *No*, but she nodded, licked her lips, and exhaled loudly.

With the ride underway, Sam's death grip on the safety bar turned her knuckles white, and Micah tightened his arm around her shoulders. After several minutes, she braved a glance at Aiden and chuckled nervously.

Aiden's smile turned to laughter as the rush of wind in his face blew his hair back. "See! Isn't this great?"

Micah followed Aiden's gaze to the scenery spread out before them, a bird's-eye view of the town painted in the warm glow of the setting sun and the surrounding mountains and valleys, serenely shadowed deep green and blue-violet in the fading light of dusk. As glorious a sunset as Micah had ever seen.

Sam's whole body seemed to relax on the seat beside him. "Amazing," she said in a breathy voice, her face alight with wonder.

After riding the Ferris wheel, Micah and Sam looked on as

Aiden rode a few other rides with his cousins, and when darkness settled in, they returned to the park for the fireworks, stopping by Micah's truck to grab a blanket which they spread on the grass.

Aiden stretched out on the blanket between Micah and Sam and let out a long, drawn-out yawn. Over his head, Micah met Sam's smile as they shared in the satisfaction of the fun-filled afternoon that had worn out his son.

"Got your phone handy?" Micah asked Sam. "I want to give you my number so you can send me that picture."

"Oh, sure." Sam handed him her phone, a blank contact screen ready.

He entered his info, pressed SAVE, and handed it back. "MD—Micah Daniels." A small part of him twisted uncomfortably at only using his initials. Why had he felt the need to disguise his name at all?

Seconds later, as the dark night sky erupted with a magnificent display of light and sound, his own phone vibrated in his pocket. He glanced at Sam's photo, mouthed a thank you, and then settled next to Aiden, hands beneath his head, as his insides danced a little jig. No question, it was the best Fourth of July ever.

Afterward, he insisted on walking Sam to her vehicle and seeing her home. As he followed her SUV down the pitch-black trail that led to her cabin, the scant path ahead barely visible despite her high beam headlights, he was glad he did.

She parked in front of the cabin and Micah pulled up behind her, leaving his running lights on, so she could see to unlock the door. He shut off his truck and glanced over the seat to where his son slept peacefully in his booster seat in the back, then slipped out quietly to walk Sam to her door.

On the step, she put the key into the lock and turned to him. "I had so much fun tonight. Thank you."

"You made his day." Micah nodded to his truck. "Heck, this was probably the highlight of his summer."

"He's a really great kid," she said. "But it was totally unfair of you to sic him on me. You knew I wouldn't be able to say no."

"Yeah, sorry about that, but it was actually his idea."

She narrowed her eyes.

"Honestly! He wanted you to come, even suggested he be the one to ask."

"Well, thank you again, Micah, for everything." She reached for the doorknob.

"Sam," he said.

She turned back to him, and the look in her eyes said everything he wanted to hear. She placed a palm on his chest.

Could she feel his heart pounding beneath her touch? He imagined her skin against his, warm and soft, her body beneath his. He placed a hand over hers, willing her to stay. They were so close he caught a gentle waft of her warm breath on his neck. She shook her head but lifted her face to his, staring up at him. Waiting?

"Sam," he whispered again, lowering his head ever so slightly, eyeing her mouth, his lips inches from hers.

A rush of breath fell out of her, and she pushed away, shoved the door open and disappeared inside, closing the door behind her.

Micah stumbled backward off the stoop, staring at the closed door, the emptiness before him.

*What was I thinking? She's married! Married, you idiot!*

He fought to catch his breath, took off his hat, and ran a hand through his hair, then shoved it back on as he slogged back to his truck. Behind the wheel, he stared at the little cabin until a light came on.

With a steadying breath, he started the truck but continued to sit there, thinking, for several more minutes. He'd wanted to kiss her, and had come close. How long before her divorce was final, before she'd put it behind her?

Sam dominated his thoughts the entire drive home. His heart sank like a rock thrown into the creek when he remembered she was only staying for the summer. Then she'd leave, head back to her life in Michigan, her real life.

*Oh, God help me. I'm falling for this woman and she's leaving. I can't do this, not again.*

*Too late, cowboy.*

AFTER MICAH LEFT, Sam took Bear out and brushed her teeth, then lingered naked before the small washroom mirror. Her hair was longer than she liked, but the curls she'd fashioned earlier draped gracefully over her breasts, which were still firm and full, but not overly so. She couldn't see her belly but knew it was only slightly rounded, and her legs were fine. The long walks in the woods and treks up and down the trail to the creek had made them strong and lean. She should shave more often, but what was the use.

Brent was seldom interested in sex, and when it happened, it was usually over quickly, simple and unemotional, and he didn't seem to care much about the feel of her skin, shaving, or any of that.

A man like Micah, now, he'd care. And somehow, she had the feeling he'd be exquisite, slow and steady and purposeful. The kind of man who'd kiss slowly, softly, a river of kisses to last a lifetime. The kind of man who'd use his power, his strength, to turn a woman inside out.

A stab of something started in Sam's chest and plunged to the pit of her stomach, did a little dance there. And when she looked up, the woman in the mirror was crying, small pitiful tears that ran in rivulets down her cheeks.

Frightened by the intensity of her desire for the rancher, she shook it off, splashed cold water on her face, and slipped into her nightshirt.

It wasn't a date. Nothing happened. Nothing's going to happen.

*Yeah, Samantha Jane, keep telling yourself that.*

# 11

# THE NORTH RIDGE

Hours later, Micah eased into his favorite recliner and gazed into the fire as his thoughts drifted back to Sam.

Why would God bring her into his life, so close, yet beyond his reach? If it was a test, he'd already failed. He desired her; no denying that. And if she'd let him kiss her earlier, how far would it have gone?

He chuckled. Not far with Aiden asleep in the truck.

He sighed heavily. What was it about her that captured his heart? She was beautiful, smart, and funny, but Janie was all of that.

No, there was more to Samantha Jamison that ran deeper than looks, intelligence, and a great sense of humor. She was fragile yet tough, and there was something about her delicate strength, rugged independence, and firm resolve to not let life happen to her that he found incredibly seductive.

She knew what she wanted and had the fortitude to go after it. Most of all, he admired her decision to fight for her marriage. Despite the sting, she refused to let her husband's infidelity crush her spirit. If anything, it only fueled the flames of her determination.

He wondered if she'd done anything yet with the divorce papers. The settlement agreement's expiration date niggled at Micah like a burr under his saddle. Not only was it fast approaching, but his feelings for Sam were inherently tied to it.

How could something as beautiful as falling in love be so wrong? And yet, it was wrong. Deep inside, trying unsuccessfully to hide in places he didn't want to acknowledge, Micah knew it was wrong. To covet another man's wife was a sin, one of The Big Ten. He knew it in his heart, but he still had an undeniable urge to reach out to her, to help her through her troubles.

He smiled as Janie's comment about the white horse echoed in his head. He supposed it was in his nature to want to help others. Isn't that what every man wants—to save a beautiful maiden in distress? It was a good thing, something he'd learned from his dad and his grandpa, something to be proud of.

"Oh, Lord," he silently prayed. "I can do this. I can be a friend, be there for her, and I can be patient. But please, please, give me strength."

"Daddy?"

Micah opened his eyes to find his son standing in front of his chair, a worried frown darkening his innocent little face.

"Why do you look so sad?"

"I'm not sad, little bear," Micah said, pulling Aiden onto his lap. "I was thinking and praying."

"About Sam?"

Micah's initial thought was to deny it. "Yes, actually."

"She's pretty special."

"Yep, that she is." Micah leaned his head against his son's. "Did you brush your teeth?"

"Not yet, but I will." Aiden hopped down and disappeared into the bathroom.

Several minutes later, Micah heard Aiden's voice, so he got up and went to his son's room, but halted at the doorway when he saw the boy on his knees beside the bed. Eyes closed, his small hands clasped together in prayer, he spoke to God like he would a best friend. Micah listened while his son went on about his new puppy, about his new friend Sam, and how he wanted his daddy to be happy, for the two of them to be a family, a real one. Then he blessed everyone, naming each one individually, and as Micah leaned against the doorframe, his heart warmed, overcome with the love he felt for his son.

When Aiden finished, Micah stepped into the room. His son patted the puppy good night and scrambled up into bed. Micah handed him his stuffed pony and pulled up the covers, carefully tucking them in, then sat on the edge of the bed.

"Your mama teach you to pray like that?"

Aiden smiled, as if sensing his father's happiness. "No, Daddy. I've been watching you."

Micah's eyes grew moist with the heartfelt realization that his little boy was growing up. He bent to kiss Aiden good night. "Sweet dreams, buckaroo," he whispered against his cheek.

"Good night, Daddy. I love you." Aiden's little hand tenderly brushed his father's jaw.

"I love you too, little bear."

Warmth permeated his soul as Micah gently pulled the door closed behind him. He slipped out onto the back deck, stood at the railing, and breathed deeply the cool night air. A nearly full moon hung over the mountain tops, like a bright white bulb in the black night sky, casting its glow over the hills and valleys that stretched in all directions.

He was a lucky man. The image of his little boy falling asleep in the other room brought a warmth to his heart. If only Aiden were a more permanent presence in his life. If only. It was a big if and one that killed a small part of Micah every September when he said goodbye and sent his son back to his mother in Houston.

Aiden loved spending summers at the ranch. He was a born mountain man, and some day, God willing, he'd ask to stay.

Micah rubbed his stubbled jaw. He needed a wife, to provide Aiden with a proper family. His son deserved that much.

Micah wondered what his chances would be in family court if he petitioned for a greater share of custody. Devastated, Elizabeth would fight him, but if Aiden felt the pull, that would go a long way. And if Micah had a wife, well, that might clinch it. It certainly wouldn't hurt.

He stared up at the moon and recalled Aiden's first trip to the ridge the month before. It was a night to remember; Aiden had fallen in love with Moonglow Meadow, as Micah knew he would. He hadn't been sure if his little bear could stay awake past ten o'clock, but when Micah had suggested it, Aiden had been so excited he'd taken an afternoon nap to make certain of it.

"When can I ride a horse?" Aiden had asked as he waited for his father to saddle up his pony.

Micah glanced over the back of the animal to his son, sitting on the edge of a gate in the dim light of the barn. "You think you're ready for a horse?"

"Sure! Caleb rides a horse, and I'm bigger than Caleb."

Caleb, Cody's boy, was a year older than Aiden, but Aiden was right. He was a mite bigger than Caleb. "Next time, okay, buckaroo?"

Aiden smiled, and sat a little taller. "Okay, Daddy."

Micah handed Aiden the reins of his pony and stood back to watch him mount on his own. He pulled himself up into the saddle as if born to it, and Micah smiled. His little boy was ready for a horse.

They started off together, and Micah glanced at Aiden riding beside him. His heart swelled with anticipation as he recalled heading out on a similar night so many years ago with his own father.

They entered the clearing at the top of the ridge, and Micah studied his son's face as Aiden looked across the valley, his eyes roving the breadth of it, taking it all in. A slow smile curved his lips, and Micah beamed with satisfaction.

He followed Aiden's gaze up to the heavens; the sky filled to overflowing with a million bright white twinkling stars, the blackness beyond barely discernible for all the brightness at the forefront. The entire valley glowed, pulsing with a white-hot intensity, frozen in a perfect stillness yet alive with an undercurrent of pure, unspoiled beauty.

"It's like magic!" Aiden exclaimed. "Like God said 'Pow!' and waved His hand, and it appeared, still sparkly with the power that made it appear outta nowhere." He looked over at his father. "Don't you think?"

Micah's heart laughed. He understood perfectly. "It's called glory," he explained. "The earth declares His glory to those who have eyes that see and ears that hear."

"Glory," Aiden repeated. "Right."

They dismounted and Micah put his arm around his son's shoulders, hugging him close as they continued to stare at the wonder of God's glory spread out before them.

"You know, Daddy, sometimes when I'm with Mommy and missing you, I close my eyes and go to my happy place, a place where I can see us together. It used to be sitting on your lap in your chair in front of the fire, but now, I have a new happy place." He looked up at Micah. "Is that okay?"

Micah had been so choked up he could only nod.

His heart still ached with the memory as he eased into a rocker, put his boots up on the railing, and leaned back. Yep, Aiden loved the mountains, no doubt about that.

Would Sam like the view of Moonglow Meadow? Afraid of heights, she might feel scared, standing up there on the ridge, looking out over the valley so far below. He should at least invite her. She said she'd love to see it.

Two days later, Aiden had a sleepover with his cousins, the perfect opportunity for Micah to ride over the ridge to Sam's cabin and invite her.

~

Startled by Micah's appearance well past sunset, Sam hesitated, uncertain, but when she stepped out and caught sight of the moon and how it lit up the meadow, she decided she wanted to see this amazing view he'd told her about. It must be something to have impressed the rancher who had lived here all his life.

She pulled on her boots and jacket, and within minutes, they were riding up the far hillside to the North Ridge.

A narrow trail wound through the trees, and Micah seemed to know it well, even in the dark. And in the dense Rocky Mountain woods, it was a deep, black darkness, unlike anything Sam had ever encountered. The moon barely broke through the timber to light the way.

"Is it always this dark," Sam asked, a little spooked.

"Only from sunset to sunrise," Micah answered with a chuckle.

The horses went slowly, their footing secure as they continued to wind up and up, until they emerged into a small clearing at the top of the ridge.

Micah helped her dismount, then tied the horses to a branch. Taking her hand, he led her toward the ridge, stopping several feet shy of the edge, watching her expression as she got her first glance of the valley below.

The meadow fairly glowed in the moonlight, the tall mid-summer grasses waving gently in the evening breeze, undulating in muted shades of luminescent gold and yellow-white. It took her breath away.

Stunning in its virtual endlessness and delicately framed by gently rolling hills and tree-lined ridges that rose on either side to great shadowed peaks in the distance, it stretched as far as the eye could see. The scene brought a lightness to her soul, a sense that whatever troubles she had were infinitesimal in the vastness spread before her.

Above it all, a mass of twinkling stars spread across a plush black blanket connected the mountains on either side while the stream gurgled softly, meandering through the valley floor, glistening in the moonlight like a silver ribbon flapping in the breeze. She'd never felt closer to God than she did at that moment.

"Oh, Micah!" She couldn't pull her gaze away. "It's the most beautiful thing I've ever seen. It's like I'd always imagined it may have looked on the seventh day."

"You mean when God rested, looked upon all He'd made, and said 'It is good'?"

"Yes!" She glanced his way, thrilled he understood so perfectly. Their eyes locked as she relished the profound moment of shared insight, faith, and heartfelt appreciation.

A gentle breeze whispered in the woods behind them, stirring up the crisp clean scent of pine, things moist and growing, surging with the fragrance of life. So, this was why Micah loved the land so much, why he couldn't move to Houston. He was as firmly planted in these Rocky Mountains as the aspens and sage that had taken root there since the beginning of time. For him to give up the mountains would be like anyone else giving up air.

After several long moments, she shivered with a sudden chill, and instantly, he was behind her, draping his Carhartt over her shoulders. The coat felt heavy and still held his warmth and scent: earth, horses, cowboy.

She thought about how they'd almost kissed the other night, and she wondered if he'd try again. Did she want him to?

*Oh, yes. No!* No, it was enough to know he'd wanted to.

"Sam–"

She turned and held out a hand to him. "Dance with me."

He stared at her hand, then into her eyes. His smile wavered as he took it. He stepped in and placed his other hand gently at the small of her back, keeping a suitable distance between them.

He held her with all the grace of an eighth-grader at his first school dance as they swayed to the music of the wind in the trees. She smiled up at him, and he looked away, as though she threatened to overwhelm his initially wholesome good intentions.

"Hey." She touched his cheek. "You okay?"

He flinched and stepped away. "No, Sam!" His voice broke, and he cleared his throat. "I—this," he waved a hand between them, "is not okay. I want more than anything to wrap you up, hold you, feel you, every damn inch of you against my skin, kiss you like, like ..." He laughed and looked away, rubbed his face.

"Samantha, you do things to me, and being with you like this, here, in this place," he spread his arms wide. "Beneath this incredible sky that God's shined down upon us, it's, well, it's more than a good man can bear."

Sam's breath caught in her throat as she realized the effect she had on him. "I'm sorry, Micah--"

"Don't be." He chuckled. "It's my fault. I shouldn't have brought you here. You're an amazing woman, Sam, smart, beautiful, and incredibly sensual. I'd have to be crazy or blind or both not to be affected by you."

Sam looked down and shook her head, her self-doubt returning to haunt her with images of her husband and the petite, dark-haired woman.

MICAH WANTED MORE than anything in the world to tell her how he felt. It was too much, being there with her and experiencing her reaction to his beloved valley. She was meant for him; he was certain of it.

He gently lifted her chin, and her eyes met his. "I want to kiss you, Sam." His voice sounded deeper than usual and strange to his own ears. "But I won't."

He licked his lips and breathed deeply, gathering his resolve. "Because I know you're married. And I know I'm not the one you want." He forced a smile. At least not now, he thought, as he stepped away from her and looked across the valley, finding peace in its unwavering beauty.

"But I'm glad I got to show this to you. I think you love this valley as much as I do, and I can't tell you what that means to me," he said, glancing back at her.

"I do, Micah. It's absolutely incredible, and I will never forget it as long as I live."

They stood shoulder to shoulder, a comfortable silence settling between them as they each took in the splendor spread before them, savoring its raw beauty, committing it to memory. And when thoughts of kissing her again seeped into his consciousness, he looked to the heavens for help, focusing on the multitude of stars, the constellations of which he only knew a few.

"See that constellation there?" He pointed up to the southern sky beyond her, leaning his head closer. "That big S?" He followed the outline with his index finger.

"Yeah," she said, smiling with anticipation.

"It's your constellation, Sam."

"Mine? Really?"

"Yep. You know, most constellations come from ancient Greek gods who cast demigods and mortals to the heavens for wronging them. But not the Samantha constellation."

His words came slower now as he made up the story as he went. "Samantha was a brave and beautiful warrior princess, spirited and kind, but unlike the others, she cast herself to the heavens." He glanced sideways to see her reaction. "She did. To flee the pain of betrayal when a ... a pagan chariot driver broke her heart."

Sam's brows shot up. "Yeah?"

"Yep. But legend has it that one day a gentle shepherd–"

"Of heroic proportions," Sam interjected.

Micah chuckled. "Right. One day, a gentle shepherd of heroic proportions is going to rescue her by throwing his lariat around her and pulling her back to earth, to live out the rest of her days, at his side, beloved and cherished, as fate intended."

STUNNED BY HIS BEAUTIFUL STORY, Sam felt herself falling. Hard. It was like getting sucker punched with flowers. Pretty and fragrant to her bruised ego, but it still almost knocked her out.

She didn't dare look at him, so she focused on the big S in the sky, but she felt him watching her, and her entire body seemed to smile. When she glanced his way, the unmistakable tenderness in his gaze made her breath catch in the back of her throat.

"As fate intended," she repeated, his sweet words shimmering in her head.

He gave her a quick nod and a half-laugh. "Yep."

Far off in the distance, an animal howled, and she flinched. "You think I'm running away?"

"You're here, aren't you?"

"What if—" Could she really say it aloud? "What if he really doesn't want me anymore?"

"Any man who says goodbye to you is a fool."

She recoiled at the hard edge to his voice. "And you're going to sweep in and rescue me?"

He took his time answering. "I think you've got some tough decisions to make—what with your marriage, your job, and all—and I want you to know that I wish you only happiness, whatever that looks like. But," he rubbed his chin, and when he looked her way, his smile made his eyes sparkle, "if given half a chance, I'd sure like a shot."

A laugh burst out of her. "Oh, God, Micah, you're a sweet, sweet man."

"And you're a fascinating woman. For now, I'm content to be your friend, but if your husband lets you go—Well, you're strong, and I know you'll find happiness again."

"Thank you, Micah. And thank you for this lovely evening, for sharing your amazing meadow with me."

"It was my pleasure, Sam, honestly. And it's your meadow, not mine."

When they returned to her cabin, she dismounted quickly before he could help her. She didn't think she could handle it if he touched her again, even in such a benign manner. She imagined herself falling against him, his powerful arms wrapping around her, pulling her against that solid chest of his, and she'd look up and—no, she didn't dare go there.

"Thanks again, Micah," she said, handing him first his jacket and then the reins.

"Hey, I need to ask you something." He shifted uncomfortably in the saddle.

"Yeah?" She stepped back and looked up at him.

"Well, I was wondering about those divorce papers. Have you signed them? Sent them back yet?"

She hesitated and looked away, unsure how much to tell him.

He dismounted with the grace of a man who's done it a million times, held both sets of reins, and stepped closer. "It's none of my business, I know, but as your friend and legal advisor, I thought I should point out that the expiration date is fast approaching."

Sam shuffled her feet. "I've done nothing yet."

"Well, in case you're not aware, in most states a spouse can get a divorce with or without the other's consent. *En absentia*, it's called. If you don't respond by the date, it can go through without your signature, exactly as written."

She nodded and glanced away.

"I know you don't want the divorce, and I don't blame you for not wanting to think about it."

She sighed, staring off into the distance.

"I'm sorry I brought it up and ruined the end of this perfect evening."

"No, it's okay. I'm glad you did. I want to make a few changes before I send it back, but I don't have a scanner or a printer."

He cocked his brows. "Oh. Well, I can help you with that. If you'd like."

"Really?"

"I'm not a divorce attorney, but as long as it's fairly simple, I'm sure I can handle it. If not, I can always run it by my Uncle Will. He's a practicing attorney in town."

"Oh, it's simple," she assured him.

"Well, I've got a busy day tomorrow, so why don't you come by the day after, early, and we'll take care of it before Aiden wakes up."

"I will. Thank you, Micah, for everything. You're a good man and a good friend."

He seemed to cringe at the word friend, then nodded, as if accepting that was all she could offer him. "Thank you for coming with me tonight. I thoroughly enjoyed sharing it with you, and I'll never forget it either."

## 12

# BREAKFAST WITH AIDEN

When Sam showed up at the ranch two days later at half-past nine, Micah teased her about her idea of early. "Hey," she said, breezing past him. "You didn't exactly set a time. For me, nine-thirty is plenty early."

"The early bird gets the worm," he said.

"The early worm gets eaten," she shot back with a giggle.

"Seriously, you don't love mornings? Waking up with a nice steaming hot cup of coffee," he raised his cup, "enjoying the quiet solitude in the cool morning air as you watch a glorious sunrise?"

She laughed in disbelief. "Honestly, Micah, don't you love evenings? Relaxing after a long, hard day, sharing a nice bottle of wine with someone special in the warm evening air as you watch a magnificent sunset?"

She'd mocked him perfectly, and with his own cadence. "Snuggling in the morning?"

"Dancing in the moonlight?"

He let out an exasperated chuckle and stared at her, a light in his eyes she'd seen before.

She knew full well where his thoughts had gone, and her insides shimmied. Would it have evened up the argument if they'd spent the night together? She would've liked to find out if snuggling with him in the morning was as wonderful as dancing with him in the moonlight. She stashed the shameful thought away and remembered the reason she'd come.

"Okay, so what do you want to do here?" he asked, taking the envelope from her and motioning for her to sit at the kitchen table. "Want a cup of coffee? I can warm it up."

Sam laughed again at his not-so-subtle reminder of how late it was. "No thanks, I'm good."

She sat as he slipped into the chair beside her and pulled out the document.

"I want to add a condition," she said. "I want him to agree that he won't remarry for at least twelve months."

Micah's facial expression changed from curious to surprised. Was that a totally unreasonable request, or was he wondering at her motives behind it? "And I want the Colorado property with the hunting cabin on it. I'll put thirty-five thousand into his side of the real estate trust."

Micah nodded. "Ok, simple enough, but," he hesitated, as though choosing his words carefully, "are you sure you want to add the twelve-month condition? You realize, if you ask it of him, he can turn around and ask it of you and what if ..." He rubbed his jaw. "I'm sorry. I—"

Guessing at his hesitation, Sam felt compelled to explain. "I don't want our children to know their father cheated on me." Her voice faltered as she fought to contain her emotions. "It would absolutely ruin their relationship with him, especially my son's. He'd lose all respect for his father, and I can't take that away from him, from either of them."

Micah placed a hand over hers. "Okay. It'll take me a few minutes to type this up, so make yourself at home." With that, he disappeared up the stairs.

While he was gone, she wandered to the back deck to look out over the valley and the mountains in the distance. It was almost eleven o'clock in Michigan. On a normal workday, she'd be at the office, already halfway through the workday by now. She hated getting up early, but had still made it a point to be in the office by seven. And where did that get her? Nowhere near where she wanted to be.

Would she go back to that job? Don't think about that now. Think about that later, in August. She mentally scheduled an appointment in her head and pushed the worry away.

"Sam!" Aiden cried as he burst from the sliding glass door.

She turned at his voice and knelt on the deck to catch him up in her arms, astounded by the intensity of the hug he gave her.

"Hey, little man!" When he let go, she stepped back. "Good morning!"

"Mornin'!" he replied with a sleepy smile. "Did you sleep over?"

"What? No, I got here a few minutes ago." She felt her cheeks redden. "Your father is typing up something for me."

"Oh," Aiden yawned and stretched his arms wide, his Sheriff Woody pajama shirt rising with his arms to show his soft, white belly. "Well, since you're here, you can make me breakfast. Come on." He grabbed her hand and pulled her into the house.

WHEN MICAH CAME DOWNSTAIRS a few minutes later, Aiden had joined Sam at the table and was slurping from a bowl of Cheerios, a plate of strawberries at its side. They were talking about Aiden's trip up to the ridge and the glory he saw. Seeing the two of them together brought a jagged edge to his heart. *She's not just meant for me. She's meant for us.*

"Morning, buckaroo." Micah ruffled his son's hair.

"Morning, Daddy. Sam made me breakfast."

"I see that. Did you remember to--"

"Thank you, Sam," Aiden blurted out.

"You're very welcome, Aiden."

Micah set the papers and envelope on the table next to her. "You'll want to review it."

Sam checked the pages he'd tagged with sticky markers. "Looks good. Thank you so much." She stood and tucked the papers into the envelope.

"Glad to help. You'll need to sign it and have it notarized before mailing it back, and there's an extra copy for you to keep. Both the post office and the bank have notaries."

"I'd better get going." Sam walked around the table and gave Aiden a quick kiss on the cheek. "Bye, little man."

She looked back at Micah. "Thanks again."

"Bye, Sam!" Aiden called as she moved to the door.

Micah watched her go, then turned to find Aiden staring at him with a perceptive grin. "What?" He eased into the chair Sam had vacated.

"Nothin'." Aiden popped a strawberry into his mouth.

# 13

# FRIENDS

Cresting the North Ridge on horseback, Aiden following behind on his pony, Micah stopped to study the meadow below. The small hunting cabin stood quiet in the afternoon heat of late July, the back deck empty save for a small table and chair. Sam wasn't at the creek either, at least that he could see. He stood in his stirrups to glean a better vantage point but still couldn't make out if she might be lying on her blanket beneath the cottonwood.

Aiden reined in abreast of him. "We're stoppin' by Sam's? Yes!"

"We are but we can't stay long. Isaac and the hands are expecting our help in moving the herd." Micah turned his horse toward the trail leading down into the valley. "Stay close, you hear?"

Nearing the cabin, Micah saw no sign of Sam anywhere, until they rounded the cabin, and she was right there, stacking a pile of splits between two tree stumps.

She jumped back, startled, when she noticed them. "Oh, my God! You scared me half to death!"

"Hey, Sam!" Aiden called as he slipped off his pony.

"Sorry." Micah dismounted, grabbed the reins of Aiden's pony, and made a mental note to talk with the boy later about holding onto his mount. "You didn't hear us coming?"

"Didn't hear anything over the sound of wood splitting." Sam removed her safety glasses and wiped sweat from her eyes with a handkerchief tied around her wrist. She wore jean cutoffs, an exercise bra-top, and hiking boots. With no make-up, and covered in wood chips, dirt, and sweat, she looked as rugged and brave as any woman he'd ever seen, the way he'd always pictured Tolkien's Luthien.

"Can I play with Bear?" Aiden stood on the step while Bear spun in circles, barking on the other side of the screen door.

"Sure. Go on in." Sam collapsed onto the front step looking thoroughly exhausted. "His leash is on the hook if you want to bring him out."

Micah nodded toward the pile of neatly stacked wood. "Looks like you've been at it a while."

"Yep, nights are pretty chilly up here and I was getting low. Wish I'd passed on my morning yoga though." She rolled her shoulders, first one, then the other, and took a long pull from a water bottle. "Something to drink?"

"No thanks. We've got to get on." Micah trekked past the woodpile and tented his eyes, studying the sky to the south. "Come here. I want to show you something."

Sam remained seated, stretched out her legs, and retwisted her hair into a messy bun, but it was little improvement. "The mass of dark clouds? Saw it. Smelled it." She wrinkled her nose and it was so dang cute, Micah almost laughed. "Wildfire on Wolf Mountain. Thankfully I have internet up here through my phone. I signed up for Routt County's Emergency Alert program. I didn't miss an evacuation notice, did I?" She picked up her phone, glanced at the screen.

Micah shook his head, amazed at her independence. He'd never met a woman so self-sufficient, so less in need of saving. "Not yet. But it grew from two acres to over four hundred this afternoon.

Sounds like emergency responders have it under control now though, but if it gets any closer and we need to evacuate, we'll swing by to pick you up."

"Micah—"

"Don't argue. Wildfires are serious business up here. You may even wake in the morning to a cabin full of smoke. It's not unusual for it to settle in the valleys overnight. If that happens, drive up the hill, come to the ranch, or head up I-80. Don't head south, into town, until we get the all clear. You hear?" He hadn't intended to sound like he was talking to Aiden. Sam was a grown woman used to taking care of herself.

Sam studied him for a long moment, appreciation, sadness, a hint of something more in her smile. Then she blinked, nodded, and looked away. "Thank you. For stopping by. For being concerned about me."

Micah kicked her boot. "What are friends for, anyway?"

~

A FEW DAYS LATER, Brent called and asked first about the kids. She'd gotten weekly letters from Emma, three from Zach, but Brent, too busy to write to his children at camp, hadn't gotten any. Just what he deserved, she thought. She wanted to remind him you get out of a relationship what you put into it, but he should know that by now. She told him how they were doing, as usual, filling the gaps in his less-than-adequate attempt at fatherhood.

"It's good to hear your voice." She hated how weak she sounded. When had she gotten weak?

"When you coming home?"

"I don't have to be back to work until after Labor Day—"

"Shit! Another month?"

"But I thought I'd come home before the kids get there. I want to spend time with them before they head off to school again." She heard papers shuffling, imagined him looking for their itinerary, which she'd tacked to the fridge. She decided to give him a bit of grace, even though he didn't deserve it. "They'll be home the last Saturday in August."

"Thanks."

The silence lingered. She didn't have much to say. It hurt too much to remember how much she'd once loved him, how he could melt her insides with just a look, how—

"Think you can give me another chance?"

"Think you deserve it?"

"Baby—"

*Don't call me that.* "You still haven't said you're sorry. And if you really wanted another chance, you'd be here by now." There. That sounded much stronger.

"This is a busy time of year for me. You know that."

Work, work, work! And still no apology. No, she couldn't go back to that. She didn't know why, but she needed this time alone, to find herself, to figure out what she wanted *her* future to look like. Because this, being with a man she could no longer trust, certainly wasn't it.

Her older brother had warned her about Brent. "You can do better, Samantha Jane," he'd said.

When she'd pushed him for more, he shut down, as if some sort of guy code prevented him ratting out a friend, even to his own sister. She'd known Brent was engaged when they first met. At their college, it was a tradition for young men to *give a ring by spring* of their senior year. But he'd broken it off to go out with her. And within months, he'd charmed Sam into bed, an unexpected pregnancy, and a late summer wedding.

"Our anniversary is coming up," he said. "Does that still mean anything to you?" She could hear him tapping on his keyboard, multi-tasking, as always giving her a mere fraction of his attention.

"Are you still seeing her?"

"I can come there. If you'll have me. We'll go to dinner in Steamboat."

*Seriously? Was he even listening?* "I asked if you're still seeing her."

Silence hung in the space between them, as vast as the twelve hundred miles that separated them physically.

Oh, my God! What she needed to hear was *Of course not. You're the one I love. You're the one I married.* But, inadequate on so many levels, he said none of those things. She wanted to hang up on him. And she did.

# 14

# TIME SPENT FISHING

Engrossed in the story bursting forth from her fingertips as they flew across the keyboard, Sam didn't notice the distant hoofbeats until Bear raced from beneath her deck chair, barking and spinning in an excited circle. Sam glanced up from her laptop as a horse crossed the stream. She finished her sentence, then squinted to make out Aiden in the saddle, riding behind another boy she didn't recognize. She stood and swiped at her eyes, surprised she'd been crying.

"Howdy, Sam!" Aiden called as they trotted up the trail to her back deck. "This here's my cousin, Caleb."

Sam pulled herself from her story and found a smile. "Hey, Aiden. Nice to meet you, Caleb."

Caleb tipped his hat. "Ma'am."

"We're goin' fishin'. Want to come?" Aiden asked.

Sam looked at their rods. "Fly-fishing?"

"Yep," Caleb answered. "Only way to catch brook trout 'round here."

"I'm afraid I don't know how to fly-fish," Sam said, trying to sound cheerful.

Aiden looked at her sideways, as though sensing something

wasn't quite right. "I can show you. Come on. I brought an extra pole for 'ya." He reached behind the saddle to jiggle the three rods there.

Sam looked toward the stream. A breather from the sad story she'd been weaving might help her frame of mind. It was breaking her heart, and she worried it was getting far too sad for anyone else to want to read. "Okay, sure. You guys go on ahead. I'll be right down."

"Great." Aiden's smile reminded her of his father's when she'd agreed to go to the picnic with them.

Inside the cabin, Sam rinsed her face, washing away the telltale signs of her melancholy, and found herself looking forward to Aiden's sunny disposition. As she strolled the well-worn path, she tied her hair into a braid, and joined the boys at the stream in time to see Aiden, waist deep in the water, hook a lively catch. He stumbled and almost fell when the fish broke through the surface. Regaining his footing, he whooped, Caleb cheered, and something inside of Sam warmed to see two young boys so happy and carefree.

She remembered the first time she and Brent had taken the twins fishing off their dock. They were little, maybe four or five, and they'd screeched with excitement as—six hands on the pole—they reeled one in. It was a picture she'd added to their photo album. Her eyes stung with fresh tears as she longed for those joy-filled days of her children's youth.

"Sam?" Aiden asked. He may have been staring at her for several moments; he was still holding his fish in one hand, the pole in the other. "It's just a fish, and I'm gonna toss it back."

She blinked away the sadness, forced a smile, and moved to join Aiden in the water. "Teach me how to do that."

Aiden freed his line, lowered the fish to the water, and shot her a grin as it swam away. "Okay, watch. When you cast, you gotta make the line go in a circle over the water. The fly's gotta float just on top, like this. Like a real fly."

He showed her, sending his line out about fifty feet in front of him, a perfect loop, and the fly danced over the water like it had a life of its own.

"You gotta relax, feel it. You watchin'?" He did it again, and a fish jumped from the water to take his fly. "Oh! See?" He laughed and Sam laughed with him, and for a moment she wasn't sad anymore.

He fetched the extra rod and she tried it several times, each attempt less awkward than the last, as Aiden continued to instruct and encourage. When she got a bite, he told her how to bring it in, then netted it when she pulled it close enough.

"Nice one, Sam!"

"Let me see," Caleb hollered from downstream.

Aiden held up the fish for his cousin.

"Good job, Sam!" Caleb called.

As Aiden retied the fly on her line, Sam stared off into the mountains. What would it be like to live here, where it felt good to be alone, where it was okay to spend an entire afternoon just fishing?

"You know, my daddy says time spent fishin' doesn't count against your life clock," Aiden said, as though reading her mind.

Sam chuckled. "That sounds like something your daddy would say."

"It's true, you know. His grandpa told him so."

She thought how relaxing it was to stand in the middle of a stream, making a line dance in circles, and she could certainly buy into the truth of it. Fishing was good for the soul.

When their legs grew numb from the cold water, they took a break and sat on the bank, warming their limbs in the afternoon sun. Sam gazed longingly across the grassy valley dotted with broad stands of aspen and into the sun-washed mountainsides, astounded by their unspoiled beauty. She always loved coming here. It was a simple life, a little rough, but uncomplicated, stress free, and God knew she needed that right now.

When the boys were ready to head back to the ranch, Caleb fetched the horse from where it stood tied beneath the cottonwood, while Aiden lagged behind. “It’d probably be best if you didn’t tell my daddy we came by today.”

“Oh?” Had the boys ridden off without permission? They seemed awfully young to be riding around the ranch on their own.

“He said I shouldn’t bother you.”

“Okay, I won’t say anything.”

“Thanks. And thanks for letting us fish here today. You got the best spot on the whole darn creek.”

“Anytime, Aiden. I mean that.”

She’d keep his secret, honored he trusted her that way. But it saddened her to know his innocence would one day be shattered when he discovered the real world, where secrets destroy lives.

# 15

# GOOD INTENTIONS

On a blistering hot day in early August, Micah met Cody in the south pasture to herd up strays that had wandered onto their neighbor's land. They rode abreast, headed toward the break in the fence.

"I saw Sam in town this morning," Cody said.

"Oh?" Micah panned the sections of down wire, posts lying on the ground.

"At the Rexall. She hurt her hands pretty bad. Rope burns. I practically had to drag her across the street to my office so I could properly bandage them."

"Rope burns?"

"Gashes, more like. Said she was trying to haul a dresser up to her loft, and it slipped, but she didn't know where her little dog was, so she held on, didn't want it to land on him. Must have hurt something awful."

"She's pretty tough."

"Think so?"

Micah gave him a side eye. It was a look he used with those he knew well, a look that said, *don't-question-me* and *end-of-discussion* rolled into one.

"I don't think she's as tough as she lets on. She was in pain, but it wasn't all in her hands. There's a deeper hurt in her. In here." Cody thumped his chest.

"Did she cry?"

"Oh, no. She wouldn't cry. Not that one."

Right, not Sam. She was strong. At least she tried to be. But Micah had seen her cry her heart out twice now.

They rode in silence, nearing the fence line, as Micah tried to push Sam from his mind. But it was hard not to worry about her. He knew the depth of her struggles, and Cody was right. It was down-deep damage, the kind that shattered a person.

He could feel his cousin's stare, and it unnerved him. What did Cody expect him to do? Micah couldn't fix Sam's problems, no matter how much he wanted to.

"What?" he said, returning Cody's stare.

"You don't think she'd intentionally hurt herself, do you?"

Micah thought back to the night of the storm. He'd never heard a more painful heartbreak, but she'd held it together. That night. When the divorce papers came, now that was a different story. She'd tried to hold it in, but it was too much, even for her. Maybe something else had happened, something that hit hard.

What if she'd gotten the divorce papers back? Signed. Final.

"Micah?"

"What!"

"Sam wouldn't try to hurt herself, would she?" Cody repeated, reining in his horse.

Micah halted. "No. What? Aw, hell!" It had been almost a month since he'd helped her with the divorce papers, and he didn't know if she'd sent them back. It couldn't be final already, could it? "I don't know. She's going through some stuff, but no, she's not the type to give up. She wouldn't do something like that, not on purpose."

*Would she?*

They rode on, through the down section of fence and broke off in opposite directions to herd up the cattle that had gotten through.

Cody's question gnawed at Micah. What if she did? And what if she tried again, and he'd done nothing to stop her?

He needed to go check on her. Now.

Coming back together on the far side of the herd, they pushed them toward the opening.

Micah considered making an excuse to get away but stopped short. Cody knew his heart too well. And he certainly didn't need to put a shine on anything for his cousin's sake.

"I'm worried about her." Micah reined in alongside Cody. "She's got a lot going on. Her husband cheated on her, wants a divorce. Aiden fessed up that he and Caleb went over there to fish the other day—after I'd told him not to—and he said she'd been crying." Micah shook his head. "I don't think she'd intentionally hurt herself, but—shoot! I should go check on her."

Cody scanned the handful of cattle left in the Henry's pasture. "You go on. I got this. The fence and ol' Ms. Henry too."

Imagining the worst, Micah rode hard for nearly an hour to reach Sam's place, his mind near panic by the time he neared. As he crested a ridge and peered across the valley, he saw her standing in the stream. He slowed his horse to a trot, forced his heart to a normal beat, and headed down the hillside, studying her as he approached.

What in the world was she doing? Standing waist deep, she held a long stick in her hand. As he neared, he guessed she was washing her hair, or trying to, with the stick, which, upon closer inspection, was a wooden fork. She wore white latex gloves, the kind Cody used. A towel and blanket roll lay in the grass at the stream's edge. A rifle stood propped against the trunk of the cottonwood.

When he reined in beneath the tree, she glanced up, straightened, and flipped her wet hair over her head. She swiped the back of a wrist across her eyes and squinted at him through shampoo bubbles.

"What are you doing?" he asked, suppressing a laugh.

She giggled. "Trying to wash my hair. Without using my hands."

She collapsed against a nearby boulder, looking thoroughly exhausted.

"Need a hand?" he offered with a chuckle. "Or two?"

A faint smirk played on her lips. "I can manage. Thank you very much."

She flipped her hair forward and resumed her task, but while her words told him she didn't need or want his help, her utter incompetence said otherwise.

Micah dismounted and looped Buck's reins over a nearby branch, tugged off his boots and shirt, and entered the water. When he took the fork and set it on the rock beside her things, she didn't fuss or say a word.

"Come here." He led her to deeper water and eased her back over his arm, first wiping the soap from her eyes then massaging her scalp with his free hand. His fingertips slowly worked the shampoo into a thick lather, then drew it through to the ends with a focused sense of purpose.

Her eyes closed, and Micah took full advantage of the opportunity to appreciate her slim body. Her breasts beckoned full and firm, their hard peaks visible beneath the fabric of her modest bikini while her stomach stretched taut across her pelvic bones near the water's surface, the soft curve of her hips disappearing beneath.

He eased her back and carefully splashed water up over her head, rinsing the suds away. Arched backward over his arm, he felt her weight, ran his fingers through her wet gold-blonde hair, lost in the perfection of her drenched skin.

*God, he needed her!* Not just physically, but deep down in places he hadn't even known were hollow and crying out to be filled. He'd waited a lifetime for her to appear on his mountain, to fill the vast emptiness of his sad, lonely life, add warmth and meaning to his desolate existence. And here she was. In his valley, in his stream.

Resisting a primal urge, he forced himself to tear his gaze away and silently berated himself for thinking he could take this on.

When he raised her to stand upright, he gently wiped the water from her eyes with the pads of his thumbs, hoping she wouldn't see what was in his heart when she opened them.

She stared at him with a tentative smile as a mild breeze swept through the meadow, setting the tall late summer grasses to whistle a soothing tune.

Micah's throat tightened, as the ache intensified in the pit of his stomach, twisting violently into a solid, single-minded knot. His heart raced as he imagined leaning down to kiss her, taking her into his arms, taking all of her, making her his in every sense of the word.

But it was wrong. All wrong. She was another man's wife, and adultery was a carnal sin as old as time itself. His parents had raised him better than that. His morality was as much a part of him as his brown eyes and ranching. But Samantha was a woman who could make even a good man come apart, and he burned for her with a longing that threatened every fiber of his well-intentioned soul.

When she rested her cheek against his bare chest, over his heart, there was no hiding how madly it beat for her. It took every ounce of his waning resolve not to wrap his arms around her. "Samantha—"

She stepped back. "Conditioner?"

"Sure." His voice sounded strange, a hoarse croak. He shuffled to the rock, grateful for the respite where he could think, breathe, collect himself, before having to do it again.

He grinned at her hair products, their labels all touting *eco-friendly* and *phosphate free,* obviously chosen with a thought to the environment. He squeezed a small amount of conditioner into his palm, then turned to show it to her. "Is this enough?" She nodded and watched as he waded back to her.

She smiled up at him as he spread conditioner over her hair, worked it through to the ends, and struggled to not get lost in the depths of her baby blues.

"That's good." She turned her back to him and leaned into his arm again for the final rinse.

He glanced away as he tried not to notice how perfect she was, how the water glistened on every curve of her body, how willingly she trusted him as he supported her, splashed water up over her hair, and ran his fingers through its silky length.

When he lifted her up, he again wiped her eyes, but his fingertips lingered, brushed gently over her cheeks, traced across her mouth, as he floated away in her sky-blue gaze. Her lips, full and soft, parted at his touch, and a breath fell out of her.

"Did you," he was so tied up he could hardly breathe, "send the divorce papers back yet?" After a long moment, she lowered her head. "I'm sorry. I shouldn't have asked that. I have no right."

Several more heartbeats ticked by, the unanswered question darn near killing him. He needed to know. And he *had* a right to ask. He was falling in love with her. He deserved to know if she was still married. With a fingertip, he lifted her chin. "Sam, tell me, please."

"I did." There was a profound sadness in those two paltry words, like the voice of a woman admitting to a heinous act foisted upon her.

He let out a ragged breath, happy she'd at least taken that one major step in the right direction—his. But still married. His desire—no, love—for her remained wrong on so many levels, as forbidden as that first sweet apple.

And yet, with every sense he possessed, he knew she was meant for him, for this very moment. *Oh, God help me. I'm losing myself here!* He closed his eyes, grasped to hold on to his resolve. *It's not too late. You can still walk away.*

*Go! Go now!* His mind shrieked. He felt himself caught in a lariat of love and passion and need—intense, overwhelming need—tightening around them both, drawing them together into one captured beast. *Getting a divorce. Still married.*

*Just ... walk ... away*, the voice, now whisper-soft as if from the faraway reaches of his mind, was barely audible beneath the spiral of desire that wracked his soul, pulling him down, down, down.

The first secret to holes, he could hear his dad say, is to stop digging.

But it was too late for that. He was already in over his head.

He smiled, knowing he'd lost the battle—pleased that he'd lost it—as he gazed at the remarkable woman staring back at him, waiting. Wanting? When she returned his smile, he gave over to it, gently cupped her face in his hands, and bent to kiss her, laying his lips on hers with a feather-soft touch. When he withdrew, her breath shuddered, and he kissed her again, tenderly at first and then with a startling intensity.

Helpless to resist her as she elicited sensations so long foreign to him, he ached with a longing that threatened to dissolve him completely, and when he pulled away to stare at her in wonder, she whimpered softly in protest, a sound so faint, so innate, it undid him.

He swept her off her feet and into his arms and started for the riverbank. With her head cradled against his chest, he felt the pounding of her heart against his skin.

Up, up, up the riverbank he went to the cottonwood. He was wild with excitement. She was his, for now, and this was his dream, a dream from which he never wanted to wake. There was no stopping now.

She sighed as he set her on her feet, draped her towel around her shoulders, and peeled off her gloves. He spread her outdoor blanket, knelt upon it, and extended a hand to her, beckoning. She took it and knelt before him with a shy smile. He melted at the nervous look on her face. She had never looked so beautiful.

Holding her hands in his, he gently kissed the clean, dry, white bandages on each palm as she watched him, eyes narrowed, anticipating. He laid her down then and bent to kiss her with a tenderness and completeness that blew away everything from his mind but the soft ether into which he floated and her warm breath on his skin.

He trembled, driven by powers beyond his control, as his lips, his fingertips, drifted over her warm, willing body. She whispered things he didn't hear, her touch evoking sensations long forgotten.

He was floating, and she was there with him, sighing softly as he swept her away, and for a few precious moments she was his—all his —and there was nothing but this moment, only the currents and his body covering hers. She tried to speak, and his lips fell upon her again.

Suddenly, he had a mad pleasure such as he had never known: rapture, exhilaration, yielding to forces so strong, lips so soothing, time that passed so slowly.

For the first time in his life, he had found someone who loved the wild like he did, someone he could give everything that was his to offer, someone who *wanted* everything he offered.

Her arms were around his neck, and she trembled beneath him as they rose up into the heavens again, a soft, swirling heaven that suspended them in a magnificent flight as he chased her across the sky.

Sometime later he opened his eyes to the dappling rays of the afternoon sun blinking through the cottonwood boughs above. He was still holding her, and had he not felt her warmth beside him, he would have thought the afternoon just a glorious dream.

*Married!* His mind screamed. *Oh, God, what have I done?*

Did he deserve forgiveness for taking a married woman? Should he even seek it? Because he wanted her again. He wanted her now, and for always. He hadn't the strength to keep it from happening again, so why even try?

She was meant for him; he felt certain of it. Wasn't it The Spirit, who'd told him to stop that day? Micah hadn't even seen her until he'd backed up. And what they'd just shared was so incredibly beautiful, it couldn't possibly be wrong. She was everything he'd been waiting for, praying for. She was getting a divorce, and it would be all right then. Wouldn't it?

He dozed off, waking with a start as he imagined she'd gone. When he realized where he was and felt her in his arms, her head on his chest, he relaxed, but his mind resumed its painful onslaught. Somehow, he had to find a way to make it right and keep her in his life.

"You ever think about staying here?" he asked. "Beyond the summer, I mean?"

She took a minute to respond, and he wondered if she too had fallen asleep. "I can't live here, in this cabin in the winter with no heat, only the one little fireplace. I'm not that hearty."

"What if you had a little nicer place, bigger, with heat and electricity, and a bathtub?"

When she lifted her head, there was a sadness in her eyes. "I have a job back in Michigan—"

"That you hate."

She returned her head to his shoulder. No argument there.

Propping himself on an elbow, he pushed her hair from her face, and ran his fingertips through the long damp strands that curled and tumbled loosely around her shoulders.

"I suppose if I sold my novel and could actually make a living writing, I could live anywhere." A glimmer of hope he'd not seen before shined in her eyes.

He smiled, pleased that she'd consider it. Did he dare tell her how he felt about her? Would it make her want to stay if she knew? Or would it push her away, make her afraid of getting involved with someone new too soon?

He breathed heavily and bit his tongue. No, he needed to be patient. She needed time to heal, time to accept her divorce, time to welcome someone new into her life.

But oh, God help him, he needed her.

"How's your book coming?" He trailed a fingertip lazily down her arm.

"Okay," she said. "I think it's going to be a great story."

"Yeah? What's the name of it?"

"Broken Fences."

His brows shot up. "As in ranching?"

She giggled. "Yes."

"What do you know about ranching?" It couldn't possibly be enough to write an entire book.

"Oh, I've been paying attention these past few months," she said with an impish grin.

He chuckled as he recalled all of her questions, how she'd gotten him to go on and on, telling her all about his family, his life, how he spent his days. "Am I in it?"

Her eyes danced with mischief. "Don't worry. I won't use your real name."

"The hero?"

"Of course."

Satisfaction swept over him. "What kind of story is it?" he asked, mesmerized by the play of the sun on the strands of her hair as it trickled like molten gold through his fingertips.

She pushed him onto his back and leaned over him. "A love story," she whispered, excitement on her breath.

*A love story.* And he was in it. He considered what that meant as a pair of sandhill cranes lit at the water's edge, momentarily drawing his attention. "Does it have a happy ending?" He looked back at her, hoping.

She took a long, deep breath and held his gaze. "I don't know yet. I haven't gotten that far."

He knew she could see, plain as day, the way he felt about her. And he was glad. "Don't break his heart."

Her smile faltered. "I'll try not to."

His breath caught when she moved over him, then leaned back, her bandaged hands caressing outward from the center of his chest, across his shoulders, and down his arms. Her soft smile reappeared. "You're a beautiful man, Micah Daniels."

"This," locks of her hair dripped through his hands to tumble over her breasts, her pale skin peeking through, teasing, mesmerizing, "is beautiful." His voice was hoarse with emotion, his whole body taut with need.

She bent to kiss him, her hair falling loose around his head, covering them both, and he was back to that beautiful place where they floated together, and she was his. Her fingers laced through his hair, the medicinal scent of gauze and her sweet-smelling shampoo mingling together as he lost himself in her touch, in her warmth, and her lips on his.

"Samantha," he murmured. "Oh, darlin', stop."

She shook her head and kissed him, hard, demanding. She continued to consume him, his body, his breath, his very heart and soul, and he was powerless to stop her.

His resistance, what little remained, was spent, and he let himself take what his body longed for, drawing strength from her strength, her softness devouring his hardness, taking all of him, everything he offered, everything she needed.

Willingly, he gave over to her, and she drove him crazy with desire as her raw, almost feral need dominated his body, burning like a rampant wildfire, ripping up the mountainside, consuming everything in its path. Setting aflame the dry tinder of her parched soul as she raged wildly out of control. When he couldn't stand it any longer, he groaned with exquisite relief, and she arched back, laughing and breathless.

It took several minutes to recapture his sanity, and when he did, he held onto her with a fierce determination not to move a single muscle. She was his, their legs, their bodies tangled in one blissful knot, skin on skin, her breath warm against his neck as she lay in his arms.

She wanted him. She *needed* him.

Lovely in her uninhibited hunger, sensual beyond anything he'd ever imagined, she was a woman made to be loved.

"You are incredibly beautiful, Samantha," he choked out, his heart still pounding in his chest.

She sobbed against his neck.

*What the heck?* With a scowl, he lifted her face to his. She pulled away, rested her head back on his shoulder, but not before he glimpsed the tears.

Moisture cooled on his skin beneath her temple. He pushed her hair aside to peer at her. "Sunshine, what's wrong?"

"Nothing." She tried to pull away, but he held tight. "Please, let me go."

"I can't, Sam. Don't ask that of me. Anything but that." Something was terribly wrong. What did he say? Was she frightened by the way she needed him? The way he needed her?

He rolled over, trapping her beneath him, and cupped her face, forcing her to look at him. "Talk to me."

"It's been so long," she blinked back her tears, "since I've felt beautiful, since I've felt any of the things you make me feel."

His teeth clenched; that pissed him off something fierce. What kind of man was she married to? He breathed deeply and exhaled the anger. "If you were mine, I'd never let you forget." Longing to give her what she'd gone without for far too long, he kissed away her tears with a tenderness he hoped bespoke his promise.

"Micah, I have to—"

"Shhh."

"Micah, please," she murmured, squirming beneath him.

"Please what?" He trailed kisses across her shoulder, leaving a trace of wet that he cooled with a soft warm breath.

"Please ... don't."

He wanted to laugh. While her words pushed him away, she wriggled against him, her body reaching for his touch. "Please don't what?" He ran the tip of his nose down her cheek.

"Please ..." Her eyes closed. "Don't ... stop." Her voice trailed off, little more than a breath. The gurgle of the stream was louder.

Thrilled by her desire, he felt arrogantly pleased he had the power to excite her. And when he made love to her for the third time, it was slow and easy, all about giving her not only what her body yearned for but also what her heart and soul had been denied.

Beyond satisfied with the effect he had on her, he wrapped his hands in the hair at the back of her neck, pinioning her mouth for his leisurely taking. Within minutes, her whole body shuddered as the first glorious wave washed over her, leaving her gasping and breathless. And as one wave subsided and her breath returned in short little gasps, another one built, catching her up to soar once more, her whole body trembling wildly with the sheer power of it.

She lay beside him quivering and breathless long afterward. When her heartbeat returned to normal, he felt her relax, like a cloak of tranquility had settled over her. And before he even lifted his head to see her face, he knew she was happy.

Three times. Maybe he was the hero.

They clung to one another, her long legs entwined with his, her head nestled on his shoulder, and for that moment, she belonged to him.

It would have to be enough, for now.

# 16

# ALL GOOD THINGS

Micah led Sam back to the stream to cool off and drew her into his arms in the waist-deep water. "You're amazing," he murmured into her ear, then he stepped back, brought her hands up, and kissed each palm through the gauze bandages. "Come home with me. Let me take care of you."

She stared back at him with such tenderness he felt certain she'd say yes. But tears pooled on her lower lids and she tore her gaze away. Her eyes landed on her wedding ring, and she pulled her hands free.

"I can't, Micah," she said, with a slow shake of her head.

She turned, stepped from the stream, dried off, and pulled on her clothes. It was over. The closeness they'd shared had come to an end.

He was alone again.

He splashed water up over his head and rinsed his face, but it did little to cool the heat of his emotions. As he moved toward the edge of the stream, Sam collected her things and started up the path.

"Sam, wait. At least let me walk you back up."

She stopped and her shoulders slumped under the weight of … what? Worries, shame, regret? Whatever it was, it broke his heart.

He dried off, threw on his clothes and boots, and tossed the towel over his shoulder as he went to fetch Buck. Leading his horse, Micah silently followed Sam up the hillside.

*Oh, God, please let this brave, passionate woman be mine.*

At the back deck, Bear greeted them from behind the slider, his stubby tail wagging eagerly. What a perfect dog for Sam—smart, bold, and soft, like her.

Micah looped the horse's reins over the deck railing. "Hey, how about I have a look at that dresser? See if I can raise it to the loft for you."

Sam led him inside and cautioned him about the broken floorboard beneath the dresser where she'd dropped it. Without too much trouble, he wrangled the dresser up into the loft, positioned it where she wanted then put the railing back on.

She watched while he worked, her expression never wavering from the faraway, wistful gaze he'd seen before she'd walked away. Would she ask him to stay or was she simply waiting for him to finish and leave, so she could be alone? It was hard to tell.

Back on the ground floor, he inspected the hole in the floorboard. "Do you have any extra wood around? I'd be happy to fix this for you, too."

"Maybe underneath the cabin."

A quick search turned up an extra board. He pulled it out and eyed the length of it. "This should work." He leaned it against the side of the cabin. "But I'm going to need a few more tools, at least a saw. Let's find something to cover it for tonight, and I'll come by in the morning to fix it properly."

"Sounds good. Thank you." A hint of a smile curved her lips.

"You bet. How's your water holding up?" He nodded toward the road where the water tank sat.

"It's okay." When he raised a questioning eyebrow at her, she shot him a sheepish grin. "Actually, it's getting low, but I can get that next time I'm in town."

"Or I can get it tomorrow when I'm going to be there. You've got a second tank back there. I'll stop by and pick it up on my way into town and bring it back when I come to fix the floor."

"Thank you."

They covered the hole in the floor with a rug and a cooler for the night, then Sam walked him outside to where he'd left his horse. He took her hands and pulled her around to stand uphill in front of him.

"Thank you for this afternoon. You're an incredible woman and I—" He stopped short when she looked away uncomfortably.

Was she afraid he was going to tell her he loved her? Was he? Did he? It didn't matter. She didn't want to hear it, any of it.

"What is it, Sam?" He leaned in, recapturing her gaze. "Tell me."

When she looked at him, he hoped his gaze told her everything he couldn't find the words to say.

But her eyes fell away again. "Micah, I can't be with you like that. I'm still married."

"You're getting a divorce."

"I," her shoulders seemed to curl inward, "didn't sign it. I couldn't. I can't give up on my marriage. I still love him."

He winced, as if she'd stabbed him in the heart. "He's divorcing you."

"I know but—"

"Sam, he cheated on you!"

"People make mistakes."

"So what? If he comes crawling back to you, you'll give him another chance? Just like that?" Forgiveness was a virtue, sure, but one he could darn well do without in this instance.

Her lower lip quivered. "Yes," she said so softly he barely heard it.

Micah turned away in frustration.

"I made a vow. A promise before God, and that means something to me. You, of all people, should understand that. I have to at least try. If he wants it. And I have to make him want it. I have t-to —" her voice broke, "at least try."

He turned back to face her. God, she was beautiful, even in her brokenness. "Oh, Sam." He pulled her into his arms, held her closer than he had a right to. He admired her commitment to her marriage, but that man didn't deserve her. And dang-it-all, *he* wanted her!

*Now what?* He held her head against his chest and breathed in the fresh, clean scent of her hair. *Let her go, be patient. Let her choose her own path.* Hopefully, her marriage really was over. A momentary pang of guilt assailed him for wanting that for her.

*Oh, God, please*—No, it was plain wrong to pray for her marriage to end.

He withdrew and when she didn't look up, he gently lifted her chin, saw the unshed tears she fought to contain. "You know I want to be with you, right?"

She nodded.

He licked his lips, studied her face, memorizing every inch of it. "But it doesn't have to be like today. I want to be your friend, Sam, until you're ready for it to become something more. Okay?"

She nodded again, tried to smile but it was tight, holding back her sadness.

"So, you'll call me if you need anything, right? Even if it's for something as simple as washing your hair."

She rolled her eyes and gave him the sweetest half-laugh. A tear escaped when she blinked. "Yes."

"Okay." He wiped the errant tear away and kissed her on the forehead.

"I promise this won't happen again."

It was a hard promise to make, but one he knew she needed to hear because the way she looked at him in that moment said clearly, she wanted it to happen again. Needed it to happen again. She was a woman who needed to be held, loved, cherished. And he wanted to be the one to do it—the one to tell her how beautiful she was, how incredibly sexy and intriguing she was. The one to rebuild her confidence, soothe her broken spirit, and crush the self-doubt embedded there by her husband's infidelity.

But what came out instead was, “Your husband’s a very lucky man.”

She cringed, his words landing like mere shadows on her shattered, disbelieving heart. He turned to the deck railing, freed Buck’s reins, tossed them over the animal’s head, and swung up into the saddle. “See you tomorrow morning then.”

Sam climbed the few steps to the deck. “Not too early.”

“Right.” With a tip of his hat, he turned his horse away.

“Micah?”

He reined Buck around to face her. “Yeah?”

“Thank you.”

Her eyes went misty, and he had the unmistakable sense she’d heard all the things he’d been unable to say.

SAM’S HEART felt swollen and achy as Micah rode off. Her head spun amidst a turmoil of conflicting emotions, torn between the marriage that was almost assuredly over and the gentle rancher who wanted to be with her when she was ready. A part of her felt ashamed that she’d let it happen—now she was no better than Brent—but another part was overjoyed to have found something so beautiful.

When Micah stopped to glance back before heading up the far hillside, she waved. She had never known a sweeter, kinder, more tender man.

“Jesus,” she breathed. And in that moment, all of the loneliness, hurt, and betrayal of the past became a distant memory, and she fell in love with Micah Daniels, rancher from Providence, Colorado, who drove an old white pickup, wore a cowboy hat and boots, and had a son named Aiden.

*Don’t break his heart.*

She sighed heavily, closed her eyes, and leaned against the deck rail, her legs weak from being wrapped around him all afternoon, her body still thrumming from the passion they’d shared.

That first scintillating taste of his fingertips on her scalp, like a lover's touch, had been her undoing. How could a man so big and hard and powerful be so tender? He'd known exactly what she needed, things beyond the physical, things she hadn't even realized she hungered for. It was like he could read the story of her wounded heart.

She didn't want to hurt him, but knew full well she would.

THE NEXT MORNING, Micah pulled into the trailhead to Sam's cabin and shut off the engine. While Cody walked around the truck and peered down the hill, Micah flipped the tailgate open and climbed into the truck's bed to offload the water tank he'd picked up and filled in town.

"Was she expecting company?" Cody asked.

"Not that I know of." Micah craned to see the cabin far below.

A silver pickup sat parked next to her black Escalade. Micah's gaze honed in on the truck's license plate, the same color as hers. No doubt her loser husband.

He offloaded the water tank, set it on the ground beside the other one, then trudged down the hillside for a closer look. Sure enough, it was a Michigan plate.

"Dang!" he muttered.

Micah stomped back up the hill to where Cody waited, leaning against the truck's hood.

His cousin straightened. "What's up?"

"We'll come back another time." Micah slid into the driver's seat, slammed the door, and started the engine, then stared down the hill at the silver pickup, as Cody climbed back in.

"Y'all right?"

Micah's jaw tensed. "Fairly certain that's her husband's truck."

"Let's meet him," Cody said with mischief in his eyes.

Micah shot his cousin an *as-if* glare and jammed the truck into reverse.

"HEY, buckaroo, I'm going to Sam's for a bit, but Avery will be here in case you wake up, okay?" Micah said as he tucked Aiden into bed that night.

"Can I come? I want to see her too!"

Micah ruffled his son's hair. "No, little bear. It's something I need to do alone."

Aiden frowned. "You'll tell her howdy for me?"

"I will."

Aiden tucked his stuffed pony into the crook of his arm and yawned. "Good night, Daddy."

"Good night, buckaroo." Micah bent to kiss his son on the cheek, lingering to savor the softness of his cheek and his warm, fresh-bathed scent.

An hour later, Avery showed up. After checking in on Aiden, Micah saddled Buck and headed over to Sam's. From the top of the ridge, the dark outline of the cabin was barely discernible in the valley below. He followed the ridge around to where it met the road and continued to the trailhead that led down to her cabin.

His heart sank when he saw the faint outlines of the two vehicles still parked in front, the haunting shape of the silver pickup, reflecting like a sharp blade in the scant moonlight.

Micah sat astride his horse in the darkness for several minutes. His chest tightened and his mind formed painful images of the husband and his wife in the little cabin below. He admired her determination to save her marriage, especially after everything that had happened, but for his own selfish reasons, he'd hoped it was beyond saving. She'd already lived through the worst of the heartbreak.

He imagined how painful it had been for her to discover the betrayal, to know her man had been with someone else. He wondered if it was someone she knew.

The way she'd handled receiving the divorce papers amazed

him. Oh, she'd been upset, unprepared to be sure, and she'd cried. But she was a lot stronger than he had been.

His heart warmed when he thought of holding her while she'd wept in his arms, then waking up beside her the next morning. He should've seen it coming.

That was the night he fell in love with her.

His mind flitted back to the first time he saw her from the top of the ridge, bathing in the stream. Or maybe that was when it happened. His mind went back to the stream again and the afternoon they'd shared beneath the cottonwood. Was it only yesterday? It seemed a lifetime ago.

*Oh, God, if it's Your will to save her marriage, I'll accept it but ...* He struggled to find the words. *I love her. If You'd give me a chance—another chance—I can be the loving husband she needs.*

Warm rivulets cooled on his cheeks. He took off his hat, rubbed his sleeve across his eyes, then replaced his hat and rode away.

# 17

# BITTERSWEET FORGIVENESS

Cody returned to the card game with a fresh beer for Nick after his cousin knocked his last one off the table. Luckily it only contained dregs, didn't break, and only a few drops splattered on the wood floor, and the dog quickly lapped them up.

The aroma of alcohol, leather, and sweat, and the clinking of glasses filled Cody's dimly lit dining room. The sound of shuffled cards and murmurs of conversation created a tense atmosphere, matching the gloom that had settled over his cousin, Micah.

"Ante up, Micah," Nick barked, slapping the table beside his brother, causing drinks to rattle.

"Easy, Nick," Cody said, not thrilled at the prospect of cleaning up another of his cousin's messes.

Micah's hands trembled as he studied his cards through bloodshot eyes. "I'm out." He threw in his cards, tossed back the rest of his whiskey, and slammed the glass on the table with a thud.

Cody scowled at his cousin, then glanced at the others: his two brothers, Rory and Jonathan, and his cousins, Isaac and Nick, wondering if any of them were as worried as he was about Micah's dark mood. The man's head was not in the game tonight. Typically the best poker player among the six of them, Micah had already lost most of what he'd started with and seemed much more intent on drinking himself into a stupor than playing cards.

Aiden dashed into the room and stopped beside Micah. Seeing his father was out of the hand, he interrupted. "Daddy," he whispered. "Can I sleep over?"

Micah barely glanced at his son. "Nope. We're going home tonight, buddy."

Cody overheard and his concern for Micah grew tenfold. Had he seen the husband's pickup still at Sam's cabin on their way into town? That had to be what was haunting him, driving him to get so stinking drunk. But no way would he let his cousin drive home.

Cody threw in his cards as Aiden skipped off to the other room. The hand ended with Nick scooping in the winnings.

"Micah, you should stay," Cody said.

"Can't, but thanks." Micah stood to fetch another drink.

"How's that long-legged flatlander girlfriend of yours, Micah?" Nick asked as Micah returned to the table. Their *friendship*, as Micah referred to it, was no big secret; They'd all seen Micah with Sam at the Fourth of July picnic. And Aiden couldn't stop talking about her.

Cody glanced up from shuffling to see Micah narrow his eyes at his younger brother, like sighting down the barrel of a rifle.

"She's not my girlfriend."

"Right, she's married," Nick said with a snicker.

The muscles in Micah's jaw twitched as he glared across the table at Nick.

Cody leaned forward. "Nick. Let it go."

"I heard her husband showed up yesterday, got a room in town, but never came back down." Nick smiled at the others, then raised an eyebrow at Micah.

Cody shook his head. Nick never knew when enough was enough. "Pull your horns in, Nick," he said, on edge as he dealt the next hand, the two brothers locked in a stare-down.

Micah slouched in his chair like a cornered wildcat, his anger barely suppressed as his gaze bore into Nick.

But his little brother wasn't done.

Nick grinned, apparently satisfied by Micah's obvious fury. "Now I'm guessing there's not a lot to do in that tiny little cabin of theirs 'cept maybe–"

Micah exploded from his chair, sending it crashing to the floor as he lunged around the table to yank Nick up by the shirtfront and pin him against the wall. "You'll shut your mouth if you know what's good for you!"

The others launched up to pull him off, but not before Micah, with the finesse of a pro steer wrestler, sent Nick sprawling to the floor, flat on his back.

Winded, it took Nick a minute to regain his feet. "Damn! I was only joshing with you, man. What the hell?" Still half bent over, he eyed his older brother, firmly held back by Isaac and Jonathan.

Surprising them all, Nick took a swing, connecting with a solid cross against Micah's jaw.

Micah's head rolled, blood spouting from the corner of his mouth. Cody and Isaac pushed Nick away while Micah wrenched free of the others, swiped the back of his sleeve across his bloody lip, and stormed out the door.

Twenty minutes later, Cody found Micah sitting on a bench in the park, elbows on his knees, head hung low. Cody sat beside him.

Micah glanced over. "Sorry for starting a fight in your home."

"I saw it coming," Cody said, brushing it off. "We all saw it coming. That brother of yours never knows when to stop."

Micah sighed and lifted his face to his cousin. "I sure hope he grows up someday."

They sat in silence for a long moment, chirping crickets and the gurgling water, the only sounds filling the cool night air.

"Hey." Cody shoulder-nudged Micah. "What do you say we head to South Arm tomorrow, so I can check out that dead heifer Rory and Jonathan found near Fish Creek Pond? We'll take Aiden and Caleb and bedroll it for a few nights. It'd be fun for the boys and give me a chance to check out the herd down that way."

No response.

Cody exhaled. He didn't know what was going on between his cousin and the pretty blonde, but whatever it was, it was damn near killing him.

He draped an arm around Micah's shoulder. "Come on, it'll be good to get away for a couple of days."

Micah stared at the ground between his boots. "I made love to her."

Whoa, that explains a lot.

Micah glanced up to gauge Cody's reaction, then bent his head and took off his hat, turning it over and over in his hands. "She's married."

"Micah—"

"Married. What the hell was I thinking?" He shook his head as his whole body seemed to curl in on itself.

Dismayed by the intensity of his cousin's shame, Cody struggled for words of comfort. "So, you're human. We all make mistakes. Ask for forgiveness and move on."

"I can't." Micah rubbed his forehead. "'Cause I know if I had half a chance, I'd do it again." He wiped his sleeve across his eyes and stared at his boots.

Cody squeezed Micah's shoulders. "Hey, man, even Jesus didn't want to do the right thing all the time."

Micah's gaze wandered as he seemed to search his inner Bible for the story. Coming up empty, he shot Cody a curious glance.

"Book of Luke. In the garden, before the soldiers came for Him. 'Father, if you are willing, take this cup from me.'"

Micah nodded, and gave Cody a brotherly hug. "Thank you."

God, his cousin was a soft heart and a damn fine man. Cody smiled, pleased he'd remembered the verse. Usually, it was Micah quoting the Bible to him. It was mighty rare he got to pull one out for him. "So, South Arm tomorrow?"

Micah nodded. "Yeah, sure."

"Come on, let's go home." Cody helped Micah stagger back to the house, settled him on the couch, and when he mercifully passed out within minutes, Cody rummaged through his pockets, found his keys, and took them to his room with him.

IN THE MORNING, back at the Homestead, Micah saddled a fourteen-hand mare for Aiden for the day's ride to South Arm.

Standing on a mounting block, Aiden launched his little body up into the saddle and smiled proudly.

"How's she feel?" Micah asked, gazing up at his son.

Aiden shot him a cheesy grin. "Pert'near perfect!"

Micah adjusted the stirrups up one more notch, then patted Aiden's thigh. *Five years old – didn't it go by in a blink?*

"Thanks, Daddy."

They met up with Cody and Caleb and spent most of the morning following game trails through thick aspen and pine before breaking out into the lowland pastures, where masses of blue lupines and yellow mule's ears grew wild in broad strokes of color amid the knee-high grasses and sage. They followed Homestead Creek down the mountain and when they crossed over around lunchtime, they stopped to eat and rest the horses in the shade of a stand of cottonwoods.

The sun cast a warm glow on the meadows teaming with Homestead cattle, and this year's calves looked healthy. Micah and Cody pointed out wildlife along the way, herds of antelope on the hillsides or mule deer bounding away at the sound of their approach, and the boys watched in awe.

A gentle breeze brushed against Micah's skin, adding a soothing touch to the day, while a smattering of puffy white clouds dotted the sky that stretched from peak to shining peak, the same pure blue as Sam's eyes. What he wouldn't give to have her riding at his side, showing her firsthand how he spent his days.

That night, gathered around the campfire, while Cody instructed Caleb on the finer points of whittling, Aiden leaned his head against his father's shoulder. "Do you think Sam would like it here?"

Micah followed his gaze skyward, where a blanket of stars lit the night sky. "Sam the dog or Sam the woman?" Micah felt the need to clarify. It still irked him Aiden had named his new puppy Sam.

Aiden smiled. "The girl. I know my dog would love it."

"She's a woman, Aiden." Micah wondered if he should take advantage of the opportunity to explain the difference, then decided there'd be plenty of time for that when he got older.

"She's still a girl."

Micah pondered Aiden's question. Sam might be as much a mountain soul as he was. She loved the beauty and splendor of the wide-open spaces, wasn't afraid of the wild animals—wary, but not afraid—and seemed to enjoy the isolation. Hadn't she roughed it all summer in that tiny little cabin of hers with virtually no plumbing or electricity and only her little dog for company? "I think she'd love it here."

"Me too," Aiden said. "We should've asked her to come."

Micah draped an arm around his son as he imagined a path that would lead to him and Sam being together with Aiden. She could be their chance at a proper family.

Several minutes of silence settled between them, and Micah wondered if Aiden missed Sam as much as he did.

"I'm gonna count the stars," Aiden said, raising a fingertip to the sky.

Caleb nudged Aiden's knee. "That would take a lifetime."

Micah smiled and his thoughts wandered back to Sam as he found her constellation in the southern sky.

"Daddy?"

"Yeah?"

"Do you think she's looking at the same stars we are right now?"

"Only one set of stars," Caleb said, poking the fire with the stick he'd been working on.

Aiden leaned closer to Micah and whispered, "Have you kissed her yet?"

"Aiden!" Micah sat upright and scowled. "You can't ask me that."

Aiden smiled knowingly and rolled his eyes.

## 18

# GENTLE SOULS

*Who is this cowboy who speaks with a poet's soul, hears music in nature, and loves me with a heart as vast and pure as the Colorado sky?*

From her lawn chair on the back deck, Sam stared at her laptop screen, but her mind refused to hold the words of her story.

She absently twisted her wedding ring as her mind drifted back to the afternoon beside the stream with Micah and the passion they had shared. His touch lingered on her skin, his big, strong hands that belied a gentle grace she hadn't expected and would probably never feel again.

Soon, she would have to tell him goodbye. And Aiden too.

She sighed heavily, dreading what lay before her.

*Don't think of that now. Think about that tomorrow.*

Pushing the thought away, she returned to her manuscript, reread the last few chapters, made one minor correction, and called it quits for the day. Relieved to have nearly finished her story, she clicked SAVE, closed her laptop, and set it aside on the little table beside her.

Bear ventured from beneath her chair, his stumpy tail wagging eagerly. She patted his head. "Okay, buddy." Inside, she grabbed her outdoor blanket and rifle, then put Bear on his leash, and headed for the stream.

Beneath the cottonwood, she spread the blanket on the soft grass, where she and Micah had once lain together, and Bear curled up at her side. She stared into the powder blue Colorado sky, basking in the beauty of it all—the mountains, the valley, the woods and the stream. The pure serenity brought an unexpected healing to her soul.

God, but she was going to miss this place.

She sat upright suddenly and looked around, taking in the sheer, unspoiled beauty of the surrounding landscape. She could be happy here.

Lying back down, she wishboned her arms behind her head and let her mind wander as she relaxed in the fading warmth of summer, haunted by memories of powerful arms and whiskey-colored eyes. Was this where she belonged?

RESIGNED to Sam's determination to save her marriage, Micah had stayed away, but after two weeks of sleepless nights and endless hours of fruitless attempts to push her from his mind, he came once again to the ridge to wait, hoping to catch a glimpse of her.

Buck nickered beneath him, uneasy, as Micah gazed over Moonglow Meadow from the top of the ridge. Sam's cabin nestled against the hillside amidst the trees while Homestead Creek flowed gently through the valley with its gurgling music, subdued now in mid-August. It had been a splendid summer with plenty of rain, the herd was thriving with the abundance of grass and water, and as far as ranching went, it had been a peaceful summer.

Of all the valleys and hilltops he rode all summer long, this one kept drawing him back, and his insides shimmered as he considered the reason. This was where Sam had first enchanted him, where they'd played in the water with Aiden, where Micah had washed her hair, caressed her skin, and she'd been his, not once but three times.

He felt his body respond and quickly pushed the thoughts away. *Wrong*, she'd said.

Oh, God, how could something so natural, so beautiful, so perfect, be wrong?

She emerged from the back door and headed toward the stream. He eased Buck back, fading into the tree line as his eyes followed her along the path to the water's edge, where she spread a towel on the ground and lay on it, her little dog curling up beside her.

She bolted upright suddenly, scanned the valley, and Micah stiffened. Did she sense his presence? When she lay back down, he relaxed. What he wouldn't give to be down there lying beside her. He took off his Stetson, wiped the back of his hand across his brow, and sighed as he settled the hat back in place.

The worst part was he couldn't do anything, except be patient. Wait for her to realize her marriage really was over. His heart ached with emptiness, as if someone had scooped out his insides, leaving only a hollow shell of the man he'd been just days before, when she'd completed him.

Her husband's pickup had been there when Micah and Aiden left for South Arm on the third day, and three days was more than enough time to set things right with a woman who'd already decided to forgive. Before long, she'd head back to Michigan, to the husband undoubtedly awaiting her return.

Micah closed his eyes as the harsh reality hit him full force. Like a blow to the gut, it sucked the breath right out of him.

"Good luck, Sam," he whispered. "Be happy."

Sam intentionally arrived late and sat in the rear pew of the small, white-steepled church in the middle of town. She rubbed her hands together and straightened her skirt. It had been ages since she'd walked into a strange church, but she desperately needed a dose of meaningful spiritual reinforcement.

She smiled at a young couple with an infant as they slipped into the pew beside her. Aiden and Micah sat in the third row beside Janie. Had they come together?

The message was about forgiveness, not at all what she needed to hear. How could she forgive a man who didn't even want it. Disheartened, she rushed out as soon as it was over. A step away from her SUV, she heard Aiden call, "Sam! Wait up!"

Sam rested her head against the glass of the driver's side window and gathered her resolve. Finding a smile, she turned to face Micah's son. "Hey, little man!"

"You weren't even going to say hi?" His voice sounded small, accusing.

Sam looked into the sad little face of the innocent child caught in the middle of it all and felt a stab of guilt. "I'm sorry, Aiden." she said, not sure how much he would understand. "I didn't want it to be awkward for your father."

Aiden glanced over his shoulder toward the church, then back at Sam. "'Cause of Janie? He doesn't like her, Sam. He likes you."

Touched by his bare honesty and the certainty in his tone, Sam didn't know what to say. "Oh, Aiden." She took a knee. "You're such a sweet and gentle soul, so like your daddy. Don't you change that as you grow up, okay? You hang onto that goodness, you hear? 'Cause it's special and rare." She blinked back tears and leaned forward to kiss him on the forehead, then hugged him.

Aiden looked about to cry. "Was that goodbye?" He stared in disbelief, his soft brown eyes full of hurt.

"I suppose it ought to be." Sam tried to force a smile, willing herself not to cry in front of Micah's tender-hearted little boy.

"You're leaving?" he asked, disappointment etched on his little round face.

"I have to go back to Michigan."

"But I want you to stay. And Daddy does too." Tears pooled in his puppy dog eyes.

"I'm sorry, Aiden." She held his thin shoulders and set him purposefully away from her as she struggled to contain her own emotions.

Aiden shot her a crooked grin but they didn't hide the almost tears. "I'm glad I got to meet you, Sam, and I sure do hope we'll see you next summer."

Sam's heart softened, warmed by the enduring hope of a child. She nodded and stood and bit her lip to keep it from trembling. "Maybe next summer."

Aiden nodded, then turned and trudged back toward the church, his shoulders slumped and head hung low.

Sam slipped into her SUV and drove away.

Less than a mile outside of town, she had to pull over when the tears broke loose. Sometimes the smallest things take up the most room in your heart, she thought.

"Do we have to go to Janie's for Sunday dinner?" Aiden asked as Micah exited the church parking lot.

"Not today, buckaroo."

"Good!"

Micah glanced at his son in the rearview mirror. Aiden craned from his booster seat as though searching for something beyond the truck's windows, then with a frustrated sigh, he sat back and met Micah's gaze in the mirror. "I want to go to Sam's."

Micah took a deep breath and blew it out. This was near about the hundredth time his son had asked to go to Sam's, and Micah was losing his patience, having run out of excuses days ago.

"Sam didn't invite us to Sunday dinner," he told his son calmly. "But Aunt Anna and Uncle Cody did. You'll get to play with Caleb," he said, hoping to redirect his son's attention.

"I want to see Sam."

"We can't see Sam," Micah stated in a firm tone he hoped would brook no further argument.

When Aiden didn't object, Micah glanced again at the rearview mirror, and when he didn't see his son, he turned to glance over his shoulder. Aiden's head lay resting on his arms.

Micah pulled off the road and turned around in his seat. Aiden's shoulders shook softly as he silently cried.

Micah leaned against the headrest and sighed. It was bad enough Sam had him all tied up in knots. He hadn't expected his son to fall hard, too. He turned off the engine, got out, and climbed into the back seat. Unfastening Aiden's car seat, he pulled the boy onto his lap.

"I know you miss her, little bear. I do too."

"I saw her at church, Daddy, and," Aiden sniffed, "she told me goodbye. She's leaving. Going back to Mich-gan."

No surprise there. Micah knew she'd be leaving soon, but he hadn't expected her to say goodbye to Aiden and not to him.

"You were with Janie," Aiden explained, as though guessing his father's thoughts.

"What did she say?" Micah asked.

Aiden sniffed again and wiped his eyes. "She said you were a sweet and gentle soul, and that was something special and rare." He gave his father a weak smile. "And she said she might come back next summer," he added, sounding hopeful.

"Yeah?" Micah allowed a glimmer of hope to seep into his own troubled heart.

Aiden nodded, then looked out the window, searching again. "How old do I have to be before I get to decide where I live?"

"Why? Where do you want to live?" Micah hoped Sam's leaving hadn't broken Aiden's heart so badly he never wanted to come back to the ranch.

Aiden rested his head on Micah's shoulder. "I want to live here with you, Daddy," he answered very matter-of-factly, "and Sam."

Micah's heart warmed at the thought of having Aiden and Sam both a more permanent part of his life. "It might be a few years until you're old enough to decide that, and besides, Sam doesn't live here."

Aiden perked up. “Not yet, but she might if you asked her. Our cabin is a lot nicer than hers. Ask her, Daddy. Or I’ll ask her. She won’t say—”

“Whoa, there, half-pint!” Micah laughed. “This isn’t a picnic invitation we’re talking about here. You let me do the asking on that one, you hear?”

“You’ll ask?”

“Aiden.” Micah shook his head, realizing he’d lost control of the conversation. “I can’t ask her to come live with us.” He rubbed his chin, struggling for words his son would understand. He didn’t want to build false hope, but he didn’t want to crush the boy either.

“When the time is right, she might come back,” he said, gazing into his son’s face, making sure he was listening, “But that time is not right now. And it may not be for a while yet, okay?” Aiden seemed to process what he’d heard, and Micah hoped he’d accept it.

“Maybe next summer?” Aiden asked.

Micah smiled. “God willing.”

## 19

# SURPRISE VISITOR

Snuggled on the couch, laptop on her knees and Bear at her side, Sam put the finishing touches on her novel and yanked another tissue from the box to wipe her eyes and nose. *Don't break his heart.*

Sam jumped at the sound of something tapping against the rear slider. Bear growled, instantly alert. Sam closed the laptop, set it aside, and listened for the sound again as she eyed the rifle propped in the corner. As though sensing her anxiety, Bear jumped down, ran to the slider, and barked non-stop. Sam crept to the window and peered through a crack in the drapes. She could barely make out a small shadow. Aiden? With a gasp of relief, she hushed Bear and opened the door to Micah's son.

"Howdy, Sam."

"Aiden! You scared me half to death. What are you doing here?" Behind him, only one horse stood tied to the deck railing. She yanked the boy inside and slid the door closed. "You rode over here alone?"

"I have to tell you something."

"Aiden–"

"Sam, don't go. You can't go! My daddy likes you, and we want you to stay."

"Does your father know you're here?"

Aiden shook his head.

"It's late. Don't you think he'll be worried about you?"

Aiden shrugged. "I had to tell you." His voice broke.

Sam studied his red-rimmed eyes, the sadness in his face. What had she done to engender this kind of affection? "Wait here while I call him, okay?"

A slight nod was his only response, but he let go of her hand. While she retrieved her phone, Aiden settled on the couch, Bear on his lap.

Returning, Sam sat and faced Aiden, but before she could speak, Aiden whispered, "Please stay, Sam. My daddy and I both want you to stay."

She stared into his solemn, hope-filled gaze, searching for words that wouldn't crush his tender little heart. "I can't stay, Aiden. I'm married. Do you know what that means?"

He frowned. "Think so." He seemed to find comfort in petting Bear.

"I have a husband back in Michigan, a man I promised to love forever, the only man I would love forever. Do you understand?"

"But my daddy loves you too, Sam. He prays for you all the time. I've heard him."

She had to close her eyes against the image of Micah bent in prayer, the sound of her name on his lips.

Reopening them, she looked into Aiden's soft brown eyes, so much like his father's. "I can't be with your father, Aiden. I made a commitment before God to another man. Do you know what commitment is?"

Aiden's brows furrowed as he thought for a moment, then he shook his head.

Sam took a steadying breath. How does one explain commitment in terms a five-year-old can understand? "A commitment is like a promise. You know your little puppy, Sam? You love him and you made a promise, a commitment, to care for him, right?"

Aiden nodded and shot her his crooked grin.

"Well, you don't up and leave him when he does something naughty, like potty in the house, right? And you certainly wouldn't leave him if he got sick or old, just because he wasn't as cute or as much fun anymore, right?"

"Right. I love Sam, and I'll always take good care of him."

"Well, that's sort of what marriage is like—it's a promise to love and care for someone, until, well, until one of you dies. A commitment, a marriage, is supposed to last a lifetime. Do you understand?"

Aiden lowered his head. "All's I know is I don't want you to go."

Sam took his hand, and when he leaned into her, she wrapped an arm around his shoulders. "I'm sorry, Aiden."

He leaned back to look at her. "Don't you want to live with us?"

A tiny tear slipped down his cheek and she almost choked. *Oh, Aiden, you're killing me here.*

She had to look away, and it took several heartbeats before she trusted her voice not to break. "I can't live with you, Aiden. My home is in Michigan. I'm only visiting here this summer. Like you are, right? In the fall, you'll go back to Houston and—"

"I don't want to go back to Houston. I want to stay here." He swiped at his eyes with his sleeve. "I want to live with Daddy and with you, Sam. If you stayed and I stayed, we could be a family, a real one. Daddy would be so happy."

*Oh, don't cry, little man. Please.* "We can't always have everything we want, Aiden."

"It's not fair."

"You're right. It's not fair but it's life. And life isn't always fair."

Aiden fell into her arms with a sob, like his little heart was breaking in two. And she was done for. Despite her best efforts, her eyes stung with tears, as she held him while he cried.

When he pulled away, he wiped his eyes with his fists, stood, and faced her. He held out his hands, and she took hold of them. "I love you, Sam. But I think I understand why you can't stay."

Sam was speechless. The little man before her, telling her he loved her, was a miniature replica of his father, totally unafraid of putting himself—his whole heart and soul—out there. Her heart almost burst.

BREATHLESS FROM THE frantic ride over, Micah tied his horse to the railing and bounded up the steps of the deck. Sam met him at the door. "I'm so glad you called! I searched everywhere."

Sam nodded and slid the door closed behind him.

Aiden looked small as he sat, shoulders slumped, hands in his lap, in the middle of the couch. Micah knelt before his son, lingering a moment to take in his cried-out eyes before pulling him into a hug. "I was so worried about you. You are never to ride off alone, do you hear? You scared the daylights out of me. I thought something had happened to you."

"I'm sorry, Daddy."

Micah leaned back and held Aiden by the shoulders. "Promise me, Aiden."

"I promise. I just wanted to ask ..." Aiden looked into his father's eyes. He didn't need to finish; Micah knew what he'd needed to ask.

And from his son's tearstained cheeks, he knew what her answer had been. "Go mount up. I'll be right out."

When Aiden moved to the door, Sam touched his shoulder and knelt to hug him. Micah overheard her whisper, "I love you too, Aiden, and I hope to see you again."

Aiden forced a crooked grin. "Me too, Sam."

She stood and Aiden walked outside, his small shoulders hunched in defeat.

Micah turned to her. "Thank you for calling me."

"Of course."

"I'm sorry. I don't know what to say. He really took a shine to you, and this is harder on him than I thought." *Harder on both of us than I ever imagined.*

"I'm sorry, Micah. I really am. I never meant to—"

He shook his head. "It's not your fault you're so dang easy to—" He was going to say *love* but stopped short. "Like," he finished unconvincingly. "Aiden said you're planning to leave soon."

She nodded.

Micah shuffled his hat from one hand to the other. "Come by the ranch to say goodbye before you go?"

Her eyes lowered. He knew it was a big ask, especially after tonight.

"Please, Sam. It would mean the world to him." With a fingertip beneath her chin, he lifted her face, recapturing her gaze. "To us both."

She stared at him, seconds disappearing in the silence of the candlelit room and the warmth of her skin. "Okay."

Micah drew open the sliding glass door. "Good night, Sam."

"Good night, Micah." Sam peered into the darkness at Aiden, already astride his horse. "Good night, Aiden."

"Bye, Sam." Aiden touched his hat and turned away, but not before Micah caught the sorrow in his shadowed eyes.

# 20

# LETTING GO

Sam pulled to a stop in front of Micah's cabin and parked beside his pickup. She'd left early hoping to catch him before he'd gone off to tend animals and before Aiden woke up.

She rapped gently on the front door. When no one answered, she looked toward the barn. If Micah was in there, wouldn't he have heard her truck pull up like he had before and come out to greet her?

Finding the cabin door unlocked, she crept inside and listened for the shower or some other sign they were awake. Only silence greeted her, so she set the printout of her story on the kitchen table and looked around the room. It was a cozy little home, warm, open, and inviting, like the men who lived there.

Her hand still on the pages, a worry popped into her mind. Aiden probably couldn't read yet, but that little man had a way of surprising her, and she sure didn't want him to find it first. Deciding to leave it in Micah's bedroom instead, she retrieved the manuscript and tiptoed through the living area to the rooms beyond.

She peeked in the first one and glimpsed Aiden asleep, a stuffed pony tucked in his arms. She smiled at the tender sight and continued to the next room, assuming it would be Micah's.

It was a large room, done in denim blues and rich browns, and dominated by a king-size bed and wide French doors that led out to the back deck. She set her manuscript on the end of the bed.

Tentatively, she plucked Micah's pillow from beneath the quilt, lifted it to her face, and breathed in the scent of him, clean and masculine, like he carried the outdoors around with him. Overcome by intense longing, hot tears stung her eyes.

"You can rest your pretty head on that any time you've a mind to," Micah said softly from where he leaned against the doorframe, hat in hand.

Sam jumped and whirled to face him. "Micah!"

"Sam." He entered the room, then quickly stepped back into the hallway, away from the heart-stopping woman looking too good to be true standing beside his bed, his pillow to her chest.

Sam stared at him wide-eyed and dropped his pillow to the bed like a hot coal. "I came to say goodbye."

Micah tossed his hat on the bed and took two long strides to stand before her. Looking into those Colorado sky eyes, he wondered if there was anything he could say or do to make her stay. And if he should even try.

What he wanted to do more than anything was to pull her against his chest, hold her, kiss her, push her back onto the bed, and make wild passionate love to her until she surrendered to him completely, changed her mind about everything, and begged him to never stop. Like the afternoon beside the stream. His heart raced as the fleeting dreamlike images raced through his mind like tendrils of an early morning mist on a rolling mountain meadow, sweet, promising, elusive.

He cleared his throat, and like a gust from an afternoon breeze, the thought-mists vanished. Straining against his will, he brushed a fingertip along her cheek as he lost his soul in the warmth of her gaze shining back at him, like drowning and being saved at the same time.

Several heartbeats later, he found his voice. "He wants another chance?" Why else would her husband have come to the cabin?

Sam nodded and dropped her gaze.

"And you're going to give it to him."

"I—"

"Of course you are." She wouldn't be the woman he fell in love with if she didn't try. Damn her sweet, forgiving heart.

When she looked at him, a million *I love you's* shined in her eyes, but she only swallowed.

"You know I only wish you happiness, Sam, whatever that looks like," he said with heartfelt sincerity. "Despite what that leaves for me."

"I know," she whispered, nodding. "And I wish the same for you, Micah. I truly do."

He wanted to ask if he'd ever see her again, but was afraid of what the answer might be. He glanced at her left hand. The ring was still there, where it had always been, where it belonged.

He pulled her into his arms and squeezed his eyes shut as he savored her warmth against his chest, the subtle sweet scent of her filling his nostrils, her body melting into his. *Let her go!* His head fell back. A breath emptied out of him. *How can I?*

He pulled back to see her face, to see if this goodbye was as hard on her as it was on him, but she wouldn't look at him. Burying his hands deep in her hair, he fully intended to give her one last kiss, but she brought her arms up between them and pushed against his chest.

"I have to g-go," she said, her voice breaking. When she looked up, tears hung on her lower lids, unshed.

He nodded. *Yes! Go! Go now before I change my mind!*

She broke free and fled the room.

He stood there for several minutes, frozen in the moment's finality, unable to move as his ears registered the front door squeak open then ease shut, her car door closing, the engine roaring to life. He waited for the sound of tires on gravel as she drove away, out of his life, but only the steady idle of the vehicle lingered.

*She can't do it.* Something inside of him snapped, urging him. *Don't let her go! At least tell her how you feel! She doesn't even know!*

He hurried to the front door, but stopped short as he gazed through the screen. She sat in her SUV, head down, her shoulders gently shaking. What a brave soul she was. If only she knew his heart. He tapped on the glass.

She lowered the window, wiped her cheeks, and gave him a fragile smile. "I'm so weak."

How could she think that? She was the strong one, the one who knew what was right and had the courage to do it. "No, you're not. Love is always worth fighting for."

She dared a glance at him, and his heart broke at the pain in her eyes. "I shouldn't have to fight for it."

She was right; she shouldn't have to. But he knew she would because that was who she was. Torn between being the friend who should encourage her to do the right thing and being the man in love with her who wanted her to stay, he let his selfishness win out, placed both hands on the edge of her door and leaned in. "Stay."

Her head fell back against the headrest, eyes closed. "I have to go," she said, her voice whisper-soft.

He'd promised himself he'd never fall for another flatlander again, yet here he was. And somehow, this time was worse. "I'll wait. You'll come back?" he asked, unwilling to accept the hopelessness, the emptiness of his life without her in it.

She swiped at her wet cheeks, sat up, and looked at him with a forced bravado. "I don't know what the next few months will hold for me, Micah, but I have to try to save my marriage. Please understand. I have to give it everything I've got. I can't have a fallback if I fail. Don't do that to me. I can't do that to you."

His heart and mind warred in the quiet that ensued, and he had to look away. While his heart screamed, *tell her!* his conscience countered, *No. Let her do what she has to do.* What came from his mouth was a bitter defeat. "He doesn't deserve you."

She jumped at the vehemence in his tone. "Micah, I did this. It's my fault. And I need to be the one to fix it. Our marriage deserves at least that much."

"You deserve better."

She bit her lower lip.

"You know where to find me," he said, willing her not to look away.

She nodded again, then squeezed her eyes shut in a futile attempt to stem the flow of tears.

While her words told him how determined she was to save her marriage, her tears told him exactly what his heart needed to hear.

"Be happy, Sam." He leaned in to kiss her tenderly on the cheek, the salt of her tears lingering on his lips, the familiar taste of a shattered heart.

WITH AIDEN BATHED and he and his puppy tucked in for the night, silenced filled the cabin as Micah relaxed in his favorite recliner before a dying fire and let his thoughts drift back to Sam. Somehow, she seemed to haunt every quiet moment, and after several days of it, he gave up and let his mind linger there.

He wondered how she was doing, whether she and her husband had patched things up, if she was still married. Or not. He refused to pray for the *not,* but he still hoped it, deep in his heart. He was only a man, after all. A man in love.

He tried to picture her there beside him, sitting on the couch, reading or writing or knitting—does she knit, he wondered—or better yet, sitting on his lap, arms wrapped around his neck, gazing down at him, asking him with a seductive smile if he's ready for bed. He smiled at the thought as his heart tightened painfully in his chest.

The clock on the wall showed the lateness of the hour, and he added two hours for the time in Michigan. He imagined Sam, a self-proclaimed night owl, getting ready for bed. Alone or with her husband?

The thought was torture on his battered soul, and he struggled to push it away. He downed his iced tea, set the empty glass aside and leaned forward, elbows on his knees. He stared into the flames, remembering their first evening together as they became acquainted in front of the fireplace in her cozy little cabin.

He should have seen it coming. She'd totally captivated him that night, the light of the fire dancing on her flawless skin, the subtle sweet scent of her, her soft laughter that almost hid her pain.

He shook his head. He hadn't stood a chance. From the beginning, he'd known he was going to fall in love with her. Married or not.

*Oh, God, why her?* Of all the women on this earth, why did it have to be someone who belonged to another? Was it a test? If it was, he'd failed miserably.

Tormented beyond his breaking point, Micah lowered his head to pray. He'd given up asking for her to come back—that meant praying for her marriage to fail which he wouldn't do—so he prayed for her happiness, whatever that entailed.

Bent over, wavering between prayer, remembering, hoping, and suffering, he felt a gentle touch on his shoulder and looked up into the tear-filled eyes of his son. He blinked back his own and pulled Aiden onto his lap.

Aiden buried his face against Micah's shoulder and sobbed. "I miss her, Daddy."

He rubbed his son's back and kissed the top of his head. "I know, little bear, me too," he choked out. "Me too."

After several minutes, Aiden stopped crying but remained as he was, snuggled against Micah's chest. "Can we go visit her sometime?"

Micah winced. "No, I don't think so."

"'Cause she has a family already?"

"How'd you know that?"

Aiden leaned back to look at him. "She told me. She's married. That's how come she had to leave. She really wanted to stay—she didn't say so, but I could tell—but she said she made a commitmen, like I made to take care of Sam, my puppy. She had to take care of her husband. And that's why she couldn't stay."

It saddened Micah to think his little guy should have to grasp such things, and he wondered if Aiden really did. "You understand all that—marriage and commitment?"

"Think so. Her husband loved her first," he said. "But I'd still like to go see her."

Micah smiled. It was better understood than he thought a five-year-old would be capable of. "Me too, little bear, me too."

Aiden laid his head back against Micah's chest, and after several minutes, as Micah wondered if he'd fallen asleep, he spoke again. "Do you think she'll ever come back?"

Micah sighed heavily, wishing he had a better answer for his son, for himself. "I don't know, buckaroo. God willing, I suppose."

"I could pray for it, couldn't I? She'd come back if I prayed it."

Micah hesitated. It wasn't like Aiden was praying for her marriage to end. He simply wanted her back, and there wasn't any harm in that. "Yeah, I suppose you could."

"Good. I will then."

Micah patted Aiden's back, uplifted by his son's faith and glad that at least one of them was praying for her return. "Let's get you back to bed."

In the moments before sleep, Micah imagined himself and Aiden, hand in hand, walking from the barn to find Sam leaned against her Escalade parked in front of the cabin. Micah smiled as the imagined gave way to the dream.

# PART II

## MENDING FENCES

**June 2014**

*“It isn’t possible to love and part. You will wish that it was. You can transmute love, ignore it, muddle it, but you can never pull it out of you. I know by experience that the poets are right: love is eternal.”*

— E.M. Forster

# 21

# FAMILIAR EYES

"Whoa there, little one," I say, catching a toddler who'd run into my legs in the frozen food aisle.

"Michaelyn!" A young woman rushes forward. "I'm so sorry, mister," she says, then turns to scowl at the little girl. "You can't run away from me like that!"

"You're not the boss of me!" the little girl spouts back, hands on her hips.

I stifle a laugh and kneel before her. "Michaelyn, what a pretty name." An unusual name, too. I gaze into the face of the toddler and I'm captivated by the pretty brown eyes staring back at me, so much like Aiden's. When she shoots me a crooked grin, my breath catches.

"Today's my birf-day," she announces.

"Is that right? Well, happy birthday, sunshine! How old are you today?"

"Free." Michaelyn frowns in concentration as her pudgy little hands work to make the right number of fingers stay up.

"Is that right? Well, you're practically a young lady already."

She beams back at me.

"You know, Michaelyn, young ladies ought not to run away from their mammas."

The young woman steps forward. "Oh, she's not—"

"I want ice cream," Michaelyn says, with a heart-wrenching pout, the kind only a three-year-old can pull off.

When the young woman rolls her eyes, she looks so much like Samantha Jamison, a memory burns like an ember in my chest. "I told you, we can't get ice cream." She takes Michaelyn's hand and leads her away, then stops and turns back to me. "Thank you," she says with an apologetic smile.

"My pleasure." I tip my hat to the pretty young blonde. "And happy birthday, Michaelyn."

Michaelyn shoots me a wide grin. The woman regains her attention, gives her a hand signal, and the toddler quickly adds, "Thank you."

As they walk away, I notice for the first time the orthotics on the little girl's ankles, and I wonder what kind of sad malady necessitates that kind of clumsy hardware on such a delicate slip of a child.

Returning to their cart, the young woman lifts the girl into the basket, and the toddler gives me that enchanting smile again. My heart tightens in my chest. How wonderful it would've been to have another child, a younger brother or sister for my son.

When I finish my shopping, Aiden's waiting for me at the checkout. He's been next door at the hardware and carries a small brown paper bag. Saturday morning, the market is as busy as it gets meaning there's someone in front of me at the one and only checkout lane. It's Cody's receptionist, Milly Peterson, and we exchange pleasantries. As she runs her credit card through, I take a peek at the fly-tying minutiae Aiden's purchased. He's become quite the angler this summer. My daddy'd be proud.

As we approach the exit of the parking lot, a black Cadillac Escalade pulls in, and I scrutinize the driver, as I always do whenever I see that make and model. Not many of them come through the small town of Providence, only a couple in the past few years, but I always look. Like I always check for fresh tracks whenever I pass by the trail that leads down to the old Baker cabin. I haven't totally lost hope.

When I see a blonde woman behind the wheel, I hit the brakes and crane my neck around so hard it hurts as the vehicle passes by.

"It's her," I utter.

The SUV stops in front of the market, and I shoot Aiden a quick glance before spinning the steering wheel to do a three-sixty. I park behind the SUV and jump out. "Sam," I call, as she steps from the vehicle.

She whirls to face me, and a surge of elation races in my pulse as I close the distance. Her hair is different, shorter and wavy with bangs, but she still takes my breath away. Her eyes narrow as she studies me then she blinks and takes a half step backward. It's enough to tell me something's off.

"It's me. Mac." I stare, dumbfounded by the look on her face, like I'm a complete stranger to her.

"I'm sorry—" Her eyes dart around wildly as her mind seems to search for something lost. "Do I know you?"

*Seriously?* The lump in my throat is so huge, I can't swallow. "Yes, I, we—"

The little girl from the frozen food aisle bursts through the door of the market. "Mommy! Mommy!" With the clumsy ankle braces, her dash toward Sam is more of an awkward waddle than a run. The young woman with her earlier hurries to catch up, dragging along their cart full of groceries.

Sam bends to scoop up the little girl and smiles happily as she kisses her cheek. "Hey, baby-girl!" She turns back to me as the young woman approaches. "These are my daughters, Emma and Michaelyn. Girls, this is Mister ..."

"McKennon," I finish for her, crushed that she doesn't remember my name. But her smile is the same and still makes me lose my center.

Turning to Emma, I tip my hat. "Daniel McKennon. Folks call me Mac." Aiden appears at my side, and I place a hand on his shoulder. "My son, Aiden."

Emma's eyes grow wide as she stares at my son, and her jaw falls open, but she quickly recovers. "Nice to meet you both."

"Pleasure's all mine," I say, forcing a smile.

"Howdy," Aiden says, staring at Sam with the same puzzled look I must be sporting.

Michaelyn stares at us, all smiles, until Sam says, "Michaelyn, can you say hello to Mr. McKennon and Aiden?"

"Hello," Michaelyn says, leaning her head against her mama's shoulder, suddenly shy.

Sam stares at me for what seems like a hundred heartbeats, but is probably only two. Michaelyn wriggles in her arms and Sam sets the toddler on her feet in front of her, hands on her shoulders. "I'm sorry I don't remember—"

"My mom suffered a traumatic head injury in a car accident and has no memory of her life from about eighteen months prior to the wreck," Emma blurts out as if she's recanted the explanation a hundred times before.

Sam glares at her eldest daughter.

Air rushes from my body like I've been sucker-punched. I glance between the two women. "An accident?"

Sam nods. "A few years ago."

I rub my chin and stare in disbelief. "So, you don't remember me—us," I glance at Aiden then back at Sam, "at all?"

"I'm sorry." Sam's gaze is soft, apologetic. She seems to have at least a vague idea of the effect the news is having on us. "I think I have a photo of you, though," she says to Aiden.

"Me too," Aiden says with a nod.

A breath escapes me, and I look away, struggling to grasp it. Finally, after four long years, she's back but doesn't remember me. What's a man to do with that?

Sam loads the groceries into the back of her SUV while Emma helps Michaelyn into her car seat. I stand by speechless, unmoving, flattened like I've been stampeded.

I suppose it's better than what I thought had happened. I pinch the bridge of my nose and close my eyes, letting it sink in. Or is it?

She doesn't know how I felt—still feel—about her, how she once felt about me, what we'd found together that summer.

I catch Aiden's gaze, and he looks as dumbstruck as I feel. Neither of us knows what to make of it.

Regaining my senses, I help Sam with the last few bags. "Hey, can I take y'all across the street for ice cream? I heard it was someone's birthday today." Sam's brows shoot up, and I nod toward her girls. "We ran into each other in the market."

"Oh." Sam hesitates, as if considering. "Thank you, but we should probably get these groceries put away."

I can't just let her go! God only knows when I'll see her again. "Yeah, me too," I say, nodding toward my truck and struggling for calm. "But I'd still like to buy you an ice cream."

"Pease, pease, pease, Mommy," Michaelyn chirps, almost rocketing from her car seat.

AT A TABLE in the ice cream shop, I plant a small pink candle in the center of Michaelyn's bowl. "We have to sing to the birthday girl," I say with a wide grin. Holding out a lighter, I look to Sam for the go-ahead.

Sam gives her daughter an excited smile, and Michaelyn looks at me, adoration dancing in her pretty brown eyes. Sam nods her approval.

I light the one little candle. "I know you're three today, but the girl behind the counter only had one candle. Now don't get too close, little darlin', okay?"

My heart swells with a warm sense of family as we all sing "Happy Birthday" to Michaelyn, sitting there looking so much like Sam, with her perfect baby-soft skin and long blonde hair. But those eyes—is it possible?

When the song ends, Michaelyn giggles.

"Now you get to make a wish and blow out the candle," Sam says.

"A wish?" Michaelyn asks in her squeaky three-year-old voice.

"Something that will make you happy," Sam explains as she kneels beside her little girl's chair.

"I'm already happy, Mommy. I got ice cream!"

Sam shoots me a look of gratitude and my heart melts like the wax beginning to drip down the side of the tiny pink candle. Sam leans in to kiss her little girl on the cheek.

"Oh! I thought of something, Mommy!"

"Okay, don't tell. Close your eyes and wish it, and then we'll blow it out together," Sam says.

Michaelyn closes her eyes, and when she reopens them, she looks at her mother and together they blow out the flame. Everyone cheers and Michaelyn claps with delight.

Emma stands as Sam slips back into her chair. "Michaelyn," she says, turning to her little sister, "want to go outside and eat?"

As Sam helps Michaelyn down, Emma turns to Aiden. "You're welcome to join us."

With a reluctant glance from me to Sam, Aiden stands to join the girls. Emma gives her mother a surreptitious grin as she leaves the table.

Aiden holds the door for the girls, and when the kids settle at a picnic table, I turn to Sam. "They're beautiful girls."

"Thank you. And Aiden, well, you've got a real gentleman there," she says. "He looks like a miniature version of you."

"Yeah, I suppose he does at that." My eyes fall to Sam's left hand, which is holding her bowl of ice cream, and my hope plummets at the sight of an enormous diamond on her ring finger. I can't take my eyes off of it. Leaning back in my chair, I struggle to make sense of it.

I catch her gaze. "Did you and Brent get back together?" Suddenly, my throat is so dry I can hardly breathe.

"You know Brent?"

"Not exactly. I provided you legal advice when he sent the divorce papers to your cabin."

"Oh. My attorney. Right." A sadness seems to settle on her. "I was wondering how we knew each other."

"So," my eyes dart back to the ring, "you and Brent?"

She looks into my eyes, and I have to look away, afraid she'll see my apprehension.

She shakes her head. "No, his name is Stephane, Stephane Desrosier."

"Desrosier. French?"

Sam nods. "Montreal."

"How long?"

"Sorry?"

"How long have you been married?"

"Oh. I'm not. It's an engagement ring."

A breath escapes me in an audible sigh of relief, and I scrub a hand across my mouth to hide the upward curve of my lips.

Sam smiles uncomfortably, and I realize I'm doing a poor job of hiding my emotions. She takes a bite of ice cream.

I clear my throat, shake my head, trying to clear it too. "Congratulations."

"Thank you." She peers at me like she can see right through my forced pleasantries.

"He didn't come with you?"

"He's on set in British Columbia. He's a film director. But he's going to meet us here midweek if he can."

I nod. "Staying at the cabin?"

Sam chuckles. "Yeah, it'll be interesting with all five of us. My son, Zach, is flying in tomorrow too. The kids tell me it's pretty rustic and tiny, short on conveniences and long on work."

I linger for a moment with the fond memory of her simple little cabin. "It is at that. How long ya'll plan to stay?"

"Just a week. Friday we'll head to Boulder. Emma's going to med school at C.U. and has an internship there for the summer. Zach will join her there in the fall for seminary school, but in the meantime, he and Michaelyn and I will head home. And Stephane will return to his movie set."

*A week!* My heart races. I've waited three and a half years for her to come back into my life. I can't lose her again.

I lean forward and place a hand on hers. It's soft and warm. "Tell me about your accident. What happened?"

She eyes my hand on hers but doesn't pull away. A small smile plays at the corners of her mouth. "A car accident. I don't remember it. I woke up in the hospital with a head injury. According to the police report, I was rear-ended at a stoplight and pushed into the path of an oncoming car." With her free hand, she rubs her forehead beneath her bangs. "And I couldn't remember the last eighteen months of my life."

"Nothing?"

"My last memory was of dropping off my twins at a youth camp for the summer." Her voice nearly breaks, and her eyes go far away as if reliving the moment. "I'd quit my job that day, too."

*Quit her job?* My head spins and I want to laugh, but the levity vanishes in the irony of it all. "What day was that?"

"The day of the accident."

*Oh, God, no!* What if it was the same day I'd left to return to the ranch? I called her that evening and left a message. She never called back.

If only I'd stayed. I might've helped her recover, helped her remember. We could've spent the last four years together. "Oh, Sam. I'm so sorry."

"Funny thing is, I have no idea why I quit." She flashes me a wry smile. "It was a good job, from what I recall."

I know why. She chose me. She'd decided to change her path, and it had everything to do with me. "How," my voice catches and I have to clear it again. "How long ago was that?"

Sam looks out the shop window at the children and I follow her gaze. The lower half of Michaelyn's face is one chocolate smear. "Little over three and a half years ago. I had just gotten pregnant with Michaelyn."

My mind races to do the math, and realization dawns like a knockout punch. *My trip to Michigan!*

For years, I'd clung to a memory that had grown wispy and vague as the months ticked by until I didn't know which parts were a dream and which parts actually happened. Did she really tell me she loved me in the wee hours of our last night together?

I'd called her so many times, left so many messages in those first few weeks that her voice mail filled up. After several months, I sent a long letter, but it came back undeliverable. By then she'd moved. What a huge mistake, accepting that she'd chosen a different path, that she didn't love me after all, or at least not enough to come live on the ranch. Or that our weekend together at her place had been nothing more than a dream.

How could I have been so faithless? Three and a half years—wasted. All those cold, lonely, sleepless nights, haunting dreams, mornings that came too soon.

I want to ask about her little girl's father, but I can't manage it. From her side of the table, I'm little more than a stranger.

I consider reminding her how in love we were and suppress the disappointment at not being remembered. Outside, the kids are getting up from the table. Sam stares at me with a wistful look in her eye.

"When can I see you again?" I ask.

A smile that could mend a broken heart stretches across her lips as she seems to see something in my gaze I can't hide. Then, in a blink, the smile is gone. "I'm engaged, Mac."

"Yeah." *Be cool. Don't panic. She'll be here all week.* "I know. But you were the best friend I ever had. I'd still like to be friends, even if it's only for a few days."

"We need more napkins," Emma says as she hurries past us.

"Thank you for the ice cream," Michaelyn says, shuffling up beside my chair.

I look into the eyes of the little girl smiling at me, a mess of gooey chocolate spread ear to ear and down her front, and she's the most beautiful thing I've ever laid eyes on. An ache starts deep in my belly for the possibility I'd secretly yearned for, the love I'd given up on, the years I've missed.

My voice sounds hoarse as the words find their way out. "You're welcome, sunshine."

As we part ways in the parking lot, I'm certain I'll see them again. And soon. I haven't quite figured out how, only know it's inevitable. I've been given a second chance, and by God, I'll make it count this time.

# 22

# ALL IN

Sam's SUV leaves the parking lot ahead of us, and we follow her as far as the gas station, then wave as we roll past.

"What?" I feel Aiden's stare as we head out of town toward home.

"What the heck! She doesn't even remember us," Aiden says, his voice quick and sharp.

"For everything a reason," I say. "Sometimes God has his own way of doing things."

Aiden shrugs, the *whatever* dismissal of youth. He folds his arms across his chest and stares out the window. "Must've been a really bad crash."

My gut tightens as I consider how to respond, and all I can come up with is, "Yep." I wonder what else he and her girls talked about.

"Emma says they're only here for the week." The raw disappointment in his faraway gaze makes my heart ache. He pounds a fist on the dash. "Dang her!"

"Hey, it's not her fault. She didn't set out to make us fall in love with her. We did that on our own. You were too young to understand, but she was married the last time she was here. Her husband didn't treat her right, but she remained committed to her marriage. That's why she had to leave."

"Oh, I understood. She told me all about commitment when I rode over there that one night." And while *it still hurt* remains unsaid, it's written all over my son's face.

I wonder what kind of understanding Sam had given a five-year-old that remained with him all this time. "Well, she's not married anymore, so what do you say we convince her to stay this time."

On the dirt road now, a billow of dust trailing behind us, Aiden continues to stare out the window, silent.

I nudge his shoulder. "Come on. I'm gonna need your help. You in?"

Aiden shoots me a pitying look, and I realize I'm grasping at this one small chance for a different outcome. I try not to think about the definition of insanity. "I'm in," he says.

"Great!" I'm so proud of his bravery and resilience, something sprouts inside me—hope. "We only have a week so we've got to move fast. How about—"

"Hey," Aiden turns in his seat to face me, "we oughta do all the same stuff we did last time 'cause I think she really wanted to stay, don't you?"

"Yeah, I think so too. Deep down. Which is where it counts."

"Only this time it's gonna be different, right, Dad? This time she don't have a husband to go back to, right?"

"Right, she doesn't." I wonder about the fiancé and immediately push the thought away. We'll cross that bridge when—and if—he arrives.

I pat Aiden's knee, happy and relieved to have his help and, most of all, his understanding. He might have been more affected by her leaving than he'd let on. The photo of the two of them sits on the boy's dresser, and I suspect I'm not the only one who still stares at it from time to time.

When we get to Sam's cabin, I pull off to the side of the road and get out. I lean against the truck door, cross my ankles and arms and wait. Aiden joins me.

Minutes later, Sam pulls into the trailhead that leads down to the cabin and parks. Sam waits for the dust to settle, then lowers her window and peers at me. "Hey!"

I tuck my sunglasses into my shirt pocket as I cross the road. "Hi again," I say, tipping my hat. From the passenger seat, Emma leans forward, watching us with a curious grin.

"Thought you might need help offloading that water tank." I nod to the back of her vehicle.

Sam turns to her daughter, then back to me. She looks puzzled.

I wink and give her a reassuring smile. "You had one the last time you were here."

When I slip back behind the wheel of the truck after positioning their water tank at the top of the trail, Aiden high-fives me. "Nicely done, Dad."

"Come on, Mac. You playing tonight or what?" Isaac taps his cards on the table.

I know I'm distracted, but when the pressure comes from my brother Isaac, the most patient man I know, I figure it's time to throw in. "I'm out."

I stare at the cards, face down on the table in front of me, and I can't remember what they were. For all I know, I threw in a winning hand. But it doesn't matter. Nothing matters except what I'm going to do for the next six days.

Despite the front screen door and back slider being wide open to catch a scarce mid-summer breeze, my house is stifling, filled with the pungent scent of beer and whiskey and the banter of men's voices, shuffling cards, and clinking poker chips.

A few minutes later, I'm picking up a new deal, and as I lift the edges, I peer unseeing at the blur of red and black. Instead, I see an image of Sam standing on the back deck of her lake house, wearing nothing but my red flannel as she holds out a steaming cup of coffee to me.

I let the cards fall back to the table. It won't be my turn again for a while. I rub the tension from the back of my neck.

When I glance up, my cousin Cody is studying me from across the table. "You look like you saw a ghost, Mac. What's up?"

"A ghost?" I chuckle. For a cousin, Cody reads me better than either of my two brothers. "Yep, that's about right." I glance around the table. We're all family here, my two brothers and three cousins. I push through a momentary hesitation about sharing this in front of them all and plunge ahead. "Sam is back."

"Sam who?" Rory asks, glancing around at the others to see if they all know something he doesn't. Growing up in Cody's shadow, Rory has never been one to be left behind.

"Samantha Jamison." My eyes stray to my little brother, Nick, a few seats to my right.

Nick pretends to choke on his beer. "Flatlander Barbie? You don't say!"

I want to laugh. The others do. I keep a straight face as I say, "Don't call her that. It's demeaning."

"What? It's a fittin' compliment. Pretty, tall, blonde. And she's from California." Nick glances around at the others, all chortling and nodding in agreement.

I dig deep for tolerance. The youngest of us all, Nick has always had a tendency to entertain. "Michigan. But close, Nick."

Nick tosses a one-chip into the center. "I'm in. So how long's she staying this time?"

"A week. She's got her family with her."

"I'm in." Isaac adds his one-chip to the pot.

Nick taps his cards on the table. "Her family. How perfect. Now you can meet that husband of hers."

I scrub a hand over my face, regretting having mentioned Sam.

"She's not married anymore." I glance at Cody. His eyes go wide and he smiles.

Nick leans back in his chair, stretches his legs out to the side and crosses his boots at the ankles. "Just 'cause trouble comes visiting don't mean you gotta offer it a place to sit."

Ignoring Nick, I glance at my cards again, actually looking at them this time, then at the card turned up on the table, and I toss in my ante. "She's engaged, though." I look at Cody again, knowing my cousin will appreciate what that means to me.

Aiden appears at Nick's side, glances at the pot and then at me. "She's got a pretty daughter, too. Name's Emma. She's gonna be a doctor. Going to C.U. in Boulder. And a little girl—"

I set down my beer a little too hard. "Aiden, go on now. Go play with your cousins."

Nick doesn't miss a beat. "A daughter? College age? Must be real smart to be going to med school." He leans forward. "When can I meet her?"

As if I'd ever in a million years introduce my youngest brother to any woman I know. "Never."

"Aw, come on now."

"She's way out of your league."

"Hey, now, I'm a real catch," Nick says with indignation. "Least ways, that's what the barrel racers tell me. Ain't that right, Jonathan?"

Jonathan laughs. "Sure enough, Nick."

"In your dreams, little brother," I say.

Nick leans his elbows on the table and stares hard at me, all joking aside. "Says the man who stares at stars."

I glare back.

"Whatever happened to you and Janie?" Cody asks, directing the question to Nick.

"Aw, Janie. She's a real sweetheart, but I think she's still got her sights set on Mac. 'Sides, I'm in the mood for someone I can talk to, settle down with, and a real smart girl might be just the ticket." Nick's goading me.

Cody nudges Isaac. "Did you talk to that kid from Abeline I told you about?"

"Yeah," Isaac says. "Seems like a good guy. Grew up on a ranch in West Texas before his family moved to Oklahoma. He'll make a fine hand. He's coming next weekend to see the place. Probably hire on."

I appreciate Cody's effort to change the subject, but when I glance at my little brother, Nick whispers, "You know I'm gonna meet her."

I shrug. Emma can handle my little brother. It's not like he's dangerous or anything. Heck, he's about as harmless as a newborn calf and almost as slippery. Maybe meeting someone like Emma—and realizing just how out of his league she is—will convince him it's time to do something more with his life besides rodeo, party, and when he gets desperate for money, hire on at cowboy pay.

Nick's sense of responsibility has always been something he can turn on and off, like a shower. Trouble is, it runs cold most of the time. But then again, when it comes time for calving, branding, or roundup, he's always here when we need him. Maybe all he needs is a good reason to turn the shower on more often, and keep it running.

The evening winds down and when the screen door slams behind Isaac, only Nick, Cody, and the younger boys remain. As I collect empty bottles from the table, I hear Nick in Aiden's room, grilling him about Sam's daughter.

Cody shuffles the chips back into their case and stifles a laugh.

"He's serious, isn't he?" I ask, shaking my head.

"He's intrigued. I know I am. And I'm a happily married man," Cody says.

"She looks so much like her mother that when I first saw her, I immediately thought of Sam."

While Nick interrogates Aiden about Emma, I fill Cody in on running into Sam and her girls at the market, her car accident and memory loss.

"Whoa, she doesn't remember coming here that summer?"

I grimace. "Nothing."

"So, what are you going to do?"

"I've gotta win her back."

"You said she's engaged?"

"Yeah. The fiancé might be here midweek or so. I figure I have a few days at best."

"Well, she fell in love with you once, and you're the same man you've always been."

"Yeah, that's about what Aiden said. Thing is," I hesitate, afraid to admit it to Cody, because I'm struggling to accept it myself. "I don't know if I can do it again."

Cody closes the lid on the box of poker chips and squeezes it into its spot on the bookshelf, between a Lord of the Rings trilogy and Lonesome Dove. He scratches his chin and eyes me for a long moment. He always knows how to lift me up, but this time he's struggling.

"I had an entire summer last time," I say. "And she needed me. She was going through a tough time with her marriage. We drank together. She cried on my shoulder. I was her legal advisor, her friend."

"You don't think she needs you now?"

"Not like then."

"Mac, she's a single mom, raising a child alone. She probably needs you now more than ever." He collects the empty snack bowls and I follow him to the sink with a handful of bottles. "Who's the little girl's father, anyway? How old did you say she was?"

I give my cousin a side-eye. Cody's sharp. He's done the math, just like I'd done earlier.

I empty the dregs from the bottles and toss them into the recycle bin beneath the sink. "Three today."

Cody leans against the counter, crosses his arms, and narrows his eyes at me. "You went to see her in—damn. Mac, you gotta ask."

"Oh, I will." I peer across the living area toward Aiden's room, not wanting to be overheard. "She won't leave without me knowing, but I have to do this right. I don't just want a daughter. I want Sam, too."

Sam's the one I've been waiting for, yearning for, dreaming of, for going on four years. It's always been Sam. And while the possibility of a daughter is beyond my wildest dreams, the thought of loving another child from afar splits me in two.

I cannot let that happen again.

## 23

# SUNDAY, FULL OF GRACE

After church, when Aiden asks if he and Caleb can go fishing at Sam's Bend, the name he'd given to the spot on the creek behind her cabin, my first reaction is, "No, absolutely not. I know it's a great place to swim and fish, but it's on her property and you boys have no right to trespass, especially with her and her family staying there this week."

Aiden cocks a brow my way. *Follow me on this, Dad,* it says.

As they ride off in the direction of Sam's place, I busy myself in the barn, check on the ailing calf Isaac brought in, take my time saddling up Buck, and try not to look at the time on my phone every five minutes. Unlike Isaac, patience has never been one of my virtues.

An hour later, I look across the meadow from atop the North Ridge. Caleb stands on a flat rock at the water's edge while Aiden wades knee deep. Downstream from Aiden, stands another kid, a good bit taller, blond hair spilling from beneath a baseball cap. I figure he must be Sam's son, Zach. Sam—no, Emma—sits on shore, a fishing rod dangling out over the water. Further up the bank, Sam and Michaelyn sit on a blanket beneath the cottonwood.

I nudge Buck's sides and we ease down the mountainside,

winding through aspens and pines. I lose the scene below a few times as I make my way along the switchbacks, but when I hear Aiden's voice ring from below, "You got one on, Zach!" I stop to watch where there's a clear sightline through the trees.

Zach yanks his line hard. I wince, certain before I even see the pole spring back that he's pulled the hook right out of the fish's mouth.

"That's okay," Aiden shouts. "Try again. They're bitin' somethin' fierce today!"

When I emerge from the trail into the open meadow, a few hundred yards upstream from the others, Zach is drawing in his line and casting it out again. The line loops out over the water in a perfect fluid circle, the fly dancing at the end of it, hovering above the surface.

Either Sam's son has done this before or Aiden and Caleb are right fine teachers because the next fish doesn't get off so easy. Zach plays it, pumps the rod while simultaneously reeling in the slack line. The fish jumps from the water and Aiden shouts, "Lower the rod, don't give 'em leverage!"

Zach follows instructions and seconds later, Aiden is at his side, net poised in the water. When he raises it, they've landed a nice size trout. All three boys whoop for joy.

Michaelyn struggles to stand on the blanket and claps. "Yea, Zachy! Again! Again!"

Sam jumps to her feet, a restraining hand on Michaelyn. Recognition alights on her face the instant she sees me. I wave and her whole body seems to smile. Or perhaps I'm imagining that. She points my way and bends to say something to Michaelyn.

With a hand to Sam's ear, Michaelyn whispers something, as if I might overhear. When her gaze returns to me, an excited smile lights up her face and I think if she wasn't wearing those cumbersome ankle braces, she'd run to meet me. It's amazing what a lasting impression ice cream can make on a three-year-old.

I cross the creek upstream so's not to disturb the fishing, then skirt the edge as I make my way toward Sam and Michaelyn beneath the cottonwood. Caleb catches sight of me and waves. Aiden and Zach, facing downriver, are hyper focused on casting.

"Whoa." I rein in a few yards away. "Howdy," I say with a tip of my hat.

Michaelyn backpedals, as if frightened by the size of my horse. She stumbles and Sam picks her up.

"How-dee!" Michaelyn echoes, carefully enunciating each syllable with a wide grin from the safety of her mother's hip.

I laugh, it's so dang cute. "I hope they're not bothering you." I hitch a thumb toward the boys.

"Oh, absolutely not. They're fine. In fact, I think they're teaching Zach a thing or two about fly-fishing. From the looks of it, it's quite a bit different than fishing with a rod and reel."

"It is at that."

I turn to study the boys. I feel Sam's gaze on me as I wave to Aiden.

"Hey, Dad," he calls from where he wades knee deep at the near edge. He nods in the direction of Sam's son, downstream. "This here's Zach."

I wave to Sam's son. "Hey, Zach!" I call. "Nice job landing that brookie!"

"Thanks," he shouts back with a proud grin. "It was all Aiden."

Aiden sports a satisfied grin, throws out a perfect cast, and I'm reminded of all of the lazy afternoons spent fishing right here, just the two of us. *Life is short, and childhood is even shorter. Savor every minute because there's nothing more precious or fleeting than the love of a child*, Sam had once told him. The memory settles soft and comfortable-like.

As I turn back to Sam and Michaelyn, I catch Emma's gaze and wave, but she and Sam are sharing a silent moment as if they've talked about me.

I dismount and loop Buck's reins around a sage bush. "Did I miss something?" I grin as my gaze darts between Sam and Emma, and I wonder if I've got my hat on backwards or my shirt buttoned wrong.

Sam tries to suppress a smile. "Nope. We just ... little girl here's getting bored, so we thought we'd go for a walk, explore, see what we can find." She touches foreheads with Michaelyn. "Weren't we, baby-girl?"

"Well now, I can show you where there's a nice crop of Juneberry bushes not far from here."

"Juneberries?" Sam says.

"Saskatoon berries, they're sometimes called."

"Oh." Sam's eyes lower and dart side to side as if searching for a memory.

"They're like wild blueberries," I say.

Sam sets Michaelyn on her feet. "Would you like to go berry picking, sweetie?"

Michaelyn nods enthusiastically.

Minutes later we ride off, Michaelyn in front of me, and Sam on Aiden's horse. Michaelyn bravely twists in the saddle to glance up at me, but her grip on the horn is so tight, I can see the whites of her tiny knuckles. She smells like baby powder and softness and family.

While we ride side by side through the meadow, Sam and I catch up. I ask about her job and she tells me she writes children's books now, has for the past three years. "I don't make much but it's enough to eke out a modest living."

She asks about the ranch and I tell her about my family, brothers and cousins, the history of The Homestead Ranch and roughly how many cattle and acres we've got. She seems impressed.

"The main house is just over that ridge," I say, turning to point behind us. Michaelyn wants to see animals, so I point out a few of our cattle in a distant pasture.

I stick to the open grasslands and head for a stand of Juneberries alongside a small tributary that converges with Homestead Creek. There are many more berry bushes along the wooded trails, but the last thing I want is to run into a bear today.

"Still have your little dog, Bear?" I ask while we're picking berries.

"No, he died shortly after Michaelyn was born." There's a sadness in her voice, as if that little dog was her last surviving link to a forgotten past.

"I'm sorry. He was such a tough little guy." I consider telling her about the dog's run-in with the eagle but decide against it. No need to frighten them.

On the way back, Michaelyn falls asleep in my arms, and I feel like I'm riding a cloud. I can't help but grin every time I glance down at her angelic face, lolled against my chest in perfect slumber. My heart tightens when I consider the good-byes at the week's end.

Sam watches me, her gaze warm and understanding.

"I always wanted a little girl," I say.

"Maybe someday you will."

By breath bottles up in my chest as I look again at the child in my arms. If your mother only knew what all I hope for.

We return to find the kids have caught a whole passel of brook trout, and Sam invites us to stay for dinner. While Aiden and Caleb fetch their horses and pack up their gear, Zach helps me clean and prep the fish creek side, and Sam and her daughters trek up to the cabin to make a pie from the berries we'd picked.

We're almost finished when Zach stares off into the distance, to where the creek disappears around a bend. "I can't believe, all the times we've been here, and we never fished the creek. What a miss," he says, wonderment in his voice.

I follow his gaze, my heart light with the satisfaction of witnessing someone finding something beautiful in life they almost missed, and I wonder again, as I have my entire adult life, how I could ever live any place else. "Your mother said you and your dad used to hunt elk here."

"Yeah, years ago. I miss it."

"Was coming here your idea?"

He shakes his head absently, his gaze still far away, roving.

"Emma's." His attention snaps my way. "You were Mom's attorney, huh?"

"More friend than attorney," I say, bending to retrieve a fish head that slid off the boulder, our makeshift cleaning table. "I'm not licensed to practice in Michigan. I gave her some free legal advice, made a few changes to the settlement when your dad sent it here."

He studies me so long the silence grows uncomfortable. "Ever been to Michigan?"

I gut the last brookie, stuff them all into a bag, and wonder how far this conversation will go. "Yep. It's beautiful."

Aiden and Caleb race up on their mounts and rein in at the last minute. Startled, Zach jumps out of the way. I shoot Aiden a narrow-eyed look, but save the scolding for later. I've got other things on my mind. Their saddlebags bulge with fishing gear, the poles in cases are tied onto the backs of the saddles. Aiden dismounts, hands me a pail, and I swipe the fish remains into it and hand it back to him.

Before I can suggest it, Aiden offers Zach his horse, then pulls himself up behind Caleb. I sling the bag of cleaned fish across my shoulder, mount up, and we ride off single file to the cabin, Caleb and Aiden in the lead followed by Zach, then me. I take a steadying breath, but I know it's only a matter of time before Zach and Emma realize there was more than a friendship between their mother and me.

On the back deck, I lay the fish on the grill, and Emma comes out to join me. "Mom thought you might be thirsty." She hands me an ice-cold beer.

"Thank you," I say, twisting off the top.

"Sure thing." Emma turns toward the door.

"Hold up there, darlin'. Stay, I could use the company."

Emma peers inside, and I follow her gaze. Her little sister sits at the table, coloring, and her mom is busy in the kitchen. The boys are out burying the fish remains.

"Okay." Emma leans against the deck railing.

I close the lid on the grill and take a long pull from the beer as I eye Sam's daughter.

"You know she's pretty much a vegetarian, right?" Emma says, eying the grill which now exudes a billow of fragrant steam and smoke: lemon, onion, rosemary and thyme.

I nod. "I recall her telling me that once." It rankles a bit along with the memory of my empty stomach after the weekend at her place. I push the thought away. "But I think she may like this. Tell me, what do you think of your mom's beau?" Might as well be direct. I don't have much time here.

Emma shuffles her feet and turns to look out over the valley. "Her fiancé? He's nice enough," she says. "I suppose."

Not exactly a stellar commendation. I wait for more.

She spins around to face me, leans against the railing. "He's a filmmaker, a director actually. Spends most of his time in LA. When he's not filming, that is."

A movie director—interesting, probably exciting too, but not exactly the stable home life Sam might be looking for to raise a child. "How'd they meet?"

"My mom and Michaelyn were at the park in Falls Creek, swinging, and one of his crew came over and asked them to leave. Nicely, of course, but ..." She shrugs. "They were filming nearby, and my mom and Michaelyn were getting in the shots. Anyway, as they were leaving, Stephane ran after them and apologized, and I suppose one thing led to another, and he asked her out."

"How long ago was that?"

"Last fall."

Hmm, not that long. That's good. "Your mom said he might join y'all here this week."

"Probably wishful thinking on her part, if you ask me. He's on location somewhere in Western Canada. There's no way he can leave in the middle of filming, even if he wanted to."

I nod, relieved but not totally dismissing the inevitable. "Have they set a date?"

"For the wedding? No. Actually ..." she trails off, as though she's said too much already.

"What?"

She eyes me skeptically. "Technically, they're not engaged yet. Mom hasn't said yes. But he talked her into wearing the ring anyway. I guess he thinks it will persuade her or something."

From what Emma's telling me—or more from what she's not telling me—I get the distinct impression Sam's daughter doesn't want her mom to marry the man. "Think she'll say yes?"

Emma shrugs. "I think you should ask her that."

"Yeah, I did, this afternoon."

"What did she say?"

"It wasn't what she said. It's what she didn't say. Kind of like you, now."

Emma shoots me a raised brow.

I open the grill to turn the fish over. "Think I have a chance?"

"I wouldn't say you're holding a royal flush or anything, but I don't know."

"Better than a pair of twos?" Having flipped the last fish, I close the lid.

Emma grins.

I'm taking that as a yes; I'm holding the winning hand where Emma's concerned. But I'll have to play my cards close to the chest this go-round.

WRANGLED into a game of cards after dinner, I lean back in my chair and watch as Sam descends the ladder, having put Michaelyn to bed in the loft. "All tucked in?" I ask as the kids ante up for the next round.

Sam nods with a smile. "Out like a light." She studies the game. "Another beer?"

"No, thank you, I'm good."

"Anyone else need anything?" she asks.

No takers, she leans against the counter to watch the game. "Texas Hold'em?"

"Yeah," Zach says. "Aiden's killing us."

"Only 'cause my Dad's laying down," Aiden says, giving me an exaggerated scowl.

"Laying down?" I say with a chuckle. "How's this for laying down?" I push my remaining chips to the center. "All in."

"Aw, now that's not fair. Not on this hand." Aiden throws in his cards.

Zach smiles and I know I've timed it perfectly. Zach wins the hand and rakes in the pile, much to Aiden's chagrin.

Strategically and successfully out of the game, I join Sam at the counter. I think about asking for a whiskey—I could sure use a bit of liquid courage about now—but think better of it. Best keep my head on straight. "There's an incredible view of your valley from the North Ridge, and it's a beautiful night. Want to go for a ride?"

## 24

# REVISITING THE NORTH RIDGE

The waning gibbous moon blinks in and out of sight above the treetops as I lead the way up the winding narrow trail through the forest. We emerge into the clearing where I dismount, help Sam down, then lead the horses to the treeline and loop the reins over a branch. When I return, Sam is standing at the edge of the ridge that overlooks the valley—her own Moonglow Meadow.

Apparently, she's no longer afraid of heights. Seems some things *are* best forgotten.

It's not the full moon I'd hoped for—no time to wait for that—or the pow of glory like last time, but it's enough.

She gasps; it has taken her breath away. Again.

The stars seem brighter and more numerous than ever, a brilliant galaxy of twinkling white sparks on a lush blanket of black, the mountains on either side faint grey sentinels, a perfect frame for Sam's lovely little piece of land. My heart and soul drink it in, and like always, I'm amazed by how this view sates my inner being.

"Oh, Mac!" Sam's gaze is riveted on the valley below. "It's incredible!"

"Like it may have looked on the seventh day?"

She stares at me, her skin kissed by moonlight. "When He rested and said, 'it is good'?"

A small laugh escapes me. She's my Sam, sure enough, the same woman I fell in love with that summer. "Exactly."

Locked in the moment, several heartbeats pass before we return our gaze to the valley below. I wonder if it's too soon to draw her into my arms like I'd done so long ago.

Is she cold? Will she ask me to dance tonight? Should I tell her how often I come here to remember her, to pray for her?

I rein in my impatience and turn her way. "Glass of wine?"

"You brought wine?"

"You still like wine, right?"

Her smile is answer enough.

I return with the saddlebags and spread out a blanket, draping the back edge of it over a log. Sam bends to help, then sits beside me as I remove the bottle of wine and two glasses.

She holds the glasses while I pour, and when she hands me a glass, I raise it to hers.

"To second chances," I say.

She tilts her head. "Second chances?"

"Our friendship," I say, a little too quickly. "And to this heavenly vista and all the glory God made for us."

"And to you, Mac, for showing it to me." She touches her glass to mine with a soft *ting* and smiles at me warily over the rim.

She asks me about the summer we met, and I describe the time we spent together. She listens carefully, unsmiling, as though struggling to remember even the smallest detail. There's a sadness in her eyes and it breaks my heart.

I wonder what it's like to hear someone describe your life, and not remember any of it. Is it like reading a poorly written poem or novel, supposedly poignant but only felt from afar?

I stretch out, rest my head against the log, and gaze at the stars. Sam settles beside me, leaving enough space between us to park a small car. Several quiet minutes pass while I think about the question that has haunted me since the ice cream shop.

I rub my jaw, searching for the right words. "Tell me about Michaelyn."

"The ankle braces, you mean? She walks on her toes. It's a condition called Idiopathic Toe Walking, ITW. Sometimes it resolves itself, but not always."

"Is it genetic?" I hadn't heard of it before, but that meant nothing.

"No. Sometimes it's associated with autism, ADHD, or cerebral palsy, but she doesn't have any of those. She walked at nine months, though, which was early. Hopefully, the braces will correct the problem. If not, she'll need surgery to lengthen the Achilles tendon."

"Surgery?"

"Yeah." The fear in her voice is that of a mother's worst nightmare.

"Oh, Sam. I'm sorry."

"It's not your fault."

"No, but ..." I was going to say I should've been there for her, for them both. Shouldn't I? What if Michaelyn *is* my child? I have to know, but I need Sam to fall in love with me again, not out of obligation, but the real thing. I want what we had before.

She glances my way, as if expecting me to finish my sentence, and her smile tells me everything I'd hoped to hear, except the one thing I have to know.

She once told me she and her husband had tried for years to have another child, and I recall Brent visited her at the cabin toward the end of that summer. Suddenly, I know exactly how to broach the subject.

"Another child must have thrilled Brent."

A small breath falls out of her, so slight I barely catch it. She turns away, to hide her disappointment, or is it shame she doesn't want me to see?

"Did you know Brent came here that summer?" I ask. "He stayed a few days."

"She's not Brent's."

"Oh," is all I can utter.

"He's positive. And believe me, if there were any chance she were, he'd be the first to claim her. He always wanted more children. We both did."

I wait patiently, hoping for more, but all I can think is *I have a daughter!*

"She was born almost nine months after the accident and," her gaze falls away, "I don't know who her father is."

*She's mine!* I want to shout it from the mountaintop.

"Someone named Micah left a note that said he loved me. I always assumed he was her father but he never came back, never even called."

*I called a hundred times!*

Part of me wants to tell her about the weekend we spent together at her place in Michigan. A bigger part wants her to fall in love with me all over again.

She looks at me, wide-eyed, as if she'd heard my inner thoughts. My throat tightens. It's like she wants to ask outright, *Are you my child's father?* But she doesn't. Maybe she doesn't want to ask for the same reason I don't want to tell her.

I shake my head, find my voice. "That must've been hard."

It's lame, I know, and I have to turn away to hide the whirlwind of emotions wracking my heart.

"So many stars," she says, gazing skyward.

The moment for raw honesty has passed, and I'm simultaneously relieved and terrified. Am I making a huge mistake not telling her right this minute? I breathe in, find my center. "Do you know any constellations?" I ask, hoping but not expecting her to remember.

"The Big Dipper, but that's about it."

I'm not surprised. "Well, did you know there's a Samantha constellation?"

"Really?" she says with a disbelieving chuckle.

I glance over at her. "Right there." I place my face beside hers and point to the large S high in the sky. "Want to hear the story?"

"There's a story?"

"All constellations have a story behind them. Most are about ancient mortals or demigods cast to the heavens by the Greek gods they'd wronged."

"Yeah?"

"Yep. Except for Samantha. She actually cast herself to the heavens." I glance at her before continuing, "To flee the pain of betrayal when a pagan chariot driver broke her heart. But legend has it that one day a gentle shepherd of heroic proportions is going to rescue her by throwing his lariat around her and pulling her back to earth, to live out the rest of her days at his side, beloved and cherished, as fate intended."

She goes silent, and I can almost see her mind swirling through endless vague shadows, searching for the tiniest snippets of recollections, struggling to form a real memory.

She rubs her forehead and frowns. "I think, I may have heard that story before."

"You have. We made it up together. The 'heroic proportions'," I chuckle. "That was all yours."

She giggles, but it dies away almost as quickly as it had burst forth, as if in one instant, she'd tried and given up on catching the memory and reeling it in. "I have a feeling we had something special. Something more than friendship."

"We did." I take a breath as unsteady as moonlight on water. "We definitely did."

The moment of serenity blossoms in the cadence of night song that surrounds us—the steady hum of insects, the far-off gurgling mountain stream, and the gentle rustle of leaves blend in a perfect natural harmony, whispering to me, awakening my long-abandoned hopes and dreams.

She stands and takes a few steps toward the ridge. Her arms hug her middle.

There's something so incredibly seductive about her uncertain posture, something that turns back the years since I'd last seen her. I stand to join her. "Cold?"

She rubs her arms. "A little."

I drape my Carhartt over her shoulders then gently turn her around and extend a hand. "Dance with me?"

She slips her arms into my jacket, takes my hand, and places her other one atop my shoulder while I pull her closer. Slowly, we begin to sway.

"This is my favorite music," I murmur.

She laughs, a soft feminine sound, perfect for the moment. "What music?"

"Really? You don't hear it? The soft breeze whistling through the pines, more beautiful than any woodwind." I lower my voice to not drown out the melody I'm enticing her to hear, the rhythm of the night. "Close your eyes, Sam. Let the darkness bloom and sing." The *scritch-scritch-scritch* of mountain squirrels form a steady cadence, as an owl hoots not far away. Foxes bark a staccato like poodles. In the distance, coyotes howl and an elk herd mew, bugle, and glug, lending their voices to the exquisite nature-song. I pull back slightly to watch her listen. "Do you hear it now?"

When she gazes up at me, there's a light in her eyes that wasn't there before. "I do."

I hold her in my arms while her scent, like jasmine, drifts up to entice me. It seems so right, everything I'd longed for. I peer over her shoulder to the stars above, and my heart swells, feeling huge, full, whole.

*Thank you, God!* I am so elated, a burst of laughter escapes.

"What's funny?"

"I'm happy, Sam, to be dancing with you again." I lead her away from the ledge and spin her out and around and dip her backward over my arm, and she laughs along with me. When I pull her up, our eyes lock, and I fight the urge to lean in, run my nose down her cheek, thread my fingers through her hair to the nape, where I know they fit so well.

Time stops, the music plays on, a breeze catches her hair, sending long blonde wisps to circle her face while my heart soars with the love I'd closeted away for so long. I wonder how I could love her so much and have survived nearly four years without her. With a sigh, I edge so close that we share the same air. I touch her cheek, trail a fingertip across its softness as my eyes search her face for some remnant of what we once shared.

"Mac," she braces a palm against my shirtfront, "I'm with Stephane." She lowers her gaze as if she sees my emotions spilling from me like a tidal wave she can't withstand.

"Not now," I whisper. And when she looks up at me, her lips part slightly as my fingertip grazes her lower lip. My breath catches and I know the moment is right. I lean in, my lips slowly brushing hers, soft and gentle. Her warmth and the lingering taste of wine drown my senses. It's our first kiss. Again. And I will remember it always. Just like the one in the creek. Our *first* first kiss.

Only this time there is no conscience screaming in my head, demanding I stop, walk away. This time, the voice only urges me on —*kiss her, kiss her like you've longed to kiss her, kiss her like she is meant to be kissed.* And when her tongue shyly welcomes mine, I do.

Remembering it's technically our first date, I resolve to not take more than she's ready to give. When I break away, her gaze caresses every part of my face, a tenderness in her expression I thought I'd never see again. "Mac," she whispers.

As I look into Sam's eyes, I'm overcome with emotion. I let go and say, "Yes." I cup her face between my palms. "Yes. You know me, Sam."

She takes my hand, lowers it, and tiptoes to place her cheek alongside mine. "I wish I remembered. I'm sorry I don't."

Over her shoulder, I stare at the stars, twinkling brightly on their blanket of black. *Oh, me too, darlin'. You have no idea.* I push sway the thoughts and lead her back to the blanket where we stretch out side by side, hands touching.

A gentle breeze whispers across the clearing, stirring layers of scent—aspen, distinctly pure and clean, and Ponderosa pine, like vanilla and butterscotch, intermingle, sweeping me up in a rich, woodsy, and immersive sensory experience. I close my eyes and inhale deeply.

I turn to her, contemplating how to describe what we'd found that summer.

"What?" She returns my stare.

I shake my head and lean back against the log. "It's too soon." I find my glass of wine, take a sip, and try to break free, looking out over the valley.

"What's too soon? Tell me."

I roll to my side, prop myself on an elbow, and I'm sunk, drowned by the pretty blue eyes that have stolen my breath away. "We fell in love that summer. At least I did. And I thought you did too."

Her eyes widen. "I did?"

"Fairly certain."

She bites her lip, and I know exactly what she's so hesitant to ask. "Did we—"

I slowly shake my head, conflicted about how much to tell her. "You were still married. And you were determined to save your marriage. So I didn't tell you. But I loved you all the same. I always hoped you'd come back one day."

Her head relaxes back against the log while her gaze returns to the stars. This has to be overwhelming for her.

I settle back beside her and gaze skyward. "But hey, don't worry. It'll come back if you give it a chance. Everything in God's perfect time."

She doesn't respond and I wonder how far I should push. Going all in, I turn onto my side again to face her. "Let me—" My voice breaks and I have to clear my throat. "—make you to fall in love with me again."

She turns my way, and her smile is slow and sweet. Her face reveals an inner peace, as though she's been waiting for this exact moment. "You do?"

I nod. "And if you sense something familiar, let it settle down deep, warm, and comfortable-like, and know that it's right. That it's exactly as it should be."

She takes a long time answering, and I wonder if she's thinking about her engagement, reluctant to revisit the past because she's already promised her future to someone else.

"Oh, Mac." She studies my face, as if searching for a memory there, or memorizing it for the very first time. "We only have a few days, and I'm—"

"It'll be enough." I take her hand and kiss it. My false bravado brings a smile to her face, and the warmth in her eyes tells me she wants to say yes. Despite her engagement, despite the possibility of her fiancé arriving midweek. Despite everything, she wants to take the chance. On me. On us.

"What if I don't?"

"You will."

"You seem so sure."

"Yep."

She laughs but quickly grows somber again as she peers at me, seeming to recognize the depth of my feelings for her.

I place a hand alongside her cheek, willing her to give in to me. "It happened once. It'll happen again. I'm the same man I've always been. Give me half a chance and I promise you *will* fall in love with me again."

She places a hand over mine and leans into my palm. Her eyes close. She inhales, long and slow. Seconds tick by. The night song plays on. I can see she's conflicted, and my hope wanes.

"Oh, Mac, is it right to rekindle this love story? I'm with Stephane—"

"Please, Sam." I stare into her eyes, willing her to say yes, but realizing, this time, I'm asking for too much.

"I'm engaged, Mac."

*Argh!* That stab in the heart again.

"And he'll be here in a day or two."

I have to look away as the knife twists.

A twig snaps in the woods behind us, and the horses snort and stomp. I lumber to my feet, resisting the urge to move too quickly and risk frightening her. With my ears perked and my insides tight as a knot, I move slowly to where the horses are tethered. "Shhh," I say to calm the animals, "Hey, hey." I touch Buck's neck, give it a little scratch, then do the same for the mare. When I'm certain they won't bolt, I free the reins and lead them to the clearing where Sam is standing with the blanket roll under her arm and the saddlebags at her feet, having packed away the wine and glasses.

We mount up and I lead the way back down the trail, traversing the switchbacks single file, enveloped in darkness, my ears alert to the slightest sound. I pass an opening in the trees, and I hear her pull up. When I turn, she's gazing at her cabin below with a look of misery I haven't seen since the night I arrived at her place in Michigan.

I shift in the saddle and let my mind carry me back to that cool September evening when I'd stood in the shadows of her side yard, hesitant and second guessing my decision to go see her.

She sat in a cushioned chair before a fire pit, a bottle of wine and a half-full glass on a table beside her. Elbows on her knees, she stared at a small computer, her face illuminated by the haunting glow of the screen. The night was eerily quiet, the lake like her eyes, shining, smooth and vacant. After several long moments, she closed the computer, set it on the table, and brought the glass of wine to her lips, while her little dog rested his head on her thigh.

I'd expected to find her like that, not exactly sitting before a fire lost in a computer screen, but I knew she'd be down. My name and address had been on the returned divorce settlement, so I'd gotten a copy of the final version, and I was surprised the twelve-month stipulation she'd asked me to add had been removed.

But the document had her signature on it; she'd agreed to it. I wondered what it meant for her and if her marriage was actually dissolved, not simply in the legal sense, but in her heart, where it mattered.

I rubbed a hand across my forehead. Having driven straight through, twenty-three hours on the road, only stopping for gas and bio breaks, I was exhausted. But I knew she'd need me, and I wanted to be there for her. And yet, the last few hours, as I'd gotten closer, uncertainty settled in. Was it too soon?

She'll need time to accept the finality of her divorce, put it behind her, and heal.

No, I decided. God had put it in my heart to come, and I trusted in that.

I stepped from the shadows, and her little dog bounded from her lap and ran toward me barking.

"Hey, Bear." I crouched, hand extended.

Bear quieted instantly and wagged his stubby tail as I rubbed his ears.

"Mac?" Sam set her glass on the table and started toward me.

"Yeah, Sam. It's me." I straightened and took several long strides to meet her in the middle of the well-manicured lawn.

Sam hesitated, and then as though a brief inner struggle resolved, she embraced me in a warm hug.

I wrapped my arms around her and relished her long soft length against me, her warmth against my chest, the familiar scent of her beneath my chin.

It was one of the longest hugs I'd ever had, but I was loath to end it. I wondered if, when we parted, I'd find tears in her eyes. I caressed her long gold-blonde hair that tumbled loosely down her back.

After several long moments, Sam pulled back to look up at me. "How did you know I needed you?"

I gazed into her eyes shining in the faint light of a crescent moon. "I will always be here when you need me, darlin'."

Her warm smile said clearly she was happy I'd come, and suddenly, every doubt I had melted away. "Nice fire you got going there." I nodded to the wrought iron table and the small gas flames burning from its center.

"Come, join me." She took my hand and pulled me forward. "Something to drink?"

I eyed the bottle of wine but thought better of it. I was so tired one drink would totally wipe me out. "No, thanks, I'm good."

I dropped into the chair beside hers, looked out at the lake, and then at the house. So this is what a one-point-four million-dollar place looked like. It was a two-story with a walk out basement, so from the back it looked like three stories, much bigger than I'd first imagined when I'd parked in the circle drive up front. A deck ran the entire back side of it, the central portion nestled beneath a gabled roof. A dim light shone from the windows beneath the covered deck, but other than that the rest of the house was dark. "You have a beautiful home."

"Thank you." She glanced at the house with a look of unmistakable sadness. "It was a great place to raise kids." When she turned back to the water, I wondered if she was recalling happier times spent out there on the lake, with her children and the husband who'd once loved her.

She picked up the computer, opened it, and it flashed on with the same image she'd been staring at earlier. She held it out to me. "Isn't she pretty?"

An image of a dark-haired woman in a wedding gown, her hair elegantly pulled up into a flowing white veil stared back at me with dark, empty eyes. "She doesn't hold a candle to you, darlin'." I handed the computer back.

Sam forced a tight smile, like someone holding a crying child, and I knew she didn't believe me. "The new and improved Mrs. Jamison," she said, her voice calm and controlled, devoid of emotion.

Her eyes strayed to the emptiness of the dark night sky, as though searching for an explanation there in the ether. She took a sip of wine, then another. "You know he came to the cabin."

"Yep."

"He spent three days trying to talk me out of the twelve-month condition. I thought he wanted me back." She set her glass aside and pulled her knees up under her. "It wasn't until I got home that he let me know the real reason he wanted it removed." She was quiet for several minutes then smiled, that forced smile again, barely curving her lips and far from reaching her troubled eyes. "She's pregnant. He married her today." She dropped it like the wrecking ball it was.

There were no words to console her, nothing I could say to help her overcome the hopelessness she was dealing with. Her husband was starting over with someone else. It was the absolute finishing touch that meant *final*, in the most definitive, permanent sense of the word.

I stood, pulled her into my arms, and held her for several minutes, the quiet coolness of the early autumn night enveloping us in its sweet tranquility. When I pulled back to look into her eyes, I was again startled to find them dry and empty.

"I don't know what to do, Mac," she admitted, her voice breaking under the weight of her crushed hopes and lost dreams.

I silenced her with a fingertip to her lips, then bent to kiss her, and suddenly I knew what to do. "Let me make you feel loved tonight," I whispered against her lips.

It took a minute, but she smiled, that same hesitant smile she'd planted on me in the stream, not huge but genuine, and she slowly nodded.

"Mac?" The sound of her voice yanks me from my reverie, and I can tell by the look on her face she's been watching me for a while.

"Yep?"

She nudges her mount forward, closing the distance between us. "Would you and Aiden like to join us tomorrow afternoon for a swim in the creek?"

A swim. At least it's something. "We'll be there."

She shines that same hesitant smile my way, the one full of distant possibilities of which I can only dream.

As we emerge from the woods and start across the valley, now riding abreast, I ask about her plans for the rest of her stay, and she describes activities she and the twins have planned—kayaking, visiting the hot springs in Steamboat, four-wheeling in the forest, and whitewater rafting—likely just Emma and Zach on that one. I graciously offer my services, and Aiden's, to be their personal guides for the entire week. Or until Stephane arrives.

She agrees, and once again I believe in miracles.

# 25

# WHITEWATER

Early Monday afternoon, Aiden and I pull onto the trail that leads down to Sam's cabin, park beside her Escalade, and hop out to unload three kayaks from the bed of the pickup.

Sam comes out to greet us, Michaelyn scurrying awkwardly behind her. I grin at the sight of them.

Michaelyn holds her arms out to me, so I scoop her up and give her a bear hug hello, then kiss her cheek and turn to Sam, Michaelyn beaming in my arms. "I thought we'd launch from here, if that's okay? It's about a three to four-hour ride down into town. My brother Nick will come by later to drive my truck to our pullout."

Sam eyes the kayaks. "I thought we were going swimming today."

I glance at Aiden, now standing beside me. "We thought kayaking would be more fun." I set Michaelyn on her feet. "And look at this day!" I raise my arms to the sky. "We can swim any day. The creek's perfect for kayaking, nice and smooth, only one fast section the whole way. We scouted it this morning."

Sam's brows knit together. "Maybe Michaelyn and I should stay here."

"Don't worry. There's only one rock above water to steer clear of. I'll take Michaelyn with me." Sam nods and I turn to the toddler. "Are you ready for a boat ride, sunshine?"

"Yea!" Michaelyn cheers.

Zach and Emma come outside to help, and a short time later, kids and kayaks are creek side. When Sam finishes zipping Michaelyn into her life jacket, Emma takes her sister's hand and leads her toward the creek. "Michaelyn, come with me. Mommy's going with Mr. Mac."

"No!" Michaelyn yanks her hand free. "I'm going with Mr. Mac!"

Emma rolls her eyes, shakes her head, and laughs when she catches my empathetic smile.

MINUTES LATER, we're paddling downstream at a steady clip. The water's fast enough to race along, but not so fast that we can't relax and enjoy the scenery. Michaelyn and I are in the lead kayak, with Sam and Aiden behind us, followed by Emma and Zach. I point out passing wildlife to Michaelyn: an osprey, a beaver pond, a family of foxes, a pair of eagles high above. Aiden and Sam's conversation floats across the water from behind.

"Those are eagles, aren't they?" Sam asks.

"Golden Eagles," Aiden says. "They're sky dancing."

"Sky dancing?" Sam's voice holds a sense of wonder.

"It's how they mate."

"In mid-air?"

Nestled in front of me, Michaelyn watches, entranced by the flight of the two birds, one following the other as they circle, soar, and plummet together as though connected by a string.

"Yep." I hear Aiden's paddle make several smooth, deep strokes in the water.

"Look how erratic that one is." I glance back to see Sam pointing skyward.

"Probably the female."

I chuckle, certain that my son has no idea how chauvinistic that sounded.

I glance back to see Aiden looking up, his hand tented over his eyes. A wide grin shines on his face, like he's just caught sight of an old friend. "We've seen that pair before. She's injured. Dad says someone yanked her to the ground and broke her wing a few years back. Uncle Cody patched her up, but she's never flown right since. Her mate doesn't care, though; she can still sky-dance. That's all that matters. Eagles mate for life, you know."

I make a couple of strokes myself as Aiden's words settle into my heart with the knowledge that I've taught him well the beauty and reverence of nature.

"I didn't know that," Sam says, her voice colored with awe.

When I glance back a few minutes later, she's studying my son in the bow of the kayak with a look of unabashed adoration. She catches my eye and her smile widens. Was she falling in love with him again? It's certainly not the first time my son's charm has preceded—or surpassed—mine.

I TURN TO SHOUT, "WHITEWATER AHEAD!" I nestle Michaelyn between my legs, and navigate into the surge. The roar of rushing water through the steep canyon-like walls grows louder as we enter the turbulent shoot. A splash comes over the bow, soaking us both, and Michaelyn gasps at the icy chill. "Woo-hoo! Isn't this fun?" I say, raising my voice to be heard over the maelstrom of water.

Michaelyn giggles, but her death grip on my calves as our kayak bounces up and down belies her fearlessness. I alternate my strokes from side to side to keep us headed straight through the tunnel. When we come to a large rock jutting from the center of the current, I lean in, forcing the kayak into a controlled spin and we circle around it.

I glance down at Michaelyn. Her eyes are as wide as saucers, but when she looks up at me, she laughs. "Good job, sunshine! You're a born kayaker." The water smooths out as the creek widens, and I paddle us over to the side and back into an eddy to watch the others come through, Aiden and Sam first.

"Straight down the middle, Aiden," I call.

I watch with a mixture of pride and anxiety as my son guides the kayak through the chute, doing a fine job of keeping the craft straight until they approach the rock protruding from the surface like an ominous sentinel.

Aiden paddles like crazy, trying to veer hard right to avoid it, but the current drives them straight for it. Aiden leans away from it, and before I can call out, I hear Sam. "No, Aiden! Lean into it, not away from it."

And sure enough, he does and their kayak spins right around the rock. Relief washes over me as Aiden and Sam paddle forward. "Good job, son!" I say, as they join us in the eddy.

Soon, Zach and Emma come through the chute the same way, cartwheeling around the exposed rock like they'd done it a hundred times before.

We paddle from the eddy and catch up to the twins.

"Wow! Good job, Mom!" Zach calls. "I can't believe you remembered how to spin around a rock like that!"

"Like riding a bike, I guess," Sam calls back, her face alight with surprise.

I glance over at Sam as our kayaks continue the journey side by side down the widening river, and I want to burst with laughter.

*She remembers!* And if she remembers how to navigate whitewater, she might remember other, deeper things, like how she'd once loved me.

~

THE LATTER HALF of the kayak trip is uneventful, the river running much slower as the drop in elevation tapers off. It's late afternoon when we land at the takeout in Centennial Park on the edge of town.

I land first and step out with a sleepy Michaelyn nestled in my arms. I drag my kayak up the bank and out of the way as Aiden and Sam land next to me. When I turn to help Sam out, I'm stopped short. Aiden has already hopped out and turned to offer Sam a hand.

"Sam, there're a couple of blankets in the backseat," I whisper, motioning to my truck parked in the nearby lot. I carry Michaelyn, now snuggled against my shoulder, to a large oak tree about ten yards from the water's edge, and wait while Sam and Emma hastily spread the blanket over the lush green grass. Then I ease the little girl down to finish her nap, careful not to wake her.

The boys and I load up the kayaks and from my truck bed, I notice one of the ranch's horse trailers parked across the street. I can make out horses inside, as they stamp their feet impatiently. When we finish with the kayaks, Emma and the boys set off to buy soft drinks at the Conoco down the block. As they turn onto the sidewalk at the park's edge, Nick appears from behind the horse trailer and jogs across the street to join them.

I chuckle to myself, not the least bit surprised. When my little brother sets his mind on something, there's no stopping him.

I join Sam in the shade beneath the tree where she lay on the blanket facing her little girl. I stretch out on the other side of Michaelyn and lean on an elbow. *My little girl—if only.* A mild breeze kicks up and I gently cover Michaelyn with the second blanket. Sensing Sam's stare, I push my longings back down where they're not so obvious.

"Can I take y'all to dinner tonight?" I ask, reluctantly pulling my gaze from the sleeping toddler. "There's a nice little diner in town, nothing fancy but good home cooking."

"All of us?"

"Of course. You fed the three of us last night."

"Sounds nice. Thank you."

"Great." Lying on my back, I wishbone my arms behind my head and close my eyes, trying hard not to let my smile wrap clear around my head.

I feel Sam's gaze rake over me, so I feign sleep, letting her take her time about it. After several long minutes, I open one eye to find her studying my abs, then my chest, my shoulders.

When she realizes I'm watching her, she smiles, unabashed. "Do you always spend your days like this?"

I stretch and sigh. "Lying in the shade being ogled by a beautiful woman or floating down a river?"

She laughs at the compliment. "I wasn't ..."

My brows shoot up as I roll to my side and prop myself on an elbow to face her.

Sam's cheeks redden.

"It's okay. I liked it."

"Yeah?"

I nod. Most definitely. And from the look on her face, she liked it too.

"So?"

"Oh, right. No, sorry to say, I don't get to do this as often as I'd like. Fact is, I work pretty hard most days. Up with the sun, feed the animals before myself, typical life of a rancher. But when Aiden's here, I try to do something like this, the two of us, at least once a week."

"I hope he doesn't mind us intruding on your time together."

"Are you kidding? I think he was almost as happy to see you again as I was. And he's had a great time hanging out with your kids these past few days. He adores Michaelyn."

Sam chuckles. "Yeah, that's one smitten little man."

"Like his dad," I say, twinkly eyed.

Sam's response is a shy smile, and her breath catches when I lean over to kiss her. When we part, we both glance at the sleeping child between us.

I stand and offer a hand. "Come on."

"Where are we going?"

"Not far."

We walk hand-in-hand the few yards to the river's edge, and sit shoulder to shoulder on the soft grass. "It's nice to have a few minutes alone with you."

Sam looks out over the gently flowing water that smells like mud. Leaves and tall grasses dance in a subtle breeze on the opposite bank. "It's beautiful here. Peaceful."

I nod as I take in the view, feeling anything but peaceful. The sun bakes the back of my neck and I wished I'd gotten my hat from the truck. "Yep." I turn to face her, hoping she won't see the turmoil roiling inside of me. "You—" I gulp down a momentary hesitation, "could stay."

Sam sighs, as if the idea was sheer fantasy.

"Seriously," I say, gently nudging her shoulder.

"I can't."

"Why not? You love it here. You always have."

"This isn't real, Mac. This week is a vacation for me."

"Oh, it's real, Sam, as real as you want it to be. It's my life, and it soothes the soul in ways I can't even begin to describe. Ranching's not much of a living, but it's a great life. You could make this home, and we could take our time getting to know each other again."

The way she looks at me, I can almost see a sliver of hope welling up, pouring out in her gaze, in her smile.

"Tell me you'll at least consider it?"

"Oh, Mac." She gazes out over the water again, and the hope is gone. "I'm with Stephane."

My jaw clenches. The sting of her fiancé's name has stolen away the warmth and comfort I'd basked in moments earlier, and suddenly, the lazy afternoon is rushing by way too fast. The week is draining away like snowmelt in June, gushing down the mountain, cutting painfully through the bedrock of my heart's desire.

Determined, I push on. "Do you love him?"

She glances at me with surprise, as if it was an absurd thing to ask. She turns her focus to the ring on her finger, twisting it around and around. "I'm going to marry him."

So why hasn't she said yes to him? Why wasn't he here with them now? And more importantly, why can't she answer the dang question? I want to ask them all, but what comes out instead is the same one I already asked. "Do you love him?"

She glances back to check on Michaelyn.

I follow her gaze. "She's fine," I say with a forced calm.

*Dang-it-all!* Why can't she answer that one simple question? I wait, watching her as she seems to be searching inward.

She brushes an ant from her knee, then glances back at me and exhales a long deep breath. "He's a good man."

I turn away to hide my knowing smile. *She can't say it!* So why would she marry a man she doesn't love?

She stares at her hands again, eyeing the ring.

A loud splash captures our attention. An osprey soars above the water, a plump cutthroat clutched triumphantly in its talons.

With a fingertip beneath her chin, I gently turn her face to capture her gaze. "I can make you happy, Sam. No one will ever love you as much as I do."

Sam stares back at me as I declare my love for her and again, I wonder if it's too much, too soon. Am I still someone she barely knows? But when I lean in to kiss her, she melts against me, as if it no longer matters. And when I pull back to gaze into her eyes, I see a softness I haven't seen in a very long time.

She touches my face. The tip of her finger traces my lower lip, and there's a longing in her touch, an ache to recapture something precious and lost—her love for me. She threads her hands into my hair and pulls me to her for another kiss.

And I know with a certainty I can't explain that she yearns to feel that way again.

~

At the diner, the owner, Franny, seats us at a large corner booth. "Best seat in the house," she says with a cheek-plumping smile. But I know it's the only seat in the house big enough to fit the six of us. Thankfully, or strategically, Nick declined to join us, saying he had to deliver those just-broke horses, inferring he was the one who broke them. Not likely, but I didn't call him out on it.

While Sam asks the kids about the young cowboy—my little brother, Nick—I study the menu.

"Hey, Aiden," a familiar female voice breaks in.

Aiden nudges me. "Hi, Janie!"

I jump up to give Janie a friendly hug. As I return to my seat, a hint of sad recognition lingers on her face as she peruses the others at the table. "Janie, this is Samantha Jamison and her children." I sweep a hand carelessly across them, awkward, like the moment. "Emma, Zach, and Michaelyn."

"Nice to see ya' again, Sam." Janie's smile looks forced. "We actually met a while back at The Homestead."

"Oh, sure." Sam nods, not letting on that she doesn't remember.

Janie's smile disappears as her gaze hops from Sam to Michaelyn to me, and then back to Michaelyn. "What a pretty little girl."

"Thank you," Sam says.

"What can I get ya'll to drink?" Janie asks, the forced smile firmly back in place.

Sam watches my every interaction with Janie, almost as if she senses the relationship we once had, one-sided though it was. Isaac's wife, Isabelle, once told me I'd have to be blind in one eye not to notice how pretty Janie was and blind in both not to realize how she felt about me. Janie is still a beautiful young woman, and I wonder if Sam feels a hint of jealousy.

While Sam orders chicken tenders and apple sauce for Michaelyn, her phone vibrates deep in her purse. Ignoring it, she adds a southwestern salad for herself. As the others take turns ordering, Sam digs out her phone, glances at the missed call, then tucks it away and shoots me an apologetic smile.

"You can call him back if you want to," I say softly so as not to be overheard as I eye her purse on the seat between us.

"Later," she says.

Emma offers to take Michaelyn to the lady's room with her, so I stand to lift Michaelyn from her booster seat and set her on her feet beside her big sister. Then I slide back in beside Sam.

The phone inside her purse vibrates again, so I slide out. "Go on."

"Thanks, I'll make it quick. I'm sorry."

"Don't be. It's fine. Take your time."

Sam makes her way to the front of the restaurant and steps outside. I can see her through the glass and I have a hard time looking away. She doesn't love him, I tell myself. She's not married yet. I still have a chance, God-willing. But what if she doesn't want to live on the ranch. It's all I have to offer, and it wasn't enough for Elizabeth. But Sam isn't Elizabeth. And Sam quit her job the day of the accident. She was changing her path to be with me. Will she make that same decision again?

Forcing the doubt from my mind, I ask the twins about their other must-dos for the week ahead, and it's enough of a distraction that I stop thinking about Sam, if only for a few minutes. But I can't help an occasional glance.

While the kids play table football with a drink coaster, I glimpse Sam scowling outside. She turns her back to the restaurant, holds the phone away from her ear. Then she lowers it, stares at it, and her whole body seems to slump. The phone disappears, and she turns back to the restaurant. We lock eyes and hers are filled with uncertainty, despair, maybe even anger. She shoots me a wry smile, blinks, and squares her shoulders as though gathering resolve, then moves to the door.

Janie arrives with our meals as I stand to let Sam slide in.

"Everything okay?" From her body language during the call, I suspect things are far from okay.

Sam nods and smiles, but it doesn't reach her eyes. Janie leaves and while Zach says a blessing, I reach under the table to squeeze Sam's hand.

While the children chat among themselves—Zach and Emma challenge Aiden to another game of Texas Hold'em—I lean over to whisper to Sam, "He's coming, isn't he?"

"I asked him not to."

I mull that over for all of two seconds. "He'll be here tomorrow."

Sam looks at me sideways. "You sound pretty sure of that."

"I know what's at stake." I consider the incredible woman at my side. "And I know what I'd do if I were him."

"Except you didn't."

Her words are a slap in the face. I look away, stunned, not wanting to believe I'd heard them from her lips.

She touches my arm. "I'm sorry. That wasn't fair."

I want to agree. But it's true. "Let me see your phone."

She hands it to me. I find and open her contacts. There it is—MD. I show it to her. "I've been here all along, Sam."

I can see her mind racing as she stares at it. Is she thinking about all the times she'd skipped past that entry, not giving it a second thought beyond the likelihood that it may be a doctor she didn't remember, one of the many people in her contacts she didn't remember?

She looks up, shoots me an apologetic smile, and then silently slips the phone back into her purse.

After dinner, on the sidewalk outside the diner, Aiden asks if we can go down the street for ice cream. Michaelyn cheers when Sam says, "Of course." As the children walk on ahead, I overhear snippets of their conversation.

"Does this town have a doctor?" Emma asks.

"Nope," Aiden answers. "Not since Doc Grady shot up our herd a few years back."

Sam laughs softly.

"What's so funny?" I ask, taking her hand.

Sam shakes her head, raises her eyes to the stars, then turns to me, eyeing me as though she has plenty to be happy about. "It's a beautiful night."

I raise my gaze to the dark canopy above, the bright white half-moon and the millions of stars shining softly upon us, and I squeeze her hand. "They're all like this, darlin'."

## 26

## SAM'S BEND

"Wait." Emma stops me with a hand on my arm.

Tuesday, day three of their visit, I stand waist-deep in the creek, sporting a smile just this side of laughter, while Sam and Michaelyn splash together a few yards away. How long has Emma been watching me? The empathy on her face is unmistakable; she senses how I feel about her mother.

"She's happy here." Emma eyes her mom.

"Yep." We watch Sam do a pirouette with Michaelyn in the water. They're both giggling.

"I always thought my parents would move out here, build a real house, after Zach and I finished school. Maybe if they had ..." She catches herself and shakes off the melancholy thought. "She's happiest when she's living in the moment."

I step closer to Emma, anticipating whatever wisdom this young woman plans to impart. "How's that?"

"She gets really sad when she tries to remember and can't. It's frustrating for her. And the recurring failure results in depression." Barely a pre-med grad, she already sounds like a doctor. "She can't go through that again."

I look back at Sam. Her easy laughter makes me smile again.

"She doesn't remember anything about those months before the accident?"

Emma shakes her head. "Nothing. And she probably never will."

I feel her stare, but I can't tear my eyes away from Sam and her little girl, right there in front of me, everything I've ever dreamed of. I move toward them.

But Emma's not finished saying her piece. "Can I make a suggestion, Mr. McKennon?"

I stop and turn back to Emma. "Sure, but call me Mac, please."

"Okay, Mac," she says. "Forget the past. Don't waste time trying to help her remember. She won't. It'll only make her sad and disappointed, and if that's what happens every time she sees you, well, after a while ... She's pulled away from every one of her old friends, says it's just too hard."

My hope plunges at the thought that Sam may never remember me.

"Make new memories." Emma gives me a nod of encouragement. "Like yesterday. And today." She eyes her mother, laughing and playing in the water with her little sister. "Look how happy she is."

I follow her gaze to where Sam and Michaelyn are giggling, their heads together as if sharing a quiet secret. I turn back to Emma. "Thank you."

Emma grins. Sam's grin.

When Zach douses Sam and Michaelyn with a huge splash, they scream in unison.

Sam clutches Michaelyn to her and ducks away. "Zach, stop! I don't want to get soaked!" She holds Michaelyn out to me, and I twirl her around, causing another fit of happy giggles.

Sam trudges from the stream, dries off, and spreads a blanket near the cottonwood. Michaelyn's braces lie amid the pile of towels on the ground beside her. Sam settles back on her elbows, face to the sun, as I continue to twirl Michaelyn around in the water. We surprise Aiden with a soaking splash and then Zach. I glance to the riverbank often, where Sam sits watching us, lost in something that looks like bewilderment.

A few minutes later, I carry the giggling toddler over my shoulder up the riverbank and plop her gently at her mother's feet. I grab a towel and wrap it around Michaelyn's shoulders, stealing a kiss on her cheek before finding my own towel.

Sam pulls Michaelyn onto her lap and rubs her down, warming her. My heart aches with longing.

"What?" Sam asks, as Michaelyn snuggles against her.

Realizing I've been caught with my love-light shining again, I wrap my towel around my waist and sit beside them. "Nothing. I'm excited. Been looking forward to this all day. All night too, if you want the God's honest truth."

My gaze wanders into the branches of the giant cottonwood and the memories it invokes. What I wouldn't give to relive that afternoon again—the way she'd written it this time.

"We've been here before, haven't we?" Sam asks.

I glance back at her, hope flooding in. "You remember?"

Sam seems to search inwardly and her smile fades as she comes up empty. "No, it's just the way you've been looking at me all afternoon. And the tree."

I search for words as I look from Sam to Michaelyn, then back to Sam. I want to tell her this was where it all began, but what comes out instead is a nonchalant, "We've been here before."

A wry smile of disappointment clouds Sam's features, and she fluffs her wet bangs, carefully covering the long scar that creases one temple.

Helpless as I watch her retreat into sadness, I think about Emma's advice. Tossing my towel aside, I sit in front of them and take Sam's hands in mine, turn them palms up, and tenderly kiss the red scar that runs across each one. The souvenirs she'll never lose. I give her a reassuring smile.

"You're beautiful, Sam, even with your scars." I tenderly brush aside her bangs and kiss that scar, too.

"Oh," she murmurs, and the smile in her eyes sends a shiver

of excitement straight to my core. It's the same smile she'd fixed on me the day I'd washed her hair. She's beginning to come around.

"Did this happen that summer?" She eyes her palms, then me.

"Yep. But the one you left on my heart is much deeper."

Sam's gaze strays to somewhere behind me and her smile vanishes, replaced by concern. I whirl around and look straight into the eyes of her son, who glares at us from the edge of the creek. How long has he been there?

Sam smiles, but the worry on her face is unmistakable. "Zach?"

Zach scoffs and shakes his head, then snatches his boots and shirt, and stomps up the trail toward the cabin.

Sam withers like a November sunflower.

I spring to my feet and place a hand on her shoulder. "I'll talk to him." I pull on my T-shirt and socks, step into my boots, and hurry after Zach.

I find him at the woodpile beyond the cabin chopping wood. "Want help with that?" I bend to collect the pieces already split.

"No, thanks," he says, not breaking stride to look my way.

I watch for a minute. His back is to me, but I can sense the tension that stands between us as solid and unrelenting as the hardwoods he's splitting.

"Did I do something?"

If Zach hears me, he gives no indication of it. He places another log on the chopping block, swings the ax, kicks aside the splits, and reaches for the next one.

"Zach—"

Zach whirls on me. "Look, I don't know any other way to do this, so I'm just going to ask straight out. And I expect an honest answer. Are you Michaelyn's father?"

Surprised by the vehemence in Zach's voice, I rub my chin as I think about how to answer.

"Oh, my God! You are." Zach turns back to the block, heaves the ax around, and hits the spike with a blow hard enough to send both sides flying ten feet in each direction. Head down, his shoulders slump and his chest seems to curl inward. He turns to face me. "You have to tell her."

"I plan to."

"What the hell are you waiting for?" He sets another log on the block, then glares at me, expecting an answer.

"Don't worry, she won't leave here not knowing. I love your mother, Zach, more than I ever thought possible. And she loved me too. Once. I need her to fall in love with me again, for me, not because I'm her child's father."

Zach takes a swing, sending pieces flying, then drops the ax and walks to the woodpile and heaves several more logs toward the block. Returning, he looks at me, concern etched in his young face. "Why? So you can totally destroy her when she finds out how you abandoned her?"

I nudge one of the logs at my feet closer to the block. "I didn't abandon her."

Zach sets the log on the block. "You sure as hell did! What kind of man are you? You took what you wanted and left her! And now, we're supposed to believe you love her?" His next swing embodies all the power and anger of his words.

"I didn't know—"

"Because you never bothered to find out!" Zach drops the ax to his side. His whole body is shaking. "You have no idea what she went through to have Michaelyn. She was so bad off after the accident and then to find herself pregnant. And everyone knew it wasn't my father's. Everyone thought she was the one who …" Zach's eyes grow dark, and he turns back to his log splitting.

*Oh, God, no!* Zach thinks the divorce was her fault, that she cheated on his father. Does everyone? Does Sam? How much did she tell her children before the accident?

Zach blinks and reaches for another log.

"I love her, Zach. I made a mistake in waiting so long." My voice breaks. "A mistake I've paid for by missing out on the first three years of my daughter's life, missing all that time I might've had with them both. Not a day went by that I didn't think of your mother."

Zach glances sideways at me, then goes right on swinging, taking out his anger on the logs he is ripping to smithereens.

"I was married once. To Aiden's mother. She left me. Didn't like living on the ranch, said it was too remote, too lonely. When your mom didn't come to me," I rake a hand through my hair, facing my deepest regret, "I figured she'd patched things up with your father or chosen a different path. That she plain didn't want the only life I had to offer."

Zach flings the ax toward the woodpile and collects the pieces he'd split. "What makes you think she wants it now?"

I've asked myself the same question time and again over the past few days, and I still haven't come up with a good answer. "She may not. But I have to at least try. I love your mother, Zach. I have to make her see that." I bend to pick up the splits near my boots. "I'm not letting her go this time, not without a proper fight."

Zach pauses with an armload of splits to look me dead in the eyes. "If it weren't for Michaelyn, you wouldn't stand a chance, because I'd tell her what kind of man you really are." He tosses the wood on the pile and turns to stacking the rest.

"For a man set on spreading the word of God, I'd think you'd be a mite more forgiving."

"I'm a man *of* God. I'm not God." He drops the last of the wood on the pile, stomps away and disappears inside the cabin.

But I do have Michaelyn. And for now, for a few more days anyway, I have Sam. And God willing, Zach doesn't spoil it all.

I MEET Sam halfway down the trail to the creek. She's on her way up, carrying Michaelyn, whose head lolls on her shoulder. "Nap-time," Sam whispers.

I offer to take the sleeping child and Michaelyn wakes and holds her arms out to me. With a surprised grin, Sam hands her over.

Michaelyn wraps around me like a little monkey and nestles

her head on my shoulder. Then she perks up and looks at me. "Will you read to me?"

Sam circles her palm over her heart—which I now recognize as their covert sign language for "please"—and Michaelyn dutifully adds, "Pease?"

I'm almost undone by the tender brown eyes smiling up at me, but I manage to choke out, "I'd love to, sunshine."

In the cabin, I carry Michaelyn to the loft and while Sam changes her from her swimsuit into a pair of pink PJs covered with tiny unicorns, I peruse the small stack of books on the nearby dresser. I pick *Go, Dog! Go!* and show it to Michaelyn. "How about this one?"

She smiles at her mother like I've just magically chosen her favorite. Sam lays her in a travel crib, hands her a stuffed bunny, and steps back. I take a seat on a small stool next to the crib and start reading. Michaelyn lies on her side watching me, and as her eyelids begin to close, her thumb finds its way into her mouth. Sam watches for a minute, her features alight with reverence. Then she turns and disappears down the ladder.

Four pages in, Michaelyn is out, but I'm enjoying the moment so much, I keep reading. I gently remove her thumb from her mouth, and read on to the end, then sit and stare at the sleeping toddler. There's an inexplicable beauty in a child at rest, an innocence, a sense of peace. And I wonder, am I doing the right thing here?

I hear Sam in the kitchen below, the sounds of dishes and pans being pulled from cupboards, the fridge door opening and closing. She's probably getting ready for dinner. I hope she'll invite us to stay again.

At the sound of an engine outside, I stand to peer out the front window and see a white Lexus SUV making its way down the two-track.

Sam's footsteps move toward the door and I hear her suck in a breath. She opens the door as the Lexus pulls to a stop in the small clearing in front of the cabin.

A man steps from the vehicle wearing a dark grey crew neck, black slacks, Italian loafers, and a confident grin. The color of his shirt matches the streaks of grey at his temples. The rest of his head is a thick mane of coal black waves that spill over his collar. The look is a little artsy, very distinguished, and totally Hollywood.

"Ah, *ma chérie*!" the new arrival says as Sam emerges from the cabin. He opens his arms wide, as if expecting her to run into them.

She doesn't.

I'm torn. Part of me feels I should make my presence known, but the part that wants to see how this plays out wins over, and I sit back down, out of sight.

"Stephane." Sam's tone is controlled. "I asked you not to come."

"I had to come, my darling. You know I did."

"Let's take a walk."

"He is here?"

"Yes. Putting Michaelyn down for a nap." I hear footsteps, but only one set.

"I am not dressed for a hike in the woods, my dear."

I suppress a chuckle, picturing him facing that uphill trek in those ridiculous shoes.

"I know. I'm sorry, but please." There's a pause. "We won't go far."

I hear them move off together.

"You look lovely, *ma chérie*. This agrees with you, all this fresh mountain air."

"Thank you."

When I hear them again, their conversation is barely audible, their voices far away and muted. I move closer to the window and peek out. They're sitting on a log halfway up the steep slope, and I'm impressed he made it that far. I eye the floor beneath the window, considering whether to stay and listen, then resign myself not to eavesdrop. With one last heartwarming gaze at Michaelyn, I head downstairs.

I stack wood in the fireplace, and despite the noise, I can still hear them through the cabin's front screen door as their voices rise with tension.

"I flew two thousand miles to see you! Left a whole crew—"

"I asked you not to!"

"I had to see you."

I can't hear Sam's reply, only sense resolve in the restrained tenor of her voice.

"A child." Stephan's voice, while no longer a shout, still carries down the hillside, and this time, with impending defeat. "Michaelyn is—"

"I don't know. Maybe. And, you know me. I wouldn't—"

"Oh, I know well, Samantha, how you feel about *that*."

They haven't slept together? I almost laugh with relief. I look around the cabin for something to do, but the place is spotless. Even Michaelyn's toys are stowed neatly in a basket at the end of the sofa. I should leave, but I don't want to interrupt. I also can't leave Michaelyn alone. I peruse the board games stacked neatly beneath the coffee table, straighten the coasters, all while trying not to listen. I'm eyeing the back deck when I hear Sam's voice again, soft but insistent.

" ... this week ... what's left of it ... to figure things out ... on my way home in a few days."

"I cannot—"

"You don't get to say no. This is—"

"Samantha, I cannot stay! ... full production crew ... over budget and behind schedule ... come with me. Please, *ma chérie*. You must."

I can't make out Sam's response, but there's a question in it.

"I cannot allow you to stay here, alone with this man! While you play at house and, and ... I am no fool."

*"Allow?* This is my life, Stephane! Mine! You don't get to *allow* me anything. And I won't marry you if you don't respect me enough to make my own decisions."

I can't bear it any longer and I head to the back deck, closing the glass slider silently behind me. The boys are fishing in the creek while Emma reads on a blanket beneath the tree. Another five minutes pass in blessed silence, then I hear Sam's and Stephane's voices growing closer. I imagine them walking down the hill together. I whistle to Aiden and motion for him to come. It's beyond time for us to go.

As I head through the cabin, I hear Stephane say, "May I stay here this night? It is late. Or is he—"

"He doesn't sleep here." Sam's voice is terse, indignant even.

"That is good."

"Of course you can stay, but I warn you it's not the accommodations you're used to. You'll be on the couch."

When I step out the front door, hat in hand, Sam gives me an awkward smile, and I'm not sure which of us is more uncomfortable. She introduces us and I shake Stephane's hand. When Aiden appears behind me, she introduces him too.

"Thank you for having us over, Sam," Aiden says.

"It was fun," Sam says, then turns to me. "Thank you for reading to Michaelyn."

"My pleasure." I tip my hat to her, nod to Stephane, and Aiden and I head for the truck.

When I glance in the rearview mirror, only Stephane remains on the front step, and by the look on his face, he knows he won't be the last man standing.

## 27

# LAST MAN STANDING

My first thought when I wake Wednesday morning is Sam with the smarmy Frenchman. I can't push the image from my head. When Aiden asks to spend the day in town at Caleb's, I readily agree, anxious to drive by her cabin to see if Mr. Director's rented Lexus is still there.

It isn't. But neither is her Escalade.

I figure Sam and her kids have gone rafting on the Elk River, or they're making a day of it in Steamboat Springs. Whatever they're doing, I'm disappointed Aiden and I weren't invited. I try to imagine the Frenchman rafting and then decide he'd never. More likely, he'd use Michaelyn as an excuse and talk Sam into whiling away the afternoon in a trendy riverfront café, while Zach and Emma do the whitewater trip on their own. That would explain why both vehicles were gone.

Or, he flew back to his movie set. *Over budget and behind schedule*—right.

As I spend the rest of the day riding fences, fix a few weak sections, and note a few others that need replacing, Sam and Michaelyn are never far from my thoughts. It's late afternoon when I settle into a rocker on my deck, iced tea in hand. I lean back, close my eyes, and relive the last few days with Sam and Michaelyn, wishing I had more.

Images of Sam and Michaelyn with Stephane invade, the three of them together at the hot springs—steamy kisses exchanged while Michaelyn, like a sleeping angel, naps beside them on a blanket in the shade.

*No, wait!* My eyes flash open and I sit up and chuckle. That's my dream, and most of it happened on Monday.

Frustrated, I toss the rest of my iced tea and storm back inside, determined to find something to do, anything to keep my mind off Sam and the Frenchman.

I tidy the cabin and make a grocery list on the off-chance I can have Sam and her family over for dinner before they leave. Then I head into town to shop before I pick up Aiden.

With a slight cringe, I place lettuce in my cart and my phone rings. It's Cody.

"Hey man, thought you'd want to know," he says without preamble. "Dallas Ray just brought in his dog. Mountain lion damage by the looks of it: puncture wounds, lacerations, huge chunk missing from her haunch. I got her stitched up and I think she's gonna make it but—hey, with the Rays being the other side of the valley from the Baker cabin, you might wanna—"

"I'm heading there now." On the way out of the store, I stop at the checkout to let Susan, the cashier, know I'll be back later for my groceries. I jump into my truck and race up the mountain, calling Sam's cell phone.

She doesn't answer. I keep trying. Combing through a tangle of uncertainty, I pull onto the trail to Sam's cabin and minutes later skid to a stop beside her Escalade, the one and only vehicle in front of her cabin.

Dread and relief wash over me in equal measure. I'm glad she's here, and the Frenchman isn't, but I worry that she or the kids might be in danger. I yank my Winchester from the rack behind the seat, check the chamber, and reach under the seat for the box of ammo. I load the gun and drop two more shots into my pocket as I head for the front door.

My knock unanswered, I race around to the back.

The air is still and dry, and it's so quiet I wonder if Sam and the children are at the creek. Rounding the back corner of the cabin, I stop short. Dressed in skinny black yoga pants and a tank top, Sam's exercising on the deck, holding one of her funny poses. From the shine on her face and arms, she's been at it a while.

I clear my throat and lower the rifle. "Afternoon."

"Oh, hey, Mac!" She wipes her upper lip with the back of her hand.

"Where is everyone?" What I really want to know is where Michaelyn is, and I'll admit, I wonder what happened with the Frenchman.

"The kids are exploring the homestead." She tents a hand over her eyes as she looks down the valley in the direction of the dilapidated building. "Stephane left."

I follow her gaze and keep my expression neutral, but in my head, I do a little dance. "Left?"

She rolls up her exercise mat. "He had to get back to his set. Over budget, behind schedule, you know."

My little dance becomes a full-on two-step. "Oh, I'm sorry."

Tucking her mat under her arm, she turns to me with a knowing smile. "No, you're not."

I let my smile shine.

She laughs and sits to pull her boots on.

"Y'all go rafting today?" I take a few steps toward the homestead, my eyes trained on it and the surrounding trees. I can barely make out Zach and Emma bent over amidst the broken-down half-walls that are all that's left of the 150-year-old structure.

"Zach and Emma did." Sam hops down the deck steps to join me. "What's with the gun?"

"Where's Michaelyn?"

"With Zach and Emma."

With a renewed rush of anxiety, I march off down the hill. As I get closer, I slow my stride, hearing Sam huffing to catch up. "Michaelyn!" I call.

Sam touches my shoulder. "Mac, what's wrong?"

I see the little girl's blonde head, all that's visible above the tall meadow grass. She's looking up into a stand of aspen.

"Michaelyn!" Sam calls, concern edging into her voice.

"Mommy, look! A kitty." Michaelyn points into the tree as she turns our way.

I panic, raise the rifle, eye to scope, and frantically search the tree's lower limbs in the crosshairs.

"Mac." The worry in Sam's voice is nothing compared to the dread that fills me as I scan the boughs.

I fire. Sam screams. Michaelyn screeches like a banshee as the mountain lion falls at her feet. She backpedals and falls. I reload and sprint forward. Sam is right behind me.

When we reach Michaelyn, she's lying on her back screaming, eyes closed, hands over her ears. Sam scoops her up, but she goes right on screaming. Zach and Emma come running as I nudge the animal with the Winchester to be sure it's dead.

I turn to Sam and cringe at the terror in her eyes. "I'm sorry. There wasn't time."

She turns away, sheltering Michaelyn's face as Zach and Emma skid to a stop, eyes wide as they stare at the dead animal.

"Oh my God!" Emma covers her mouth with her hands.

Zach nudges it with his boot, then with wide eyes, looks at me.

"It's okay, baby. Shh. It's okay." Sam's voice is shaky as she strokes her daughter's hair, whispers in her ear, and the child's screams diminish to choking sobs.

I place a hand on Michaelyn's shoulder, and she recoils at my touch, cries harder, and nestles into Sam's neck.

Sam glares at me and with a shake of her head, does an about-face and starts toward the cabin.

"Sam, wait. She needs to see it," I say.

"No!" Sam marches away.

"Yes!" I chase after her, step in front of her, blocking her path. "Sam, trust me on this. Let her see it. It'll help her understand."

"Under-stand?" Sam's voice cracks.

Michaelyn raises her head from her mother's shoulder, and I can see a flash of curiosity, bravery even, behind the teary brown eyes.

I gently brush away the tears. "It's okay, sunshine. Nothing's going to hurt you. I promise." Michaelyn cranes to search the ground behind them, but Sam tightens her grip on her daughter, pressing her head against her collarbone. I put an arm around Sam's shoulders and lead them back to where the animal lay.

Michaelyn stares at it, but after one quick look, Sam gasps for breath, raises tear-filled eyes to me and I think she might collapse right there in front of me. I place a steadying hand on the small of her back.

"I'm sorry, Mom." Emma's eyes are filled with tears.

"We shouldn't have let her get so far away from us," Zach adds.

"You know how to use that thing?" I eye the sidearm strapped at Zach's hips.

The young man narrows his eyes at me. "Of course I do."

"Well, don't forget there's a reason you're wearing it."

"How'd you know?" Sam is still shaking, still looks as though her legs might give out any minute, but in her eyes is something akin to relief.

"Cody called. A neighbor just brought in their mauled dog. They live on the other side of the valley." I nod in that direction. "So I came to warn you."

"Mauled—" Sam shakes her head, as though refusing to imagine it. "Cody," she whispers, and I realize she doesn't remember him.

"My cousin. He's a vet, in town."

Zach stares at the wildcat, mouth agape. "That was some shot."

"Had to be." I turn back to Michaelyn. "You okay, sunshine?"

Michaelyn nods and sniffs and peers at the animal. "Can I pet him?"

"No!" Sam cries, backing away. She almost stumbles and I steady her.

Michaelyn's eyes go wide with fear at the terror in her mother's voice.

I rub my chin, considering what needs to be done and how best to handle it. "Why don't you take her inside?" I say to Sam. "I'll be right in. Emma, go with them."

Emma follows Sam and Michaelyn to the cabin while Zach hangs back. "Need a hand?" he asks.

"You bet," I say, grateful for the offer. It's a large cat, a male by the looks of it. I nudge the animal with the rifle one more time. It was an excellent shot, straight through the vitals.

We each take an end, haul it to the front of the cabin, and toss it into the bed of my truck. I'll have to take it in, report it. I grab a narrow piece of firewood from the pile, spread the animal's jaw, and insert it.

"What's that for?" Zach asks.

"Keeps the jaw from locking shut. The DOW will want a tooth sample to determine the animal's age. They keep a steady pulse on the wildlife 'round these parts."

When we enter the cabin, Michaelyn is having a snack at the table, her sister at her side. Emma eyes her mother with a worried expression. Sam sits on the couch, elbows on her knees, a tissue in her hand. She doesn't move as I approach.

"We're leaving," she says in a voice that's resolute.

*No!* "Sam—" I'm at a loss for words, imagining her terror—I can't even let *my* mind go there.

Taking her hand, I pull Sam outside to talk. I lead her away from the open windows then turn to her and take a deep breath, trying my best to find calm. "You have to teach her about wild animals, Sam. You can't bring a child to the mountains and leave her unattended. Do you realize how close she came to getting killed today?"

She stares at the ground. A sob escapes and when she looks up at me, her eyes are filled with fury. "Of course I do! She was with Zach and Emma, and they're responsible."

"They weren't today! She was a good fifty yards from them. Alone. There are birds that have picked up bigger than her. Can you imagine watching her get carried—"

"Stop it!" With both hands, Sam pushes against my chest, causing me to stumble backward. Fresh tears course down her cheeks as she glares at me. "Just stop!"

I soften my tone. "It's scary, I know, but it's the way it is here. As her mother, you have to teach her, teach them all."

Sam backpedals, covers her face with her hands.

My heart goes out to her. As terrified as I'd been, it had to have been so much worse for her. "I'm sorry. Oh, darlin', come here." I pull her into my arms, and she sobs against my shirt. "Shh. It's okay. She's fine."

Sam sniffles and pulls away, wiping her face with the heels of her hands. "No. You're right. You're absolutely right. It's my fault." She collapses onto a downed tree.

I hand her my handkerchief, which elicits a smile.

"You carry a handkerchief?" She manages a small giggle through her tears.

I grin, fondly remembering a past conversation. "All cowboys do."

She dries her tears and looks at me with those sky-blue eyes, and my breath catches. "Thank you."

"Anytime." While she collects herself, my thoughts return to that whiskey-soaked night so long ago. One shot, straight to my heart, and I was a goner. If only this night could end as that one did.

"Tell you what, why don't y'all come up to the ranch tomorrow, spend the day? We'll teach Michaelyn together. We've got quite a few critters for her to see. Course, the dangerous ones are stuffed, either on Aiden's bed or wall-mounted."

Sam sucks in a steadying breath that shakes on its way out. "Okay." She glances back at the cabin. "Oh," she says, rubbing her forehead. "I almost forgot. Tomorrow's our last day, and Emma and Zach wanted to take the ATV up to the forest."

"The Routt National Forest? They're not planning to go alone, are they?" I don't mention that her ATV that's been stored beneath the back of the cabin for nearly four years isn't likely to start, let alone make it more than a stone's throw without breaking down.

Sam looks away, biting her lip.

"Sam, there are literally millions of acres of trails up there."

"I know it's big."

"It's *really* big, darlin'. But hey, The Homestead butts up against the Routt and we've got a few ATVs. They can leave from there, with Aiden, who knows his way around. And you and I and Michaelyn can spend the day with the animals."

She agrees and as I walk her back to the cabin, I think ahead to tomorrow. I'll have Sam and Michaelyn all to myself.

For one more day.

It'll have to be enough.

# 28

# AT THE RANCH

Thursday morning, I'm in the kitchen clearing away breakfast dishes when I hear a vehicle cross the cattle guard at the ranch entrance. I glance out the front window as Sam's Escalade creeps up the gravel drive, kicking up dust. It hasn't rained in weeks and the earth's parched for moisture.

Zach, riding shotgun, points to my truck, which is parked in front of my cabin. Across the way, I see Isabelle sneak a peek from an upstairs window of the big house. She's almost as excited to see Sam as I am. I think she has high hopes for a bit of female companionship.

Aiden comes running from the barn.

From the back seat Emma seems to be looking everywhere, her face shining with awe, and I stand a little taller. It takes a lot of work to keep it all going: the buildings in good repair, the fences straight and true, the animal dung and broken-down machinery stored out of sight or hauled away.

Sam parks beside my truck as I hang the dish towel on a peg beside the sink.

Michaelyn points toward the paddock beside the barn where several horses graze near the split rail fence.

Sam stares straight ahead at my modest little log home, The Cabin, we call it.

I walk out to the front porch to greet them, but Sam sits behind the wheel, her expression reverent, like she's experiencing a flashback.

She slides out and stands behind the open door, and her smile reminds me of the night we spent together, tender and inevitable. "It's like a Christmas platter I have," she says, but as quickly as her euphoria arrived, it evaporates like a raindrop in the desert.

Emma has unbuckled Michaelyn, who comes running now from the other side of the vehicle. "Mr. Mac!" She throws herself at me.

I scoop her up and wrap her in a bear hug and kiss her cheek, a ritual for us now. When I straighten, Sam's still standing behind the open door, staring straight ahead. She seems distant, as though struggling to capture a memory.

"Sam?" I step forward. "Something familiar?"

Slowly, Sam brings her eyes around to focus on me, and the sunshine returns to her broken smile. "Yeah."

"That's good." My grin stretches my cheeks beyond their measure. "Real good."

I turn to Michaelyn. "Now, where did those big kids run off to?"

Michaelyn flings a hand toward the barn, where Emma, Zach, and Aiden are coming out, helmets in hand.

With Michaelyn in one arm, I take Sam's hand, and we head toward the barn.

A Border collie bounds forward to greet us before being called back by Aiden. "Sam, come!" Obediently, the dog returns to Aiden's side, where he stands wagging his tail.

Sam looks sideways at me. "You have a dog named Sam?"

"Aiden's dog. Named after someone he really took a shine to," I say with a chuckle.

Sam laughs and shakes her head.

We meet the kids in front of the barn, where they're already strapping on helmets, each standing beside an ATV. I eye the pistol strapped to Zach's hip and catch his gaze. I nod and he knows it's a reminder of what happened yesterday. I review the bare necessities with Aiden—plenty of water, PBJs for lunch, his compass, matches, a pocketknife, and after words of caution directed to all three of them, they race off in a three-pronged cloud of dust down the drive.

We watch them disappear around a bend, the dust settling and the smell of exhaust lingering in their wake. "You sure they won't get lost?" Sam looks at me, her brows furrowed.

"They'll be fine. Aiden's been up there dozens of times. He knows not to go too far in. Come on, we've got the entire afternoon, you and me and this sweet baby girl. What would you like to do first?"

Michaelyn perks up. "Horsies!"

Sam gives her a hand signal—open palm circled over the heart—and Michaelyn quickly adds, "Pease."

"Well, then little darlin', let's start the grand tour in the barn, shall we?" When she nods excitedly, I reclaim Sam's hand and we continue toward the barn.

We visit a few horses with foals and a couple of cows with young calves, which Michaelyn wants to pet. From there, we make our way to the paddock, where there are more horses, and beyond in the grassland, a number of the Homestead's cattle idly graze. I saddle up Aiden's pony and lead Michaelyn around the corral while Sam looks on from atop the fence.

There's a sadness in Sam's eyes, and I wonder if she too is thinking ahead to tomorrow's goodbyes. I give her a reassuring smile but find it near impossible to mask my own foreboding. We're running out of time. And I think we both know it.

In the big house, I introduce Sam and Michaelyn to Isabelle, who's laid out a kid-friendly luncheon of chicken tenders and grilled cheese sandwiches for us. Michaelyn's a good eater, but Sam barely touches her food. Maybe her stomach is as tied in knots as mine is.

After lunch, I take them through the great room and Isaac's study, which used to be our father's and before that our grandfather's. Between the two, there must be over fifty different species wall-mounted or stuffed. I name and describe each one of them for Michaelyn: elk, moose, pronghorn, mountain lion, mountain goat, lynx, a bear skin, beaver and several other smaller game animals and birds.

As we leave the big house and head back to my place, Sam asks why Aiden and I don't live there with Isaac and Isabelle, and I explain that I like my privacy. Actually, it was my wife, Elizabeth, who wanted to have our own place, and after she moved back to Houston, the idea of leaving the cabin empty just didn't sit right.

I grab animal books from Aiden's room and sit on the sofa. Michaelyn crawls onto my lap and Sam sits beside us. We start with a book about tracks and scat and she thinks it's funny that you can tell the animal by its poo. Toward the end of book two, I see Michaelyn's perfect little bow-shaped mouth stretch into a wide yawn, and my insides shimmy. After a light snack, it'll be naptime. I pray she will be able to fall asleep in Aiden's room. I sorely need time alone with Sam before the older kids get back.

In the kitchen, I pour us all water, while Sam slices a banana and places it on a plate with a handful of almond crackers for Michaelyn's snack. We sit at the kitchen table, and my mind goes back to the morning I'd amended Sam's divorce settlement for her.

I'd come downstairs from my office to find her sitting at the table with Aiden, who was five at the time. Seeing Michaelyn and Sam sitting in the exact same spots now gives me the same delicious sense of feels-so-right.

Minutes later, Sam returns to the kitchen, having put Michaelyn down for her nap. "She's out."

Drawn to Aiden's room, I peek through the cracked door to see our precious little girl sound asleep, Aiden's stuffed pony clutched in her arms. And the fear crashes into me, sudden and treacherous, so sharp it steals my breath, my strength, my resolve. Will this be the last time I'll see her like this? First Aiden and now Michaelyn, it's more than a man can bear.

I grab my guitar from the living room and join Sam on the back deck. Elbows on the railing, she's gazing out over the vineyard. She turns around, her face aglow with happiness.

"Come sit with me." I lower myself into a rocking chair and pat the one beside me.

Sam eases into the rocker and eyes the instrument. "You play guitar?"

"A little." I strum it a few times, making sure it's still tuned. Satisfied, I turn my chair to face hers, and she smiles at me.

I play the song from the poem she'd written, and though I'd practiced it at least ten times the night before, I choke on the words, the memories they invoke washing over me like a tsunami, drowning any semblance of control I may have held over my emotions.

I stop and stare at my hands. Like my voice, they, too, have betrayed me, unable to play. "I'm sorry. I thought I could do this."

"It's okay." She touches my arm. "Mac, it's beautiful."

I breathe, breathe again, and raise my eyes to meet hers. "It's yours." I strum a few chords. "You wrote it for me."

With a perplexed smile, she says, "I did?"

I nod and muster the courage to try it again. And this time, the song flows straight from my heart, through my voice, my hands. And my music, my words—her words—find their home again in her heart.

"Mac—"

"I know you don't remember, and it's okay. But I wanted you to have it to take with you." I set the guitar aside and turn back to her with a wink. "A new memory."

"You've given me a lot of new memories this week."

My heart smiles. It's a start. I only hope this time I've given her enough to last.

Zach, Emma, and Aiden return on the ATVs, a bevy of excitement as they each tumble over one another to describe their excursion into the Routt National Forest, over a million acres of nothing but wilderness. They're covered in trail dust and mud; the only clean skin is the white circles around their eyes where their goggles had been. They'd come across a whole herd of elk on a hillside, seen moose and pronghorn and a black bear. They'd taken selfies in California Park, with the snowy peaks of the Continental Divide in the background. They made it up to Bears Ears and saw the start of the Elk River which they'd rafted the day before. On the way back, Aiden had shown them an abandoned gold mine, and they'd stopped to explore. "But we didn't go inside," Aiden assures me.

Over dinner, they're still gushing over the adventures of the week, the fly-fishing, kayaking, swimming and four-wheeling, and they all agree it was one of the best trips ever. Sam and the twins thank us more than once.

For me, it's been the single best week of my life, having reconnected with Sam, and I'm as sure as ever that she's meant for me, for us. I lean back in my seat, and for several long minutes I watch Sam and the children interact, and again I sense that everything is exactly as it's meant to be, not only for the moment but for all time.

I've been living a monotone life for far too long. This, here and now, is the full-color picture of the family I've always wanted. I imagine the six of us years down the road, Zach and Emma bringing their mates to the table, Aiden and Michaelyn grown, becoming teenagers, then young adults themselves. This is what family means. And this is *my* family.

After dinner, while Aiden takes Michaelyn and the twins to see a new litter of kittens in the hayloft, Sam and I retreat to the deck to watch the moon rise over the vineyard. I pour us each a glass of wine and set the bottle aside.

Sam studies the label. "Homestead Creek? This is your wine?"

I nod and raise my glass. "Like it?"

"It's wonderful."

"It's young, but it has promise."

She takes another sip and eyes me over the rim.

I set our glasses aside, stand and hold out my hand. "Dance

with me?" It isn't quite the full moon I'd hoped for, but between the lights from within and the stars above, it's plenty.

Sam takes my hand, and I pull her in, slowly moving to the faint melody left playing in the cabin. The subtle scent of her hair, like jasmine, drifts up to tease my nostrils, while the cool evening air draws me to seek her warmth, and suddenly, the thought of her leaving in the morning hits me like an avalanche, bowling over my control, leaving in its wake an icy panic.

Can she feel my heart racing in my chest? Does she have any idea how much I need her, how much I love her, how long I've waited for her return?

"Sam." The sound of my voice sounds foreign to me, deep, and laden with anxiety.

She raises her face to me, a question there.

"I ..." *Tell her! She knows. I've already told her. Tell her again! If I don't, I know I'll regret it, later tonight, tomorrow, and for the rest of my life. It can make a difference this time. Tell her!*

I swallow and regroup before trying again. When I cup her face in my hands, my words from years ago echo in my head. "I love you, Sam. I've loved you from the start and every day since. And I will always love you, whether you remember me or not."

The front screen door slams once, twice, three times. The kids are back.

I drop my hands to my sides, and Sam steps back, takes a shaky breath. "We're out here," she calls.

I find my glass of wine. Despite my shaking hand, I manage a good long drink.

Sam kneels and holds out her arms and Michaelyn stumbles into them. I watch and listen as she describes the kittens, how "coot" they are. Sam sinks back into the rocker, Michaelyn on her lap. I settle myself into the rocker next to Sam's and move her wine glass to a small table on the opposite side so it doesn't get knocked over.

"Do we have time for a game of cards?" Zach asks from the back door.

Sam looks at me and I nod. Beside me, Michaelyn snuggles into Sam's chest, starting to slow down. "Sure, but make it a quick one," Sam says.

Michaelyn raises her head to look at her mother. "Can we have a sleepover, Mommy?"

I grin. Sounds like a nice idea to me, but I know Sam's answer before she says it.

"Not tonight, baby-girl."

"I like it here, Mommy."

Sam smooths Michaelyn's hair away from her face. "Me too, sweetie." When she gazes at me over the top of the child's head, there's a warmth in her eyes.

A gush of happiness and something like triumph washes over me. Sam shoots me a knowing smile, leans her head back, and rocks her little girl to sleep while I look on. Is she considering staying? My heart feels huge, swollen beyond its limits by my love for this woman and her child, my child.

Before long. Michaelyn's tired little eyes close. A few minutes pass, and I offer to take her to Aiden's room.

She wakes when I lift her from her mother's lap, and when she sees it's me, she snuggles against my shoulder. I tuck her into Aiden's bed, then sit on the edge and gently tug her thumb from her mouth. I watch her sleep for a minute—or maybe it's five—while my mind races over the challenge ahead of me.

I bend to kiss my little girl's cheek one last time. "Love you, sunshine," I whisper.

A small, "Oh," comes from behind me, and I turn to find Sam standing in the doorway.

As I pull the door closed, I hear Michaelyn's squeaky little voice, barely audible from the brink of slumber, "Love you more."

It stops me in my tracks. I hadn't dreamt it!

Sam had said those same three words, exactly like that, our last night together at her place. Michaelyn had to have learned it from her mother. Or did all children use that phrase? No, Sam did love me. Once.

I turn to Sam, searching for a hint of recognition. Did she hear it? Does she remember it too?

Sam nods toward the closed door. "She'll have a hard time of it tomorrow."

My breath hitches in my throat. "She's not the only one."

## 29

# ALL FOR YOU

At the dining table, the three older children play cards. I take Sam's hand and lead her across the hallway. "I want to show you something."

We walk through my bedroom to the master bath, and I push the door wide and step aside to let her enter first. She gapes wide-eyed, taking it all in—the oversized footed tub set before a bank of floor-to-ceiling bay windows, the tile work, the matching vintage vanities and mirrors, the view beyond of the moonlit vineyard sloping down the hillside.

"You told me you only missed two things that summer, music and bubble baths," I say.

She whirls around and catches my gaze, and I see her mind putting pieces together. A spark of hope inside of me burns brighter.

She turns to look again at the bathroom. "You did all this for me?"

I pull her into my arms, her back against my chest, my lips to her ear. "I wanted you to be happy here."

"Oh, Mac."

I can see her profile in one of the mirrors, and I watch her eyes caress every loving detail. It's a beautiful room, I have to admit, similar to the one she'd enjoyed so much in her big house on the lake, but this one holds a rustic warmth and agelessness that's all Colorado mountain cabin. I know she doesn't live in that lake home anymore, and I wonder if she misses it.

She turns in my arms and smiles up at me, places a hand on my cheek, and kisses me. It's soft and tender, tentative at first then grows bolder as she threads her hands into my hair and kisses me again and again.

Her tongue finds mine and I'm lost. I don't want her to stop. Ever.

When she pulls away, she's breathless and trembling in my arms.

I'm on fire, thrilled by the way her body speaks to me. "Stay with me, Sam."

Time stands still as she stares back at me, her gaze caressing every inch of my face, as if searching, or remembering. Or falling again. With every ounce of my being, I will her to say the three words I long to hear, the words that will bind her to me forever.

She stares at my chest and places a palm there. "Zach and Emma—"

"We can put them on a plane."

"Stephane."

"You don't love him."

She steps back, eyes lowered. "Mac, I—"

"Sam, please." I take her hands in mine, hold them against my shirt. When I speak, my voice sounds tense, hoarse, desperate, but I can't help it. "I need more time."

Her eyes narrow. "More time?"

"For you to fall in love with me again."

"Oh, Mac." Her face darkens with a sadness I don't understand. "I can't do this." She pulls free and rushes past me.

I sit on the edge of the tub, exhale a long centering breath, and close my eyes. Elbows on knees, my head falls into my hands. There is still time, I tell myself, but it is fleeting, faster now with every heartbeat.

*Oh, please, God, please! Help me to find the words to make her stay this time. I can't lose her again.*

I square my shoulders. At the sink, I splash cold water on my face, hang the towel back on the ring, straighten my hair, and turn toward the tub.

Did she recognize it? It's not exactly like the one she had in her lake house, but it's close. I picture us lounging there the morning after our first night together, her back to my chest, my legs straddling her, suds up to our necks. Who knew bubbles actually served a purpose, kept the water warm for hours?

I run a hand along the white porcelain and remember the snowy November day Cody had helped me install it.

We'd trudged through the freshly fallen snow to the end of the front porch, where I pulled a tarp off the massive cardboard box on a wooden pallet. I took out my pocketknife and slit open the top, folded back the flaps, and pulled out the packing material.

Cody leaned over my shoulder. "Holy cow, cuz'! Now that's a bathtub."

It was like Sam's, except on feet. Placed in front of the new bay window, it would have a spectacular view of the valley and the mountains beyond. I could hardly wait to show it to her, enjoy it with her.

Normally, Cody would have given me a hard time about such a frivolous expenditure, but my cousin knew me well and understood about the tub. I had shared enough of the details of my weekend in Michigan that Cody knew the renovated bathroom I had been working on since I'd returned in mid-September was something special I'd wanted to do for Sam, for when she returned.

The tub set in place, I stood back to admire it. "She's going to love it."

"Is she coming soon?"

"God willing," I say.

"Seems to me you leave a whole lot up to 'God's willing'." His voice rang with doubt. I knew my cousin didn't rely on his faith the way I did. Cody's way was to take things into his own hands.

"Worst case," I said, "She might be here late spring or so."

Cody shook his head. "Whew! You really going to wait that long?"

"She said she needed time to think things through. When she comes, it'll be for the right reasons."

"You're a patient man, cuz'."

"Some things are worth waiting for."

But I'd waited long enough. Maybe too long.

Heading through the bedroom, I catch sight of her manuscript sitting on my nightstand—my last card.

I find her on the back deck, glass of wine in hand, rocking. "Want to take a walk?"

She raises her gaze to me. "Is it safe?"

I extend a hand. "You'll always be safe with me, darlin'."

As we stroll through the rows of the vineyard, I parlay all I'd learned about viniculture, the art of growing grapes for wine-making, how I'd chosen the vines I'd planted, and my modest success with our first bottling the year before.

"One of my favorite movies is about a workaholic stockbroker turned country vintner," she says.

She's telling me about the movie we'd watched that rainy afternoon at her place, snuggled together on a pile of quilts before her fireplace. I smile as my gaze traverses the long, even rows of vines I'd so carefully tended for the past three years, while I'd waited for her return, anticipating this very moment.

"He inherits a vineyard—" She must read my face because she stops and looks at me. "You know that."

I grin and give her a side-eye.

"Oh, Mac. This too?"

I turn to face her and take both of her hands. "There's nothing I wouldn't do for you."

"I don't know what to say."

"Say you'll stay."

When she falls silent again, we walk on. I drape my arm around her shoulders, and she leans into me. My heart warms.

We return to the house, watch the kid's card game for a few minutes, and discover Aiden is once again dominating, much to Zach and Emma's chagrin. Then Sam peeks in on Michaelyn.

When she closes Aiden's bedroom door, I take her hand and lead her to my room.

Flicking on the light, I walk straight to the nightstand and pick up the manuscript. I say a quick, silent prayer—*Oh, please, God, please*—then turn and hold it out to her.

"What's this?"

"It's your story, the one you wrote that summer."

She sits, almost collapses, onto the edge of the bed, and gazes at the manuscript in her hands, the title *Broken Fences* in large bold font, with her name just below it. Her mouth falls open as she raises her eyes to me. "I wrote this?"

I nod, encouraged by her excitement. "It's a beautiful story. You should read it." I say. "Before you leave."

She thumbs through the pages, two hundred and two to be exact. *No way* is painted clearly on her face.

"Please, Sam." I can't help the agony in my voice but I'm fighting for my life here, for our life together.

The baleful silence of the bedroom disappears in the peals of laughter coming from the card game in the other room.

"Okay." She stares down at the manuscript.

Now, if only it's enough to spark her memory. Or make her fall all over again.

She stands. "I suppose we should go then."

While I'm disappointed to see her leave, I'm encouraged too, knowing she's going to read her story. Our story. I drag in a breath. "Can I see you tomorrow?"

"We're leaving mid-afternoon—"

"I'll come by early, make breakfast for y'all." I need one more private conversation after she reads her story. "Sound good?"

She nods. "We have little food left in the cabin."

"I'll bring it."

"That'll be nice." She takes a deep breath, and I wait, hoping she'll tell me how she feels, give me something to hold on to. "Thank you for the time you've spent with us, for the memories you've given us, for being the man you are."

My throat is suddenly so dry I'm certain my voice has turned to dust. "I love you, Sam."

She tilts her head and studies me. Her smile is soft and sweet and speaks volumes. "Still?"

"Always." I trail a fingertip across her bottom lip. "I never stopped loving you. Hold onto that, okay?"

She nods slowly as she stares back at me, and I wonder if she has any idea what she'd done to me that summer. Do I dare tell her how many nights I've lain awake dreaming of her coming to me, how many times I've stood on the North Ridge looking out over the valley—her valley, the creek, the cottonwood, reliving every cherished moment we spent together?

Seconds drain away like grains in an hourglass, as my mind shudders at the last three and half years of longing, waiting, wanting. And now, here she is, in my life, in my arms, in my bedroom where I'd dreamed of her so many times.

I cup her face in my hands and lean in to place a kiss gently upon her lips. I fully intend to keep it light, a short good night kiss, nothing more, but when I taste her sweet, wet warmth, my whole heart and soul awakens to remembered moments, the passions of the past. As her body surrenders, melting into mine, my kisses grow intense, searching, demanding, yearning to rekindle what they'd once known.

On the verge of losing myself completely, I draw back, search her eyes. The fire is there again, and my insides shimmy with a hint of satisfaction. She can't possibly spend the night, but despite the knowing, I have a hankering to ask, anyway. With a wild, almost animal desire, I long to hear her need for me voiced so sweetly, like she'd done more than once that lost September weekend.

My heart thunders, and I wonder for an instant if she can hear it, feel it beneath her palms resting against my chest. I focus to slow my breathing as I search for calm.

"Promise me you'll read it? Tonight?"

She gazes up, but doesn't speak.

"Please, Sam."

"I promise."

I EASE Aiden's door closed after tucking him into bed. In the living room, Avery, Isabelle's daughter, sits cross-legged on the sofa with a computer on her lap.

"Finals?" I ask.

She glances up, tucks a long strand of straight black hair behind one ear. "You know it."

"Thanks for coming over on such short notice." I grab my Carhartt from the peg by the door and slip it on. "I won't be long."

"Sure, Mac. Anytime."

Long after I return from my ride to the North Ridge, Aiden's questions still haunt me. *Think she'll stay this time? When does our will get to matter?* I peek in on him and my heart aches. I want more than anything to hang my—our—future on God's will, but I can't seem to manage it. Not tonight. *Don't worry, Dad. Love never forgets.* I pray he's right.

Hours later, sleep eludes me. I lay in bed, arms behind my head, staring at the ceiling. I imagine Sam curled up on her couch, reading her story—our story—and I wonder if she'll recognize any of it: the characters, the scenes, the events. The emotion, desire, passion.

Her story, infused with obvious and heartfelt affection for the hero—for me—had touched me deeply. Even if she doesn't remember, she'll fall in love with the man she'd written about.

My entire body tingles with delight as I recall her portrayal of our afternoon beneath the cottonwood. God, how I long to make that scene a reality.

I pray again for the one thing that dominates my life—recapturing her love. With a torment that threatens to rip me in two, I look forward to seeing her in the morning. I'll have one more chance to convince her to stay. Or tell her good-bye.

I glance at the clock on the nightstand. The digits glow bright red, two twenty-eight. I'll be dog-tired tomorrow. I recall the last time I'd pulled an all-nighter, the time I'd driven straight through to Michigan, thirteen hundred and fifty-two miles, and my mind wanders back to relive one of the best weekends of my life, the precious few days when she'd been mine.

The morning after I'd arrived, I'd awakened in a strange bed, rolled over, and reached for Sam, but found only emptiness beside me. *Dang-it-all!* I hadn't dreamed it, had I? Again?

I bolted upright and discovered I was indeed in Sam's bedroom. Relieved, I fell back to the pillows and stretched, lingering blissfully with the memory of the night before. When I glanced at the clock beside the bed, it showed 9:15, so I rousted myself up, showered and brushed my teeth in the on-suite bathroom, and wandered out to find Sam on the covered deck. Wearing my red flannel shirt, she sat nestled in a blanket on a double chaise, staring out through the rain at the lake, an empty coffee mug on the table beside her. She looked content, happy, relaxed.

"Good morning, sunshine." I settled beside her and when I pulled her into my arms, she nestled into me, soft and warm.

"Morning, cowboy. Would you like coffee? I can heat some up for you." Her eyes playfully teased me for sleeping so late.

"Hey!" I laughed, indignant. "First of all, it's not even sunup in the mountains, and second, I drove straight through to get here last night."

She looked sideways at me, suddenly serious. "You did?"

I tapped her chin. "I did. Something told me you might need me."

She placed a hand on my cheek, rough with two days' growth. "I did." The look she gave me in that moment held a tenderness I'll never forget. "I'd love to make you some fresh coffee." She started to get up, but I pulled her back down for a deep, leisurely kiss, then watched with my insides spinning, as she disappeared into the house on lean bare legs.

Whew! She looked good in my shirt. I wondered if she wore anything underneath it and looked forward to finding out. I stepped to the railing to look out at the water. It was a beautiful setting, a large lake that disappeared around peninsulas in both directions, dense woods directly across with a few estate homes tucked in.

I wondered what Sam's life had been like when her children were little, when the house had been a home, filled with the joy of a happy family.

And I wondered what her life was like now. Beyond telling me about her cheating husband and the job she hated, she'd told me very little about her life in Michigan. We always talked about my life, ranching, and the mountains.

I made a mental note to make this trip all about her and her life. And getting her into my life.

"How do you take it?" she called from the door.

"Barefoot."

She giggled. "Barefoot? Is that cowboy parlance for something?"

I chuckled. "Black."

She returned a minute later and handed me a steaming mug. "Thank you." I raised it to my lips for a cautious sip. "Mmm."

"Would you like your solitude now?" she asked, still teasing about how I loved mornings.

I laughed and set the mug aside. "No way." I pulled her onto my lap on the chaise and wrapped my arms around her. "I was looking forward to waking up and snuggling with you, though." Then, I whispered against her ear, "I had a dream, Sam. For just one night, I held the stars in my arms. And I loved her."

A happy moan escaped her, and she turned to straddle me, and what breath I had left was captured by the deep kiss that followed as I closed my eyes, let my hand caress down her back and slip beneath the shirt to feel her nakedness.

Oh, God, what I wouldn't give to relive that entire weekend, and stay just one more day.

# 30

# BELOVED AND CHERISHED

"No," Sam whispers. "Oh, God, no! It can't end that way." The words blur and a tear falls to the page. She swipes it away, then notices other similar stains. His?

She hurls the manuscript aside and rubs her eyes, haunted by the story—that she'd written. Was it their story?

Her heart aches for the characters she'd created, and she wonders how much of it is true and how much is pure fiction: drinking whiskey, bringing down an eagle, and writing a poem for him. And oh, the afternoon in the meadow—was that really her?

She smiles, mostly pleased with the woman she may have been. The woman she always wanted to be—daring, brave, bold.

And what about Mac—Micah? Did she love him once? If so, how could she have left such a wonderful man who was so obviously in love with her for a husband who didn't want her?

Mac waited three and half years for her, but why didn't he at least call?

Exhausted, her head falls back against the couch and she yawns. She has no idea what time it is, but it's still dark outside; she's been reading for hours. She should try to get some sleep. It's already Friday and they have a long day ahead of them.

Instead, she goes to the slider, parts the drapes, and stares out over the valley, beautifully lit by a half-moon hanging low in the sky. The stream below is barely a glimmer, the cottonwood beside it a towering shadow.

Did they really make love beside the stream, in the middle of a wide-open valley? Her cheeks grow hot and she smiles at the thought, then glances back to the pages scattered across the floor.

*Michaelyn!*

When she picks up the manuscript, an envelope drops between her feet. She stoops to retrieve it and holds it to the light. Sent to her old house, it has NO LONGER AT THIS ADDRESS stamped across the front in broken black ink. The return address reads M. Daniel McKennon, Attorney at Law, Homestead Ranch, Providence, CO.

M for Micah.

She sinks back onto the couch and stares at the envelope. It's thick, at least four of five pages, and postmarked three months after her divorce was final. She holds a breath as she uses a fingernail to slice it open.

*Dear Sam,*

*I hope this letter finds you well and above all else, happy.*

*It's hard to believe it's been months since we said goodbye. I can still taste the sweetness of that last kiss as it lingers on my lips, haunts my days, fills my nights. In my memory it definitely said goodbye.*

*But I didn't think it said forever.*

*I realize now that perhaps I asked too much of you. It was incredibly selfish of me to expect you to give up all that's familiar to you —your career, your home, your friends—with no thought to what that would mean to you. I didn't even offer the promise of a future, no commitment, only a heartfelt "I love you" as though that should be enough.*

*I took Aiden to the airport this afternoon—another heart wrenching goodbye. They never get easier. Now, I find myself sitting beneath the cottonwood at the creek behind your cabin where I come often. I feel you here. When I close my eyes, I imagine you here beside me, your long blonde hair blowing gently in the breeze, and you smile when I turn your way.*

*You said I helped you see your life more clearly; that the things I'd shown you that summer made you wonder what else you hadn't left room for. I want you to know, you did that for me too. All my life I've lived on this ranch, loved the mountains, the land, the woods, the animals; all the while so certain this was where I was meant to be.*

*But until you came, I never stopped to consider what I might be missing. I've blindly followed this path set before me by my heritage, my boots firmly set upon it by my forefathers, a trail blazed by my ancestors over a century ago.*

*But it's a lonely road I walk. And it's not enough. I want love. I want you. Without you, this life holds nothing. Without you here to share it, there's no satisfaction in working the ranch, no joy in the beauty of the land, no wonder in the magic of the stars.*

*There's nowhere I look that doesn't hurt. Even the places I didn't show you haunt me because I wish I had: the waterfall up Epley's Pass, the herds of wild horses on the Ute Reservations, the lowland meadows bright with mule's ears and lupines. I come to the North Ridge at night and look out over Moonglow Meadow, and I feel only a desolate emptiness, an intense longing that brings me to my knees, and I cry out your name and wonder how much more I can bear.*

*I once told you to take a good hard look at your life, and if it wasn't all that you hoped for, then it was time to stop, turn around, choose another path, one that leads to what's most important in life. Well, it's time I took my own advice. I'm choosing a different path, one I hope will lead me back to you.*

*I love you, Sam, and I know you loved me too. I knew even before you said the words our last night together. I felt it in your touch, saw it in your eyes, heard it in your voice. God brought you to my mountain. We're meant to be together. And I know I can make you happy. We can build a life together, wherever that needs to be. I only know I have to walk this path of life with you at my side, beloved and cherished as fate intended.*

*You can have my office upstairs to write. It'll look out over our vineyard one day. Or if you'd rather live in town, I could build you a fine home in Providence. My Uncle Will has been hankering for years for me to take over his law practice.*

*I want to give you what you need, whatever that might be. I love you, Sam, more than I ever thought humanly possible, and I can't imagine living the rest of my life without you in it.*

*Come to me, Sam. With every word I write, every whisper of breath, I pray that you'll come to me. Forgive me, Sam, for needing you like I do, but you have to know, I will never stop loving you.*

*Still, always, forever,*

*Yours,*<br>*Micah*

*P.S. I loved your story—our story—until I got to the end. We need a better ending, so I took the liberty of writing it. I hope you like it. Make it yours, Sam. Make it ours.*

Sam slips the envelope and its contents behind the last page of the manuscript and hugs the bundle to her chest, leans her head back against the couch, and stares at the rafters as she fends off sleep.

A million thoughts spin in her head like an out-of-control merry-go-round that she can't jump off, and her heart races as a familiar panic sets in. She takes a deep breath, then another one.

*You know what to do* she tells herself. *Breathe, just breathe.*

She straightens, stares out the slider at the moon, and pictures herself sitting beneath the cottonwood, the creek trickling by. She can almost hear the water gurgle and splash as it meanders down the gentle slope of the valley floor, as the wind whispers through the branches above and the meadow grasses wave gently, peacefully, calmly around her.

With another purposeful inhale, she's focused, ready to think, determined to figure out what to do. She sets the manuscript on the coffee table and tidies the pages into a neat pile. *Oh, Mac.* His ending wasn't exactly a resonant happily-ever-after, but ...

She smiles at his words, *Make it yours, Sam. Make it ours.*

*Oh, if only.* If only she remembered. If only he'd called or come back for her. Is it fair to blame him for that? After all, she was the one who left first, to save a marriage to a man who didn't want her.

Sam closes her eyes and imagines a future with Mac—a good man, thoughtful with a poet's soul, his physical strength matched only by the core of his moral fiber. And he's still in love with her.

Is it too late for them? They have a daughter, the product of their love, and Michaelyn deserves to know her father. Has he really been waiting for her all this time? Or did he give up on her? Like Brent did.

And what about Stephane? He's a good man too.

Whatever she decides, someone will be hurt.

## 31

# BREAKFAST

When Aiden and I arrive in the morning, our arms laden with foodstuffs, Emma greets us at the door. "Mom just left for a walk," she says.

We're no sooner through the door than Michaelyn jumps into my arms, and I give her a bear hug and kiss her cheek. Carrying her, I walk to the glass slider and see Sam nearing the creek's edge. She's wearing my red flannel, the one I'd left at her place, and I take that as a good sign.

Anxious to speak with her alone, I set Michaelyn on her feet. "Aiden brought something for you." I toss the sausage into a skillet and ask Emma to keep an eye on it while I go fetch her mom.

As I near the trails end, I consciously slow my pace to hide my apprehension. My heart is in my throat as I wonder if the story spurred a memory. I whisper a silent prayer, the one I've prayed so many times—*God, please bring her back to me.*

"Morning, sunshine!" I call as I approach.

She's sitting beneath the cottonwood, her knees pulled up, arms wrapped around them. At the sound of my voice, she shoots me a smile. "Morning, cowboy."

I sit beside her and follow her gaze out over the creek. As

nervous as a pimply-faced teenager asking the prettiest girl in class to prom, I struggle over what to say. There's so much I want to know, so much I want to tell her, but where to start?

She obviously stayed up late. I can see it in the dark circles beneath her eyes, although she's still radiant in the soft morning light. I can't wait for her to ask about the manuscript. Does she realize it's our story?

I shoulder her. "Nice shirt."

"Yours, I assume?"

I want to tell her how she'd taken her sweet time unbuttoning it the night I'd arrived at her place, how she'd laughed when I told her I hadn't washed it since the night she'd cried on it. But my words catch and, "Yep," is all I can manage.

She reaches for my hand, twines her fingers in mine and stares at them.

I can almost see her mind churning, figuring things out. "It's a beautiful story, isn't it?"

"Yeah." She turns back to the splendor of the daybreak, looking wonderstruck as her gaze drinks it in. Sunlight dances on the water and shimmers on the tall grasses while tiny tufts of cotton swirl like snowflakes. Her lips curve into a slow smile. "Is this real?"

"It's as real as you want to make it."

Sam glances up into the tree, then looks at me. "Did we really spend an afternoon making love here?"

I grin, remembering that day, the two of us standing in the water as I'd washed her hair. She was so trusting, relaxed over my arm, so vulnerable with her damaged heart. When I'd finished with her hair, she straightened and her gaze landed on me, and I was done for. I never wanted anything more. It must have been written all over my face because she detailed it so perfectly in her story, right down to the voices screaming in my head, urging me on, yet warning. Like now. Wracked with desire, I have an overwhelming urge to lay her down right here and now, make her mine again, for once and for all, forever.

Entranced by the mere thought of lying beneath her in the tall grass, her long legs tangled up with mine, I'm startled by the gentle touch of her fingertip on my cheek. I snap back to the present to find her staring at me, brows raised.

I try to speak, but my throat's so dry my words stick.

"No." My gravel whisper seems to grind from my vocal cords. "I washed your hair that day, we kissed in the water, and I held you closer than I had a right to. But we did the right thing. We spent the afternoon lying on your blanket, talking. About your book mostly. That's when I told you my first name was Micah, named after my grandfather, but I went by Daniel, my middle name, to avoid confusion. You said you liked Micah better."

"Oh." She sounds disappointed as her eyes fall away, and I want to laugh.

"But everything else in your story is real."

"So, Michaelyn?"

I hesitate. This is it. I hope she won't be angry for not telling her sooner. "She's mine. I came to visit you after your divorce was final. We spent the weekend together. Best few days of my life."

She slowly nods, seeming to pull the pieces together. "The note."

Yes, the note I'd left beside the photo of her and Aiden. *When you're ready, you know the path to where I am. Love, Micah*

I study her; she's on the verge of tears. The silence that hangs between us is swept away by a soft breeze that swishes through the grasses, gently rustling the leaves above and setting the cotton tufts swirling.

"You told me you needed time. To heal. To choose your path."

"Sounds like something the old me would say." She eyes the engagement ring, absently twisting it.

She has a focused look about her, like someone trying to solve a difficult math problem, and it hits me. "You're remembering something."

She closes her eyes. "It's ..."

"Tell me."

"You removed my wedding ring."

"Yes, reel it in, Sam."

She rubs her forehead, the scowl there.

"We were standing in your bedroom."

"Candlelight."

"You were so lovely in your near nakedness."

A half-smile curves her lips as if she's picturing the scene. "You put it in a drawer."

"Yes, in your dressing table."

"There's a photo—"

"Of you and Aiden." She turns to look at me, a softness in her smile. She remembers!

She blinks, and the softness vanishes, taking the smile with it. "I can't—that's all I've got. That may be all I ever—"

"It's enough!" It's far from enough, but it's something.

She looks out over the valley and takes a long, deep breath, as though on a precipice of a decision. "I want to see the waterfall at Epley's Pass."

*Fantastic. She not only read the entire story, but she found my letter too, and my revised ending for her—our—story.* "I'd love to show it to you." My heart soars with renewed hope.

"This afternoon, when Michaelyn goes down for her nap?"

"Perfect." It'll be just the two of us, and I look forward to telling her—no, showing her—how I once loved her.

There's a hint of trepidation in her smile when she looks my way as if she heard my thoughts.

"Hungry?" I stand and pull her to her feet, then hold her hand as we trek back up to the cabin.

Breakfast, like all our meals together that week, is a family affair. While I turn out pancakes, Sam puts water on to boil for the dishes, Emma gets Michaelyn's booster seat, Zach pours orange juice, and Aiden and Michaelyn set the table.

When the conversation turns to their leaving that afternoon, I offer to stay and help pack up, but Sam suggests I play with Michaelyn instead.

"Keeping her occupied is help enough," she says.

So while Sam and Emma tear apart the beds and toss down their belongings, Zach attends to the outdoor tasks of closing up the cabin: taking down the solar panel and screens, filling the cistern one last time, so they'll have water for the rest of the day, then fetching the water tank from the top of the hill and stowing the hose.

After a quick lunch of leftovers, I take Michaelyn for a walk and once again find myself beneath the cottonwood. I sit with her and show her how to blow a whistle through a blade of grass. I chuckle at her failed attempts to make her chubby little fingers hold the grass right. But she seems enchanted enough to hear me do it and giggles with delight at each ear-piercing blast.

"Are you coming with us, Mr. Mac?" Michaelyn asks, suddenly serious, her eyes searching mine for the answer her three-year-old heart needs to hear.

My hands fall away from my lips as I search for words that won't crush her. There aren't any. "No, sunshine, I'm not."

Her smooth little brow wrinkles. "Then I don't want to go. I want to stay here, with you and Aiden." She grins up at me. "I like it here."

"Oh, Michaelyn, I would love for you to stay, you and your mama both. But—"

"I don't want to go!" She stands and throws her arms around my neck and buries her face against my neck.

I close my eyes, savoring the warmth of the tender young soul clinging to me. "Want to learn how to skip a rock?" Distraction is always the best approach for a frustrated toddler. I remember that much from Aiden's early days.

I take her hand and lead her to the water's edge, and for the next half hour we throw rocks into the creek. Michaelyn counts the hops of each one, and lucky for us both, I can't skip a stone more times than she can count. When she rubs her eyes, I know it's naptime.

In the loft, Michaelyn is reluctant to go to sleep until I assure her that I'll be back before they leave.

While I sit beside her travel crib, holding her tiny hand, my mind works to find a way to keep her in my life. I hear Sam and the kids outside, packing the truck, and I stare out the window, picturing the six of us at dinner the night before, how perfect it had seemed.

My mind replays the rainy weekend together at her place, aching to pinpoint what I said that convinced her to quit her job. I have to do it again.

I first asked her to come home with me on Saturday, late morning. We were in her bathtub, up to our necks in warm bubbles, discussing her story and how it needed a better ending. How *we* needed a better ending.

That evening, at the end of the movie about the workaholic stockbroker turned country vintner, I pondered how closely it mirrored Sam's life—working excessively, sacrificing everything for her career, only to realize that life held more than just climbing the corporate ladder.

I began to build the argument in my head. By inviting her home with me, I'd already planted the seed; now I needed to nourish it, encourage it to grow, build upon it, like an excellent trial lawyer would.

We were lying together on a quilt before the fireplace, and I leaned on an elbow to face her. "Sam," I said, placing a hand alongside her cheek. "I love you. I've loved you from the start and every day since, and I want to be with you."

Her smile was slow and sweet as she leaned into my palm.

"You love the mountains. I saw it in your eyes. I know you can never get around what you've gotta go through, but when you're ready to move on, let it be with me. I don't need an answer today, or even tomorrow. But think on it. Consider your life here, what's left of it, your job, that you hate. You can write in my office upstairs."

She took my hand and twined her fingers in mine. "I'll think about it, okay?"

I nodded and raised our hands to kiss hers. "Okay." I tried to give her an encouraging smile, but I'm not sure I pulled it off.

"Thank you, Mac, for coming, the incredible summer, and being a wonderful friend. You don't know what it's meant to me." She laughed softly. "I wrote a poem, and a real live cowboy sang it to me. I trusted a little boy who held my hand on my first Ferris wheel ride. I napped in a meadow, danced in the moonlight, and looked down on heaven. It makes me wonder," she seemed to lose herself in my gaze, "what else have I not made room for?"

*What else, indeed? How about what's happening this weekend? Right this minute. How about love? An ideal soil for planting a dream.* Satisfied Sam was at least considering embarking on the path I'd led her to, I didn't pursue it again until Sunday night. With the glorious weekend coming to an end, I felt my closing argument had to be physical, one final miraculous night that would linger long after I'd gone.

When I led her back to the bedroom, I showed her the depths of my love as I caressed, kissed, and cherished every inch of her, setting her on fire with my burning need to make her mine until she quivered and shook from the passion I reaped from deep within her.

Sublimely sated, we fell asleep in each other's arms as the sound of the rain calmed to a soft drizzle. In the wee hours of the night, I woke to find her smiling at me. I blinked several times, wondering if I was dreaming again. It was like a dream, one I'd had so many times. "I love you," I murmured, still half asleep.

"Love you more," she whispered back.

The next morning, I woke to an empty bed and the sound of the shower in the on-suite bath.

I threw off the covers, slipped into my jeans, and fetched a cup of coffee before heading to the living room. Staring out at the lake, its dark surface smooth and silent in the early morning light, I wondered what more I could say to convince her to come back to the ranch with me.

"Good morning."

I turned at the sound of her voice and her smile evaporated at the disappointment I couldn't hide. "Morning." My eyes travelled the length of her, from her neatly pulled back hair to her long slim skirt and heels. She's dressed for work. "You look nice."

"Thank you." She moved to the kitchen and poured coffee into a travel mug. "You'll be here when I get home? I won't work late. We'll have dinner together, okay?"

I closed the distance between us and took her hand, squeezed it. "It's never too late to change your path, Sam. Promise me you'll at least consider quitting your job. It's killing you, darlin', even you can see that. Don't keep following the wrong path just because it's the one you chose long ago. At some point, you *can* turn around."

"Oh, Mac. You're such a romantic. You make it all sound so logical, so easy."

"Just follow your heart, darlin'."

"I have to work, Mac. I have to live."

I rubbed my chin in frustration. I knew from experience following your heart was seldom easy. "It's just a living, Sam. But what kind of life is it? You could sell this house and live on it for years." I spread my arms wide, gesturing to the enormous room we were standing in.

She surveyed her possessions, the decorations and furnishings, photographs and knickknacks amassed over the years, all in an attempt to create a happy home for her family. But what they truly craved, her husband at least, was more of her time. "But this is my home."

"It's an empty house, Sam! A desolate shell of your former life."

She recoiled at the harshness of my tone. "I have to go, Mac," she said, her voice breaking. "Will you stay one more day? Please?"

My answer was a quick kiss on the cheek. "Have a great day at work, Sam."

It came out sounding flat and insincere, and she winced, tried to cover it with a smile like it didn't matter. Yet her eyes revealed a different story.

"I'm sorry." I ran my hands over my face. "It's just so damn hard watching you continue on this road, knowing what it's cost you already. I can't stand by and watch you make the same mistakes again."

"I have to go." She stepped back, blinking away tears.

"The hardest thing is usually the right thing, Sam."

She cupped my face and kissed me goodbye, and it was long and sweet. She gave me her heart in that kiss, and when it ended, she pulled away.

The door closed with a finality that rocked my soul. At the kitchen window, drowning in a sea of regret for not trying harder, I watched her pull out of the driveway.

I should've kissed her back, really kissed her. I should've pushed her against the wall and kissed her like I'd never kiss her again. Then taken her back to bed, made love to her, slow and sweet, leisurely taking my time with her, enough to make her late, inexcusably late. Make her writhe and moan and plead beneath me. Make her forget everything but the way my touch turned her inside out. Maybe then she would've chosen to take the day off.

Yeah, I should've made that kiss into something more. But maybe because I didn't, she felt free to follow her heart. She'd decided to quit her job that day, so whatever I said and did, it worked.

Now, I must do it again. Convince Sam that her life is here with me, that her path, the one she'd chosen that morning, was leading her to me.

I gaze at Michaelyn, her breathing steady and even.

It's time.

# 32

# WATERFALL

Sam closes her eyes and leans back, the water cascading over her head, and she gasps. I know the feeling of crisp mountain water on hot skin—exhilarating beyond words. When she opens her eyes, she catches my stare.

She worries her lower lip and gives me a seductive smile. I touch her hair, let my fingers thread through the long, wet strands, then with surer hands, I caress her scalp, smoothing her hair back beneath the fall of water.

"Jesus, Sam," I say in a hoarse voice. "You are so beautiful."

Her lips stretch into a real smile, as if she has waited as long to hear those words as I have to utter them. She closes her eyes, and I kiss her, soft, so soft, and tender, so tender, first her lips, then her cheeks, ears, neck. She arches back, giving over completely to my possession of her, and my lips are on hers again, teasing, demanding, devouring.

I draw her in, wrap her in my arms and switch places with her beneath the water, relishing the feel of her cool skin against my chest. My hungry stare travels from her eyes to her mouth, then lower still before returning to her face.

I trail kisses where my eyes had roamed. Water runs down her front, over my head, while I cover her with kisses, whispering words of love along the way. "I want you to be the blessed sunshine that wakes me every morning." My lips linger at the edge of her bathing suit top, but I resist the urge to push aside the fabric.

"The cool breeze that sees me through my days." My mouth travels to her shoulder, and I whisper in her ear as the water crashes over us both, "The warm blanket that tangles me up at night."

Her breathing is ragged as she succumbs to the desire I've awakened in her. "Oh, Micah."

At the sound of my name on her lips, I pull back and our eyes lock. I cup her face between my hands. "Yes, Sam. I'm the same man you once loved."

A moment of recognitions seems to pass across her features, followed by the most delicious sigh I've ever heard.

My lips speak against hers, "Let me." Then, as though her body acquiesces of its own accord, her knees give way and I scoop her up and carry her to the riverbank.

I set her on the towels, kneeling over her while my eyes caress every detail of her face. "You know," I say in a soft, reverent tone. "I almost raced by that day. I was thinking about Aiden, when I heard a voice say, 'Stop. It's her.' I slammed on the brakes, backed up. That was the first time I saw you."

I trace the outline of her jaw with a fingertip and drown in the tenderness of her gaze. "I knew, even then, that you could never be anything but mine."

"Oh," she sighs, and her head falls back as her defenses crumble beneath the ruthless onslaught of my words. My mouth crashes onto hers, stirring a fire meant to consume the very last spark of her waning resistance.

Her hands shoot out to stop me. "You left me," she says, her voice weak, her body weaker, her resolve weakest of all.

I shake my head, my eyes not leaving hers. "No, Sam. You said you needed time. You sent me away." I inch closer, brush the tip of my nose down her cheek.

She turns away. "No, you abandoned us. You never even tried to—"

"I called. For weeks I called you."

"I lost my phone in the crash."

My head spins as I vet possibilities. "But when you got a new one, you would've seen—"

"There was nothing—"

"I wrote to you."

"One letter! After months." She shoves me away and jumps to her feet. "No, you gave up on us."

I stand and grasp for her hand. "I *never* gave up on you!"

She backpedals. "You did. All those months I waited for you."

"*I* waited for *you*."

"Your note said you loved me. I held onto that. I thought you'd come back, and you never did."

"You were supposed to come to me."

"Oh!" She pushes me away, reaches for her shorts and yanks them on.

I rake both hands through my hair and let out an exasperated sigh. "Okay, you're right. I gave up on you. I gave up. This is my life, darlin'." With arms outstretched, my gaze sweeps the woods, the waterfall, all of our surroundings. "This is where I belong. I can't live any place else. I've tried. I needed you to come to me, and when you didn't, I figured you didn't want this life. I already had one woman leave me." I look away, surprised that the memory of Elizabeth still crushes me. "I knew I wouldn't survive it a second time."

She shakes her head as though struggling to not let the first tear fall. "No, I won't cry for you. I've already shed way too many tears over you, all those long lonely months of my pregnancy, as I waited and wondered and cried for the father of my child, some faceless man who hadn't bothered to stick around, even in my memory."

I take her hand. "Sam, come on. Think about it. How was I to know you'd had an accident? That you didn't remember me?"

She continues to shake her head then looks down, my despair or her own wavering heart too much to bear.

With a fingertip, I lift her face to mine. "I love you, Sam. I want a happy ending for us. Like the one I wrote in my letter. You read that too, right?"

She nods. Good.

"And I want to be a father to Michaelyn. She's my child."

She falls to her knees, overcome.

"What do you want from me? Tell me what I have to do to—"

"It's too late—"

"Don't say that!"

"I needed you, Mac. Someone who believes in me. A man who will fight for me, not give up when things get uncertain."

"Like Stephane? He left you here—with me—to go back to his movie set."

"I sent him away."

"Like you sent me away."

"No." She buries her face in her hands.

"Yes." I gaze at her and I hate myself for what I've done to this beautiful woman. I drop to my knees before her and soften my tone. "If you're so in love with him, why haven't you accepted his proposal?"

Her head jerks up and her face grows red-hot angry.

"It's because you don't love him, darlin'. I can see it. Emma sees it. He offers you security, an exciting lifestyle, things you think will make you happy, but Sam—please, look at me."

She raises her chin. Her eyes are dry, her expression defiant.

"What will you do when he's off on set somewhere, like now?"

"Go with him."

"With Michaelyn?"

"Yes."

I take a deep breath and unclench my teeth. "That might be fine for now, but what about school, friends? What kind of life is that for a child growing up?"

"It'll be a good life."

"Don't settle for good, Sam, not when you can have great. You'd have a great life here, with me, with us." I think about Aiden and how devastated he'll be if she leaves again. "You don't love him."

Her head jerks up, and she glares at me. But she doesn't deny it.

"Not like you once loved me."

"I'm going to marry him." She stands and reaches for her boots.

I struggle to my feet, at a loss for how to turn this around. A moment of silence vanishes in the roar of the waterfall crashing behind us. I step forward and grasp her shoulders. "I didn't leave you, Sam. You forgot me." I say it with a calm finality as if it were the ultimate failing—hers, and hers alone.

Her breath catches. When I pull her in, she collapses against my chest, the last of her defenses falling away as hot tears sear my bare skin.

*Yes, she had forgotten me, but it wasn't her fault.*

"Let me go." She pushes against my chest.

I hold on. "Don't ask that of me. Anything but that. I've let you walk away twice now, and I've lived with three and a half years of regret. I can't do it again, Sam. I can't."

My heart pounds fiercely beneath her wet cheek as my mind reels against what's happening. I can't bring myself to accept it.

She loved me once. And I can still see it in her eyes when she looks at me, taste it in the way she kisses me, feel it in every inch of her skin on mine, in the way she speaks to me with a melancholy longing, as if overcome by a deep-seated desire to push away the hurt and find that happiness again.

When she lifts her head to gaze at me, I see it as clearly as I see the blueness of her eyes and the Colorado sky. She loves me, she wants me; there's no mistaking it. She couldn't possibly feel something more for Mr. Director.

"Tell me you love him, Sam, and I'll let you go."

"He's a good man—" She sniffs and swipes at her cheeks with the palms of her hands.

"Tell me!"

"Mac!" It's Cody, shouting down from the road.

I glare up at him, furious.

"Mac, there's a fire up near the Routt. We need you, man!"

## 33

# FIRE AND RAIN

Bad news never has good timing. A fire is the last thing I need. My mind races as I do a mental accounting of where the herd is: over twelve hundred head up near the Routt. It'll take every man we've got to rustle them down the mountain.

I set Sam from me, cup my mouth, and call back to Cody, "Meet me at Sam's in ten minutes."

"We don't have that kind of time."

"I have to drop her off. You got the horses?"

"Isaac and Nick've got 'em. Meeting us at the fork. They've got Aiden and Caleb too."

My eyes dart to Sam. *This cannot be happening. Not now.* "Ten minutes, Cody. It's on the way."

"All right, all right."

Cody disappears from the edge of the road, and I turn to Sam, afraid to ask, dreading what her answer might be. My heart races while my eyes hold hers captive and I search for the right words. I can't afford to have her say no. "You know I have to go."

She nods.

"Wait for me, Sam. Please?"

When she doesn't answer, I pull her against my chest and hold her, savoring the warmth of her near nakedness. My voice is a hoarse whisper when my plea tumbles out again. "I don't know how long I'll be but, please, Sam, promise me you won't leave until I get back."

She frees herself from my embrace, takes a step back, and reaches for her shirt. "I have to go too, Mac. I'm sorry."

*No! This can't be how it ends.* My mouth goes dry, and I struggle to draw breath as a knot in my stomach twists violently. She slips her shirt on as hopelessness crashes over me.

I take my T-shirt when she hands it to me, pull it on, then hold her hand as I lead the way to the trail, my feet on autopilot as my mind races to come up with something more to convince her.

As we speed down the mountain, despair settles in every second of the awkward silence that hangs between us like a coiled rattler, and every bit as fateful. I glance her way. She stares out the passenger window, so lost in her own thoughts she may as well be on the moon. I wonder what she's thinking, if she's at least considering waiting. Or something more.

How can I possibly convince her in the next ten minutes that she's choosing the wrong path? Again.

My insides slump and I rub my chin. If only she knew now what she knew then.

"Sam," I begin, and she looks my way, her eyes questioning. "Look, I'm sorry. You have no idea how sorry I am that I didn't come back. You told me you needed time to sort things out, think things through, choose a new path. I thought I was doing the right thing. I was doing what you'd asked."

I glance her way again to see her staring down at her hands, absently twisting the engagement ring on her finger.

"When you didn't answer my calls or return any of my messages in the first few weeks, I thought you needed to be alone. So I waited. I waited for you, Sam. For three and half years I've waited for you. I didn't abandon you. I loved you. From the first time I set eyes on you and every minute since, I've loved you." I grasp her hand and shoot her a pleading glance. "I never stopped loving you."

When I look her way again, I see a tear escape down her cheek. Not bothering to wipe it away, she turns back to the window.

*That's a good sign, right?* Pride forces the tears back, but the heart lets them fall. "You once told me you loved me."

Her head jerks my way, and her eyes widen, as if that were a revelation she'd wondered about before. I smile as I focus on the road ahead of me.

"It was our last night together at your place. I woke in the middle of the night to find you staring at me. I told you I loved you, and you put a finger to my lips and said, 'Love you more.' I lived on that for three and half years. I knew you loved me and you'd come back to me one day."

In my peripheral vision, I see her head turn to the window again. I know she doesn't remember, but I hope she's trying to picture it. "After a while, I began to wonder if it was a dream. If not for the story you left me, I'd have thought it all an incredible fantasy—meeting you that summer, our friendship, that weekend together."

"I don't remember any of it."

The fist around my heart squeezes painfully. "I know you don't, darlin', and that's what makes it all so sad."

She sighs and swipes her cheek. "I don't want to be sad anymore, Mac. Stephane is a new start for me. He makes me happy."

I want to tell her I can make her happy. I had for a time. That weekend, nothing had ever felt so right. And nothing has felt right since. I have to convince her I'm the safe bet, the better man. I can't sit back and watch her make the same wrong choices again, knowing what it cost her the first time around.

"So, why didn't he come on this vacation with you? Oh, right, he had to work."

"He works hard."

"For all the wrong reasons, I'm sure," I mumble under my breath.

"What's that?"

I reach for her hand and hold on to it. I have something to say and I have a feeling she'll find it difficult to hear, like a surgeon sharing a patient's terminal prognosis. But I have to let her know. "As your friend and someone who cares about you, I have to tell you you're heading down the wrong path again."

"And what path is that?"

"The same one that brought you here four years ago. Working too hard for all the wrong reasons."

She stares at me, as if measuring the truth of my words. "You think that's why my husband cheated on me? I told you that?"

"Not in so many words, but yes."

"This is different. Stephane is different."

"Okay, it's him, not you, working too hard this time, but it's the same path with the same damn destination!"

Her eyes go wide at the anger in my voice before she looks away again, resigned. "Don't we all have the same destination?"

"I suppose we do, but life is in the journey, darlin'. Choose the path that holds your happiness because nothing else matters."

"Stephane makes me happy. He loves me."

"*I* love you."

Silence hangs between us as my old truck rattles down the mountain. Too many minutes of excruciating silence. "I have your shirt," she says, her words so soft it's almost like she hadn't meant to voice them.

I can't help but smile as I picture her as I remember, naked beneath my soft red flannel that hung to her knees. She'd spent an entire weekend in and out of that shirt.

I fishtail onto Sam's road. My heart squeezes tighter in the unrelenting grip of failure. "Keep the shirt, Sam. Or better yet, bring it back to me after you drop off Emma."

She sniffs. "I can't."

It's barely a whisper, but it hits me like a thunder clap. I clear the knot from my throat. "Why not?"

"I'm supposed to marry Stephane." It sounds like an automatic response and lacks any semblance of emotion or conviction.

"*Supposed* to?" I almost choke on her choice of words.

"I'm marrying Stephane!" She glares at me. At least the emotion is back. I ought to be grateful for that. Finally, she's feeling *something*.

"Why?" We're almost at her cabin. I have only minutes left. "Why are you so intent on marrying that man?"

Her jaw clenches before she turns away.

Then it hits me. Her reason for marrying Stephane has nothing to do with love and everything to do with Michaelyn. The man is obviously wealthy and wanting the best for your child can be a compelling reason for a bad decision.

I turn onto the trail that leads to her cabin and ease the truck through the narrow path of switchbacks down the steep incline. "Do you need his money? Is that it? For Michaelyn's surgery? I can help with that, you know. She's my child!"

Silence.

"You don't love him." I will her to look my way as we round the last bend. Why can't she face me?

Suddenly, it all becomes clear. "That's exactly why you're set on marrying him, isn't it? Because he's safe. When he leaves you—like every other man in your life has done—you won't be hurt. That's it, isn't it? You think because you don't love him, it won't hurt when he leaves you. Deep down, you're afraid of being abandoned again."

"You don't know anything! How do you know if I love him or not?" Now she's facing me, her gaze hot, challenging.

I stop behind her SUV, slam my truck into park, and face her. "Darlin', tell me you're in love with him, and I'll drive away."

Glaring at me, her mouth opens, but no words come out. With a huff, she turns and hops out, slamming the door behind her.

I bolt after her, catching sight of Cody pulling in at the top of the trail as I skirt the hood of my truck to grab her hand before she makes it to the front step. "Sam, wait—"

"And what were you afraid of, Mac?" she shouts, whirling on me. "Three and a half years—"

The door flies open, and Michaelyn darts out. "Mac! Mac!" she cries, running, nearly stumbling, to me. I kneel to scoop her up and greet her with a forced bravado. I give her a hug and a kiss, then hold her in my arms as I level an insistent gaze at Sam. “Tell me.”

Sam’s almost tears betray the smile she tries to fake for our daughter’s sake. “Baby, Mr. Mac has to go. Give him a hug and say goodbye.”

Michaelyn cups my face between her chubby hands, worry creasing her little brow as she stares at me. “You come back?”

I take in a stuttering breath and glance sideways as Cody’s truck skids to a stop behind mine. “Soon, sunshine, real soon.” I kiss her forehead, then hug her tight as my eyes implore her mother.

Sam holds out her arms to Michaelyn, but when I lean forward to hand her over, Michaelyn clings to me. Even the child can sense the finality of the moment.

“No! Don’t go. I want you to be my daddy.” Tears, pure and innocent, spill from her eyes as she clutches at me.

While Sam wrenches my child away, I peel her little arms from around my neck and

choke on a strangled sob as my baby girl writhes in her mother’s arms, reaching for me.

"No! I wished you to me!" she cries, and I can’t take any more. I whirl around. Cody stands next to his truck, arms raised impatiently.

When I turn around again, I think I have myself together. But I’m wrong. I have to blink several times as I nearly choke on the bitter taste of this soul-crushing defeat.

I take a long, deep breath and stare at Sam. “Tell me, Sam, please.”

My breath catches in the back of my throat and a slice of time hangs between us, a moment where eyes don’t blink and hearts don’t beat.

Sam shakes her head, and her eyes go misty.

Michaelyn sobs, “Mac,” and reaches for me.

“Mac,” Cody calls.

“Tell me, dammit! Tell me you love him, so I can go.”

Michaelyn stares at me wide-eyed, startled by my outburst, and then buries her face in Sam's neck, her sobs muffled against her mother's shoulder.

I knew it. She doesn't love Stephane. If she did, she wouldn't kiss me like she does.

I place a hand on Sam's shoulder, and I wait. For the words that will set me free to save my ranch or bind me to her forever.

"I love him," Sam says, her voice little more than a breath. The low, steady moan of the breeze in the trees is louder.

*No!* My breath leaves my body in one huge rush, like I've been gut-punched. I look at her long and hard, not believing I'd actually heard it. But she nods, and my heart shatters like crystal on concrete. I take her face in my hands and kiss her hard, like I'll never kiss her again—and likely I won't.

When we part, she smiles weakly, tears hanging on her lower lids, and she runs a fingertip over my mouth the way she once did. "Be careful."

"Always." I kiss her finger.

She pushes me away. "Go."

"It's never too late to choose another path, Sam." I turn and stagger toward my cousin's truck on legs as unsteady as a newborn foal.

# 34

# EMBERS

Hours later, in a steady downpour as darkness descends, I return to Sam's cabin for my truck, physically exhausted but emotionally charged, as I anticipate setting things right with her. My brother Isaac stops at the edge of the road to drop me off.

"Do me a favor," I say, hitching a thumb toward the back seat where Aiden is fast asleep, "put him to bed for me?"

"No problem," Isaac says. He cranes forward to peer down the two-track. "Think you'll make it out of there?"

I follow his gaze. It'll be tough, all right, but if by some miracle Sam waited for me, there is no way I'm not showing up. "May have to put the chains on, but I should be fine. I'll be along shortly." I turn up the collar of my duster, pull my hat low on my head, and step out into the rain to begin the slippery trek down the wet trail.

When I can make out the cabin, my heart withers. Even beneath the moonless sky, through the driving rain and the shadowy timber that stands between me and the cabin, I can see it's completely dark. No hint of light peeks from the edges of the windows, no outline of Sam's Escalade sits in front. Only the faint silhouette that's my old white pickup, which is parked right where I'd left it.

As I near, I picture myself on her front step the first time I'd stopped by, drenched and seeking shelter from another storm. She'd welcomed me in, into her cabin, into her life, into her heart.

If I'd known it would come to this, would I have knocked on her door that night? I trudge ahead, focused on the cabin, picturing her within, standing before the fire, handing me a glass of whiskey, her almost smile that caught at my heart even then.

My chest tightens as I think about all the good times I would've missed—drowning our heartaches in whiskey and laughter, holding her while she cried over her failed marriage, waking with her in my arms after that terrible storm, riding the Ferris wheel, dancing in the moonlight, the glorious and intimate weekend at her place. And Michaelyn, our beautiful baby girl.

Yeah, I would've knocked. I wouldn't have missed one single minute of it, not for all the hay in the barn.

I remember telling her, "When you can't stand the pain any longer, kneel," and I fall to my knees on the wet earth.

"Oh, God! Take this pain from my heart. I did all I could, and it wasn't enough. It wasn't enough!" I lift my face to the dark night sky, welcoming the cleansing rain while the wind blows, bending the pines and aspens to its will. Lightning flashes, illuminating the cabin in its eerie light, and still I ache. For another woman who doesn't want the life I have to offer, for another child I'll forever be telling goodbye, for the simple dream of a family that once again has slipped through my fingers.

Am I destined to spend my life alone? Are these the wages for my sins? For coveting another man's wife, almost giving in, not waiting until we wed? "Oh, God, forgive me. For being impatient, for not trusting—"

"Dad!"

I whirl at the sound of Aiden's voice as my son shuts down the ATV and jumps off.

"Aiden!" I lumber to my feet. How long have I been on my

knees? I can't believe I didn't hear the ATV approach. "What are you doing here?" I say, collecting myself.

"I thought you might be stuck."

"Right. That trail's slick as snot." I don't want to admit I haven't even tried.

"Kind of figured. Want a ride home?"

"You bet." I throw a leg over the seat and Aiden climbs on behind me.

I press the auto-start button, but nothing happens. I hit the gear pedal, making sure it's in neutral, then look at the gauge, try again. Nothing.

"It was cutting out a bit on the way over," Aiden says, peering around me.

I'm spent, physically, mentally, emotionally. The last thing I want to do is mess with a persnickety engine.

"Let's stay here. I don't think they'd mind. Zach showed me where the key is, in case we ever needed it."

Minutes later, stripped of our wet things and warming before a roaring fire, I let my thoughts drift back to Sam and the night our friendship began, right where I sit now on the braided rug before the fire. I'd been soaked through that night, too.

Aiden settles in beside me. "It's a little weird, ain't it?"

My thoughts are elsewhere when I turn to my son with a raised brow.

"I mean, being here without them."

"Yeah, guess so."

There's a long stretch of silence as my gaze roams the cabin, seeing Sam in every detail—sitting at the table with Michaelyn on her lap, standing at the sink doing dishes, laying on the couch in my arms with her little dog curled up in front of her. If I could just hold on to one single moment, that would be the one. Or it would be our first dance in the moonlight overlooking the valley. I'd never felt so alive.

"So," Aiden shoulders me, "when are we leaving? We're going after 'em, right?"

I turn and stare blankly at my son, and I realize mine isn't the only heart breaking tonight. "No, buddy, not this time." He doesn't know about the last time—he'd been back in Houston by then—but I don't remember that until the words are already out.

"But, Dad!"

"Sam's decided to marry someone else. She told me so."

"That guy who showed up the other night?" The look of utter disgust on Aiden's face would have made me laugh if it wasn't so shamefully genuine.

"Yep." An image of Mr. Director stepping from his Lexus flashes in my mind. The way his eyes had brightened at the sight of her sears an angry green scar on my heart.

"She doesn't look at him the way she looks at you."

I glance up to see Aiden's serious young face, a mirror of my own painful heartbreak.

"She doesn't," he repeats.

"How do you know the way she looks at him?"

"Zach says so."

*Zach?* "Well, he's the one she wants to marry, not me. There's nothing more I can do."

Aiden is silent for several long minutes and I think the matter is settled, but when I glance sideways, tears stream unchecked down my son's cheeks and I nearly choke on a strangled sob.

I place an arm around his shoulders. "I'm sorry, buckaroo."

He pushes me away. "God helps those who help themselves. Ain't that what you always say? Ain't it?"

I drag a hand down my face. "That isn't anywhere in the Bible." I know because I looked last night.

"You can't just give up on her!"

I can only stare at my son. Is that what he thinks, too?

*I didn't give up on her!* My head falls to my hands as I struggle for words my son will understand. But there aren't any. How can I possibly make Aiden understand when I don't understand it myself? *Did* I give up on her?

Aiden places a hand on my shoulder, and I hear him sniffle. "We gotta go after 'em. We gotta!"

"Aiden! Stop! You can't make someone stay if it ain't where she wants to be!"

Aiden's stunned silence adds to my desolate guilt, and I let my head fall back into my hands.

Aiden stands and his voice is small but resolute when he says, "She likes it here just fine. That ain't it. That ain't it at all."

Then Aiden disappears up the ladder to the loft, and with a heavy heart, I turn back to the fire. The raging flames blur to a wash of placid yellow-orange through the exhausted red-hot tears that fill my eyes.

Lost in despair, I don't hear the ringing until Aiden calls from the loft, "Dad, your phone!"

I pick it up, and it takes several seconds before my vision clears and the name registers. My heart soars as I slide it to answer. "Hey, sunshine!"

"Hi." Her voice is soft, as if Michaelyn is asleep nearby.

"I'm so glad you called."

"You are?"

"Of course I am." I hadn't thought to hope for it, but I'm thrilled all the same. It might mean something. Something good. "Did you get Emma all settled?"

"Yeah." Sam sounds down. Or just tired after staying up late reading the night before. "The apartment's nice, near campus and the hospital."

"Good. That's good. You must be exhausted."

"Yeah. How's the ranch? The herd?"

"Fine. We were able to move 'em out in time. And then we got a nice downpour that doused the fire. So, it's all good. We'll probably keep the herd low for a while, since those pastures will be greening up nicely with all this rain. How about you? You all right?"

She takes a few beats to answer. "I'm okay."

"Heading back this way tomorrow?" I try to sound optimistic, not like I feel—wretched and lonely.

Silence hangs between us. "No, Mac. Stephane's shooting on location in BC, and he wants us to join him. We fly out in the morning to Vancouver."

"We?"

"Michaelyn and I. Zach's taking the Escalade and heading back to Stonebridge."

"Oh." My disappointment resonates in that single syllable.

"Is that Sam? I want to talk." Aiden reaches for the phone.

"Aiden wants to say hi." I hand the phone over.

"Howdy, Sam."

"Hey, little man. You're up late." I can barely hear Sam's voice through the speaker.

"I was hoping it was you." Aiden turns away from me and his words tumble out. "I love you, Sam. I wanted to say that. 'Cause I never really got the chance before. And I didn't want you to leave, not knowin'. And Michaelyn too."

The cabin is quiet as Sam talks, and I wait, watching my son with the phone to his ear.

Aiden turns back to me, his face alight with a happy grin. "Okay. I'll let you talk to my dad now. Hope to see you again real soon. Bye."

"She loves us both," Aiden whispers to me as he returns the phone.

"Hey," I say, smiling at my son.

"That's one sweet little man you got there."

"Yeah, he's pretty special, all right. Tells it like he sees it."

"Like his father." I hear tears in her voice.

"Sam?"

Silence. A sniffle.

"You okay?"

"Oh, Mac." I hear her shuffle around a bit, then sniffle again. "I don't know what to do."

I know what I want her to do and come darn close to blurting it out, letting the words tumble and fall, as Aiden had done. *Come home to me! Love me. Marry me. Make a life here with me and my boy!*

I can picture her crying on the other end and I think back to the day I'd left her house to return home, the day of her accident. She had cried then too. And quit her job. She had chosen me. And now she needs to make that choice again. "You know what to do, Sam. You've always known what to do."

"I don't remember."

"I know, and it's ok. You don't need to. You fell in love with me once, Sam. You'll fall in love with me again."

Silence. Then I hear her take a shaky breath. "I already have."

"Oh, darlin'."

"I have to go. I," Sam sniffs again, "I just needed to hear your voice."

"Don't go."

"I have to—"

"Come home to me, Sam."

"I'll talk to you soon, Mac, I promise."

"Sam—" I hear three little beeps. She's ended the call.

I set the phone down, let my head fall back against the couch cushion, and close my eyes.

*I already have.* I allow myself a small smile.

"She coming?"

I open my eyes. Aiden's leaning over the railing of the loft. "Don't think so, buckaroo. I don't know. She needs to figure things out for herself."

Aiden nods.

"But she loves us," I say.

Aiden smiles. "That's something."

"Yep, that's something, all right."

I WAKE with a start as the first blush of dawn peeks through a crack in the drapes. I bolt upright, grasping to hold on—to what, I don't know—then I realize where I am as my mind wrenches free of the dream. My arms fall limp to my sides, and the emptiness inside me returns full force. My pulse still racing, I close my eyes, seeking calm, but the dream flashes before me: Sam slipping from my grasp as I desperately try to hold on, my boots losing traction on the rain-slicked hillside. The look on her face is so loving, so trusting, so certain I'm her rescuer, I scramble, dig in, hold tighter. And then she's gone.

I groan as the reality of it slams me. I've lost her. Again!

I fall back against the couch and throw an arm across my face. *Oh, God, this can't be how our story ends.*

*I love him*, she'd said.

It's too late for us. I'm too late; she found someone else.

But she called. She'd needed to hear my voice. *I already have.*

Wavering precariously between hope and regret, I drag myself from the couch and lumber to the washroom, where I bend to turn on the faucet. Nothing.

Right, Zach drained the plumbing to prevent it from freezing over winter. Because they don't plan to come back. I turn it off and straighten, coming face to face with my reflection in the mirror.

The man staring back at me looks haunted, the face hard and shadowed in shades of shame and guilt. In the dim light of the tiny room, I stare long and hard, an intense hatred filling me for the coward I see. I failed her. Again. When it came down to it, I hadn't trusted in her love for me.

Why, I'd even believed for a time that I'd dreamt waking in the night to her stare, her touch upon my lips, her words, *love you more*. Yeah, I gave up on her. Sure enough, that's exactly what I did.

Everything inside me aches, and I'm so tired I can barely hold myself up. My chin falls to my chest, the weight of my shallow faith crushing what little self-worth remains. Tears sting my eyes, and I don't try to stem them this time as they course freely down my cheeks and fall like raindrops from the hard line of my jaw into the small metal sink with a *ting, ting, ting.*

*Every storm runs out of rain. Even the blackest night holds a bright new day.*

My head jerks up to search the mirror again, and I swipe my face dry with my shirt. I'd given Sam those words, and she'd found strength in them. I yearn to find strength in them too.

I rush to the slider and yank back the drapes, then stumble backward, nearly blinded by the brightness of the dawn. I recover my footing and squint to see her beloved valley, the foliage and treetops shimmering moist and vibrant green in the early morning light, cleansed and refreshed from the night's rain. The creek reflects like a gold band cutting the valley in two, like puzzle pieces, the mountains in the distance aglow in their purple-hued majesty. Wondrous!

But empty. Like my life. How can I ever look upon this valley and not think of Sam? And Michaelyn—there are so many things I want to show my little girl, so many things I want to teach her.

Sam's words echo in my mind, *someone who believes in me, a man who will fight for me.*

*I already have.*

*I love him.* But she didn't accept his proposal, and she asked him to leave.

I rub my stubbled chin, and an idea hits me like a freight train. She knows how important the ranch and my family are to me. She'd captured it perfectly in her story. There's no way I could've turned my back on them and she knew it. So she lied to me, setting me free to do what I needed to do.

A movement catches my eye, and I look up as a pair of golden eagles soar across the clear blue sky, one not quite as graceful as the other. Sam's eagle and her mate. My hope is restored, my strength renewed.

God brought her to my mountain. He meant for us to be together. And it's not too late; I can damn well fight for her now!

My mind races through possibilities. Mr. Director is somewhere in British Columbia, on his movie set. And Sam is on her way to join him.

But she called. That was something. And she didn't know what to do. That was something else.

I step outside onto the back deck and look east to where the sunrise floods the horizon in a pink-golden glow. It reminds me that nothing is more important than the people you love, and that beautiful beginnings can still be found at the end of cold, rainy nights.

I march to my truck and set to putting the chains on.

## 35

# MIRACLES

Sunday mid-day, after a grueling 24-hour drive with little sleep, I pull my old pickup to a stop at the end of a two-track outside of Vancouver, British Columbia. I turn off the engine and shoot off a text to Zach, thanking him for his help and begging one last prayer. With a heart full of hope, I tuck my mother's legacy of love into my shirt pocket and hop out to look around, careful not to wake Aiden, asleep in the back.

I know I'm in the right spot. Straight ahead is a large clearing, a cul-de-sac of trampled grass with a dozen or more travel trailers tucked into the edge of the woods. A large open-sided tent stands at twelve o'clock, and at three o'clock, a narrow trail disappears into dense woods. Trunks, tripods, scaffolding, and utility ATVs sit between the tent and the trail while a throng of not-so-busy-people mill among the movie-making paraphernalia.

Sam emerges from the trees, carrying Michaelyn on her hip. My stomach knots as I watch the two of them make their way up the trail. So tired from the long drive I can hardly stand, I lean back against my truck, cross my boots at the ankles, and wait. Groups of people pass between us, and I momentarily lose sight of them before they reappear again, each time a little closer.

At the edge of the clearing, Sam sets Michaelyn on her feet, takes her hand, and continues forward, heading for the tent.

Michaelyn sees me first. "Mac! Mac!" She points in my direction, pulls free and hurries forward, stumbles and falls, picks herself up and runs on, jumping into my outstretched arms as I kneel to pick her up.

"Hey there, sunshine!" I give her a bear hug and kiss her cheek.

Michaelyn holds my face, and turns to her mother. "Mommy, look! It's Mr. Mac!"

I set her on her feet and Aiden emerges from the truck, rubbing sleep from his eyes, then he too bends to hug his baby sister.

Sam stops a few steps away and when I say her name, she looks back the way she'd come, as though she'd taken a wrong turn into the past. "What are you doing here?" Her eyes are bright, yet shadowed with the darkness of an inner pain.

She closes her eyes then covers them with a hand as if she expects when she takes her hand away, I'll be gone. She no longer wears the engagement ring.

I step forward. "I'm sorry. I—" No, wait. This isn't the way I planned it. I restart the moment. "Sam—"

"You were right," she says as she throws her body against mine. Her arms wrap around my neck, and she holds me tight, like she still can't believe I'm here.

It doesn't make sense. Until it makes the only sense.

I swallow her in my arms and close my eyes, thankful beyond measure. I'm not quite sure what I expected, but this greeting wasn't even in the realm of possibilities. I hold on to her, though, reluctant to question the reason behind it. It seems to be what she needs right now.

I whisper against her ear, "I'm not giving up on you. Not now. Not ever."

She pulls away and steps back, looking up at me like she knows I have something more to say, something bigger.

And I do. I've driven thirteen hundred miles, guided by hope, flanked by fear, as I'd imagined and prayed for this very moment.

Thank God, hope is stronger than fear, and I believe in answered prayers.

Risking it all, I pull my mother's ring from my pocket, reach for Sam's hand, and drop to a knee. "Sam, darlin', you take my breath away. And I can't imagine a life without breathless moments. Will you marry me?"

A single tear runs down her cheek and I have no idea what it means. Panic beats like a drum inside my chest. My entire world depends on what that teardrop means.

I wait with bated breath as she stares at the ring in my outstretched hand. It shakes a little. A slow smile spreads across her lips. My heart dares a beat, then another. Then I lose it. "Say yes, darlin', just say yes."

"I want to live like that again," she says, a catch in her throat, "but ... can we maybe start with a nice long visit?"

A flash of disappointment, as brief as a sneeze, bursts into a full-on laugh as I exhale. "Right. Of course. You need to think things through." She's my Sam all right, the same one I fell in love with that first summer.

She nods and her smile blooms into something akin to relief.

I tuck the ring away without taking my eyes off of her. "You look beautiful."

"Think so?" There's a shine in her eyes, a wondrous joy, like someone who's found something lost, something treasured, something that completes them. It's the same way she looked at me the first time we kissed.

"Yep."

"I know so little about you."

"We've got time." I take her hand and when I turn toward the truck, Aiden and Michaelyn rush forward, hug our legs, and I wrap my arms around them all.

# MAC'S ENDING

How much longer is the path before me, and how, I wonder, will our story end?

The moon is full and bright and, like always, outnumbered by the stars, but not outshined. I shuffle my tired old legs to the ridge to look out over Moonglow Meadow. Like a turtle on a fencepost, I'm not sure how I got here, how I keep ending up here, night after sleepless night.

I breathe deeply the sweet tranquility of the cool night air. When our bed is colder than I can bear, I find myself drawn to this ridge, to be with you again.

I know how much you always loved these mule's ears and lupines, so I'll set them here with the others. God willing, one day their seeds, sown in our love, will spill down this ridge to cover our beautiful valley with their sea of yellow and blue. Like your gold-blonde hair and sky-blue eyes, a testament to God's benevolent blessing of beauty on my beloved bride. Fitting, don't you think?

I'm glad I got to tell you how much you meant to me while I had the chance, because every minute I had with you made me who I am. And I was my best when I was with you. I lived for the smile on your face when I'd surprise you with these flowers, for the gentle goodness you brought out in me. Thank you for all the wonderful years you gave me. Didn't they go by in a wink?

The kids are doing well. Emma's medical practice in town and those young'uns of hers are keeping her busy. Who knew she'd be the blessing my little brother needed to find his way? They're happy, Sam, so happy. Nick's grown into a fine man and he's a wonderful husband and father. I'm so proud of him.

Zach writes often. Sounds like his mission work in Indonesia is bringing many new hearts to Christ. I know you're smiling down on him, watching over him, keeping him safe.

Our grandchildren are growing up and the ranch is in good hands. And while it pains me to know I'll be leaving them one day, maybe soon, I find comfort in knowing we leave behind a legacy of love.

Our daughter has your head for business, a blessing to us all. I used to love watching the two of you ride off together through the vineyard. To this day, it reminds me how God works in ways we can never imagine, leads us upon paths we can only trust are true and right.

Who knew a daughter would hold the reins of the ranch one day, and so capably? She's a smart one, that girl. Diversify, she said, remember? She was right. The winery's got more orders than it can handle since our merlot won that contest in Sonoma last summer. We've got two new barns going up, new farming equipment, and irrigation in the valley. The boys say we may not need to push the herd up to the Routt next year.

Me? I suppose I'm doing all right. It's been a year, and I still miss you every day. I don't know how to be me anymore without you. Was there ever a time I was a whole person before I found you? I don't recall. I yearn to see you again, exactly when, only God can say.

I make a fire to fend off the cold that falls down the mountain to chill me to the bone. I squat my tired old legs and warm my gnarled hands over the flames, and I can't remember the last time I actually felt warm.

Tired more from the emptiness in my heart than the effort to get here, I lie down near the fire to rest a spell before heading back. I lean against the log and stare at the stars, like we so often did. My gaze is drawn to your constellation in the southern sky, and I smile at the memory. To this day 'heroic proportions' still gives me a chuckle. I love the way you saw me.

I close my eyes and savor the warmth and familiar scents of serenity—smoke, pine, aspen, moist earth—and the music that surrounds me—the crackle of flames amidst the distant call of coyotes, the soothing night breeze dancing through the trees.

And I see you, arms outstretched, beckoning.

"Come to me," you whisper, in a voice as soft and sweet as a drop of summertime honey. There are a million stars behind you, illuminating your long golden hair, and you're lovely, ethereal like the angel I once saw step from the stream. And I know, with heart-bursting joy and a surety that warms my weary soul, I am home.

IF YOU ENJOYED *HER STORY*, I would love it if you let your friends know! As with all of my books, I enable lending everywhere it's allowed. And I am always grateful for a kind and honest review.

Stay up-to-date on upcoming releases by joining my newsletter via my website KathrynSueMoore.com or the QR Code below.

# ACKNOWLEDGEMENTS

There is only one author listed on this book, but I could never have written this story without the following people:

My father. I miss your unfailing encouragement and steadfast belief in me, more than words can express.

Nicholas Sparks, Lisa Wingate, and Kristin Hannah, my silent mentors and professional crushes.

My beta-readers. To those who read early drafts of this story and offered honest and constructive critiques—Kelly Anderson, Lyn Brink, Jessica Fare, Claire Fawcett, Laura Henderson, and Nancy Mosier—I offer my heartfelt gratitude for your help in making each new version better than the last. Your feedback, support, and unfailing friendship are more than I deserve.

My children, Jake and Rachel. It's difficult to write a story without some version of you two in it, because being a mother remains the most important and rewarding thing I've ever done and will ever do.

My husband, Alan. Born and raised in Michigan, with a pure Colorado heart, you have shared my story for thirty-one years. The plaque on our bedroom wall that you gave me years ago says it all: "If I could live forever, and you would be with me ... I'd choose a house for all seasons, in mountain greenery."

## ABOUT THE AUTHOR

K. S. Moore is the award-winning author of *Angel Beneath My Wheels* and *The Bravest Among Us*. The cabin and meadow depicted in this story are fond memories of a parcel of land her family once owned in Northwest Colorado. A native of Indiana, she now lives in Michigan with her husband, Alan, and they vacation in the Rockies whenever they can. Find her online at KathrynSueMoore.com.

Made in the USA
Monee, IL
29 October 2024

68257034R00180